Mystery Women:
An Encyclopedia of
Leading Women Characters
in Mystery Fiction

Vol. 2 (1980-1989)

Colleen Barnett

Poisoned Pen Press

10 9 8 7 6 5 4 3 2 1

Library of Congress Catalog Card Number: 2001086357

ISBN: 1-890208-69-8

Poisoned Pen Press
6962 E. First Ave. Ste 103
Scottsdale, AZ 85251
www.poisonedpenpress.com
info@poisonedpenpress.com

Printed in the United States of America

This volume is dedicated
To my parents, Jerry and Mae (Heney) Clifford,
Who provided my sister, Patricia,
And me with unconditional love

And to all teachers, including parents,
Librarians, and others
Who instill in children
The joy of learning

Contents

Introduction

Growing up in the 1930's and 1940's in a household where books were important, I moved beyond the Nancy Drews and Judy Boltons to search for adult female detectives. The rare specimens available included Harriet Vane (too sophisticated for my tastes then) and Jane Marple (too old then). I delighted in Agatha Christie's minor heroines: Tuppence Beresford and Eileen "Bundle" Brent.

My interest in mystery stories was a resource to me as I moved through college, marriage and parenthood in a small town, relief for my cabin fever. They provided my tours to distant lands when travel was impossible. They created tensions, but provided solutions and involved exciting female characters. I particularly enjoyed those heroines who showed enterprise and independence.

My research into the development of the female series investigator was triggered by Maggie, my younger daughter, who requested a book with a strong heroine, and sustained by Cathie, my older daughter, who enjoyed legal mysteries. My interest in the evolution of the female mystery series protagonist combined my own early values (influenced by Nancy, Judy, Tuppence and others) with my professional awareness of the need for positive role models. As a social work supervisor and volunteer coordinator, then later as an attorney and college lecturer, I was aware of the need for positive role models in literature and the media in order that young women could see themselves as potentially capable and independent. One of the side benefits was the discovery of obscure authors and sleuths as I researched the genre.

Since 1975, I have read thousands of mysteries with female characters who appeared in at least two books. I am indebted to Michelle Slung's *Crime on Her Mind* and Patricia Craig and Mary Cadogan's *The Lady Investigates* for initial coverage. Allen J. Hubin's *Crime Fiction* series provided a plethora of names, supplemented by the editions of *Twentieth Century Crime and Mystery Writers*. I also benefited from previously unidentified sleuths found in Willetta L. Heising's editions of *Detecting Men* and *Detecting Women*. I mourn the passing of *The Armchair Detective*.

Wisconsin's excellent interlibrary system provided books not locally available. The University of Wisconsin-Platteville, University of Wisconsin-Richland, and University of Wisconsin-Madison were gracious in meeting my needs. Individual librarians particularly those in Boscobel and in Phoenix, Arizona went out of their way to help. I was able to travel to university and public libraries across the United States, Canada, and England to read books reserved to the premises.

Used book dealers and mystery bookstores made it possible for me to add to my own collection. I could never have found needed materials without the assistance of Jeff Hatfield at Uncle Edgar's in Minneapolis or Mary Helen Becker at Booked for Murder in Madison, Wisconsin.

A twenty-five year project like this could never have been sustained without help from my family. My children, their spouses, and my nieces perused card catalogs and computers in Chicago, Minneapolis, Boston, New York and the Library of Congress to help me locate obscure books. Now with Wiscat, Madcat, and the Library of Congress on the Internet, I have expanded personal access. My son Andrew, a professional librarian, initiated me into the wonders of the reference section where I could locate U.S. holders of rare books, available through the University of Wisconsin Interlibrary Loan System. I am particularly grateful to Deb Reilly of the University of Wisconsin Memorial Library for her intervention. My daughter-in-law Vonne Meussling Barnett stepped in on several occasions when I could not get access to books in holding libraries. She read them and forwarded her well thought out reviews.

As always, I am grateful to my husband, John for his support. He carried home grocery bags full of books from the local library and endured countless overcooked meals, while I read "just a few more pages".

Peg Eagan, my original publisher, and Larry Names, her husband and editor, had faith in my work at a time when I wondered if it would ever be published. When they discontinued their publishing venture, I was most fortunate to discover Poisoned Pen Press of Scottsdale, Arizona. At the 1999 Bouchercon in Milwaukee, Wisconsin, I picked up a booklet listing publishers. It referred to Poisoned Pen Press as having a dedication to the mystery novel. Publisher Robert Rosenwald was well aware that genre books are rarely good financial ventures but accepted that risk in publishing Mystery Women. I am deeply grateful. His assistant, Karen Jolly was a kind resource for a writer with limited experience. Joe Liddy, the editor recommended by Poisoned Pen Press, proved to be a wonderful choice. His professional skills were enhanced by his patience and courtesy. Both he and his wife Lisa deserve credit for their contributions to the final project.

My motivation for writing the books was to pass information on to others who enjoy mysteries as I do, and as an expression of gratitude to the genre itself for all of the pleasure it has provided me. I am particularly grateful to those authors who widened my horizons, challenged my assumptions, and explored issues of concern to women.

The books utilized in this research were reviewed in a written format. Some were boring, some distasteful, and therefore merely skimmed for basic information. Each sleuth was profiled with attention to her education, state of life, physical characteristics, and her relevance to the period during which she was published. My criteria for inclusion included: the number of significant appearances, the format (novels as opposed to short stories although some collections were noted), the exclusion of juvenile and young adult novels, and the inclusion of negative figures (women who were anti-heroines) because of their impact. The most difficult factor to evaluate was whether characters (a spouse, assistant, or lover) played sufficiently strong roles in the narratives. My decisions were inevitably subjective. For the errors, omissions, and failure to properly evaluate an author's product, I accept full responsibility and apologize in advance. I will welcome corrections and additions.

I order to make my work meaningful I increased my personal knowledge of social and legal history, women's rights, and literary developments. (See the final section for resources and references). As my reading progressed, there were observable trends which I have noted whenever possible within the biographies or historical material.

Volume I covered female sleuths who made their first appearances between 1860-1979. Because of the incredible expansion of this sub-genre, Volume II covered a much shorter period, 1980-1989. Volume III, currently in progress, will include female sleuths introduced during 1990-1999.

Section 1:

Review of Historic Aspects of Women in Mystery Fiction from 1860 to 1979

During the one hundred years since American author Anna Katharine Green introduced the first female sleuth to make three appearances, women's status in society and in the mystery novel have undergone considerable changes in status. At times these changes paralleled one another; at times, they diverged.

In literature, as in nature, a species cannot develop and flourish except under conditions that support its existence. The more complex the species, the more intricate and sophisticated are the requirements for a hospitable environment. The historical perspective of the heroine in the mystery novel shows such complexity and development. A male fictional detective might transfer easily from the present to the nineteenth century with merely a change in clothes and mode of transportation. Few of the current female private investigators, police officers, attorneys, or other professionals could have existed in the Victorian period.

Genre writers, including such luminaries as Dorothy L. Sayers, Howard Haycraft, and E. M. Wrong, have identified conditions necessary for the development of credible fictional investigators of either sex, which include:

- Respect for the legal process, including police forces, because there has been—and remains in some communities—a belief that only the powerful receive justice (which in cases may be justified);
- Widespread literacy through public education;
- An inexpensive means of publication; and

- The use of series. The popularity of sleuths was enhanced from the onset by the use of series, to which the readership became attached to a character, as in the case of Sherlock Holmes.

Initially the lack of literacy and cost of publications channeled mystery stories into magazines and newspapers in the form of short stories or serials. These proved so popular that circulation increased, which, along with cheaper forms of printing, led to the dime novel and inexpensive hardbound books. Compulsory education and the development of a public library system expanded the ability and opportunities for leisure reading. The acceptance of the legal system awaited the professionalization of the police forces, democratic selection of the judiciary, and constitutional protection for civil rights. The mystery story has traditionally flourished in those societies with broad personal freedoms. The amateur detective remained the sleuth of choice until these conditions were prevalent.

The development of mysteries featuring female investigators further required:

- The removal of legal and political barriers to women;
- Societal acceptance of women as intelligent, logical creatures;
- Personal freedom for women as shown in the clothes they wore and in their ability to move within the community;
- Access to an education equal to that provided for males and to employment based on qualifications, not gender; and
- Awareness that some, if not all, females enjoy risk-taking and adventure.

The Victorian Era—1860-1899

The budding feminist movement in the United States that emerged at the 1848 Seneca Falls Women's Convention waned under the more pressing problem of slavery. Progressive women turned their attention to the abolitionist movement, within which they were effective. Harriet Beecher Stowe's "Uncle Tom's Cabin" was credited with awakening its readers to the evils of slavery. When the war ended, only minor consideration was given to expanding the rights of females along with those of former slaves through the 15th Amendment. Married women in the mid-Nineteenth Century were unable to contract, to make wills, to transfer property, and to manage what property they owned. Even the custody of the children and the wages of the wife were controlled by the husband at this time.

Changes to these onerous conditions came slowly and piecemeal through state, not federal, action. Beginning with the passage of the married Woman's Property Act in Mississippi in 1839, state legislatures expanded women's legal rights.

The voting franchise had been awarded to women, in several Western states, (Wyoming had granted women the vote while a territory) decades before the U.S. Congress passed the Nineteenth Amendment to the Constitution.

Societal conditions were equally burdensome. Marriage or spinsterhood were the only acceptable possibilities for proper young women. The spinster, unless she was wealthy enough to command respect, was a figure of ridicule, condemned to live upon the charity of male relatives. Indeed most women worked. They have always worked. Housework and the care of children took many more hours than it does today, and only a small number of women had household help. Those who sought employment during the Nineteenth Century found it as domestic servants, underpaid workers, or in the degradation of prostitution.

But ferment existed, in life as in literature. By the late Nineteenth Century businesses seeking females for low paying clerical jobs, supported education for women. Education widened the horizons of women. It also opened a field of employment for women, as teachers. Nursing became a profession, but one that paid badly and no longer attracted men. Those professions considered suitable for women were extensions of their roles in the home. In most cases it was understood, that a female teacher or nurse would abandon her profession upon marriage. To do otherwise would infer that her husband was unable or unwilling to provide for his family.

Clothing changed to make it easier for females to work in factory settings, use such office machinery as the typewriter, and move from work to home. Domicile changed as society accepted the fact that a female might live outside of her family home in a boarding house or a private dwelling.

The educated woman, and particularly the financially secure woman, often had leisure time that could be spent in reading, and in writing fiction. The early female authors frequently utilized pseudonyms or their initials to earn public acceptance for their work. Books available to women before the turn of the century, even those by female authors, encouraged domesticity and femininity, dramatizing the problems experienced by independent women.

A fictional female in the Victorian Era might appear in an investigative capacity. Generally, this role would be justified to meet a financial emergency in her home or to prove the innocence of a loved one, father, fiancé, or husband. Once the emergency had been resolved, there would be a return to the home and an acceptance of domesticity. The skills possessed by fictional female investigators often were those of intuition; special training such as lip reading; and frequently exercised under the tutelage of a male.

Anna Katharine Green created an intelligent, self-sufficient female investigator in Amelia Butterworth, free of the constraints of a household, able to move within a large city through public transportation; and buttressed by her friendship with a male professional, Ebenezer Gryce. Although marriage was still a possibility at her age, Amelia could work with males without constraint.

A New Century—1900-1919

The first decade of the Twentieth Century was relatively quiescent, but America and England were changing. Industry and mechanization opened new fields of employment for women: typewriters, electric sewing machines, cash registers. Three-fourths of the states had granted women the right to own and control property. In all forty-eight, they were able to will their property at death, and in most they could retain their own earnings from work other than in a family business. Both single-sex and coeducational colleges and universities had expanded women's opportunities for careers; new professions, expansions of the traditional women's work, were home economics and social work. College was still reserved for more privileged classes. The emphasis remained on educating the sons in a family, because they would be "providers". Divorce was rare, and a settlement might include lifetime alimony.

Immigrant populations, as in the 1840's and 1890's, envisioned education as the ladder to higher economic status and increased income in America. Later immigrants learned English as a first step to academic work. Adult classes in English were popular. Immigrants continued to work at the lower levels of employment; as domestic servants, on the railroad or in the building trades, and later in public service as their votes provided leverage. A small number of women entered medical schools and law schools, but found it difficult to obtain employment after graduation, and were denied professional acceptance. Educated women bonded together in sororities and organizations where they exchanged ideas. Philanthropist Andrew Carnegie endowed over 9,000 libraries. Many more were begun by organized women's clubs, later to become the National Federation of Woman's Clubs.

State legislatures, recognizing the increased numbers of women and children in the workforce, enacted protective legislation limiting hours and setting work conditions. Society experienced tremendous change with the development of the automobile. Highways had to be built and cheaper automobile models developed to increase sales. When this occurred, especially in America and England, people became mobile in a new sense. Telephones connected homes and businesses, providing employment for women. Radio and films brought fashions, ideas, and dreams to small town men and women.

The First World War had two distinct impacts upon women's status. While it focused attention away from the organized movement for suffrage, the war speeded industrialization and utilized women to fill jobs left vacant when men were mobilized. Women served in factories, government offices, and in the military. Most such opportunities were limited to single women, but they had interesting side effects. Clothing was less restrictive. Women rode bicycles and learned to drive automobiles. As the double decade ended, women had bobbed their hair, wore make-up, and enjoyed more personal freedom.

The end of the war, while it decreased employment for women, still found them better organized, more ambitious, and emboldened by their success in getting state legislatures to grant them the franchise. Congressmen, aware that they faced opposition in their home states, were open to change. American suffragettes were less militant than their English sisters. Led by the formidable Pankhurst family, Englishwomen marched, protested, endured prison and forced feedings, as dramatized by "Upstairs, Downstairs", the PBS series from England. However the English franchise was limited to women thirty and older until 1928.

Postwar advances in the workforce were more difficult. It was expected that men would claim their former positions in offices and factories. The unions had not recruited women and felt no need to plead their cause.

On the literary level, there was a movement toward more active heroines. The Stratemeyer Syndicate, publisher of many adventure series for boys, learned that girls were reading their books. They developed series in which girls and young women, singly or in groups, traveled, solved mysteries, and enjoyed excitement. Carol Billman in her book on the Syndicate, commented, "Since it is in childhood, starting with the highly patterned fairy tales, that readers acquire a taste for popular narrative formulas and begin to develop their literary habits and preferences, it seems important to consider juvenile fiction as part of readers' cultural heritage regarding the mystery genre." According to Billman, the Ruth Fielding series taught the Syndicate a lesson, which affected their policy. As Ruth was allowed to mature, graduate from college, take employment, marry and have children, the popularity of the series diminished. Later series, Nancy Drew and the Dana sisters, never allowed their heroines to develop to such a degree.

The most common format for adult mysteries remained the short story, often collected into hardcover form during these decades. Mary Roberts Rinehart was recognized for her novels, but often accused of developing the HIBK (Had-I-But-Known) school of mystery, in which the heroine retrospectively regretted the mishaps she encountered because she did not plan ahead. Other types of popular mysteries during this period included those featuring scientific detectives, religious detectives, and espionage thrillers, none of which was particularly adapted to the use of a female sleuth. When women appeared in espionage novels, they were more likely to be villainesses.

Four women characters were introduced in series of three or more during the years 1900-1919: English private investigators Dora Myrl by M. McDonnell Bodkin; and Mercedes Quero by G. E. Locke (a female who utilized her initials); and two Americans; private detective Millicent Newberry by Jennette Lee and working class Molly Morganthau by Geraldine Bonner. Three of these series were written by women; three featured professional investigators; two of the women married; one indicated that she had attended college.

The Changes brought about by Excess and Depression—1920-1939

The illusion of a peace that would last and the booming of industry fueled by the capacity needed to fight a war created an illusory sense of optimism as the Twenties began. Returned servicemen welcomed by their families embraced civilian life. The stock markets boomed; jobs were plentiful. What could go wrong? Men accustomed to danger were aggrieved to find that the Eighteenth Amendment had abridged their right to drink alcohol. Smugglers from Canada, speakeasies where a password would gain access and home made booze filled glasses and energized organized crime.

There were other changes to be faced by the returned servicemen. The wife or sweetheart who had worked in an office or factory during the war had become more independent and assertive. Even their physical appearance was altered in a rejection of traditional standards. The "beauty parlor" provided short, permed hair, bright red fingernails, and pencil thin eyebrows for women who were remembered differently. The corset, long skirts, and demure blouses gave way to slim boyish ensembles with hems well above the knee. Young women were encouraged to smoke a cigarette rather than eat a sweet to maintain a trim figure. Alcohol, separate living quarters, and the closed automobile led to sexual intimacies by "nice girls" which would have been less likely before the war.

The theories of Sigmund Freud, which discouraged repression, accused women of penis envy, and blamed mental illness upon sexual experiences in childhood, may not have been well understood by most but they encouraged permissiveness. Divorces nearly doubled over twenty years, although most states required a showing of adultery or significant abuse.

Women had the vote on a national basis, but use of that privilege did not reach the expectations of those who promoted or opposed the Nineteenth Amendment. A "women's vote" did not materialize, although participating females were now included at national political conventions. The suffrage organizations, having achieved their purpose, splintered into a variety of personal and professional interest groups, including the League of Women Voters. Only a small core sought an Equal Rights Amendment.

The prosperity of the Twenties kept both men and women employed. The war had brought about a major migration of low-income whites and blacks to the North where factory work was available. Many remained in large cities after the war ended, although in lesser jobs. Educated women found additional openings as librarians, or interior decorators, but were rarities in the traditional professions of medicine and law.

For those adult women who did not work outside the home and had household help or modern appliances, there were increased leisure opportunities: bridge, matinees at the movie theatre, book clubs and lending libraries. Lending libraries and publishing houses sought light fiction, including mysteries that women would enjoy. Both the Book of the Month Club and Literary Guild began service in 1926, with hard covers selling for a dollar and under, but that was a hard-earned dollar. There were serious writers on the best seller lists: Edith Wharton, Sinclair Lewis, and F. Scott Fitzgerald, along with westerns, mysteries, and romances. Because of the large female audiences, movies were designed to attract women, portraying them favorably. The hairstyles, clothing and mannerisms depicted in the movies were copied in the cities and small towns.

The Twenties have been dubbed the "Golden Age" of mysteries. The caliber of the best and most popular writers was exceptional. The British mystery focused on the wealthy end of society as depicted by Dorothy Sayers, Agatha Christie, or Ronald Knox.

The Depression, which began on the farms as early as the mid-Twenties, then was fueled by the crash of the stock market and a loss of confidence in the economy, had major impact on the role of women in society, the work place, and literature. Family income was cut in half, eliminating discretionary items from the budget. As a result, factories closed, and the ranks of the unemployed swelled. Women and minority workers were the first to be fired. Government itself refused to hire two spouses with the result that the woman was terminated voluntarily or by fiat. School systems required female teachers to resign when they married. Because local and state resources were inadequate to care for the indigent, the Democratic administration of Franklin D. Roosevelt brought massive federal intervention.

Women were still employed but at low-level jobs—sometimes supporting their families. Single women and families moved back to parental homes. Home canned vegetables, patched clothing, and postponed medical care saved money but further depressed the economy. There were fewer divorces in the thirties. The average age at marriage increased and fewer children were born to families. Dropping out of school for teenagers became less of an option when there were no jobs available. School attendance increased.

There were some bright spots for women workers. Unlike the American Federation of Labor (A.F.L.) the Congress of Industrial Organization (C.I.O.), which represented laborers by industry rather than craft, welcomed female workers.

Radio and movies responded to the challenge of a depressed nation in several ways: bright witty comedies that ignored the problem; musicals that lifted the spirits; gangster movies reflecting the increase in crime; and heartwarming stories of sacrifice and devotion, usually by females. The plots, which featured independent, self-supporting women tended to depict them as eventually moving into married life.

There were still those who preferred a book to movies or radio. "Gone With the Wind" was a tremendous success. Readers purchased contemporary fiction, gritty and realistic by Erskine Caldwell, James T. Farrell, and John Steinbeck. The most popular mystery writer of the period was Erle Stanley Gardner, author of the Perry Mason series. Women as depicted in his narratives were victims or villainesses. His dutiful secretary, Della Street, was allowed to assist but rarely had any meaningful role. Although Gardner was more successful financially, critical acclaim in the mystery genre went to the authors of "hard-boiled" detective stories; i.e. Dashiell Hammett, Raymond Chandler, Jim Thompson. This initiated a significant sub-genre that did not supplant the traditional cozy puzzle mystery but joined it. New female mystery writers in the Thirties included Marjorie Allingham, Ngaio Marsh, and Josephine Tey. Although, like Dorothy Sayers, their primary characters were male, the heroes courted and married strong and interesting women.

Dashiell Hammett was credited with another major sub-genre in the field; the couples mystery, popularized by his book, *The Thin Man*, featuring Nick and Nora Charles. It was not the novel itself, but the series of movies that followed the book, featuring the light hearted repartee of William Powell and Myrna Loy that advanced the spousal approach to detection. "Couples" books, movies and radio programs modeled themselves on Nick and Nora who combined the male toughness and the wit and intuition of the female. The combination of male and female was not restricted to married couples. Erle Stanley Gardner writing as A. A. Fair teamed tough ex-attorney Donald Lam with ill-humored widow, Bertha Cool in an extended series.

Mystery publishing was expanded via the return of the soft cover/ paperback book. Unlike the dime novels of the turn of the century, the new paperbacks were usually reprints of hardcover books, selling for a quarter, conveniently sized for pocket or purse. The popularity of mysteries was evidenced by the increased number of reviews of detective stories in major newspapers and magazines and in the genre non-fiction which evaluated authors and trends.

Literary trends during the Twenties and Thirties included:

1. The development of the American mystery novel; the end to the dominance of English mystery writers; and more narratives set in the United States, although primarily on the East and West Coasts.

2. Additional prototypes:

   - The widow/spinster amateur emerged in a leading role. Amelia Butterworth was followed by Jane Marple; Hildegarde Withers (who became a professional late in the series); Elizabeth Warrender; Lace White; Ethel Thomas; Grace Latham; Jane Amanda Edwards

   - The daring young amateur detective—Helene Justus, Eileen "Bundle" Brent—and for juveniles—Nancy Drew, Judy Bolton, the Dana Sisters

   - The couples mystery in which the wife played a significant role, in one or more of the narratives—Jeff and Ann McNeill; Sue and Andy McVeigh; Anne and David Layton; Iris and Peter Duluth; Tuppence and Tommy Beresford; Meg Garret and Raeburn Steel

- The professional female, who encountered murder through her responsibilities, including:
  - ☐ Teacher—Hildegarde Withers;
  - ☐ Nurses—Hilda Adams, Sarah Keate, and "Davvie" McLean;
  - ☐ Private investigators—Dol Bonner, Bertha Cool; Meg Garret; Lynn McDonald; Maud Silver;
  - ☐ Police officials—the wild and incredible Palmyra Pym;
  - ☐ Psychiatrists or psychologists—Dame Beatrice Bradley;
  - ☐ Store detective—Mary Carner;
  - ☐ Authors—Harriet Vane;
  - ☐ Crime reporters—Juliet Jackson, Gail McGurk;
  - ☐ Businesswomen—Daisy Jane Mott, Susan Yates;
  - ☐ Medical doctors—Joan Marvin;
  - ☐ Attorney, though not practicing—Daphne Wrayne; and
  - ☐ Anti-heroines—Louisa Woolfe, Avis Bryden; Polack Annie; Fah Lo Suee.

3. The impact of social change on the women was shown in their professions. They were better educated, often having college degrees or technical training. Advanced degrees were noted particularly among the English females. Meg Garret had a Ph.D.; Daphne Wrayne, a law degree; Beatrice Bradley, either a MD or Ph.D.; and Palmyra Pym was an Oxford graduate.

   Pet ownership became popular—best known being Nick and Nora Charles' Asta, but the Murdoch sisters featured cats; Rosika Storey had a monkey; Hilda Adams and Kate Marsh referred to their pet birds.

   Few previous female sleuths had children. Even though most families were small in this double decade, Jeff and Anne McNeill, Tuppence and Tommy Beresford, and Beatrice Bradley had at least two children. Even more unusual for a time when maternal instincts were expected to prevail, Juliet Jackson had a son whom she farmed out to friends.

4. Establishment of long series, in most of which the female protagonist changed very little over the years. Beatrice Bradley (66 books); Maud Silver (32 books); Daphne Wrayne (47 books); Palmyra Pym (24 books); Bertha Cool (29 books); and Jane Marple (16 books). Some of these series are still in reprints.

The Second World War and Its
Aftermath—1940-1959

Even before Pearl Harbor, American industry was resuscitated by the exportation of goods to the Allies in Europe. After December 7, 1941, personal concerns, even national concerns were overwhelmed by global events. American men volunteered for service. In addition to the nursing services that dated back to 1907, segregated military units were developed for women (WACS, WAFS, WAVES, and SPARKS) who served in non-combat positions. Women filled many of the vacant positions in schools and colleges, hospitals, public offices, businesses and factories. Initially public opinion sanctioned the employment of single women. When it became clear that there were too few to meet the demand, married women were recruited. A second major migration of African-American and low paid white workers took place as the steel mills, auto plants, and airplane factories provided well-paid, skilled positions in the Midwest.

As at the end of World War I, the cessation of hostilities brought the veterans back to their jobs, and diminished opportunities for women workers. This had a mixed impact. Women welcomed the return of their fathers, sons, brothers, fiancés and husbands. Most were eager to resume family life. Suburbs and the housing developments were designed for large families, station wagons, new schools, and community activities. For some women, the need to continue to work was based on economics. Single career women, widows and divorcees, married women in low-income households had no choice. Because of continued prosperity, most of those who sought work, found it but at lower wages and in appropriate occupations for their sex. Because law and medical schools during the war had recruited them, there were more females in the professional schools and actually practicing. They were discriminated against at both levels, often shunted into "feminine" specialties. Families realized that their daughters might require a post high school education. College, which for some had been a "finishing school" or the hunting ground for promising husbands, became a serious option for those who could afford it.

However, a reaffirmation of domesticity as the natural role for women was reinforced by religion, the educational system, and the media. During World War II, working women were portrayed by the media as heroic, serving alongside their men or supporting them on the home front. Film historian Molly Haskell in *From Reverence to Rape* noted the change after the war. She identified films in which successful married women were seen as emasculating. The more acceptable role, the supportive spouse or pliant victim, was displayed in films, such as those by Alfred Hitchcock.

During the Forties home entertainment was still dominated by radio, but the Fifties moved into television. Radio series such as *Stella Dallas* and *Young Widow Brown* had emphasized the sacrificial role of the mother and wife. Many of the television hits of the Fifties were wholesome family programs where Mom stayed in the home: *Ozzie and Harriet, Father Knows Best, Leave It to Beaver,* and *The Donna Reed Show.* Books critical of the influence of women such as Philip Wylie's *Generation of Vipers* were published.

The adoption of slacks or jeans during the war years because of fabric shortages and the need to wear protective clothing while working in factories persisted after the war ended. In more formal attire and sports apparel, there was an emphasis on femininity and sexuality. The bikini made its appearance.

Personal reading was a refuge for many. Women waiting for their sweethearts or husbands had empty hours. Servicemen read while waiting in ports, on board ships, in barracks, railroad stations, and airports. Both fiction and non-fiction became more complex. Millions of Americans had been exposed to other cultures, new ideas. The mistreatment of Jews, the service records of African-Americans and Asian Americans created a reaction to prejudice and discrimination that would erupt in the Sixties. These social changes emerged in popular novels and films. Religious books and films reflected an increase in church attendance among the newly founded families.

In content, books changed. Sex became more explicit. Profanity was no longer expressed by "XQ*#" or blank spaces, but explicitly. Violence, so intrinsic to war, emerged in peacetime literature, as well. The violence and sexuality were expanded in the mystery novel, as in other literature. Profanity, brutality, and misogyny rivaled puzzles, witty dialogue, and coziness. Mickey Spillane's *Mike Hammer* and Ian Fleming's *James Bond,* each in his own way relegated women to subordinate roles, but (according to Kenneth Van Dover) became the most popular of mystery authors.

New sub-genres were added to those already identified as emerging in the Twenties and Thirties, including:

- The espionage novel that reflected the fear of Communist dominance occasionally featured women—Julia Probyn;
- The police procedural, which recognized the improbability that individual amateurs could solve complex crimes;

- The coupling of a female amateur and a male professional not only by marriage, but by sexual relationship, professional association or friendship—Henry and Emmy Tibbett; Pam North and Lt. Bill Weigand;

- Additional professional females who dealt with murder encountered in their work included: archaeologist Elsie Mae Hunt; medical doctor Mary Finney; attorney Amy Brewster (although she was a caricature);

- An early divorced series female sleuth—Emily Bryce; and

- Divorces and reconciliations—Michael and Terry Terence and Liz and Gordon Parrott.

Several of the women featured in mysteries had served in the war effort: Arabella Blake in Washington, D.C.; Liane Craufurd in the British War Office, and Emily Tibbett in the British Women's Auxiliary Air Force.

Action and Reaction—1960-79

Repressed tensions flared. Generations split on the issue of U.S. military involvement in Vietnam. Men who had served in World War II were unable to accept a new generation's attitude towards America's world responsibilities. Both sides were vitriolic, descending to charges of treason and cowardice on one side; "babykillers" on the other. The deaths of John and Robert Kennedy, Martin Luther King and Malcolm X triggered racial and class conflicts. Men and women worked together in both the peace and civil rights movements. Lyndon Johnson, a descendent of Confederate soldiers, guided equal rights legislation through the Congress but was unable to unite the nation over Vietnam.

An unexpected bonus accrued to women when Southern legislators in an effort to block rights for African-Americans added gender to the legislation protecting employment opportunities. When the administrative bureaucracy was hesitant about enforcing the provisions as to gender, a feminist organization, N.O.W. (National Organization of Women) turned to the courts to gain access for women to jobs hitherto restricted to men. Segregation was outlawed as to both race and gender, but attitudes were slower to change.

The complacency attributed to women in the Fifties had masked a growing dissatisfaction with their status. Betty Friedan identified educated wives and mothers isolated from the world of paid employment and intellectual stimulation in *Feminine Mystique*. A combination of factors had changed women's roles: the availability first of birth control, then abortion; the reduction of fault as a factor in divorces; an increase in cohabitation as opposed to marriage; affirmative action policies which favored minorities; an electorate in which women's votes had become increasingly important; homosexuals search for equal rights and their increased openness about their relationships, and a high percentage of single mothers, many of whom had never married.

Each change prompted a counter-reaction. Many religious and lay leaders strongly opposed *Roe V. Wade*, the Supreme Court decision legitimizing abortion. No-fault divorces increased the number of children raised by single parents, often forcing mothers to work while their children were pre-school. Affirmative action programs were perceived as discrimination against white males and a betrayal of equal rights. Welfare rolls expanded, creating a vulnerable subsidized class of women and children.

Women, who in an earlier generation might have married to gain economic security, earned college degrees and became self-supporting. Some who might have married to legitimize a child sued for child support and remained single. With abortion and birth control as options, women could have smaller families or none at all.

As families were changed, so were institutions. Colleges and universities did not recover quickly from the student riots that had weakened administrative authority. Women's Studies and African-American Studies became academic disciplines in universities. The anti-war and feminist movements promoted the concept of a volunteer military service in which the genders were integrated except on the battlefield. Police forces, fire departments, hospitals and law firms became sensitized not only to the percentage of females and minorities on their staffs, but to their inclusion in the higher ranks. Title IX of the Higher Education Act extended the rights of females to educational opportunities and sports previously reserved for males. Politics lagged behind. White males still controlled all major roles in the executive, judicial, and legislative branches in state and federal governments.

Not every change in society was related to sex or race. The use of recreational drugs was a problem for all ages, races, and genders. Medical science had made a longer life possible, but the cost of living and receiving medical attention after the productive years could turn a longer life into a miserable existence.

American industry suffered because international corporations had no loyalty to a country or its citizens. Production facilities were moved from high wage locations to Third World countries. Robotics, computerization, and low wage foreign plants undermined the dominance of the United States industrial base and the power of labor unions.

Television had become so overwhelming in its impact that books, newspapers, radio and movies suffered from retrenchment. Videos could be cheaper for a family than an evening at the theater. Book prices had risen over the years until a hardcover novel was priced beyond the means of many readers. Sports had become an industry underwritten by television. The movies had changed, becoming more violent, sexually explicit, and oriented towards a younger generation. The major studios had been commercialized; their products patterned for a mass production market. Feminists, long devoted to First Amendment rights, felt conflict as pornography proliferated in videos, adult bookstores, and finally on the Internet. Lyrics to many popular songs were anti-female and pro-violence.

Major publishing houses which, like movie studios, were absorbed into larger corporations wanted blockbusters, big money makers, and were less innovative in developing new talent. In novels, including mysteries, relationships and character development played a larger role. Heroes and heroines were more likely to be promiscuous or unfaithful in marriage. On a positive note, they became more heterogeneous and ethnic. There were gay, Jewish, Native American, Asian, and African-American sleuths. Due to the increased character development and issue-oriented plots, mysteries became a major genre in fiction, and female sleuths a significant sub-genre. Issues of particular interest to women—child abuse, spousal abuse, breast cancer, illegitimacy and abortion—were motives for murder or the basis for subplots in mysteries. Paperbacks performed new functions; in addition to providing affordable reprints of hardcover mysteries, they became a testing ground for new authors and sleuths, much like the "B" movies of the Thirties and Forties.

Women's employment opportunities introduced realism into narratives featuring:

- British and American female police officers and detectives: Clare Reynolds Atwell, Norah Mulcahaney, Delia Riordan, Jane Boardman, Charmian Daniels, and Christie Opara;

- Private investigators: Alison Gordon, Cordelia Gray and most promising of all, Sharon McCone;

- Fictional female attorneys: Rosa Epton;

- Medical personnel: Lucy Beck, Virginia Freer, Dr. Nora North, and Dr. Grace Severance, and

- Reporters: Helen Bullock and Jemima Shore.

These characters encountered murder on a practical level in series often written by professionals in those fields.

James Bond was cloned in female garb (Modesty Blaise, Maxine Dangerfield, and Lady Jennifer Norrington) and new espionage agents were introduced (Cody and Emma Greaves). In less likely settings, actresses (Tessa Crichton), artists (Persis Willum) and academics (Kate Fansler) were exposed to murder through their professions or associations with police professionals. The number of mysteries featuring females in significant roles expanded, causing some mystery bookstores to devote separate sections to them. As in the Twenties, mysteries with dominant male sleuths had challenging wives and lovers (Vera Castang, Emmy Tibbett, Helen Blye Horowitz, Helen Shandy, and Susan Silverman). The number of sub-genres increased to include:

- Historical mysteries: Dulcie Bligh, Amelia Peabody Emerson, and Charlotte Pitt;
- Crossovers with science fiction: Telzey Amberdon, Sibyl Sue Blue, Hildy Pace, Claudine St. Cyr, and Effie Schlupe;
- The occult: Kitty Telefair; and
- Westerns: Molly Owens and Charity Ross.

These did not replace the established sub-genres, but supplemented them. Motivations became more complex and more diverse. Although still tied to greed, jealousy, and relationships, they focused less on wills and material concerns. Environmental issues, industrial espionage particularly in the computer field, medical technologies and scientific discoveries prompted the contemporary killers. The serial killer who might have no obvious motivation was featured in an increasing range of books.

Women characters were multifaceted. They ranged from high school graduates to academics with Ph.D.'s: (Penelope Spring) and included more diverse racial and economic backgrounds and age groups; widows and divorcees (Natasha O'Brien and Anna Peters), lesbians (Helen Keremos and possibly Hon Constance Morrison-Burke), happily and unhappily married women, those who chose not to marry, and women who had been sexually assaulted (Charity Tucker, Anna Jugedinski, and Julie Hayes).

Widows were less likely to notice murder while working in their rural gardens than to encounter it on city streets (Margaret Binton, Minnie Santangelo), and often found happiness in second marriages or relationships (Persis Willum, Lucy Ramsdale, and Arlette Van der Valk Davidson). Sex outside of marriage was treated more casually. Relationships between adult children and their aging parents, between parents and their younger children, among siblings were explored through mystery narratives.

The political ideologies of the female characters were acknowledged:

- Mici Anhalt had worked for the Kennedy brothers;
- Sue Carstairs Maddox mirrored her author's more conservative viewpoint;
- Dr. Nora North extolled the British empire;
- Cody disdained both British Intelligence and the American CIA.

A religious publisher, Moody Bible Institute, developed a Christian mystery series (Margo Franklin) but most ignored the religious convictions of their protagonists. In addition to couples' series, there were ensembles with female members (Julie Barnes, Jennifer Norrington, and Betty Crighton Jones).

Women series characters in the popular espionage sub-genre, particularly those written by male authors, were often portrayed as promiscuous (Shauna Bishop, Lee Crosley, Amanda Curzon, Cherry Delight, Eve Drum, Angela Harpe, Amanda Nightingale, and Penelope St. John Orsini). Some of these verged on being soft pornography. Anti-heroines could be engaging; Lucilla Edith Cavell Teatime was delightful.

The settings for the narratives expanded, filling in the under-represented area between the East and West Coasts. Southern and Western authors were particularly successful in utilizing the unique qualities of their areas as backgrounds. Although none of the series in the Sixties and Seventies had time to equal the longevity of a Jane Marple or Beatrice Bradley, many extended into the Eighties and Nineties building a loyal readership (Charlotte Pitt, Charmian Daniels, Emily Pollifax, Emily Seeton, Sharon McCone, Norah Mulcahaney and Amelia Peabody Emerson among others). The popularity of series movies or television programs extended to the mystery novel. Some television series were adapted into mystery novels, although rarely of high quality; *Policewoman, The Mod Squad, Charlie's Angels, The Girl from U.N.C.L.E.* and *The Avengers*. The known quality, the name of the author or protagonist, prominently displayed on a book jacket produced sales. Small publishers filled an important role as major publishers merged but encountered difficulties in merchandising their products.

Americans dominated the field of mystery writing, not surprising considering the relative size and populations of the United States and Great Britain.

Section 2:
Women Sleuths of 1980-1989

Although there was considerable unrest in the global community—the Russian invasion of Afghanistan, the rise of the Solidarity movement in Poland, and continued violence in Northern Ireland—America was not at war during the 1980's. This did not mean Americans were exempt from violence in other countries. The confinement of U. S. hostages in Iran continued until Ronald Reagan's election. Chernobyl, crack cocaine, and the discovery of the AIDS virus made it clear that new problems were on the horizon. Although women had more opportunities, their second salary in married couples often disappeared in rising prices and the costs of raising a family.

On the positive side, women were taking their places in the military, the operating room, and on the judge's bench. Sandra Day O'Connor became the first female United States Supreme Court justice in 1981. Sally Ride became the first American woman in space in 1983. Some Episcopalian and Anglican churches ordained women priests. Females moved up the ladder (to the glass ceiling, anyway) in business, government, and industry. England, India, Norway, and Israel had already selected women as Prime Ministers, when Geraldine Ferraro became the Democratic nominee for vice president (but lost).

The legal structure, primarily through the Civil Rights Act of 1964 and its amendments, established a woman's right to a discrimination-free work environment. American women moved into the male-dominated areas of sports, due partly to Title IX of the Higher Education Act. Their potential competition in the 1980 Olympics was aborted when the United States boycotted the Moscow event; and diminished when Russia and other Communist nations retaliated at Los Angeles in 1984. Women tennis and golf players were hitting the sports pages. Colleges allotted a share of the budget and scholarships for female athletes.

The expansion of the market for books written by women about female investigators, frequently dealing with issues of concern to women, continued into the Nineties. Most sleuths' politics tended to be liberal, occasionally tied to earlier anti-war or feminist activities. Increasingly, the mystery explored the dynamics of gender, family relationships, and the struggle by women to balance professional and personal lives.

As female writers turned their hands to mysteries, they were more likely to have experience within the systems they explored:

- As journalists: Celestine Sibley and Alison Gordon
- As attorneys: Lia Matera, Carolyn Wheat, and Sarah Caudwell
- As medical personnel: Patricia Cornwell
- As television actresses: Eileen Fulton
- As former policewomen: Lee Martin, and
- As spies: Aline Romanones, who had served as a spy in World War II, wrote three biographical books about her adventures and one fictional account.

American heroines increasingly came from the Midwest, the West, and the South. Writers from Spain (Maria-Antonia Oliver), Canada (Doris Shannon as E. X. Giroux, Medora Sale, and L. R. Wright), and Australia (Claire McNab, Kerry Greenwood, and Marele Day) enriched the bookshelves. England continued to provide American readers with top notch authors and sleuths, among the best being the Judy Hill series by Jill McGown; Margaret Duffy's Patrick and Ingrid Gilliard; Gillian Slovo (originally from South Africa) and her free spirited sleuth, Kate Baeier; Frances Fyfield, author of two excellent series; and Sarah Caudwell who kept her readers guessing as to the gender of Hilary Tamar. American sleuths had less traditional backgrounds: African-Americans from inner cities—Marvia Plum by Richard Lupoff; Vonna Saucier in two books by J. Madison Davis; "Rat" Trapp in the Denise Lemoyne series by the Corringtons; "Hawk" who, along with Susan Silverman kept Robert B. Parker's Spenser on an even keel—were achieving recognition. Native Americans on reservations, Asians entering the mainstream (except for Tina Tamiko in the Calico Jack Walker series by Paul Bishop) and independent African-American female sleuths would have to wait another decade for significant representation.

Mysteries with female sleuths became sexually explicit, exploring inter-racial, heterosexual and homosexual relationships. Inspector Carol Ashton, police officer Kate Delafield, and restaurateur Jane Lawless appeared in well-written lesbian mysteries. Heroines had shorter marriages, but more of them; fewer children but more pets; fewer husbands and more lovers. Nurturing instincts were often expressed through nieces and nephews, foster children (Charlotte Kent) or volunteer programs (Carlotta Carlyle was a Big Sister).

Conservative religious viewpoints found a voice in the mystery genre through Jerry Jenkins—Jennifer Grey. B. J. Hoff wrote an extensive series about Jennifer and Daniel Kaine. Doran Fairweather (author: Mollie Hardwick) married a Protestant clergyman but he wavered in his faith. Isabelle Holland's Claire Aldington was an Episcopalian priest. The best that Catholics could do was a trio of nuns by Monica Quill (pseudonym for Ralph McInerny) and a more interesting series featuring Sister Mary Helen by Sr. Carol Anne O'Marie. The Jewish faith was explored through several heroines—Rachel Gold by Michael A. Kahn; Nina Fischman by Marissa Piesman, Mom by James Yaffe, but more completely in the series by Faith Kellerman featuring Rina Lazarus Decker.

Mystery heroines were less likely to be widows or wives than divorcees or single women with long term relationships. Although a substantial number of widows and divorcees remarried, others enjoyed the independence, preferring informal alliances. Where previously the age range had been heavy at the young and elderly ends of the spectrum, now the majority of female sleuths were mature women in their thirties and forties. Stay-at-home housewives were less common. Often they were single mothers paired with police investigators or Lucy Ricardo clones. The females were taller, more athletic, more likely to be skilled professionals in music or art. Flaws and disabilities were explored. Maggie Elliott had an alcohol problem. Marlene Ciampi lost one eye and several fingers. The level of education and training increased, partly due to the large number of sleuths with medical, legal, and doctoral degrees. Names became more clipped—Roz, Kat; even initials V. I., T. T.; and more androgynous—Sam.

Ensembles or couples which included a female and sometimes a racial or social minority tried to cover all bases:

1. Italian-American with remnants of parochial school education; Marlene Ciampi married Jewish Butch Karp in the Robert K. Tanenbaum series.

2. Denise Lemoyne worked with redneck reporter Wes Colvin and African-American Captain Rat Trapp.

3. Marvia Plum had both a professional and personal inter-racial relationship with Bart Lindsey.

4. Barbara Havers, a lower class police officer worked with the elegant Thomas Lynley and Lady Helen Clyde in Elizabeth George's ensemble.

The basic cozies, couples, academic mysteries, puzzles, private investigators and police procedurals were supplemented by other sub-genres and crossovers—the culinary mystery, the business mystery, the legal mystery, the medical mystery, sports and computer mysteries. Depictions of historical characters included Eleanor Roosevelt in the series identified as written by son Elliott; Gertrude Stein and Alice B. Toklas as portrayed by Samuel M. Steward; and Geraldine Farrar and Enrico Caruso by Barbara Paul. Historical mysteries featuring a female sleuth during a period when actual sleuthing by a woman was unlikely were written by Leonard Tourney (Joan Stock), Lindsey Davis (Helena Justina who was subsidiary to Marcus Didius Falco), and Kyra Keaton (Teona Tone).

Women mystery readers who traveled by car, bus, train, or plane now had access to books on tape. Paperback reprints remained a standby (even a necessity considering the prices). The tendency of paperback originals to serve as minor league experience for new writers, who might move on to hardcover, was expedited by the multiple mergers within the publishing industry. The mergers had more serious negative impacts, but stimulated an increase in small presses. The higher costs of both hard covers and paperbacks triggered the development of a large number of "used" bookstores with major mystery sections. Paperbacks were a bargain. Libraries were the least expensive and most convenient resource particularly for readers in small communities without a bookstore.

Where, a century before, a single female sleuth emerged in a three book series over decades, now several series with women investigators were introduced each month. Popularity bred duplication and imitation. Although the best (i.e. those by Linda Barnes, Nancy Pickard, Carolyn Wheat, Karen Kijewski, Sara Paretsky, Liza Cody, Jill McGown, etc) were excellent, there was a considerable amount of mediocrity.

There were commendable books featuring women sleuths written by male authors (Richard Barth, John Sherwood, Michael Kahn, and Bill Granger) and several by couples (the Corringtons and Maxwells). Still, more and more, women writers dominated the mystery field, generally with female protagonists. This is not surprising considering that Publisher's Weekly published a Gallup Survey in 1986 indicating that more females than males read mysteries and that women who worked part-time were the most frequent readers. Women mystery authors and fans banded together to form Sisters in Crime in 1986 hoping to increase clout with publishers and encourage more reviews of mystery books written by females. The best was yet to come.

Biographies of Sleuths,
Introduced Between 1980 Through 1989

(Readers are advised that when a book was first published as a hardcover only that cite is provided, but that the version used for the review may not be the original.)

Gillian Adams

Author: Nora Kelly

The daughter of a Canadian father and American mother, Gillian Adams lived and worked in Canada and England. Her father, Nathaniel, had died in his sixties; her mother, Estelle, lived on in New England. Initially Nora distanced herself from her American roots. In her forties, she was tall and slight with charcoal gray hair and eyes. She had earned a Ph.D. from Cambridge University, and was employed as a history professor at Canada's Pacific Northwest University.

In the Shadow of Kings (St. Martin, 1984) began as guest lecturer Gillian, and her lover, Scotland Yard detective Edward Gisborne, witnessed the death of Professor Ambrose Greenwood. The narrative moved languidly savoring Gillian's insights about the suspects and the setting as Gisborne closed in on the rather obvious killer. Gillian's ardent feminism surfaced in *My Sister's Keeper* (St. Martin, 1992) when she supported the Feminist Union and the solicitation of funds for a women's studies program at Pacific Northwest. After protest leader Rita Gordon's scholarship application was rejected, her death drew Gillian into an investigation, which paralleled the official efforts.

On her return to England in *Bad Chemistry* (St. Martin, 1994), Gillian weighed her relationship with Gisborne against her career. While at Cambridge, she immersed herself in the investigation of the theft of important documents at the Pregnancy Information Service and the deaths of a brilliant young research chemist and an obscure teenager.

Nora re-emerged after a five-year absence in *Old Wounds* (Harper-Collins, 1999). Prodded by Estelle, her elderly mother, she evaluated her current relationship with Edward. He had been disappointed when she chose to spend her sabbatical with the aging Estelle rather than in London with him. Nora revised her book and taught a course at the local college, where one of her students was a young woman, Nicole Bishop. The discovery of Nicole's body near a lonely road over which Nora had passed that same evening, and the police focus on a recluse whom Nora remembered from her high school years put her at odds with old friends. Edward came to the United States to be with Nora and assisted in her investigation. He was agreeably surprised at her change in attitude as to their future.

Above average with a feminist agenda, more subtle in later narratives.

Samantha Adams

Author: Alice Storey, pseudonym for Sarah Shankman

In the two books written under the Storey name, Samantha Adams was portrayed as being in her thirties, tall with curly dark hair and brown eyes. Orphaned at the age of twelve, she had spent her teenage years in the Atlanta home of her uncle, Attorney George Adams. She remained there through a year of college, but, jilted by Beau Talbot, transferred to Stanford majoring in pot smoking, the peace movement, and rebellion. She survived a Mexican abortion, a short unhappy marriage, and serious problems with alcohol, before becoming a successful investigative reporter. Samantha's sobriety was threatened when her police detective lover was killed. She returned to Atlanta and Uncle George, securing a job on the Atlanta Journal-Constitution.

In *First Kill All the Lawyers* (Pocket Books, 1988), Samantha reunited with medical examiner Beau Talbot (now divorced), investigating the disappearance of Uncle George's partner Forrest Ridley. Samantha's knowledge of Southern politics did not forestall her challenge to the unrestrained authority of a rural sheriff.

By *Then Hang All the Liars* (Pocket Books, 1989), Samantha had settled into the family home, owned an expensive car (BMW), and a thoroughbred dog (Shi Tzu named Harpo). She learned that local debutantes and their younger sisters were performing stripteases in Peachtree street bistros. She also became concerned about the mental deterioration of retired actress Felicity Morris, the widow of a very proper banker. Shankman's insights into Southern mores illuminated the problems experienced by victims of prejudice and mental illness.

Now Let's Talk of Graves (Pocket Books, 1990) written under the Shankman name as were all succeeding books, changed the tone of the series. When Samantha visited the New Orleans Mardi Gras, her hostess's brother was killed in a hit and run accident. Handsome young insurance investigator Harry Zach and Samantha worked their way through a melange of medical malpractice, voodoo, family feuds, and drug dealing to a personal relationship.

Samantha was uncomfortable in *She Walks in Beauty* (Pocket Books, 1991) when assigned to the Miss America Pageant in Atlantic City. The concept offended her feminist principles, but Zach's presence made it tolerable. Samantha, Zach, and African-American police officer Lavert Washington dealt with assault, kidnapping, and murder. The narrative was cluttered with characters (gamblers, contestants, judges, and family members), substituting zany humor for the coziness of the earlier books.

In *The King Is Dead* (Pocket Books, 1992), Samantha and Zach attended the Tupelo, Mississippi International Barbecue Cook-off. Murder victims and suspects included mercenary widows, Elvis impersonators, pill-popping truckers, and a small town socialite who paid a terrible price for rejecting Elvis.

Depressed by Zach's dalliance with a younger woman in *He Was Her Man* (Pocket Books, 1993), Samantha headed for Hot Springs, Arkansas to attend a party held by college rival Jinx Watson. When a friendly ex-hooker was murdered, her corpse was shunted from one place to another while conmen and canny women competed for a huge diamond.

Samantha had resigned herself to a solitary life, working on the second volume of her book, *American Weird*, but was thrown off balance in *Digging Up Momma* (Pocket Books, 1998) by a letter from her mother who had purportedly died 34 years earlier in an airplane accident. Samantha's life had been changed irreparably by the crash. From that experience, an unhappy marriage, and the death of a lover she had become unwilling to risk a long-term commitment to Harry Zach. Samantha flew to Santa Fe to confront her past and learn what tragedy caused Johanna Adams to abandon her only child. Their reunion was short, but focused the attention of a vengeful killer on Samantha. The narrative combined spiritualism (appearances of a deceased Indian mystic), emotional impact (the loss of a mother), and tension. Appropriately humor played a less important role in this narrative.

Impersonal Attractions (St. Martin, 1985) by Shankman had preceded the first Samantha Adams narrative. Although it was not part of the series, it bore many connections—the heroine Annie Tannenbaum had a best friend, Samantha Storey. Samantha was a crime reporter for a San Francisco newspaper who was in love with a police detective, Sean O'Reilly. Like the later Samantha Adams, Samantha Storey had an alcohol problem. Many of the characteristics of Samantha Storey were incorporated into Samantha Adams, but transferred to the South, and endowed with a new supporting cast.

Lauren Adler

Author: Victoria Silver

College students have rarely been mystery heroines, perhaps because they tread the line between youth and adult fiction. Lauren Adler, a full-figured brunette from a New Jersey Jewish family, was a coed in *Death of a Harvard Freshman* (Bantam, 1984). Russell Bernard's failure to keep their date was explained by his murder. Lauren and gay fellow student Michael Hunt believed that the killer was a member of their seminar on the Russian Revolution.

Lauren reappeared in *Death of a Radcliffe Roommate* (Bantam, 1986) occupying a dormitory suite, into which she welcomed poetess Helena Dichter, but not troublemaker Debbie Doyle. Debbie's strangulation by a harp string produced several suspects, although the intended victim might have been an Arabian princess.

Claire Aldington

Author: Isabelle Holland

Claire Aldington, a member of the Episcopalian clergy, was also the widow of an Episcopalian priest. Her husband Patrick, a social activist, had died, leaving her to care for their son Jamie and Patrick's anorexic teenage daughter, Martha. Claire's marriage had been troubled by Patrick's infidelity but his death left her financially secure. A graduate of Smith College, she had a master's degree in clinical psychology from Stanford, and a degree in theology before she was ordained. Even then, Claire worked in a subordinate position, as a therapist/counselor rather than as a sacramental priest. At thirty-five, she was slim with reddish brown hair and hazel green eyes.

In *A Death at St. Anselm's* (Doubleday, 1984), Claire's discovery of the parish business manager's corpse and her investigation of the murder occurred amidst the parish discussion as to its role in helping the homeless, and Claire's problems as a single parent.

Flight of the Archangel (Doubleday, 1985) focused on Kit Maitland, a female reporter researching a lavish estate bequeathed to St. Anselm's, using Claire as a resource and consultant. Claire's romance with banker Brett Cunningham was endangered in *A Lover Scorned* (Doubleday, 1986). Brett's son was involved in a drug investigation while Claire was preoccupied with violence against women priests.

After Claire and Brett married, she continued at prestigious St. Anselm's during *A Fatal Advent* (Doubleday, 1989). Her professional problems included a rector who challenged her role as therapist, the Norwich boy choir now singing at St. Anselm's, and murder in the parish house. During *The Long Search* (Doubleday, 1990) editor Janet Covington sought the child she had released for adoption. Claire helped Janet deal with the past but did not play a significant part in the action.

These were enjoyable narratives

Finny Aletter

Author: Yvonne Montgomery

Finny Aletter had burned out in her mid-thirties due to the fierce competition she faced as a Denver stockbroker. Her MBA had led to a well-paid position as an account executive at Lakin and Fulton. Except for the short-term affair she and her boss Elliot Fulton had when she was first employed, her personal life was unexceptional.

As *Scavengers* (Arbor House, 1987) opened, Fulton was murdered and Finny fired. Lt. Chris Barelli, in charge of the investigation, considered her a likely suspect. Finny followed the trail of street persons who had inside information about a fabulously valuable manuscript Elliot had purchased, but found the killer closer to home. Barelli had moved in with Finny by *Obstacle Course* (Avon, 1990), and she had begun a new career as a carpenter. An old friend, Twee Garrett, gave a party to introduce Finny to prospective clients, but the evening ended in the murder of a controversial judge. An early confession did not ring true to Finny, so she continued to investigate.

Liz Archer a.k.a. Angel Eyes

Author: W.B. Longley, one of the pseudonyms used by Robert J. Randisi who also wrote as Nick Carter and as Warren B. Murphy

The Angel Eyes series was identified as an "adult western", but like adult bookshops and adult movie theaters, not all adults would be interested. The sex was explicit and meaningless in terms of any emotional commitment.

Liz Archer prided herself on not being a "hired gun"; i.e. not taking money to kill, but she killed and frequently. She also saw herself as not being a whore, because again she did not take money for her generous services. The series, which extended to at least eight appearances, took place in the decade following the Civil War.

Book #4, *Chinatown Justice* (PaperJacks, 1985) placed Liz in San Francisco where she was seeking fun and excitement. For fun, she engaged in sex with at least five different people (one, a woman) over 183 pages. For excitement, she identified the killer of a young libertine.

Book #5, *Logan's Army* (PaperJacks, 1986) pitted Liz against Ed Logan who controlled 90% of everything in Loganville, but wanted it all. His brutality in a planned takeover of Honey's Place, a gambling establishment, caused Liz to align herself with some questionable allies. Before she left town, she killed a hired gunman, and turned a murderer over to the sheriff.

Book #8 *Avenging Angel* (PaperJacks, 1986) sent Liz to Mexico. She had heard that a Mexican rebel had shot the one man she had truly loved, Tate Gilmore, during a bank robbery. Tate and she became enmeshed in the struggle between the revolutionary forces of Profirio Diaz and those of the current president, Benito Juarez. Almost everyone had been killed by the conclusion, often by a trusted companion.

Others: *The Miracle of Revenge, Death's Angel, Wolf Pass, Bullets and Bad Times; Six Gun Angel.*

Inspector Carol Ashton

Author: Claire McNab

Blonde, green-eyed Carol Ashton of the Sydney Police Department had married and divorced barrister Justin Hart. The couple had a young son, David, who lived with his father and stepmother and visited Carol regularly. A married friend Christine Tait had brought Carol to the realization that she was a lesbian. Although Carol ended her marriage because of their relationship, moving to the Sydney Harbor house built by her architect father, Christine remained with her husband. Carol's investigations often risked disclosure of her sexual orientation, which eventually occurred. Over a period of time, Carol acquired a cat named Sinker.

In *Lessons in Murder* (Naiad, 1988), Carol investigated the death of high school teacher William Pagett, whose family had important political connections. In the process of the successful investigation, Carol became sexually involved with Sybil Quade, a major suspect. During *Fatal Reunion* (Naiad, 1989), former lover Christine contacted Carol when suspected of her husband's murder. Carol, although never assigned to the case, used her contacts to monitor the situation. She feared that her relationship with

Christine might be made public in a trial, but the solution made that unnecessary.

In *Death Down Under* (Naiad, 1990), Carol and assistant Mark Bourke sought a pattern to deaths by "The Orange Strangler." Sybil, now Carol's live-in lover, tutored children on a movie set connected to the crimes. *Cop Out* (Naiad, 1991) found Carol fatigued and anxious until her aunt interested her in the death of a supporter of the gay movement. Carol, believing that the police had settled for a quick resolution of the case, investigated the prominent Darcy family.

By *Dead Certain* (Naiad, 1992), Sybil insisted that their relationship become public. Justin Hart wanted Carol to tell their ten-year-old son about her sexual orientation. During her investigation of the death of an Australian operatic tenor, Carol learned that he was HIV positive. His family preferred that his illness be concealed and the death designated "accidental" in order to collect on his life insurance.

Carol had been physically injured, publicly "outed", and abandoned by Sybil by *Bodyguard* (Naiad, 1994). When she was ordered to guard Marla, a strident American feminist, Carol distinguished herself for both physical courage and alertness in saving Marla's life.

Madeline Shipley, the television reporter who sought and gained a relationship with Carol, wanted her personal attention directed to threatening letters she had received in *Double Bluff* (Naiad, 1995). Not only was Carol busy on the possible murder of Tala Orlando, a prominent television producer, but she considered her intervention in Madeline's case a conflict of interest. Sybil's decision to return from England created a second area of stress for Carol, as Madeline aggressively sought her affections.

Kent Agar, a conservative member of the Australian parliament had publicly criticized Carol's sexual orientation, but when *Inner Circle* (Naiad, 1996) began, he could not exclude her from the investigation of two murders in which he was involved. Carol was detailed to the rural community where the victims lived to probe into their lives and possible terrorist activities. Unsure of who were her allies or her antagonists, Carol was decoyed into personal danger.

The breach with Sybil had not ended when *Chain Letter* (Naiad, 1997) began, but Carol retained hope of re-establishing the relationship. The death of a fellow police officer galvanized the resources of the department into action. Only after tying his murder to a series of other suspicious deaths, each preceded by the reception of an ominous chain letter, did a motive and the identity of the killer become clear. Carol had a personal stake in apprehending him before he could kill again.

During *Past Due* (Naiad, 1998), Carol lived alone in the home her father had built. Sybil, who had been terrorized by a killer at that house, could not bear to enter. Arson and murder at a local fertility clinic could potentially affect prominent citizens, giving Carol little time to deal with her personal problems. She researched unfamiliar material in genetics, artificial insemination, and cloning before she identified a killer who had been driven by horror.

Concern about a future court appearance for son David on a charge of selling marijuana had to be put aside in *Set Up* (Naiad, 1999) while Carol investigated the deaths of men considered "predatory" by environmentalists. A group called "Gaia's Revenge" denied personal responsibility for the murders, but gloated over them. By the time Carol realized the identity of the hired killer, it was too late to prevent her escape. Although Justin would have preferred that David be spared a court appearance, Carol refused to use her position to shield him from the consequences of his acts. Eleanor, Justin's second wife, and Carol had become friends.

Freed of her need to reconcile with Sybil, who remained a friend and very close to David, Carol looked forward to attending a special training session at FBI headquarters in Quantico, Virginia as *Under Suspicion* (Naiad, 2000) opened. Her pleasure was diminished by her rude traveling companion, Inspector Peter Karfer. Although the training was worthwhile, there were tensions among the students and members of the faculty. The murders of a British inspector and an instructor resulted in Carol's arrest for the crimes. Only the intervention of Leta Woolfe, an African-American FBI agent, who was having an affair with Carol, saved her from confinement until trial. The killer's eagerness to add Carol to his victims saved her. This was not one of the better Ashton stories.

Carol had not given much attention to golf courses, unlike her Aunt Sarah who detested and protested them for their overuse of pesticides and weed killers. During *Death Club* (Naiad, 2001), the murder of Fiona Hawk, a homophobic Englishwoman then in first place in Gussie Whitlew's tournament, Carol learned about women's golf, the competitive females who devoted their lives to it, and the men who preyed upon them. Gussie, a wealthy widow, had a second motive for sponsoring the tournament. She used the event to attract young women. Leota Woolfe, who became important to Carol in the prior book, arranged a transfer to Australia.

The series had competent plotting and characterizations. The sexual passages were short, avoidable by a reader who found them distasteful. Carol did not hate men, had good relationships with male co-workers, and was devoted to her son.

Beth Austin

Author: Edith Skom

Beth Austin, an English professor at a midwestern university, had previously taught at Princeton. She owned an original Matisse, smoked, loved puzzles and music, but rarely described herself physically. During *The Mark Twain Murders* (Council Oak Books, 1989), prize-winning student Marylou Peacock, suspected of plagiarism, was found dead in the college library. An attractive FBI agent tied the death to thefts from academic libraries. Beth proved Marylou's innocence of plagiarism, but only identified the killer when he sought her out.

It was off to Hawaii for Beth in *The George Eliot Murders* (Delacorte, 1995). Having overheard a casual conversation by the woman in the next room, Beth doubted that she had committed suicide. Such incidents are played down at distinguished hotels, but Beth and two new friends took on the challenge. Beth compared suspected spouses to the ill-fated couples in George Eliot's *Middlemarch*.

The recent death of a woman in a New York City hospital during *The Charles Dickens Murders* (Delacorte, 1998) was of no interest to Beth until she connected it to her mother Laurie's concern about an unsolved murder. That killing had taken place decades before, when Laurie attended the University of Chicago. Beth reconstructed those tense years in the lives of a half dozen women (pregnancy and possible abortion, thefts of jewelry and subsequent accusations, and the death of a provocative coed during a party). As in prior books, Skom utilized classic novels (*The Mystery of Edwin Drood*, Bleak House) to point out parallels; the burden of beauty, the uncovering of past secrets. It helped if the reader had knowledge of the classics.

Kate Baeier

Author: Gillian Slovo

Kate Baeier, an investigative reporter and detective, was a leftist by birth and inclination. A Lithuanian, she had lived in Portugal before coming to England. Although the series provided little information about Kate's physical appearance, it disclosed that she played the saxophone for relaxation, had a sense of humor not always found in feminist heroines, and shared a monogamous relationship with Sam, a mathematician.

Political activity underlay the plotting in *Morbid Symptoms* (Dembner, 1985). The staff at African Economic Reports hired Kate to investigate the death of a commentator that the police preferred to write off as an accident or connected to "communist" activities.

Death by Analysis (Doubleday, 1988) involved Kate with support groups. Her therapist, believing that psychoanalyst Paul Holland had been murdered, sought Kate's intervention at a time when Kate was undecided about moving in with Sam.

During *Death Comes Staccato* (Doubleday, 1988), Alicia Wetherby, a promising young pianist, was stalked. Although Kate preferred corporate investigations, she agreed to protect Alicia. Both the stalker and Alicia's young boyfriend were murdered before Kate could pinpoint the real villain.

Kate experienced a dramatic change in the interval before the next book, *Catnap* (St. Martin, 1996). Sam, who had represented love and stability in her life, had died. She had found it impossible to cope with her memories in England, so spent five years abroad as a freelance writer, returning only for business reasons. Then, withdrawn and morose, Kate realized that her return to London was threatening someone. She could not leave until she had confronted her enemies.

Close Call (Michael Joseph, London 1995) found Kate still in London with no intention of returning to private investigation. When she was arrested as a suspect in a murder, she had no choice. She had an unlikely ally, her father, General Alfonso da Souza-Baeier, a prominent Portuguese official, with an agenda of his own. The plot was complex to a level of incredibility, unusual for Slovo.

Slovo's anti-authoritarian principles echoed in her books. She spotlighted police brutality and racial discrimination without stridency.

Jane Bailey

Author: Margaret Dobson

Jane Bailey, a chestnut-haired woman in her mid-twenties, seemed naive. Her mother had died when she was young; her dad, more recently. Jane owned a bookstore in Tulsa, Oklahoma, but traveled, leaving Aunt Minnie in charge. She met insurance investigator Phillip Decker in *Touchstone* (Dell, 1987), when her brother Ted was killed in a car accident. Jane's need to understand his death took her to romantic Aruba and into the clutches of international jewel thieves.

In *Primrose* (Dell, 1987), Jane returned to Tulsa where she and Phillip probed the murder of a paraplegic garage owner.

Soothsayer (Dell, 1987) exposed differences in attitudes between Jane and Phillip. She was aggrieved at his assumption that she should help on his cases without any payment. He had withheld important information from a client that Jane felt should have been disclosed. Finally, he scoffed at the psychic clues that his client Roxanne said would lead them to Howard, her missing son. In their search, they learned more about Howard than Roxanne had anticipated, but found the formula to end his flight from Portland.

At 38, Phillip was twice divorced, but serious enough about Jane to invite her to Hawaii to meet his father in *Nightcap* (Dell, 1987), where Jane became a murder suspect.

The Bailey series, published by Dell, was lightweight with covers that employed comparisons to a popular television program. It might be considered as young adult. Their badinage was more corny than clever.

T. T. (Theresa Tracy) Baldwin

Author: Shannon OCork

Redheaded T. T. Baldwin was an aggressive, even unprincipled, sports reporter. She was covering professional football for the New York Graphic in *Sports Freak* (St. Martin, 1980) when an acupuncture needle killed quarterback Lou Lamont during his first professional game. The bizarre touches did not end with the choice of murder weapon.

In *End of the Line* (St. Martin, 1981), T. T. and her obnoxious associate Floyd Beesom covered a sports fishing contest to probe the disappearance of a diamond dealer and his jewels. Photos taken by T. T. provided significant clues, which she withheld from the police department.

During *Hell Bent for Heaven* (St. Martin, 1983), T. T. had two assignments—covering the rodeo, and acting as a courier for the federal government. The narrative tried hard with nursery rhyme clues, drugs, porno movies, and international intrigue.

Michelle Merrill Ballard

Authors: Carole Gift Page and Doris Elaine Fell

See: Michelle Merrill, Page 195

Margaret Barlow

Author: David Osborn

Margaret Barlow, initially a widowed part-time resident of Martha's Vineyard, was an active woman. A hot air balloonist and glider enthusiast, she enjoyed personal risks.

During *Murder on Martha's Vineyard* (Lynx, 1989), Grace Chadwick had lifetime occupancy of a family mansion, while painter Algar Mikele waited impatiently to inherit the property. When an older woman's corpse was found in Grace's pond, Algar was suspected of killing her by mistake.

Scenic descriptions and reminiscences enriched *Murder on the Chesapeake* (Simon, 1992). Margaret's recollections of herself as a midwestern scholarship student at an eastern prep school for girls expanded her character. Teenaged granddaughter Nancy, who attended exclusive Bride's Hall, involved Margaret in the death of a fourteen year old student but she was not the primary in solving the case.

In *Murder in the Napa Valley* (Simon, 1993), Margaret's work as a photojournalist prompted her tour of California vineyards including L'Abbaye de Ste. Denise, where the Selfridge family struggled with a series of mishaps. When the owner-manager's ex-wife was murdered, Margaret's reputation as an amateur detective motivated the local editor to recruit her to solve the crime.

Margaret had a chameleon like quality, a persona that changed as author Osborn moved her from one setting to another.

Bertha Barstow

Author: Dicey Thomas

Bertha Barstow, a tall, slim brown-haired woman in her thirties, used her Ph.D. in metallurgy as a private consultant. She had worked for the British Museum; then spent two years in Leningrad as a teacher and researcher. Partner Caleb Saunderson loved Bertha, but his feelings were not reciprocated.

Statutory Murder (Tudor, 1989) suffered from too many characters, too much detail, and too many explanations. Shortly after Harvard physicist Aaron Hodgkins accepted an artifact for verification, he was murdered. Bertha was convinced that the artifact and death were connected to controversy about extra-terrestrials. However, she and Caleb discovered that the killer was more interested in smuggling.

Just Plane Murder (Tudor, 1992) was anything but plain. The narrative mixed metallurgy and "astronautics" with international sabotage. Bertha and Caleb challenged the FBI and a host of government agencies to find a scientific killer.

Angela Benbow

Author: Corinne Holt Sawyer

The J. Alfred Prufrock Murders (Fine, 1988) featured four elderly women seeking the killer of a quiet ex-librarian who subsidized her retirement by blackmailing neighbors. Only tiny caustic Angela Benbow and sophisticated, six-foot tall Caledonia Wingate were still available by *Murder in Gray and White* (Fine, 1989). When new resident Amy Kinseth was killed, the sprightly widows offered their services to Lt. Martinez. Aware of their utter disregard for such legal niceties as search warrants, Martinez tried to limit their participation.

Murder by Owl Light (Fine, 1992) began when two workers were killed on the retirement home premises. Emboldened by their prior successes, Angela and Caledonia expected cooperation from the police. The assigned investigator, Hal Benson, was immune to their blandishments. Only when Martinez took control, did the standard plot resume, with the women breaking rules to gather evidence against a killer.

The Peanut Butter Murders (Fine, 1993) provided a weak motive for the murders of Edna Ferrier's slick young suitor and of the secretary for the accountant who managed Edna's trust.

Friendship with Dorothy McGraw proprietor of the Time-Out Inn, a spa for women, took Angela and Caledonia away from the housing project in Murder Has No Calories (Fine, 1994). The death of a staff member, and succeeding incidents threatening the Inn's success, motivated Angela and the more reluctant, non-athletic Caledonia to combine aerobics, diet menus, and detecting in a refreshing narrative.

Ho-Ho Homicide (Fine, 1995) was centered on Christmas preparations at Camden-sur-Mer with murder on the side. "Birdy" Benton, a lover of wildlife, had managed to alienate many of the other residents before she was found dead under the Christmas tree. Angela used "muscle readings" of the suspects to find a killer, whom she preferred to protect.

Angela trolled the trashcans and dominated the interviews in *The Geezer Factory Murder* (Fine, 1996). When the beleaguered killer confronted Caledonia, she needed to be rescued by a fat cat. Camden-sur-Mer competed with the nearby Golden Years Retirement Home, so administrator Olaf Torgerson was delighted when several residents of that facility relocated at Camden. He was unaware that two victims and one killer were among the transfers.

Angela and Caledonia left the retirement home behind in *Murder Ole!* (Fine, 1997) to tour Mexico with fellow residents. Angela's determination to improve her Spanish language skills took her into the marketplaces of Tijuana and Ensenada. Her fellow travelers encountered murder, sudden illness, and accidents too frequently to be a coincidence. Although Angela misplaced her trust and endangered her well being, she exposed the guilty parties.

The plots were occasionally overwhelmed by trivia, but presented a charming view of active elderly women.

Maggie Bennett
Author: Anne Stuart, pseudonym for Anne Kristine Stuart Ohlrogge

Maggie Bennett, whose father had been a Danish Count, had been christened Margretha Elisa, but she never used her father's last name, and settled for Maggie. What might have been unusual in any other family was customary in that of Maggie's mother—Sybil Bennett. Sybil, an American actress born in England, initially believed in marriage. This led to four marriages, each of which produced a single daughter, followed by a series of relationships. Her change in approach was less a question of morality than what the public would accept.

Maggie, the eldest of the four daughters, became "little mother" as Sybil found parenting cut into her other activities. Fortunately during the early years, Sybil's mother was available to fill the gap. At her demise, Queenie, Sybil's maid, took on the responsibility. Eventually Maggie became less daughter or sister, than mother. This contributed to her uncompromising, controlling personality. She had also been deeply affected by sexual abuse at the hands of Sybil's third husband, actor Deke Robinson. The daughters, all of whom used Bennett as their last names until they married, were close and supportive.

Maggie became an attorney, serving for a time with the CIA. While working on a joint mission for the agency, she became sexually and emotionally attached to worldly Randall Carter, an international businessman who cooperated with the CIA. His apparent abandonment of her in Eastern Europe left her devastated and vulnerable. A rebound marriage lasted eight months. Maggie never took the bar examination, choosing instead to work with Third World Causes, an international agency assisting hostages.

At the request of Peter Wallace, head of Third World Causes, Maggie escorted former rock star Mack Pulaski to safety in *Escape Out of Darkness* (Dell, 1987). Pulaski had witnessed a drug exchange. His testimony could target a major criminal figure. What had been termed a three-day assignment turned into a long-term commitment as Mack and Maggie traveled from Utah to Texas to Honduras and New York City, and finally to Zurich. They were set upon by rebel armies, rogue CIA agents, and drug smugglers. Along the way, Mack helped Maggie escape some demons of her own and they were married.

Maggie's happy marriage to Mack had ended when *Darkness Before the Dawn* (Dell, 1987) began. He had been shot down two years before and Maggie was still mourning. A call from sister Kate, in the process of a child custody suit, sent Maggie to Chicago and a resumption of her on-again, off-again relationship with Randall Carter. Kate's involvement in a murder tinged with espionage forced Maggie to work with Carter. She achieved revenge for Mack's death but at a bitter price.

Devastated by charges made against Randall by CIA agent Bud Willis, Maggie shut herself off in *At the Edge of the Sun* (Dell, 1987). Even in her depression, she could not ignore the news that her mother, Sybil had been left near death by a recent lover, Flynn. The sisters rallied. Two remained in California to watch at their mother's bedside while Randall Carter joined Maggie and Holly, a beautiful model, in their pursuit of Flynn. More reluctantly they accepted help from Ian Andrews, the former British officer, who had released Flynn from a Northern Ireland police station and learned to regret it.

Happy endings abounded but not until dozens more had been killed, thousands of miles traveled, and multiple quarrels occurred between the two couples. Not to be taken seriously, but the series must be extremely popular. Paperback originals of the three sold in the used book market on the Internet at prices totaling $150 a set.

Mavis Bignell*

Author: Nancy Livingston

Also spelled as Mavis Bignall in some printings.

Not all consorts to male detectives were sculptresses or financial experts. Mavis Bignell, the plump but shapely redhead who accompanied former tax inspector G. D. H. Pringle on his investigations, was a barmaid at the

Bricklayers, a British pub. Her earthy warmth provided a contrast to the meticulous Pringle in a humorous series, reminiscent of Colin Watson.

This was Pringle's series and Mavis's participation increased gradually from not at all (*The Trouble at Acquitaine*, St. Martin, 1985), to a minor appearance (*Fatality at Bath & Wells*, St. Martin, 1987), when murder occurred at a television studio, she and G. D. H. visited. She listened to his theories, slept with him, and took care of him when he was ill, but rejected his proposals. After one bad marriage, she preferred to remain independent, causing Pringle's sister to refer to her as a "whore" in *Incident at Parga* (St. Martin, 1988).

Death in a Distant Land (St. Martin, 1989) took the pair to Australia on Mavis's gambling pool winnings. While there, G. D. H. sought a neighbor's grandson taken to Australia by his father. Good hearted Mavis, tricked into transporting heroin, fended off drug dealers when G. D. H. threw the heroin out.

In need of extra cash, G. D. H. advertised his skills as a tax preparer in *Death in Close-Up*, (St. Martin, 1990) and was hired by a television program controller. When a self-centered actress was killed on the set, Mavis had little impact on the investigation.

In *Unwillingly to Vegas* (St. Martin, 1991), Pringle escorted English performers who were to take part in an American film, not realizing he was to be the fall guy for a Las Vegas robbery. Mavis saved Pringle's life and his reputation.

Quiet Murder (St. Martin, 1992) returned the action to the Bricklayer's, where a patron gave bonuses to worthy senior citizens at Christmas. When he was found dead and the bonus money missing, the obvious suspect was a demented ex-convict trucker. Only after he had been ruled out did Pringle and Mavis focus on the killers, and why the victim "deserved to die." Interesting plots and characters.

Dr. Marissa Blumenthal

Author: Robin Cook

Marissa Blumenthal, the only daughter and youngest child of a surgeon, chose pediatrics as her specialty in medical school. After completing her residency in Boston, she took a position as an epidemology Intelligence Services Officer at the Center for Disease Control in Atlanta. She had experienced an unhappy love affair with a neurosurgeon who left her behind when he moved to California.

In *Outbreak* (Putnam's, 1987), her first assignment was to supervise control of an Ebola virus outbreak at a Los Angeles clinic. Although her supervisor, Dr. Cyrill Dubchek, relieved her, Marissa showed a continued interest in the disease. When other outbreaks followed, she ignored official protocol and risked professional retribution. She was convinced that the outbreaks were induced by a vicious conspiracy against new methods in the provision of health care.

Marriage to businessman Robert Buchanan brought conflict in *Vital Signs* (Putnam's, 1991). His mother disapproved of Robert's marriage to a member of the Jewish community. The honeymoon ended when, month after month, Marissa and Robert failed to conceive a child. She met other women who had resorted to artificial insemination, and discovered patterns that affected her as a woman and as a doctor. Lacking support from Robert, Marissa and a friend began an investigation that led her to Australia, Hong Kong, and the People's Republic of China. A powerful conspiracy of Chinese triads and greedy medical practitioners had manipulated women's lives for their own gain.

Martha "Moz" Brant

Author: Jean Femling

"Moz" Brant characterized herself by her racial heritage, finding it significant in each encounter with an unfamiliar person. Her mother Ana, an Englishwoman had been married six times. The relationship with Moz's Filipino father had been one of the shorter connections. It was unclear whether Moz had been married, then divorced, and was disinclined to marry again or if she had never married. She was tiny, with hair and coloring that confused others as to her racial identity: Mexican? Puerto Rican? Native American? Moz liked to keep people guessing. She was a competent, if impetuous, insurance investigator who went far beyond her responsibilities to the T. Ambrose Agency of Los Angeles and her boss, Leo Jablonka.

In *Hush, Money* (St. Martin, 1989), a serious injury to Rick, a former lover, prompted Moz and her new friend and subsequent lover, Gage Pfeiffer, to investigate an explosion on board a nearby yacht. The deceased owner had tangled personal and family relationships that made him a likely target.

Moz's employer had insured the elderly driver who was considered to be at fault in a car accident in *Getting Mine* (St. Martin, 1991). Moz detected inconsistencies in the circumstances. Gage and the local police dismissed her suspicions, but she uncovered a major medical fraud.

Pleasant with complex plotting.

Juliet Bravo a.k.a. Jean Darblay

Author: Mollie Hardwick

"Juliet Bravo" was code for radio messages to Yorkshire Police Inspector Jean Darblay. Three books, all published by Pan (*Juliet Bravo 1,* 1980; *Juliet Bravo 2,* 1980; and *Calling Juliet Bravo,* 1981), intertwined Jean's domestic and professional problems with the solutions to "hour length" crimes. Jean was slightly taller than average, slim with short dark hair. The only daughter of four children, she chose police work, rising to head a forty-three person squad. When her husband Tom lost his job as an engineer, he became a social worker. The narratives contrasted Tom's social services approach with Jean's commitment to criminal justice. Under pressure as a woman supervisor, Jean's consistency tempered with experience earned the respect of her subordinates. Her personal style and the couple's inability to have children were more threatening to her marriage.

The narratives ended without resolving Jean and Tom's personal problems.

Kori Price Brichter

Author: Mary Monica Pulver

Peter Brichter was a prickly man, unpopular with fellow police officers, tolerated only because he was competent and incorruptible. He met Kori (Katherine McLeod Price) through Gordie Ramsey, who had been hired to tutor her by Mafioso Nick Tellios. Tellios had become Kori's guardian after her parents died in an unsolved murder.

In *The Unforgiving Minutes* (St. Martin, 1988), Brichter learned that Kori was a virtual prisoner, ostensibly because her mental state was so fragile. Kori's role was that of victim and object of Peter's affection.

By *Knight Fall* (St. Martin, 1991, but previously published as *Murder at the War* by Diamond in 1987), they had married and joined the fantasy world of medieval reconstruction. Participants in the Pennsylvania campout assumed the names, attire, and behavior of the Roundtable era. Kori became a murder suspect when she discovered the dying Thostane, a member of the Great Dark Horde.

Peter was at risk in *Ashes to Ashes* (St. Martin, 1988) when a fellow officer used equipment from Tretorn, Kori's stable, to frame him for arson and corruption. Kori's standard poodle helped prove Peter's innocence, but her mind was on the pregnancy, which she had not yet shared with Peter.

Kori knew very little of her birth family so in *Original Sin* (Walker, 1991) she welcomed elderly cousin Evelyn McKay Biggins for a visit. Weather conditions forced Peter and Kori to invite retired Police Chief Frank Ryder and his new bride, Mary to join them. The close quarters reawakened a feud between Evelyn and Mary's families, and made Mary a suspect when Evelyn was killed.

Kori managed without Peter during most of *Show Stopper* (Walker, 1992) when she traveled to the Lafite County Fairgrounds for a dressage competition. After a brutish horseman was murdered and his body deposited in a Tretorn stall, Kori's groom was suspected. Kori had last minute help from Peter and a female police detective, but correctly identified the killer. Good buys at paperback prices.

Susan Bright

Author: Michael McDowell

Susan Bright was not easy to describe because she represented three different women, living in three distinct decades of the Twentieth Century. Author McDowell used the names Susan Bright and Jack Beaumont as labels for three different couples, sharing some basic characteristics. Because the periods in which they existed contributed to their personas, there were changes from book to book.

Susan, an actress who turned to scriptwriting when she broke her leg, and Jack, an investment broker posing as a poor inventor, met during the infant years of the movie industry in *Jack and Susan in 1913* (Ballantine, 1986). Independent filmmakers were pitted against the powerful Edison Patent Trust. An envious rival for Susan's affections stole Jack's innovations in camera mountings before he could patent the device. Light fare.

In *Jack and Susan in 1933* (Ballantine, 1987), Susan married Harmon Dodge, a rich hard-drinking attorney who rarely went to his office. Jack and his arrogant wife Barbara had opposed the marriage, perceiving Susan as a "gold-digger." Her social background was impeccable, but her father had lost the family money in the Crash of 1929. She had been reduced to singing at a "speakeasy." Susan admittedly had taken advantage of a drunken Harmon to provide the economic security that she missed. The arrangement became a farce, but a proposal from elderly widower Marcellus Rhinelander was not the solution Susan wanted. His death was determined to be murder. It didn't help that Rhinelander was Barbara's father.

Jack and Susan in 1953 (Ballantine 1985) had been published earlier than the other narratives. Rodolfo, a dapper Cuban connected to the gambling industry, was courting Susan. Jack who loved Susan was attached to "Libby", the fifth wealthiest woman in America. After a slow start, the action picked up. When Libby and Rodolfo married. Susan and Jack followed suit, going to Cuba on their honeymoon. Susan's estranged Uncle James, now a Cuban, died mysteriously, leaving her property but making her the suspect in his murder.

Susan needed to be bright. Jack was rather dim. In 1933, she had been a Radcliffe graduate, reduced to salon singer. In 1953, she had attended Smith College, spoke at least five languages, and worked as a translator.

Jane Britland
Author: Ron L. Gerard, pseudonym for Ronald Renauld

Being a president's daughter brought special problems to Jane. Her marriage to Andrew Hatch, a philanderer and heavy drinker, met his needs more than hers. He might have tired of Jane as a wife, but having a president for a father-in-law had advantages. Jane's failure to cope with these pressures led to alcohol abuse and a suicide attempt.

As *Deadly Aims* (PaperJacks, 1986) began, Jane had received help through a short institutional stay. She had to return to society and face the future. A divorce was inevitable because marriage to Andrew was part of the problem. Her dad, George Britland, defeated for a second term, was sincerely concerned about Jane. Her mother, a self-centered woman, was too busy to care. Jane made limited progress in her rehabilitation until Secret Service agent Jack Damascus was assigned to her. A former lover, J. T. Aames, obsessive in his belief that he and Jane were destined to be together, was stalking Jane. The narrative moved back and forth from Jane's resolve to get her life in order and Aames' plan to possess her. Jane was a victim, not a sleuth.

Jack (now known as Demarrest, not Damascus) was the man in Jane's life during *Deadly Sights* (PaperJacks, 1987). After a short and fiery affair they had drifted apart. Jane, hired as a reporter on the society page of a Washington newspaper, had been sober for six months. When she learned that Jack had been seriously wounded in a failed attempt to kill the newly elected president, Richard Houril, she quit her job and rushed to his hospital room in Northern Michigan. Although Jack's original prognosis would have left him a paraplegic, under Jane's care and encouragement, he had a second successful surgery and recovered the use of his legs. They returned to D.C. where Jack continued therapy and Jane worked on a book covering her experiences as a presidential daughter. Continued terrorist activities drew Jack back to work on the task force investigating former CIA agents who sold munitions, trained and led foreign terrorists and local survivalists in attacks and burglaries. Left out of the action when Jack journeyed to North Dakota where the terrorists were headquartered, Jane resumed her role as reporter and began her own disastrous investigation.

Really more of an adventure series, focused more on Jack and other government agents than on Jane's activities.

Sydney Bryant

Author: Patricia Wallace (Estrada)

Sydney Bryant, a San Diego private investigator, ended her affair with Deputy Sheriff Mitch Travis shortly after she learned that he was married, but no one else had taken his place. Encouraged by a father who loved mysteries, Sydney had majored in criminal justice in college. Her first job was with a detective agency in Los Angeles, but she preferred solo work. She was described as 5' 4" tall with ash blonde hair.

Sydney's love life improved during *Small Favors* (Zebra, 1988), when family friend Ethan Ross sought a closer relationship, and Mitch, whose marriage had been troubled, turned to her. Dr. Richard Walker hired Sydney to find his missing wife, because the police suspected him of her murder.

Nicole Halprin, daughter of a neighbor, discovered the body of a classmate on school property in *Deadly Grounds* (Zebra, 1989). Nicole hired Sydney to find her friend's killer from among the faculty members.

Sydney contacted wealthy young reporter Martina Saxon in *Blood Lies* (Zebra, 1991) to help a friend. She shadowed Martina until the young woman died in her family swimming pool. Then Martina's socialite grandmother hired Sydney to find the killer.

By *Deadly Devotion* (Zebra, 1994), Sydney had succumbed to Lt. Mitch Travis and was planning their wedding. This did not preclude her from undermining the police department's case against a coin dealer charged with the murder of his young wife.

Rhea Buerklin

Author: Mikel Dunham

Rhea Buerklin's life had been difficult. Her mother died in childbirth. A horseback accident caused Rhea to have major abdominal surgery that made it impossible for her to bear children. Although a Brazilian, she had attended a private Swiss school; then married a Munich investment banker, who discarded her because she was barren. Rhea was portrayed as self absorbed, crude, profane and promiscuous. After her relocation to the United States, Rhea and a partner Emil Orloff established an art gallery. Emil had tremendous rapport with artists, some of whom shared his recreational interest in alcohol and drugs.

As *Stilled Life* (St. Martin, 1989) began, Rhea found Emil's naked corpse in their ransacked gallery. His bequest to her of the premises on condition that she kill her Jack Russell Terrier, Crunch (possibly the only friend she had) evidenced the poor quality of their relationship. The sympathetic character in the narrative was detective John Tennyson, who came to love Rhea.

In *Casting for Murder* (St. Martin, 1992), Rhea could not understand why artist Jodie Rivers engaged in self-destructive behavior. After his murder in Italy, Jodie's father Verle underwrote Rhea's trip to Venice to discover the killer. He would take care of the punishment.

Kate Byrd

Author: Wendy Hornsby

See: Kate Byrd Teague, Page 279

Sarah Cable

Author: Michael Hartland

Sarah Cable appeared initially in *Seven Steps to Treason* (Macmillan, 1984) during which she was kidnapped by the Russians to force information from her father, Bill Cable. Bill had been retired by the intelligence services because he succumbed to torture while a prisoner. When he was restored to duty, Sarah, nineteen and in college, was accused of smuggling drugs and imprisoned by the Russians. She not only survived her imprisonment but was recruited by British Intelligence.

By *Frontier of Fear* (Walker, 1992) Sarah was twenty-six, a graduate in physics from Liverpool University, and assigned as a United Nations nuclear inspector in Vienna. She had become a tall, fair-haired young woman, marred by arrogance for cultures and beliefs other than her own. British Intelligence used her to seduce Nazim Rashid Khan, a scientist in the Pakistan Atomic program. Eventually both Nazim and Sarah were transferred to Pakistan, where he risked his personal and professional lives to save her. More of a thriller than a mystery.

Sarah stayed in the East, rebuilding her career and her stamina. Her father and his second wife were in retirement on the Isle of Wight. Nick Roper, U.S. Naval attaché at Peking became her lover. They shared his free time at her Hong Kong home. As *The Year of the Scorpion* (Hodder & Stoughton, 1991) began, Communist China was in turmoil. The Old Guard feared new and liberal elements in the party. The Chinese had a secret weapon, a disloyal officer in the U.S. Navy, code name: Scorpion. While British and American services sought Scorpion, the Chinese schemed to get the names of underground agents in China. Sarah and her friends were caught in the middle. Although she risked her life to confer with the Chinese underground, she would not surrender her loyalty to the man she loved. At the end, she had nowhere to turn.

Rosie Caesare

Author: Rosemarie Santini

Italian-American Rosie Caesare, a well-built, dark haired woman in her twenties, lived with Rick for several years. When their affair ended, he married a woman more acceptable to his New England family. Later, Rick, financially secure from a family trust, ended his unhappy marriage, and wed Rosie. She was a writer who enjoyed exuberant sex, Coca-Cola, *Casablanca*, and Lorenz Hart lyrics.

In *A Swell Style of Murder* (St. Martin, 1986), Rick, who avoided regular employment, noticed a severed hand while jogging through the streets. He intended to call the police, but was convinced by Rosie to solve the crime and write a book about his investigation.

The couple returned in *The Disenchanted Diva* (St. Martin, 1987). While Rosie was scripting a film based on the book, Rick discovered more body parts; this time, the disfigured body of a young girl in his Aunt Amanda's cellar. Although Rosie wanted to repeat their success in finding the killer, she was badly beaten when her meddling angered a Soho pimp. She spent the remainder of the narrative in bed while Rick and the police finished the case.

Jenny Cain

Author: Nancy Pickard

Jenny Cain, director of the Port Frederick (Massachusetts) Civic Foundation, was the daughter of a distinguished but dysfunctional local family. Their status had changed abruptly when her father bankrupted their clam business by absconding with the pension fund. His defection cost Port Frederick an important industry and robbed employees of their jobs and security. Trust funds insulated Jenny from the financial impact, but not from public reaction. The great tragedy in Jenny's life was not her father's dereliction but her mother's chronic mental illness, which required institutionalization. Jenny's relationship with her married sister, Sherry, was constrained. Her job was not based on nepotism. She had earned an MBA from the Wharton School of Finance.

Jenny was a 5' 7" slim blonde in her thirties when, during *Generous Death* (Avon, 1984), she met Geof Bushfield, the man who would dominate her personal life. Independently wealthy, Geof was a police officer by choice. Jenny's broken family and Geof's prior marriages made them leery of commitment. When major donors to the Foundation died mysteriously, Jenny's personal and professional lives intersected as her probe paralleled Geof's.

By *Say No to Murder* (Avon, 1985), Jenny had moved into Geof's home. Foundation support for harbor restoration drew her into an investigation when opponents to the project were murdered. While covering up for her prodigal father, Jenny challenged Geof's line of inquiry and went beyond the obvious to a hidden murder.

A visit to ailing former teacher Lucille Grant in *No Body* (Scribners, 1986) made Jenny aware that graves at a neglected cemetery were empty of the bodies once buried there. She dug up old dirt on the Pittman family that operated the local funeral home, but also uncovered a current scam.

Geof and Jenny legalized their relationship in *Marriage Is Murder* (Scribners, 1987). She was active in a crusade against domestic violence, but someone, even more incensed, was killing abusive husbands.

Jenny's personal interest in mental health led her to support a community center for chronic patients in *Dead Crazy* (Scribners, 1988). Local opposition built when a mental patient became a murder suspect. Jenny worked with Geof to "follow the money," identifying the killer.

Pickard, who lived in Kansas, took Jenny there in *Bum Steer* (Pocket Books, 1990) in pursuit of a major donation from dying Cat Benet, but she arrived too late. She remained, showing a lighter side to her nature;

surmounting snakes, gunshots, and terror until she found a killer. The real mystery was not solved until she returned home.

I.O.U. (Pocket Books, 1991) was a sensitive story. After her mother's death, Jenny searched for the cause of her mental illness. Jenny's struggle to reconstruct the guilt-ridden Mary Margaret Cain, to make peace with her father, and rebuild a relationship with her sister was engrossing and dangerous.

During *But I Wouldn't Want to Die There* (Pocket Books, 1993), Jenny's friend and colleague Carol Margolis was murdered before she could reach Jenny for help. Jenny accepted an interim appointment as Carol's replacement at the Hart Foundation in New York City to probe her friend's ethical dilemma and death. The move occurred at a difficult time in her marriage. Jenny and Geof worked it out, leaving her ready for a career change.

The question as to whether their marriage would include children could not be ignored in *Confession* (Pocket Books, 1994), when information from Geof's past revealed his need to be a parent. Young David Mayer wanted to know who killed his parents, and whether Geof was his father.

Separated from the Port Frederick Civic Foundation, Jenny established her own in *Twilight* (Pocket Books, 1995) but her crusade to control traffic on a local hiking trail met resistance. She learned of a mother's search for her daughter's killer and a wife's efforts to conceal her husband's weakness.

The Cain books went beyond the conventional mystery genre to explore relationships among women; as sisters, mothers and daughters; and between women and the men they love.

Sarah Calloway

Author: Jean Warmbold

Sarah Calloway never described herself physically or provided background material about family or education during her narration. She was an under-financed freelance reporter, who pitted herself against the medical establishment, the CIA and FBI, Cuban nationalists, and chemical manufacturers. Sarah had never married, but had multiple affairs and two abortions

Frank Winslow, once Sarah's lover, had achieved prominence as a researcher for an AIDS vaccine. She contacted him for an interview as *June Mail* (Permanent Press, 1986 a.k.a. *Dead Man Running* in England) opened. By the time she reached San Francisco, he had disappeared. Frank's long-suffering wife and his son had no idea where he had gone. His employers were unwilling to help. Her only ally was Stanley, a newspaper columnist whom she picked up (or did he pick her up?) in a local bar. Sarah was unsure as to whom she could trust. Yet she wanted to tell Frank's story.

The White Hand (Permanent Press, 1988) began when Sarah observed the murder of Diana, a young pregnant woman whose body was removed in a darkened police vehicle. Her involvement constituted a threat to drug dealers and a militaristic Cuban group formerly controlled by the CIA and connected to major assassinations.

The Third Way (Permanent Press, 1990) found Sarah in Paris covering the bicentennial of the French Revolution. Her secondary assignment was to bid on the journal of Isabelle Eberhardt, who had traveled the Mid-East during the late Nineteenth Century concealing her gender. A casual contact at the auction drew Sarah into Arab/Israeli politics, centering on a group seeking peace between the two nations. She maneuvered among powerful forces to foil a plot to spoil the bicentennial celebration by destroying a national treasure.

The narratives involved massive conspiracies, international terrorism, and business shenanigans.

Angel Cantini

Author: Robert Eversz

Los Angeles private investigator, Paul Marston, the hero/narrator of the series, described Angel Cantini as a long-legged brunette with curly hair and smoky green eyes. She was on the rebound from a relationship with Jack Carlisle, who owned her contract as the Southern California Women's boxing champion.

When Marston needed Angel's help to investigate Carlisle's fatal airplane crash in *The Bottom Line Is Murder* (Viking, 1988), he did not plan to fall in love with her, but it happened.

Angel reappeared in *False Profit* (Viking, 1990–subtitled a Marston/Cantini Mystery), but her role remained subsidiary to Marston, an insensitive bully. She had become Marston's business partner and lover, working with him to reunite a brother and sister and to discover the killer of an unreliable client. These were tough guy stories in which Angel had a supporting role.

Carlotta Carlyle

Author: Linda Barnes

Carlotta Carlyle, tall with flaming red hair, was the daughter of a deceased Scots-Irish policeman and a Jewish mother. Her Jewish identity, although unconnected to her religious views, was important to Carlotta. Her grandmother had been in a Nazi concentration camp. Carlotta's mother had never forgotten the tattooed identification number on her mother's arm. Carlotta's marriage to Cal, a musician, ended because of his drug addiction and infidelity. Although he reappeared in her life, they never remarried. Carlotta in her thirties had dropped out of law school. She had worked as a police officer, but preferred life as a Boston private investigator. While a police officer, she had been close to Joe Mooney with whom she cooperated unofficially. Her part time work as a cab driver led to a relationship with Sam Gianelli, the law-abiding member of a Mafia family. Carlotta had inherited a home, was active in intramural volleyball, and shared a "big sister" match with Paolina, a Colombian child. Her first appearance was in a short story (see *New Black Mask*, 1986).

A Trouble of Fools (St. Martin, 1987) sent Carlotta in search of a missing widower. She used her street contacts and experience to convince Irish-American cabdrivers that they were misled as to the contents of the packages they were delivering.

In *The Snake Tattoo* (St. Martin, 1989), Carlotta helped Joe Mooney (now a Lieutenant) when he was accused of police brutality and worked for a teenage boy worried about the disappearance of his girl friend. Both assignments took her to the Boston Combat Zone, danger, and the need to shoot to kill.

During *Coyote* (Delacorte, 1990), Carlotta became involved with Boston's illegal immigrants. Someone was maiming and killing Latino women, including a client referred by rebellious young Paolina. Although the identity of the "coyote" who transported, then betrayed, the migrants might be obvious to the reader, it came late to Carlotta.

Steel Guitar (Delacorte, 1991) evoked Carlotta's past, exploring her relationship with Cal and Dee Willis, the singer for whom Cal left her. They re-entered Carlotta's life: Cal, free of drugs, working his way back in the music business; and Dee, a success haunted by her past.

In *Snapshot* (Delacorte, 1993), anonymous photos of a growing child piqued Carlotta's imagination before she learned that little Rebecca Woodward had died.

Things were not going well between Sam Gianelli and Carlotta as *Hardware* (Delacorte, 1995) began. He was pre-occupied, frequently out of town, and unavailable when Carlotta and Gloria (his partner in the taxi business) needed him. Attacks on cab drivers and the reappearance of a Vietnam buddy of Sam's meshed in a powerful narrative during which Carlotta re-aligned her priorities. The Green and White Cab Company needed major repairs, and so did Sam who recuperated in Florida.

During *Cold Case* (Delacorte, 1997), Carlotta was aware that she was being followed. Mooney, her pal from police department days, believed that the Gianelli family blamed her for Sam's injury. The body of young author Thea Janis had supposedly been located and buried by the family twenty-four years ago. Evidence that she continued to write triggered reopening of the case. The search for Thea and a possible second book could have major political implications so Carlotta put herself at risk. Over the years, life had changed for Carlotta. There had been no further contacts between her and Sam. Paolina with whom she had been matched seven years ago in a Big Sister program was now fourteen. Business remained at a marginal level, although she no longer drove cab as a supplement.

In *Flashpoint* (Hyperion, 1999), Gwen, a volleyball acquaintance, talked Carlotta into providing security for a frightened widow for whom Gwen provided home-care services. It was too late. When Valentine, the elderly woman, was found dead, Gwen was arrested for her murder. Although distracted by Paolina, whose abandonment by her mother had led to an attachment to an undesirable older man, Carlotta sought the secret that Valentine had guarded until she was betrayed.

Barnes developed a heroine capable of growth, featuring complex but realistic plots with touches of warmth and humor not always associated with female private investigators.

In a prior series featuring actor/investigator Michael Spraggue, Barnes had featured his rich and resourceful Aunt Mary Hillman who assisted in his cases. She was a knowledgeable investor with contacts in the business community that she used to help her nephew.

Agnes Carmichael
Author: Anthea Cohen, pseudonym for Doris Simpson

Agnes was a strange, unhappy woman, raised in an orphanage. Hardly a heroine, she was a killer. Her greatest pleasure was the accumulation of knowledge about other people.

In *Angel Without Mercy* (Doubleday, 1984), Agnes, then a night duty nurse in a rural English hospital was determined to rise in her profession. One formidable obstacle to her advancement was Nurse-Supervisor Marion Hughes, an unhappy spinster who blackmailed those who offended her. Hughes' mysterious death after a hard day at the hospital removed her from Agnes's path, but at a cost.

During *Angel of Vengeance* (Doubleday, 1984) Agnes used her authority as a supervisory nurse to gather information on others. She owned a car, her apartment, and had become more attentive to her appearance. She even had a friend, pediatric nurse Sister Jones who interested Agnes in the problems of a three-year-old victim of child abuse. Agnes did not particularly like children but she knew how to deal with abusers.

Agnes experienced love in *Angel of Death* (Doubleday, 1985), but Professor Harold Maitland, a blind man with a difficult wife, meant only to be kind. Her efforts to solve Maitland's problems brought Agnes to a nervous breakdown.

After her release from a mental hospital, Agnes accepted lower level employment as a night nurse during *Fallen Angel* (Quartet, 1984). Her attempts to bring professionalism into the slipshod administration went unappreciated. When she found the corpse of her predecessor in the woods, she failed to notify the authorities, but planned her own punishment for the killer.

By *Guardian Angel* (Doubleday, 1985), Agnes had returned to work in a responsible position. She had two cats, a comfortable little home and garden, but was not a happy woman. She challenged several juvenile deliquents and a pro-union employee who was trying to recruit nurses.

Change came again in *Hell's Angel* (Quartet, 1986), a new job in a new facility and community. Agnes worked in the casualty department headed by an orthopedist with whom she had worked before. When his romance with a hospital employee ran into problems, Agnes knew only one way to cope.

Agnes had a dismal time on a singles tour of Italy. In *Ministering Angel* (Quartet, 1987), she returned to find her dear friend Bernadette preparing to be married. Bernadette convinced Agnes to attend a seance with unfortunate consequences for the medium. Although Agnes's participation in death was passive this time, more might have been expected from a professional nurse.

An inheritance from Beatrice Bradshaw, an elderly woman whose cat she had saved, made Agnes financially independent. Agnes enjoyed the added income, bought new clothes, assisted friends in need, adopted another cat, but in *Destroying Angel* (Quartet, 1988), she still coped through violence. A man who injured a cat deserved to be injured himself. A suitor who knew too much about her and a corrupt builder were legitimate targets for extinction.

As *Angel Dust* (Quartet, 1989) ended it seemed that Agnes had pushed one of her victims too far. She had successfully eliminated several drug dealers who preyed upon juveniles, and found true love. Stalked by a figure from her past, Agnes was too tough to die.

During *Recording Angel* (Constable, 1991), ill health caused Agnes to do home nursing in a noble English home where she dealt with family problems by her customary final solution.

Her grateful employer, Lady Gladys, had provided Agnes with a comfortable home in the Dower House in *Angel in Action* (Constable, 1992). With leisure to become involved in the community, Agnes disposed of a tyrannical parent, forced an HIV positive surgeon to discontinue his operations, and indulged in blackmail.

By *Angel in Love* (Constable, 1993), Agnes had retired on ill-gotten gains. She was a more attractive, self-confident woman, but was unable to handle a rival for the man who taught her about physical love. There was at least one intervening book (unavailable for review) *Angel in Autumn*, during which Agnes achieved some level of happiness married to Bill, her congenial neighbor on the Isle of Wight. Bill, after years of hard work, had become a successful author. He was generous in his gifts, providing her with a fine London home at Rutland Gate.

Even when married in *Dedicated Angel* (Constable, 1997), Agnes could not leave well enough alone. After only a few months of marriage, she found herself attracted to a very different man, an established novelist, who was arrogant and disinterested in other people's welfare or opinions. She became besotted with him. His death did not end the situation because Herbert had left behind evidence that might destroy Agnes's comfortable marriage.

In *Angel of Retribution* (Constable, 1998), Agnes made several life changes after Bill's unfortunate death while he was in the United States. She placed the Wight cottage and the Rutland Gate apartment up for sale. Then she settled into a rural area of Sussex, where she had no prior attachments. Her addiction to murder was re-awakened by Amanda, a young neighbor whose beloved horse had been brutally killed. The attacks on animals continued even after a major suspect was murdered. Agnes was less interested in finding the killer, than in punishing his accomplice.

Cruelty to animals was intolerable to Agnes (now known as Agnes Turner). She intervened when she saw young men tormenting a dog as

Angel and the French Widow (Constable, 2000) began. When a new acquaintance, the French widow, was murdered, Agnes assumed that she had been the target. Andy, the leader of the thugs, was also peddling drugs to children and teenagers. Agnes pursued the matter until she located a major drug smuggler. It was unnecessary for her to kill anyone. She could just stand back and let them kill one another.

The series ran to at least 16 books, many unpublished in the United States. An unusual amoral heroine.

Sabina Carpenter

Author: Bill Pronzini

Quincannon (Walker, 1985) introduced Sabina Carpenter as a supporting character in a historical Western mystery featuring Secret Service agent John Quincannon. In spite of his skills, Quincannon had become a personal risk to the agency because of his alcoholism. They sent him to Silver Creek, Idaho where possible counterfeiting presented a danger to the U.S. economy. There he met Sabina, a recently established milliner, in a town with diminishing prosperity. Silver was no longer in demand. Sabina was an enigma, tall and dark haired a good woman, who turned up in inappropriate places and complicated his investigation. Her real identity as an agent for Pinkerton investigating possible stock fraud was revealed to Quincannon late in the narrative. A prior marriage to a Pinkerton agent had ended when he was shot in a raid.

Quincannon's relative sobriety and his attraction to the comely widow, led both to end their current employment and form a partnership as Carpenter and Quincannon, Professional Detectives. Quincannon had played a significant role in *Beyond the Grave* (Walker, 1986), co-authored by Pronzini and his wife, Marcia Muller. The narrative correlated Quincannon's activities in search of religious treasures during the 1890's with a subsequent investigation by Muller's series heroine, Elena Olivarez. Sabina was referred to as present on occasion, as the disinterested object of Quincannon's affection (he even considered marriage, as a last resort).

More recently, in *Carpenter and Quincannon* (Crippen and Landru, 1998), Pronzini gathered short stories, all but one of which had been published previously in mystery magazines. Although the length of his sobriety and their continued partnership had softened Sabina's response to his ardor, she never succumbed. Most of the short stories kept her in the San Francisco office, doing research while he did the fieldwork. In *Lady One-Eye*,

Sabina went undercover as a gambler, playing a significant part in discovering a cheat and a killer. An enemy of Quincannon held her hostage in *Coney Game*. In *The Desert Limited,* she provided the information that led to the arrest of an escaped criminal dressed in female clothing.

Although the stories were worthy on their own merits, Sabina did not develop as a character.

Cathy McVeigh Carter

Author: Eileen Dewhurst

During *Trio in Three Flats* (Doubleday, 1981), Inspector Neil Carter's apartment was adjacent to those of attractive Hilary Fielding and friendly Cathy McVeigh. Cathy and Neil worked together when Hilary was accused of murder. Rather too neatly during a murder investigation, Neil came to prefer "the girl next door", Cathy.

She offered support in *There Was a Little Girl* (Doubleday, 1986) when Neil, aware that young Juliet had been a prostitute, was disturbed by her death. He and Cathy re-routed their honeymoon to rescue another teenage girl from disaster.

Married and pregnant in *A Nice Little Business* (Doubleday, 1987), Cathy discovered her blackmailing dressmaker dead. Neil, having been suspended because of his temper, resorted to detecting in drag to solve this one. Cathy wisely stayed out of it.

Sandrine Casette

Author: Michael Bowen

See: Sandrine Casette Curry, Page 64

Doran Fairweather Chelmarsh

Author: Mollie Hardwick

See: Doran Fairweather, Page 82

Emma Chizzit

Author: Mary Bowen Hall

Were stalwart movie actress Marjorie Main still alive, she would be a natural to portray Emma Chizzit, a tall, broad shouldered woman who survived widowhood and an unhappy second marriage. Emma wore old clothes, drove a truck, and had a cat named "Sourpuss", but was still attracting suitors. Before she went into the salvage business, she had worked on a small town newspaper.

In *Emma Chizzit and the Queen Anne Killer* (Walker, 1989), Emma contracted to clean out a deserted home. She discovered the corpse of a long dead baby on the premises. Her primary candidate for the child's mother was shot down in a restaurant parking lot. Reluctantly accepting help from aging police officer Vince Valenti, she found a killer and saved a friend from a disastrous liaison.

During *Emma Chizzit and the Sacramento Stalker* (Walker, 1991), she encountered ardent feminists, unscrupulous investment counselors, and a serial rapist. Valenti tagged along; eager to be with Emma, even though she showed little interest.

Emma Chizzit and the Napa Nemesis (Walker, 1992) involved Emma in a purportedly unpublished Robert Louis Stevenson novel. She risked death and romance, surviving both.

Celebrity newswoman Adelaide Simpson had worked with Emma years before. In *Emma Chizzit and the Mother Lode Marauder* (Walker, 1993), Adelaide called on Emma to help her son Jim, a reporter who opposed real estate developers in Buckeye, a decrepit ex-gold mining town. Emma and Jim worked with environmentalist Trooper Hadley until her "accidental" death.

This interesting series ended with Hall's death.

Marlene Ciampi

Author: Robert K. Tanenbaum

Although Marlene's original presence in the series featuring Roger "Butch" Karp was as an assistant district attorney and romantic interest for Karp, she emerged as a strong character. A small dark haired Italian-American, Marlene had been raised as a Catholic, attending parochial grade and high schools in Queens. Competing with three brothers, she played roller hockey, worked out at a punching bag, and drove like a fiend. She took her undergraduate degree at Barnard (a later book identified Smith College as her alma mater), was on the Law Review at Yale University, but settled for work as a low paying assistant District Attorney. Marlene wore tight colorful clothes, and had a foul mouth, but could quote from philosophers and cope with the give and take of chauvinistic fellow attorneys. She entered Karp's personal life after he learned that his estranged wife had a female lover.

No Lesser Plea (Watts, 1987) focused on Karp's determination to convict black career criminal "Man" Louis of murder. Louis had feigned an obscure form of insanity in the hope that a delayed prosecution would let him off for time served. Louis, intending to kill Karp, commissioned a letter bomb that caused serious and permanent damage to Marlene.

Her injuries left Marlene in debt during *Depraved Indifference* (Dutton, 1989) because her Workman's Compensation claim was delayed. Karp and Marlene encountered layers of intrigue when five terrorists were tried for the death of a police officer. Karp's devotion and need for Marlene was undiminished by her glass eye and disfigured hand.

By *Immoral Certainty* (Dutton, 1991), the couple shared a large loft subdivided into living areas. Marlene's probe of child abuse merged into Karp's investigation of a knife-wielding burglar.

In *Reversible Error* (Dutton, 1992), Karp's struggle against police corruption connected with Marlene's legal and physical pursuit of a serial rapist. Her pregnancy came after they decided to marry, but they barely avoided her forced retirement under the nepotism rule.

Marlene was on leave during *Material Witness* (Dutton, 1993), when a popular basketball star was murdered with drugs in his car. Karp risked his career and his knees, but refurbished his basketball image as an aging "twelfth man."

Marlene gave birth to a daughter under trying circumstances, but in *Justice Denied* (Dutton, 1994) she was no less reckless. She and her new associate Harry Bello tangled with Armenian and Turkish nationalists over a holy relic. In her spare time, she nailed a trio of rapist/killers at risk to herself and little Lucy. Marlene admitted to becoming more Sicilian, and less Smith (whatever happened to Barnard?) as she aged.

Corruption of Blood (Dutton, 1995) moved the family to Washington, D.C. when Karp accepted a short-term appointment with the House of Representatives Select Committee on Assassinations. Marlene, originally unwilling to accompany him, did so when sexually harassed by Sanford Bloom, Karp's nemesis at the District Attorney's office. Although both made significant discoveries in their investigations, the federal bureaucracy impeded any real results.

By *Falsely Accused* (Dutton, 1996), Karp, now in private practice, was suing the mayor and District Attorney Bloom on behalf of a discharged medical examiner. Not even a pre-school child and a second pregnancy kept Marlene on the sidelines. Obsessively concerned by spousal abuse, she recruited Harry Bello as her partner in an investigative agency focused on protecting battered women. Marlene and Harry were willing to bend and break the laws, operating as vigilantes. Justice of a sort was achieved, but Marlene had set her daughter on a path that she might regret. Marlene juggled three children (since the birth of twin boys), an agency which employed more than two dozen full time equivalent workers, and marriage to Karp.

Her expectations were put to the test in *Irresistible Impulse* (Dutton, 1997) when she provided security for two celebrities who had been threatened anonymously. Meanwhile, Karp returned to the District Attorney's office and personally tried a serial murder case against a crafty defense attorney. Marlene's impulse to risk her marriage, her children and her life for the excitement of her career was matched against the sinister impulses of men who wanted women under their domination.

By *Reckless Endangerment* (Dutton, 1998), the Ciampi/Karp family was growing. Zik (Giancarlo) and Zak (Isaac) were two years old. The very precocious Lucy, now 10, was a linguistic genius. Karp, as a result of internal government politics, had been moved from his position as chief of the District Attorney's Homicide Bureau to a less active post as Deputy for Special Projects. Marlene's partnership in a security agency with Harry Bello was under stress. Harry, having renounced vigilantism, sought to merge the agency with a major security firm. Two cases drew Karp back into action; then involved both Marlene and Lucy:

- The murder of a Jewish shopkeeper by youths connected to a militant Arab group; and

- The trial of two Mexican drug dealers by ADA Roland Hrcany, who had replaced Karp as head of the Homicide division.

It was difficult enough for Karp having a wife who courted danger. In *Act of Revenge* (HarperCollins, 1999), they both had occasion for concern. Lucy had become secretive, disrespectful, and reckless. She had probably witnessed a murder, but felt honor bound to conceal information from her parents and the authorities, even if it threatened her life and those of her dearest friends. Karp was engrossed in a major Mafia murder investigation; Marlene, researching a twenty year old case involving an attorney's suicide. Tanenbaum tied it all together with his usual skill.

The complications in the Ciampi/Karp family increased geometrically as Lucy became even more significant in *True Justice* (Pocket Books, 2000). Marlene, now in private practice, had not totally renounced her penchant for violence. She defended a college student facing the death penalty for infanticide. Butch was drawn out of his administrative role to prosecute in a similar case and to negotiate the fate of a child murderer. Lucy, a witness to that murder, disregarded the law, visiting the suspect in prison. Later she counseled her mother's client to accept responsibility for her role in her child's death. Each of the three operated from a different basis of belief—Marlene saw no linkage between abortion and infanticide; Butch left decision making to the legislature, but did not reject a solution which evaded the letter of the law; Lucy, a devout Catholic, found abortion and infanticide equally repellant, but recklessly compromised her father's murder case. Thank heavens the twins were still too young to add to Tanenbaum's repertoire.

Butch, Marlene and Lucy all had traumatic experiences during *Enemy Within* (Pocket Books, 2001). Butch and Marlene found themselves in unacceptable positions within their jobs. Neither hesitated to manipulate the system to excise corruption at the workplace. Both fought for justice on cases that, if handled properly, would damage Jack Keegan's (Butch's boss) chances for re-election. Marlene, suddenly wealthy because the security firm which had absorbed her agency went public, initially couldn't handle her affluence. Lucy's personal religious faith involved her with a homeless community, members of which became major players in her parents' struggle with the law. All three survived, but their lives were changed.

Marlene was a vivid character, stretching credulity in the more recent narratives. The reader may need to be reminded that the narratives took place in an earlier decade.

Kat Colorado

Author: Karen Kijewski

Kat Colorado's beginnings gave little promise of the woman she would become. She had found her alcoholic mother dead when she returned from her high school graduation. Her unknown father was reputed to be from the state of Colorado, hence the last name. Kat's closest attachment had been to a younger sister, who died when their mother delayed medical care. At thirty-three, 5' 7" tall, she was a private investigator living in Sacramento, California. She had previously worked as a reporter, supplementing her income by bartending.

Kat created a new family of her own choosing. In *Katwalk* (St. Martin, 1989), friend Charity Collins, who dispensed advice professionally but was incapable of managing her own life, asked Kat to find her estranged husband Sam and the $200,000 he took with him. In Las Vegas, Kat met Police Sgt. Hank Parker, who cared enough about Kat to offer her a lifetime commitment.

Alma Flaherty was Kat's adopted "grandmother," so in *Katapult* (St. Martin, 1990) Kat made time to investigate the death of Alma's great nephew and the disappearance of his country singer sister, Michaela. During the probe, Kat bonded with teenage hooker, "Lindy," who wanted the serial killings of young prostitutes to stop.

Kat's Cradle (Doubleday, 1992) was as much about Kat's inability to let go of her independence as about the confused Morrell family.

Still haunted by the death of a man she had trusted, Kat refused professional help in *Copy Kat* (Doubleday, 1992). Hank gave her an ultimatum, but Kat dealt with her stress by a new setting, new identity, and a return to bartending, as part of a murder investigation.

Kat rescued petite accountant Amanda Hudson from a car accident in *Wild Kat* (Doubleday, 1994), but was unable to save her from death, even though Amanda's husband hired Kat as protection. Amanda had "blown the whistle" on faulty heart valves made by her employer, incurring the wrath of management and those family members who had settled their lawsuits with the company.

Kat's world fell apart in *Alley Kat Blues* (Doubleday, 1995) when she sought Hank's comfort, and found a woman sharing his bed. Hank had become obsessed by the deaths attributed to the "Strip Stalker" who preyed on women of a certain physical type, similar to that of his former wife. Although they solved their cases, Hank and Kat's personal relationship was in trouble.

Friendship was important to Kat, so when her childhood pal, country singer Dakota Jones asked for help in *Honky Tonk Kat* (Putnam, 1996), Kat flew to Nashville. Someone from the past had been harassing Dakota; somewhere in Kat's memory was the clue to a killer. She reestablished her relationship with Hank, although not on the prior level.

Kat's determination to bring her cases to closure was tested in *Kat Scratch Fever* (Putnam, 1997). At the request of his law partner, Kat had investigated James Randolph, good citizen, family man, and supporter of charitable causes. Randolph's suicide seemed irrational. Only when she discovered the "benevolent blackmailer" who tormented Randolph and others who had secrets in their pasts, did she feel the pressure exerted by a ruthless fanatic.

The knock on the door, the entry of Davis, Hank's partner, and the news that Hank had been killed began *Stray Kat Waltz* (Putnam, 1998). Kat had waited so long to let Hank into her life, afraid that he too would be taken away from her and now it had happened. Good friends rallied around, but she was vulnerable as she had not been for a long time. She was reluctant to take on a new client, even one as insistent as Sara Bernard, who said her husband's abusive behavior would eventually lead to her death. Cat was vulnerable enough to take the case when Sara attempted suicide, but not so vulnerable as to be manipulated.

Kijewski explored "shades of gray" in her writing with complex characters, unresolved relationships, and solutions that left the reader wanting more.

Liz Connors

Author: Susan Kelly

Liz Connors, who had attended an urban American college, earned her Ph.D. from a university in Scotland. At thirty-three, she abandoned teaching undergraduates to do freelance writing.

In *The Gemini Man* (Walker, 1985), tall redheaded Liz and her dog Lucy had just moved into a new apartment when she found a corpse. She cruised the singles bars with Police Detective Jack Lingemann in search of a split personality who preyed on single women.

Connors offered an interesting view of Vietnam protesters in *The Summertime Soldiers* (Walker, 1986). Liz was teaching at the Police Academy when the People's Revolutionary Cadre resumed terrorist activities, putting both Liz and Jack on their hit list.

Carl Di Benedetto of Thatcher College recruited Liz in *Trail of the Dragon* (Walker, 1988) to find missing cancer patient Bonnie Nordgrem. When Bonnie was discovered dead of a drug overdose, Liz explored her lifestyle and connections with prominent politicians.

By *Until Proven Innocent* (Villard, 1990), Liz and Jack were lovers who did not live together. Dalton Craig, stepbrother of Jack's deceased wife, accused him of heading a secret police unit that manipulated evidence in a murder trial. Liz worked with a supportive policewoman to clear Jack, but resorted to violence.

In *And Soon I'll Come to Kill You* (Villard, 1991), Liz was threatened, possibly by an individual she had profiled in her real crime stories. Her encounter with the killer left her so fragile that she reluctantly moved in with Jack.

During *Out of the Darkness* (Villard, 1992), Liz helped crime novelist Griffin Marcus research victims' lives. She ended her relationship with Jack, enraged that he did not regard her work as meaningful. Unwilling to return to him or move away with Marcus, Liz was alone. She was unable to cope with dependency at any level.

A rather sad ending to an engrossing series.

Claire Conrad

Author: Melodie Johnson Howe

See: Maggie Hill, Page 134

Iris Cooper

Author: K. K. Beck a.k.a. Katherine Marris

Iris Cooper was a flapper in a camp presentation of the Twenties, an era which seemed idyllic when viewed through the eyes of nostalgia. Red-headed Iris had few teenage joys. Her mother had died young leaving Iris to raise younger brothers and sisters. At nineteen, she wanted a life of her own.

Wealthy Aunt Hermione (like Aunt March in *Little Women*) invited Iris to accompany her on a round-the-world cruise in *Death in a Deck Chair* (Walker, 1984). When a passenger was murdered, Iris served as police stenographer, making her privy to all interviews. Working with brash young newspaperman Jack Clancy, she uncovered international intrigue.

Iris, who attended Stanford in *Murder in a Mummy Case* (Walker, 1986), visited the family of college beau, Clarence Brockhurst. Clarence wanted to interest Iris in Egyptology, but, when they found a member of the household in a mummy, Iris preferred criminology and Jack Clancy.

Iris traveled again in *Peril Under the Palms* (Walker, 1989) when Aunt Hermione included her on a Hawaiian trip. She was intrigued by the identity of a mysterious "woman in white," and the secrets to be found in an ancient diary.

A novelty, but Beck wrote better mysteries featuring Jane Da Silva in the 1990's.

Katharine Craig

Author: Deborah Valentine

Katharine Craig made only two significant appearances in the three Valentine novels—both as victim rather than sleuth. A tall dark virginal young woman in her late twenties, she had achieved recognition as a sculptress before she returned from Europe to the Lake Tahoe area. Her meeting with deputy sheriff Kevin Bryce in *Unorthodox Methods* (Avon, 1989) came about because she was a suspect in a series of art thefts and murders. At the conclusion, she and Kevin planned to relocate in Ireland where she could sculpt and he could concentrate on writing novels.

Kevin had returned to the United States alone by *A Collector of Photographs* (Bantam PBO, 1989), urged by Katharine to help an old friend. Paul Gautier, shocked by the homosexual images in his wife Roxanne's paintings and the death of her male model friend, wanted reassurance from Kevin's investigation. Kevin explored the seamy aspects of Roxanne's imagery and the dangerous side streets of San Francisco, finding more than enough guilt to go around.

In *Fine Distinctions* (Avon PBO, 1991), both Kevin and Katharine were in Ireland, but not getting along. After a quarrel, she left in Kevin's car, which was later found abandoned. Katharine's disappearance was tied to the return of a former IRA rebel to his native land. She moved to London, then back to Dublin, where her actions in a bar precipitated a murder and death from a heart attack. She eventually returned to Kevin, still unable to make a commitment. Maybe he should look elsewhere.

Erratic plotting and an unstable heroine weakened the series.

Sandrine Casette Curry

Author: Michael Bowen

Sandrine Cassette, the daughter of a French Army officer, had been raised in Algeria. Attorney Thomas Curry, whom she later married, smuggled guns to Algerian rebels during the Sixties. He was captured by her father's troops; then, released on the condition that he would fly Sandrine, her sister and mother out of the country, leaving her father to die. She was a sophisticated young woman, classically educated, proficient in languages, even able to make her own bombs.

The relationship between Sandrine and Thomas developed in *Badger Game* (St. Martin, 1989) when she worked as an administrative assistant for the Curry law firm. Thomas represented artist Harrison Tyler in a dispute over his new painting. He accepted Sandrine on an equal basis, acknowledging her independence.

In *Fielder's Choice* (St Martin, 1991), baseball might seem a strange interest for Sandrine, now Mrs. Thomas Curry. Tom introduced her to the sport, which attracted her particularly by the intricacies of the scoring notations. This new knowledge enabled her to solve the murder of a New York Giants fan.

Sandrine seemed obsessed in *Act of Faith* (St. Martin, 1993). While she and Tom were on a photo expedition near the Burundi/Katanga border, they were taken into custody by Burundi troops guarding a vehicle convoy. She disappeared with a disreputable guide, leaving the impression that she had abandoned her marriage. Tom's faith in his wife and his ability to fly a helicopter enabled her to prove otherwise. Safe again, she announced her American naturalization and her pregnancy.

Bowen's plots were ingenious but the narration by law partner Furst inhibited the character development of Tom and Sandrine.

Serendipity "Sarah" Dahlquist

Author: Dick Lochte

Serendipity "Sarah" Dahlquist was a member of a very select group: juveniles who appear in adult mysteries without being obnoxious. At fourteen, she was small (5'), "skinny," with shoulder length hair; the daughter of Faith, an ex-drug addict now dependent on men, and Frank, a Vietnam casualty. Serendipity became an intelligent and mature teenager under the influence of her grandmother, former television soap actress Edith Van Dine and laconic California private investigator Leo Bloodworth, her co-narrator.

In *Sleeping Dog* (Arbor, 1985), Sarah was ignored by local police when her bull terrier Groucho disappeared, so she contacted Bloodworth. She became his assistant when his partner was murdered. When Gran was injured, Leo took over as her involuntary custodian, searching for Groucho through a maze of blackmailers, hyped up wolves and Mexican gangsters.

Their investigation in *Laughing Dog* (Arbor, 1988) was marred by the implication that Leo might view pubescent Sarah with a lecherous eye. He was too busy to consult with New Orleans investigator Terry Manion about runaway Cece MacElroy, so Sarah took on the case. Their paths eventually joined, pitting them against a group of actors led by a politically conscious academic.

Serendipity and Leo also appeared in two short stories in a collection by Lochte called *Lucky Dog and Other Tales of Murder* (Five Star, 2000).

Jean Darblay

Author: Mollie Hardwick

See: Juliet Bravo, Page 42

Annie Laurance Darling

Author: Carolyn G. Hart

Mystery bookseller Annie Laurance Darling was a delight to mystery fans. She would have been comfortable with those who could recognize the English titles of Agatha Christie's books, name the butlers who attended Lord Peter and Albert Campion, and remember who H. H. Holmes really was. She was a freckled ex-Texan with golden brown hair and gray eyes. Her parents divorced when she was three, ending contact with her father (see *Sugar Plum Dead* below). Her mother subsequently died of cancer. After Annie earned a Bachelor of Fine Arts from Southern Methodist University, she intended to go into the theatre. While acting in New York City, Annie met Max Darling, a wealthy dilettante. Concerned by the differences in their lifestyles, Annie was reluctant to make a commitment to Max. When Uncle Ambrose died, bequeathing her Death on Demand, a bookstore on Broward's Rock Island, South Carolina, she left New York without providing a forwarding address. Max sought her out.

Annie was surrounded by supporting characters:

- Max, whom she eventually married, realized that Annie would think less of him if he were as indolent as he preferred to be;
- "Henny" Brawley, one of Annie's best customers who vied with author Emma Clyde in solving Annie's puzzle contests;
- Laurel Darling Roethke, Max's devoted but ditsy mother; and
- The cats—Agatha and Dorothy L. Additional regulars were added as the series continued.

In *Death on Demand* (Bantam, 1987), vengeful author Elliott Morgan, who was also Annie's landlord, was murdered after he threatened to expose secrets of fellow writers. Annie was a suspect, until Max put his talents and law degree to work and identified the killer. In return, Annie saved his life.

The Historical Preservation Society in nearby Chastain planned a mystery weekend in *Design for Murder* (Bantam, 1987), hiring Annie to assist in the production. A vengeful woman, hell-bent to be murdered, was. The local police preferred to arrest outsiders, but Annie prodded the killer into a confession. During *Something Wicked* (Bantam, 1988), both Max and Annie had major roles in the local production of *Arsenic and Old Lace*. The death of an obnoxious fellow actor put Max in the role of #1 suspect, thanks to an ambitious state prosecutor.

Although the wedding ceremony took place, Max and Annie postponed their honeymoon in *Honeymoon with Murder* (Bantam, 1988) because Annie's assistant, Ingrid, had disappeared and a blackmailing retiree was dead. During *A Little Class on Murder* (Doubleday, 1989), Annie taught a course on mystery writers at Chastain Junior College. Laurel and Henny Brawley enrolled, putting their skills to work when murder occurred in the Journalism department. Laurel, Max's mother, fell in love with a married man in *Deadly Valentine* (Doubleday, 1990) shortly before his wife was murdered.

Although *The Christie Caper* (Bantam, 1991) included gimmicks to attract mystery fanatics, the underlying plot might be fairly obvious to the same reader. Neil Bledsoe was a disruptive presence at Annie's Agatha Christie Centenary, but it was his rich Aunt Kathryn who died. Max accepted a difficult case in *Southern Ghost* (Bantam, 1992), when Courtney Kimball asked him to investigate the "suicide" of the man she believed to be her father.

In *Mint Julep Murder* (Bantam, 1995), Annie served as author liaison at the Dixie Book Week on Hilton Head. Her responsibility was to meet the needs of five disparate authors who were being honored with medals. When one was murdered, Annie suspected the other four, but the local police suspected her.

The women of Broward's Rock had their own agenda for the annual Fourth of July celebration in *Yankee Doodle Dead* (Avon, 1998). They were sabotaged by library board member, Gen. "Bud" Hatch. Hatch, a newcomer on the island, joined community organizations, then set about "improving them" to meet his standards. His death during the celebration placed a young African-American student in danger of going to jail. Max, Annie, and their friend Miss Dora, focused on the real killer, not realizing how much heartache it would bring to a dear friend.

The rich flavor of familiar sleuths and authors enlivened *White Elephant Dead* (Avon, 1999). The plotting was proof of Hart's respect for the Golden Age authors. Suspects in the death of a blackmailer were all upper class, highly respectable, and identified as possessors of personal secrets.

Although Annie worked at appreciating Max's wonderful personality, she was a workaholic paired with an easy-going husband content to live on inherited money. His curiosity aroused, Max took a strong role in identifying the killer. Henny Brawley's accidental involvement in the murder disabled her from a role in the detection, but she had no trouble in winning Annie's monthly mystery contest.

Sugar Plum Dead (Morrow, 2000) had many elements of the traditonal cozy, including a wealthy widow who threatened to disinherit her stepchildren. Surprisingly, the murder victim was not the domineering widow of a movie producer, but her well-meaning sister. At first Annie reluctantly participated in the investigation. The initial suspect was Pudge, the father she had not seen since childhood. The next most likely to be arrested was Rachel, a teenage stepsister whom Annie had not known existed. The conclusion was startling, dependent upon circumstances and legalities that taxed credibility. More intriguing was Annie's gradual acceptance of her father, her fierce loyalty to young Rachel, and a deeper understanding of Max, whose more casual approach to life was a reaction to a workaholic father who had no time for his son.

The books were designed to amuse and amaze. They did.

Lisa Davis

Author: Lilla M. Waltch

Lisa Davis was a slim, dark-haired teaching assistant at Addison University. Her mother, who had been abandoned by Lisa's father, was a toy buyer eager to see her daughter married.

In *The Third Victim* (Dodd, 1987), Lisa, in 1984, came upon the murder of Professor Sheldon Silverman, a conspirator in the fatal 1968 bombing of a Page University laboratory. Professor Louis Hammer, who had provided Silverman with his alibi, was found dead. Undoubtedly the root of the murders was in the earlier crime, and Lisa worked her way to an unconvincing solution.

By *Fearful Symmetry* (Dodd, 1988), Lisa was in her early thirties, still single, and worked as a reporter for the Braeton Times. Zoo director Matt Yates, an old family friend, was suspected when Jacky Winston, the disenchanted wife of a major underwriter of the Zoo, was found dead in a polar bear cage. Matt and Lisa probed the Winston wild game farm connection to drugs. She was a traditional "Had I But Known" heroine, going alone late at night into obvious danger.

Clara Dawson

Authors: Eleanor Boylan/Elizabeth Daly

See: Clara Dawson Gamadge, Page 100

Elizabeth MacPherson Dawson

Author: Sharyn McCrumb

Elizabeth MacPherson was presented first as a naïve Southern sociology student, developed into an unsophisticated graduate student, and then became an ingenuous married forensic anthropologist. She was petite, dark-haired, slightly plump, inordinately proud of her Scots heritage, and awed by British royalty.

In *Sick of Shadows* (Avon, 1984), Elizabeth was drafted as a bridesmaid for her affluent cousin, Eileen's wedding. The cousins were aware that Great Aunt Agatha had left a tidy fortune to the first of her grandnephews or grandnieces to marry. Bill MacPherson, Elizabeth's brother, deduced who wanted the bride dead.

Elizabeth was in her early twenties in *Lovely in Her Bones* (Avon, 1985). She joined an archeological dig designed to forestall corporate takeover of an Indian cemetery. After the head scientist on the project was murdered, Elizabeth's anthropological skills provided the clue to the murderess. Her naivete almost made her the next victim.

A West Virginia Scottish festival attracted Elizabeth in *Highland Laddie Gone* (Avon, 1986) and introduced Cameron Dawson, a visiting Scots professor with whom she fell in love. The Campbells and the MacDonalds had never resolved their feuds. The squabbles turned dangerous when pride and pretense led to murder.

In *Paying the Piper* (Ballantine, 1988), Elizabeth returned to her Scottish roots to study Celtic "standing stones" on an isolated island, while Cameron, a marine biologist, worked nearby. The plot took an Agatha Christie twist as members of the expedition sickened and died.

During *The Windsor Knot* (Ballantine, 1990), Elizabeth advanced her wedding plans to attend the Queen Elizabeth's Garden party as Cameron's wife. Before leaving home, she sifted the ashes to uncover a deadly life insurance scam.

As *Missing Susan* (Ballantine, 1991) began, Cameron left on a field trip. Elizabeth joined a "Jack the Ripper" tour. She was unaware that guide

Rowan Rover had accepted a $10,000 down payment to kill heiress and fellow tourist Susan Cohen.

In *MacPherson's Lament* (Ballantine, 1992), Elizabeth played a lesser role. Brother Bill, a young attorney in Danville, Virginia, was bamboozled by a covey of elderly "Confederate Women" in search of rebel gold. The MacPherson siblings had a problem. Their parents, deciding that they had outgrown one another, wanted a divorce. Elizabeth returned to the States, hoping to encourage them to reconcile.

Through *If I'd Killed Him When I Met Him...* (Ballantine, 1995), Elizabeth stayed on, distraught by the disappearance of Cameron's small craft at sea. Bill and his feisty female partner, A. P. Hill, involved Elizabeth in their investigations of a generations old murder by arsenic in which no method of administration could be found, and a modern day death by arsenic in which a mistreated wife was the descendant of the prior suspect. The characters were well drawn, and the medical aspects of the plot worthy of Christie.

A month in Cherry Hill Mental Hospital helped Elizabeth to accept Cameron's death in *The PMS Outlaws* (Ballantine, 2000). She took an unauthorized leave of absence to clarify the identity of an elderly ex-convict who was occupying the Southern mansion her brother Bill had purchased. The investigation made it possible for her to move on. Otherwise the narrative focused on A. P. Hill, Bill's partner. She was haunted by memories of a youthful prank that may have inspired a *Thelma and Louise* couple to terrorize members of the opposite sex.

The Elizabeth MacPherson mystery series blended humor and light narrative. To experience McCrumb's merit as a regional author, a reader should try her most recent series featuring mountain woman Nora Bonesteel and Sheriff Spencer Arrowood.

Charity Day

Author: Dimitri Gat

Private investigator Yuri Nevsky was an interesting hero, assisted by attractive young attorney Charity Day. Charity, a graduate of Radcliffe and Harvard Law School, had been widowed when her husband and only child were killed in an automobile accident. An Iowa transplant, she remained in the Pittsburgh area to practice law, renting the upstairs flat in Russian-American Nevsky's duplex. She lived alone except for a cat, Tuptin.

In *Nevsky's Return* (Avon, 1982), Ludmilla Markov came to Yuri when her missing grandson was accused of murder and the theft of a valuable religious relic. Charity provided Yuri with press cards, which they used to interview other suspects. Yuri settled for a bloody and unsatisfactory ending and the rejection of his proposal by Charity.

Nevsky, a divorced man with two daughters in school, had accepted Charity's role as a friend and tenant when *Nevsky's Demon* (Avon, 1983) began. Felicia Farrow Semanova, her college roommate, stopped by to leave a large package. Charity arranged for Yuri to hide the object when the house was burgled, and Felicia was killed. Charity and Yuri retained possession of the package, while assorted malefactors and politicians killed to find it. Author John D. MacDonald's successful plagiarism lawsuit against Gat ended the series.

Sarah Deane
Author: J. S. Borthwick, pseudonym for Jean Scott Creighton

Although Sarah Deane was a college professor, the series, with one exception, did not fit the category of academic mysteries. She traveled extensively, spent time bird watching in nature refuges, went to sea in a sailing sloop, and bounced uncomfortably on horseback. Her mother was a landscape designer; her father, an architect. A huge Irish wolfhound was added later to the household.

She appeared in *The Case of the Hook-Billed Kites* (St. Martin, 1982) as a high school teacher working on an advanced degree. Sarah joined her beau Philip Lentz in Texas, where he led a bird watching group. When he was strangled, Alex McKenzie, Philip's former college roommate, took a personal interest in the investigation and in Sarah.

In *The Down East Murders* (St. Martin, 1985), Sarah was enrolled in graduate school. She and Alex vacationed on a Maine coastal island. Elspeth McKenzie, Alex's mother, introduced the couple to the island art colony; which included a murderer, a thief, and a murder victim. With her Ph.D. partially completed, Sarah accepted a fellowship at Bowmouth College.

The Student Body (St. Martin, 1986) was the academic mystery with familiar ingredients: unpopular but brilliant victim (this time a student), departmental jealousy, and a blackmailer who preyed upon the faculty.

In *Bodies of Water* (St. Martin, 1990), Sarah's concern for her restless brother, Tony, sent her out on a yacht used by religious leader David Mallory to carry supplies to his congregations. Sarah enjoyed risks, asking questions and searching staterooms when one passenger was murdered and another disappeared.

Sarah's widowed Aunt Julia (Cassidy) brooked no excuses when she invited Sarah and Alex to join her for an Arizona Christmas in *Dude on Arrival* (St. Martin, 1992). Sarah accepted, followed by Alex, to discover bodies, rustle horses, and uncover political scandals.

Sarah and Alex's plans to marry were disrupted in *The Bridled Groom* (St. Martin, 1994) by an overabundance of relatives, interfering neighbors, and threats to Aunt Julia. They managed the ceremony, but delayed the honeymoon to solve a series of murders.

The deaths of Junior and Marsden Gattling did not disturb the locals, nearly so much as did that of Dolly Beaugard in *Dolly Is Dead* (St. Martin, 1995). The Gattlings were considered troublemakers, while Dolly's family was highly regarded in the community. Alex, now a medical examiner, and Sarah, who had known the Beaugards since childhood, wanted to sit this one out. They were not allowed to do so.

Aunt Julia, who could not resist two free tickets on a garden tour of Europe, persuaded Sarah to accompany her during *The Garden Plot* (St. Martin, 1997). Though neither one was particularly concerned with gardens, both enjoyed a mystery. Sarah was interested in the murder of former schoolmate, Ellen Trevino. Those who had another agenda for the trip had not welcomed Ellen and other members of the tour staff.

As *My Body Lies Over the Ocean* (St. Martin, 1999) began, Sarah, Alex and Aunt Julia traveled on the maiden voyage of the elegant new ship Queen Victoria on their return to the United States from the European adventure. Their intent was to rest and relax, a goal made untenable by sinister crewmembers, vengeful passengers, and a trio of suspicious undercover agents. The echoes of the Titanic hovered. The motivation for the murders seemed unrealistic, but Borthwick is a good storyteller so the reader may not notice.

There were no openings for an English professor in Camden, Maine when Sarah was awarded her Ph.D. In *Coup de Grace* (St. Martin, 2000), she accepted a short term position at Miss Merritt's School in Massachusetts. She anticipated the difficulty in spending her weekdays away from Alex. She had been made aware of the formidable Madame Grace Carpenter who headed the language division. She did not expect attacks upon faculty members, including herself.

The series offered enticing locales, well-drawn minor characters, action for the heroine, and above average plotting.

Rina Lazarus Decker

Author: Faye Kellerman

See: Rina Lazarus, Page 165

Kate Delafield

Author: Katherine Forrest

Kate Delafield, a lesbian police officer in Los Angeles, had concealed her sexual orientation at work. In her thirties she was a tall woman with blue eyes and short black hair that was going gray. Both Kate and her lover Annie had grown up in Michigan, where Kate attended the University at Ann Arbor. Her last year in college, she joined the Marine Corps, serving in Vietnam. After military service, she joined the police department, working juvenile, and then homicide where she was teamed with Detective Ed Taylor. Kate had shared a home with Annie until she was killed in a fire; then moved to an apartment in Santa Monica, California.

Kate was assigned to the murder of a sexist/racist businessman in *Amateur City* (Naiad, 1984). During the investigation she was attracted to Ellen O'Neill, also a lesbian, because of her resemblance to Annie. After Kate rescued Ellen from a killer, they became intimate.

Forrest provided realistic details as to how the police might handle a crime scene in *Murder at the Nightwood Bar* (Naiad, 1987). Since the murder occurred in the parking lot of a tavern frequented by lesbians, the customers were hostile to questions. Kate, as a woman, was expected to do most of the interviewing. The narrative explored the family background of the victim—her parents' inability to accept her lifestyle (which included heterosexual prostitution), and her father's sexual problems.

During *The Beverly Malibu* (Naiad, 1989), Kate investigated the sado-masochistic murder of former movie director Otto Sinclair. Suspicion focused on other residents of the apartment complex, because Sinclair had been a friendly witness before the House Un-American Activities Committee.

In *Murder by Tradition*, (Naiad, 1991), a homosexual was brutally murdered in the kitchen of his catering business. The suspect argued that he killed Ashwell in self-defense after a homosexual advance. Kate was determined to prove that the defendant was a gay basher, and guilty of murder, not manslaughter, even if cross-examination revealed her lesbian orientation.

After a five-year absence, Kate reappeared in *Liberty Square* (Berkley, 1996) during which she renewed her contacts with other Marine Corps

Vietnam veterans. She had not sought this reunion, but was convinced to attend by Aimee, her current lover. Their hotel room door was riddled with bullets. Cap, Kate's former male fiancé who had been declared missing in action, might be alive. A lieutenant who had survived the war was murdered, and Cap was suspected.

Apparition Alley (Berkley, 1997) might be Forrest's tautest narrative. Kate was shot by "friendly fire" when her team was serving a warrant on a suspect. While incapacitated, she was drafted to represent Luke Taggart, an unpopular police officer, charged with improperly shooting a drug dealer. Taggart had lost the respect of fellow officers because he "broke the code", testifying against a former partner. Taggart's primary interest, however, was in reopening the murder investigation of Tony Ferrara. Ferrara, a gay police officer, had intended to divulge his own sexual orientation and "out" a list of other homosexual police officers and detectives.

Although she was deeply embroiled in an investigation with international and scientific implications in *Sleeping Bones* (Berkley, 1999), Kate seemed more relaxed, less strident, more pragmatic, and less polemic. New information about her birth family came as a surprise. She agreed to the use of illegal, unethical methods to drive off a wife batterer and balanced her desire for justice against national interests.

Forrest is a skilled writer, who has edited material for other mysteries.

Sr. Mary Theresa "Emtee" Dempsey
Author: Monica Quill, pseudonym for Ralph McInerny

Sister Mary Theresa (Emtee) and her companions Sister Kim and Sister Joyce represented the positive qualities in religious women; faith, hope, and considerable charity along with a high level of scholarship. Emtee, a wise septuagenarian, short (5') pudgy (200 pounds), with blue eyes behind her glasses, was a serious historian. Sr. Kim Moriarity, a brash redhead dressed in street clothes, had a disapproving police captain for a brother. Sr. Joyce, housekeeper and sports fan, provided the light touch, managing the Frank Lloyd Wright designed Chicago residence. They were the remnants of the Order of Martha and Mary, which formerly staffed a local college. The stories followed a pattern with the nuns offering refuge and support to victims and suspects, usually against the wishes of the local police.

Not a Blessed Thing! (Vanguard, 1981) introduced the trio to crime when Kim's brother, Richard Moriarity co-opted the convent as a hideaway for Cheryl Pitman, a television station owner whose life had been threatened.

Let Us Prey (Vanguard, 1982) found Sr. Kim baby-sitting a four-year-old boy, homeless because his father confessed to killing his mother. Emtee proved the dad's innocence and produced a witness to identify the killer.

And Then There Was Nun—poor English for an academic—(Vanguard, 1984) brought a former student of Emtee's, Diane Torrance, to the convent seeking marital counseling…from members of a religious order! When Phillip Torrance was murdered, Diane needed a different kind of help.

In *Nun of the Above* (Vanguard, 1985), a stranger shared his dreams of witnessing a crime, the details of which were close to those of a recent murder. The victim was a very religious young woman determined to "save" a sleazy nightclub owner.

Sine Qua Nun (Vanguard, 1986) found Emtee matched against a radical religious, Sister Faith Hope, on a TV interview show. Not only did Faith Hope fail to appear, but her substitute was murdered and the television host was accused of the killing.

Emtee championed an accused killer in *The Veil of Ignorance* (St. Martin, 1988). Lydia Hopkins, a woman convicted of killing not only her husband but also her young daughter, had corresponded with Emtee while in prison. In a classic gathering of the suspects at the convent, Emtee identified the murderer of Lydia's abusive husband.

Katherine Senski, a Chicago newswoman who appeared in many of the books, had a leading role in *Sister Hood* (St. Martin, 1991) an improbable story of religious and civic politics, leading to the murder of a cloistered nun.

Nun Plussed (St. Martin, 1993) hinged on a spurious invitation to the wedding of divorced Catholic Margaret Nelson Doyle. Her subsequent murder triggered Sister Kim and Emtee's efforts to prove former husband Gregory Doyle's innocence.

The sisters returned in *Half Past Nun*, (St. Martin, 1997) with the addition of postulant Margaret Mary Horan. Police Lt. Richard Moriarity, Sister Kim's brother, headed the task force seeking a serial killer who preyed upon women. No pattern emerged among the victims until Emtee reached into the past for a motive for vengeance.

Laura Di Palma

Author: Lia Matera

Laura Di Palma, a thirty-three year old divorcee, practiced criminal law, then a risky and unusual specialty for a woman. She was a late bloomer, who ended an unhappy marriage before attending college and law school. After an auspicious start as law clerk for a state Supreme Court Justice, Laura gained experience in the U.S. Attorney's criminal division, and then moved to a large San Francisco law firm. Once professionally secure, she employed household and yard help, owned a Mercedes, and enjoyed too much Stoli vodka. Her private life was obviously less rewarding.

In *The Smart Money* (Bantam, 1988) Laura revisited her hometown, coming into contact with her ex-husband and his current wife, her father who had been widowed when Laura was very young, "uncle" Henry Di Palma, a crooked politician, and Henry's son, Hal, an unstable Vietnam veteran who became her lover. Into that mixture appeared client Wallace Bean, acquitted for murder on grounds of insanity.

Laura was under pressure from her law firm in *The Good Fight* (Simon, 1990) to abandon criminal law and avoid left wing causes. Dan Crosetti, a Vietnam protest marcher until he lost both legs, had been accused of murdering an undercover FBI agent. Laura's concern for Hal, recovering from a stroke, took precedence over Dan's defense until he was found, an apparent suicide.

Out of work and in need of respite, Laura and Hal set out on a six-month vacation in the woods in *A Hard Bargain* (Simon, 1992). Laura's former investigator Sandy Arkelett intruded to seek Hal's assistance. Karen McGuin, the wife in an interracial marriage, had committed suicide, ostensibly with her husband Ted's encouragement. He was prosecuted for assisted suicide. Laura joined in the investigation, and found herself increasingly attracted to the handsome young African-American.

Laura had left corporate practice by *Face Value* (Simon, 1994), renting space from a public interest law firm. She was drawn into the activities of a cult, headed by charismatic Brother Mike. Mike had betrayed members of his sexual therapy group by taping sessions and making them available commercially. In this narrative, Laura came across as gullible, even irrational. Sandy Arkelett who loved her was on hand to pick up the pieces.

By *Designer Crimes* (Simon, 1995), Laura was ready to re-establish her relationship with Sandy. She was obsessed by her hostility for former employer, Steve Sayres, and the hatred borne her by District Attorney Connie Gold. Gold had resented Laura's criticism of her connections with the entertainment industry. Laura was involved in a series of attacks, one of which led to the death of labor attorney Jocelyn Kinsley. Sandy believed that someone was designing crimes of revenge for employees who could not get legal relief, and that Laura, not Jocelyn, had been the intended victim in the attack.

The characters were provocative, holding the reader's attention until their problems were resolved, but sometimes they never were resolved. Matera made no attempt to win readers with tidy solutions. Laura's narration was introspective, but the story lines were well plotted with plentiful action.

Trixie Dolan

Author: Marian Babson

Narrator Trixie Dolan gave minimal physical descriptions of herself and friendly rival Evangeline Sinclair. Perhaps the allusions to aging bodies, hair, and eyes would have been too traumatic for actresses. Despite their age, both were professionally active. Evangeline carefully guarded her star status while Trixie was content with lesser roles as she had been when she danced in the Forties musicals.

In *Reel Murder* (St. Martin, 1988), they visited England for a retrospective of Evangeline's films. Upon discovering a fellow tenant carrying a corpse, they encouraged him to dump it in the river. Martha, Trixie's devoted but staid daughter, joined them and learned of her real parentage.

During *Encore Murder* (St. Martin, 1989), Trixie was preoccupied with details of Martha's wedding to producer Hugh Carpenter, while Evangeline feuded with a rival actress. Cressida, Hugh's ex-wife, was struck by an arrow, casting suspicion on Martha, an excellent archer.

In *Shadows in Their Blood* (St. Martin, 1993), Trixie and Evangeline went on location for producer Job Farraday's *Dracula* movie. The narrative was strong on atmosphere (blood, bats, and a knitting stage-mother rivaling Madame Defarge), but had little deduction.

On their return to London in *Even Yuppies Die* (HarperCollins, 1995), Trixie and Evangeline settled for modest quarters, provided by Jasper, the grandson of friends. They realized that they were being manipulated by their fellow tenants, one of whom was a killer.

So many of the characters and their motivations in *Break a Leg, Darlings* (St. Martin, 1996) were based upon prior novels that it might be difficult for a new reader to keep track of the action. Trixie and Evangeline sought an original play in which they could return to the London stage. They visited minor productions, including those in pubs, goaded by the fact that rival actress Sweetums Carew was also play-hunting. Instead of finding a script, they acquired a clique of young friends, a massive Irish wolfhound, and a murderous betting scheme.

Trixie and Evangeline, however engaging they might be and although they eventually identified killers, withheld important information from the police. Knowing who had committed the crime was a long way from convicting the party in court.

Lorna Doria

Author: Heather Graham (Pozzessere)

See: Donna Miro, Page 201

Mona Moore Dunbar

Author: Will Harriss

Protagonist Clifford Dunbar had a wife who merited greater attention. Mona Moore, of the green eyes and dandelion colored hair, was in her mid-twenties when she met widowed English Professor Cliff Dunbar. She was currently working on a master's degree in physical therapy and kinesiology, planning to earn a medical degree.

In *The Bay Psalm Book Murder* (Walker, 1983) Dunbar, a wealthy man, decided that the Los Angeles police department would never solve the murder of his best friend, curator of the university library special collection. Why would the curator's assailants take his money and leave a valuable book, purported to be the first published in the Colonies? Dunbar's suspicion that the book might be a fake caused him to hire Mona to proofread it, checking against an authenticated copy. The investigation caused an attack on Mona, whom Dunbar took into his home for protection.

Mona and Cliff were married by *Timor Mortis* (Walker, 1986). A family interest and the challenging offer of a valuable portrait motivated him to investigate the murder of Maria de Castello Atterbury. Maria could chose which of her husband's relatives would inherit at her death. Mona took a minor role, keeping the killer from suicide, as Cliff learned why the painting held such value.

A. J. Egan

Authors: Matthew and Bonnie Taylor

Not all of Alice Jane Egan's ideas were well thought out. She could not abide the name Alice Jane, so settled for the ambiguous A. J. She did not want to remain in the Midwest so she moved to Florida. She intended to be the best reporter in the area, but rented an apartment from her potential rival, widower Palmer Kingston. Kingston was a well-to-do eccentric who collected antique cars in the ballroom of his old mansion and rented out his attic.

In *Neon Flamingo* (Dodd, 1987), Kingston was unaware that his new tenant would also cover the murder of retired police captain Haskins Delano. Palmer had been the negotiator during the kidnapping of Peter Chastain's grandson, a case that Delano, then a young cop, had bungled. A. J. and Palmer became lovers, concealing their relationship from their employers, but combining their efforts to find the ransom.

Neon Dancer (Walker, 1991) awarded A. J. an early victory when she scooped Palmer on corruption at the local zoning office. Julio Montiega felt that he was being unfairly targeted because of a boyhood tie to a Spanish Mafia family. Although Palmer was sympathetic, he and A. J. agreed to disagree when Montiega was arrested. They became bitterly competitive, to the point where their relationship was threatened. When Palmer was jailed for refusing to share information, A. J. and other reporters rallied to support his First Amendment rights. Palmer and A. J. exposed the bribery of councilmen and the improper awards of zoning permits to a corporation. She carried a subordinate but interesting role.

Dr. Janet Eldine

Author: Charlotte Epstein

Janet's mother had raised her and three younger brothers in spite of a husband who did little to provide for their welfare. Possibly as a result, Janet remained single, and wanted no children. As the series began, she was a tiny white-haired academic in her fifties. She was an accredited writer and teacher attached to Kirktown College in the United States with an attraction for Chinese culture. She traveled to Communist China to teach English to Chinese students who planned to further their education in the United States.

As *Murder in China* (Doubleday, 1989) began, Janet awakened during the night at her room in the Foreign Student's Building. Madame Li, a Communist hard-liner on the campus, had been murdered. Foreign students and academics, including Janet, were suspects. Because Janet was known to have worked with the Philadelphia police, she was asked to intervene by her fellow students. This was difficult because she had been accused of implanting foreign ideas into her students. Janet spent time in a Chinese jail before identifying the killer, but made an important contact with an unnamed police official.

Murder at the Friendship Hotel (Doubleday, 1991) returned Janet to China to establish an English department in a new Chinese University in Inner Mongolia. En route to her new assignment, she was lodged on a Beijing college campus. Dr. Ian Chen, a Chinese-American geneticist on staff, seemed to accept the pro-life stance of charismatic guest lecturer, Mary Allen. Nevertheless, when Allen was slaughtered in her dormitory room, Chen was suspected. The investigator was the same official with whom Janet had worked in *Murder in China.* Birth control through abortion was a provocative issue in a country intent upon decreasing its population.

Epstein had undeniable background and expertise for her stories, but lesser narrative skills.

Maggie Elliott

Author: Elizabeth Atwood Taylor

The death of Maggie Elliott's husband precipitated her alcoholism. Her reckless behavior continued after sobriety. She had interesting characteristics: an ex-Texan; an Ivy League education; interests in massage, Tarot cards, and the implications of her dreams (although few of them were seriously explored). Maggie was strongly committed to protection of the environment and socially concerned about Native Americans in Northern California and Central America, where she had worked as a volunteer.

The trigger to Maggie's recovery from alcoholism had been the fatal accident to her half-sister Celia, followed by the death of Celia's daughter, Lindy. Even after her addiction was controlled through AA membership, Maggie did not connect the deaths. During *The Cable Car Murder* (St. Martin, 1982), she met ex-cop Richard O'Reagan, a witness to Celia's "accident." O'Reagan and Maggie combined their efforts as private investigators, but her temperance and freedom were threatened before they trapped the killer.

In *Murder at Vassar* (St. Martin, 1987), Maggie attended her fifteenth class reunion. Local officials were unimpressed by her California detective license when fellow alumna Pudgie Warner Brown was arrested for the murder of an affluent aunt. Undeterred, Maggie focused on Aunt Chloe's other heirs, particularly those who would benefit if Pudgie were eliminated.

There was a chameleon-like character to Maggie. First, she was a Los Angeles urban professional suffering from alcoholism; then a Vassar alum returning to the East. In *The Northwest Murders* (St. Martin, 1992), she was portrayed as an environmentalist suffering from Chronic Fatigue Symptom. O'Reagan, no longer an important figure in her personal life, supplied Maggie with a vacation cabin in the North California woods. An unidentified killer had murdered and scalped a man; then raped and almost killed his companion, young Sally Stephens. Maggie befriended Hermina, a child who had seen the killer. Maggie's attraction to Jim Pepper, O'Reagan's cousin, personalized her interest in Native Americans and their treatment by the Forest Service. She and Pepper found romance, a treasure trove, and a killer, but survived only with the help of a female bear.

Lydia Fairchild

Author: D. (Doris) R. Meredith

The images of attractive, independent females on *Hill Street Blues, L.A. Law,* and *Law and Order* advanced the entrance of women into the justice system in real life and in mystery fiction. Even when introduced as supporting characters, female attorneys had the potential to earn vital parts in the series, as was the case of perpetual law student Lydia Fairchild in the John Lloyd Branson series. Branson, a formidable criminal attorney, was tall and handsome with a mysterious injury and a hidden sorrow. He selected as his Watson, tall, slim, blonde Lydia Ann Fairchild. Lydia, who somehow maintained her status in school, came whenever Branson whistled, even occupying an apartment over his garage. Branson, conscious of the difference in their ages and status, was circumspect.

They met in *Murder by Impulse* (Ballantine, 1988), when Lydia interned for Branson in Canadian, Texas. The dialogue was heavy handed, but the action, swift. With Lydia's help, Branson proved that his lifelong friend Jim Steele had not killed his wife.

In *Murder by Deception* (Ballantine, 1989), Branson needed Lydia to defend a local farmer from a murder charge. They connected the death with the use of adjacent land for storage of nuclear waste.

Lydia had a more active role in *Murder by Masquerade* (Ballantine, 1991) when she disguised herself as a hooker to trap a serial killer. She was depressed as *Murder by Reference* (Ballantine, 1991) began, haunted by a man she had killed in self-defense. Branson diverted her with the murder of the curator of the Panhandle-Plains Historical museum. She worked through her post-traumatic anxieties in time to redirect Branson and the police to the killer.

During *Murder by Sacrilege* (Ballantine, 1993), Lydia shared Branson's investigation, although she opposed his defense of a minister accused of murdering his young wife. Her mood was not improved when Branson's courtroom tactics negated a possible insanity defense or manslaughter verdict. Lydia had been promised a full partnership when she graduated, enough to make any savvy law student suspicious of Branson's intentions, as his defenses against her gradually crumbled.

Doran Fairweather

Author: Mollie Hardwick

Doran Fairweather's world of antiques was one where a female could compete and where fraud and subterfuge might be anticipated. She was tall, slim, brown haired and hazel eyed, twenty-six-years old, living and working in Abbotsbourne, Kent, England. An educated woman, the daughter of a deceased Oxford don, Doran had inexplicably failed her college finals. She had spent time working in a bookshop and as a secretary. Her partner in the antique business was Howell Evans, whose homosexuality was treated without exploitation. Howell's mother, Gwenllian, played a role in the series.

In *Malice Domestic* (St. Martin, 1986), Doran and widower Rev. Rodney Chelmarsh confronted Mumbry, an ex-solicitor who brought a sinister element into Abbotsbourne. When Mumbry was poisoned, suspicion focused on Rodney and his disabled daughter, Helena.

In *Parson's Pleasure* (St. Martin, 1987), Doran and Rodney were reluctant to marry because of Helena's opposition. Although at times, it played a secondary role to romance, the mystery arose from stolen antiques.

By *Uneaseful Death* (St. Martin, 1988), the couple had married. Rodney was experiencing a crisis of faith. Doran was uneasy in her role as stepmother. While she was traveling, a dead body was deposited in her car. All suspects were isolated by a storm.

In *The Bandersnatch* (St. Martin, 1989), Doran seemed irresponsible. Even though the family finances were stressed by the birth of son Christopher (Kit) and Rodney's career change, she spent an exorbitant amount of money on a carved wooden cherub. The cherub's value was so great that Christopher was placed at risk to force Doran to surrender it. One element of mystery was Rodney's acceptance of her disregard for the child's safety.

Helena, obsessively attached to her father, had died by *Perish in July* (St. Martin, 1990), but the Chelmarsh marriage remained troubled. When the small church in which Rodney worked part-time needed money, the parishioners decided to "give a show." The death of a performer on the stage was worrisome to Doran. So was evidence that Rodney was flirting with her old school chum.

In *The Dreaming Damozel* (St. Martin, 1991), the focus returned to Doran's antique business. Howell's departure caused her to concentrate on Pre-Raphaelite art. She was drawn into murders in which the victims were attired as models in pictures of the Rosetti period. A windfall solved the family financial problems, but security did not bring happiness.

As *Come Away, Death* (Fawcett Crest, 1997) opened, Doran was restless, and bored with Rodney who seemed more interested in his research. An opportunity to occupy a rent-free apartment in London seemed the answer. Leaving her children and Rodney behind, she submerged herself in the literary and historical London she so enjoyed. There were unexpected snakes in her Eden. Gwenllian's crude lover was murdered. An avaricious housemaid menaced Doran's children. A handicapped and lonely man tempted her into infidelity. The underlying motive for the murders stretched credulity.

Doran was impulsive. Her recklessness necessitated rescues by Rodney, Howell, his mother Gwenllian, and/or local officials. Rodney was not involved in detection, but had a "sense of evil" that occasionally surfaced. The side references to literature, art, and antiques were informative.

Geraldine Farrar

Author: Barbara Paul

Real persons as series detectives have included such disparate individuals as Eleanor Roosevelt, Gypsy Rose Lee, and Gertrude Stein. Opera star Geraldine Farrar may be less well known, but had been distinctive in her time, an American prima donna. The blue-eyed brunette, born and raised in Massachusetts, studied and made her debut in Europe before returning to sing at the Metropolitan Opera in 1906.

In *Prima Donna at Large* (St. Martin, 1985), Geraldine shared the spotlight with Arturo Toscanini and Enrico Caruso. The resident tenor was unable to perform *Carmen* because of ill health. A temperamental understudy substituted but was plagued by accidents, taking his own life when his throat was irreparably damaged.

By *A Chorus of Detectives* (St. Martin, 1987), Geraldine believed that her voice had deteriorated, and that Rosa Ponselle, a former vaudevillian, was being groomed as her successor. When a young member of the chorus was poisoned by orange juice left in his dressing room, Farrar and the ailing

Caruso enlisted fellow singers to solve the murder. With the help of police detective O'Halloran, they set a trap to identify the killer before the comeback appearance of Caruso on Christmas Day.

Interesting historical pieces. Readers may be interested in Paul's other series, featuring police detective Marian Larch.

Nina Fischman

Author: Marisa Piesman

Jewish elder-law attorney, Nina Fischman solved New York City crimes with the help of her mother. Ida Fischman had graduated from Hunter College where she had a brief interest in the Young Communist League. In her later years, she dedicated herself to introducing Nina to eligible young men, interfering in her legal cases, and righting the wrongs she identified in the community.

In *Unorthodox Practices* (Pocket, 1989), Ida was concerned about malfeasance by a member of the board of directors of her co-op apartment building. It was she, not Nina, who traced the insecticide found in several apartments. It was Ida who proved that tenants, not cockroaches, were meant to be eliminated. Nina was preoccupied because her five-year relationship with fellow attorney Grant Miller, son of a Lutheran minister, was going nowhere.

Personal Effects (Pocket, 1991) revealed that Nina, who had worked as a secretary and a cab driver, had been seeing a therapist for years, and that her deceased father, Leo, had been a Communist. African-American detective James Williams, investigating the murder of Susan Gold, Nina's best friend in high school, believed the killer would strike again and that Nina would be the target. After she helped to trap the killer, Williams convinced Nina to resume serious dating.

During *Heading Uptown* (Delacorte, 1993), Nina's role as alternate executor of a will and her compassion for a teenager motivated her to investigate the death of the girl's father. Without any current NYC beau, Nina became involved with Tom, a former lover who practiced law near the setting of the father's death.

Tom was on a two-week canoe trip with his daughter in *Close Quarters* (Delacorte, 1994). Nina joined a predominantly female household on Fire Island for her vacation. The "house manager" had slept with several of the residents over the years, so when he was poisoned, there was a house full of suspects.

Nina had a steady beau, Jonathan, in *Alternate Sides* (Delacorte, 1995), but that did not keep her out of trouble. While she was trying to decide whether or not to move in with Jonathan, someone put a corpse in his car. Nina juggled murder, her emotional ties to her own neighborhood, and the fear of commitment, but survived.

She moved to California with Jonathan when he was transferred, but by *Survival Instincts* (Delacorte, 1998) realized she could never live there. Nina returned to New York City in need of an apartment and a new job. Ida provided a temporary place to live. Nina's sister Laura set her on the trail of the killer of a young researcher whom Nina had dated years before. She found herself relieved to have left her prior relationship and unwilling to return to the practice of law. A temporary assignment as a researcher for an investigative newspaper columnist turned into an extended alternative.

Piesman's narratives had been enhanced by her witty characterizations, descriptions of the neighborhood settings, and the ethnic and social interactions.

Phryne Fisher

Author: Kerry Greenwood

Her name was not the only unusual aspect of the Hon. Miss Phryne Fisher. Raised poor in Australia, Phryne relocated to England at twelve when her father inherited a title and landed estates. At sixteen, she ran off to join Queen Alexandra's Volunteers, serving overseas as an ambulance driver in the First World War. Having experienced poverty, Phryne denied herself nothing—the finest food and drink, loyal servants, the best in cars, clothes, and furnishings. She enjoyed sex for the physical pleasure it afforded her, scorned "meaningful relationships," and was attracted to criminal investigations because they provided excitement and risk. Phryne was physically small with dark hair. Still in her twenties during the Roaring Twenties when she returned to Australia, Phryne set up housekeeping, and began detecting. She was proficient with guns and knives and not reluctant to use them.

Death by Misadventure (published in Australia in 1989 as *Cocaine Blues*, in the United States by Fawcett 1991) was episodic, explaining how Phryne gradually built her menage: young maid Dorothy (sexually harassed by a prior employer); Socialist cabbies Cec and Bert; and Dr. Elizabeth MacMillan who joined the crusade against inept abortionists. When drug smugglers tried to discredit Phryne, she and Melbourne police detective Robinson trapped the dealers instead.

Two investigations kept Phryne busy in *Flying Too High* (Fawcett, 1992). A worried mother hired her—first, to prevent a young aviator from killing his domineering father, and then to prove him innocent of the death. Phryne professed to dislike children; still she worked even harder on the abduction of a three-year-old girl, but found time to cavort in bed with a young doctor.

By sheer chance, Phryne was on the scene when a young but boastful anarchist was gunned down by his associates in *Death at Victoria Dock* (Penguin Australia, 1992). She was outraged at the youth's death and the scattered shots that smashed her windshield. Between finding the killers and thwarting their bank robbery, Phryne rescued a missing fourteen year old from her dysfunctional family and comforted a discouraged anarchist.

Murder on the Ballart Train (Fawcett, 1993) re-emphasized Phryne's concern for the vulnerable, her enjoyment of pleasure, and her ability to handle violence. The murderer of an irritable old woman, pulled by a rope out of a railroad passenger car, was easy to identify. The killer's descent into madness lacked credibility.

During a visit to the Green Mill, a Melbourne dance hall in *The Green Mill Murder* (McPhee Gribble, 1993) Phryne witnessed the death of a marathon dancer. When her escort, Charles Freeman ran off from the scene, he was considered a suspect. Phryne was hired by Charles' mother to find Charles and his shell-shocked brother Victor who had disappeared into the outback. Along the way, Phryne involved herself in the problems of Tintagel Stone's Jazz Makers, and those of other marathon dancers. As usual she provided sexual comforts to the vulnerable.

The discovery that a fellow boarding house resident was not only dead but, while posing as a male, was actually a female, sent several "carnies" to Phryne for help in *Blood and Circuses* (McPhee Gribble, 1994c). "Carnies" were not part of the exclusive circus family, but ran booths and sideshows that accompanied the circus. The Farrell Circus had been plagued by a series of accidents. This recent death might be an escalation of the attempt to put the Farrell family out of business. Phryne went underground as "Fern," a novice equestrian, shedding her usual helpers, but acquiring new friends. She slept with a clown and survived a gentle lion, but was happy to return to her gilded world.

During *Ruddy Gore* (McPhee Gribble, 1995), Phryne met Lin Chung who lasted longer than most of her lovers. He was an Eton and Oxford graduate who had returned to Australia where he managed a silk business. Phryne had intervened with attackers to rescue Lin Chung's grandmother. Her immediate problem was an investigation of dangerous incidents occurring backstage and on stage during performances of *Ruddigore*, the Gilbert and Sullivan operetta.

Chung became Phryne's escort when in *Urn Burial* (Penguin, 1996), she was invited to the isolated home of publisher Tom Reynolds. She was unaware of the hidden personas, concealed crimes and violent emotions she would encounter as the rising waters enveloped the house.

Phryne would be unusual at any period in time. She was free of discrimination by race, sexual preference, or class, but had little discrimination in her own sexual choices.

Ginny Fistoulari
Author: Reed Stephens, pseudonym for Stephen Donaldson

Mick Axbrewder was the tough private investigator. Ginny Fistoulari was his boss and partner in Fistoulari Investigations. What a mixed-up pair! Narrator "Brew" turned to alcohol when he mistakenly shot his policeman brother, Dick. Ginny, who suffered from depression, gobbled vitamin pills, lived like a slob, and had no hesitation about drawing her .357. Obviously they were meant for one another. Motherless since childhood, Ginny had grown into a tall, slim blonde with gray eyes who acquired a broken nose, and lost a hand during her adventures. She was hardheaded and logical except when it came to Axbrewder. The other continuing character in the series was super-criminal, El Senor.

In *The Man Who Killed His Brother* (Ballantine, 1980), Ginny hauled Brew out of an alcoholic binge when his thirteen-year-old niece (Dick's daughter) disappeared. The police handled the matter as a runaway, but the disabled duo operated on the theory that Althea was the latest victim of teenage kidnappings.

The Man Who Risked His Partner (Ballantine, 1984) had Brew sharing Ginny's apartment and bed. He had been sober for six months because she needed him due to her recent amputation. Bank official Reg Haskell said El Senor threatened him because he could expose money laundering. Ginny saw very little action. Brew blundered through the investigation, also seeking the murderer of a young Mexican boy. This time he ended up in the hospital. No narratives were published for six years, possibly allowing the hero and heroine to heal.

By *The Man Who Tried to Get Away* (Ballantine, 1990), Brew was still on El Senor's hit list, so Ginny accepted an "easy" assignment. They were to pose as participants in a mystery game at an isolated mountain resort, while providing security. There were real murders interspersed with psychological insights into their personal problems. At the end they went off into the sunset to start a new life, hopefully with medical insurance.

Fiona Fitzgerald

Author: Warren Adler

Police officer Fiona Fitzgerald had two successive personas. Initially, she, the daughter and granddaughter of street cops, had FBI experience and a master's degree in criminology from American University. Eight years later, Daddy had been upgraded to United States Senator (defeated because he opposed the Vietnam War) and Fiona had attended the more exclusive Mt. Vernon Jr. College. Both versions of Fiona worked on the District of Columbia police force and were assigned Randolph Cates, an ex-Trinidadian, as their partner. She was the only white woman on the squad, but Cates had his problems too.

Fiona managed a working relationship with her ambitious African-American supervisor, who operated under pressure from the political bureaucracy governing the District Police Department. She had an African-American "rabbi," police pathologist Dr. Benton, but no personal support system; instead an assortment of lovers over the series. Narrative tensions often arose from her problems: her "married with children" lovers, her role as a mistress, and her desire to have a child.

American Quartet (Arbor, 1981), about a murder in the National Gallery of Art, and *American Sextet* (Arbor, 1983), an investigation into a possible suicide connected to a political exposé, were raunchy and sexually explicit with Fiona as the stereotypical redheaded, green-eyed rebellious female.

Adler revamped the series on the wave of mystery heroines, reshaping Fiona, possibly to attract a female readership. In *Immaculate Deception* (Fine, 1991), Fiona's longing for a child by her married lover affected her response to the suicide/murder of a pregnant pro-life Congresswoman. Involving Fiona in the pro-life/pro-choice controversy was risky. The outcome might not satisfy adherents of either cause.

Senator Love (Fine, 1991) featured a married senator so sexually attractive that Fiona could barely control her libido in his presence. They met professionally when recently discovered bones were connected to the disappearance of a young woman. The victim had worked on a Congressional committee the Senator had headed.

Fiona was unattached in *The Witch of Watergate* (Fine, 1992) when assigned to the killing of Polly Dearborn, a vicious gossip columnist. Assigned to work with a resentful African-American policewoman, Fiona risked disciplinary action for concealing evidence. Her partner argued that Dearborn had committed suicide. Fiona and medical evidence indicated otherwise.

The explicit details of Fiona's degrading treatment by an older lover when she was eighteen began *The Ties That Bind* (Fine, 2000). They were significant in explaining Fiona's emotional reactions to the investigation of a sadistic murder of a young female attorney. Fiona's memories of her own mistreatment focused her attention on a possible suspect, now a United States Supreme Court justice. His exalted position did not protect him from Fiona.

Anne Fitzhugh

Author: Carey Roberts

Fictional policewomen seem to have Irish sounding names more frequently than those of other ethnic groups (Mulcahaney, Fitzgerald, Cagney, O'Neill). Anne's came from her husband, Congressman Rob Fitzhugh, killed in a random shooting. She was a petite brunette, daughter of widower John Tyler, a Virginia district attorney. Her decision to abandon the practice of criminal law came after Rob's death. After training and early service, she was assigned to the District of Columbia homicide department under Captain Terry Wilson.

In *Touch a Cold Door* (Pageant, 1989), former football player Lt. Don Dakota was appalled to have Anne assigned as his partner. Anne's classmate Nina Bibesco, a Georgetown artist, had contacted her. Nina wanted an investigation of the mugging and subsequent death of an art-loving attaché at the British Embassy.

The relationship between Anne and Dakota, punctuated by a one-night stand, remained stormy in *Pray God to Die* (Scribners, 1993). Caroline McKelvey, beautiful daughter of a former ambassador to the United Nations, was discovered with her throat slit. To add to the importance of the case, major suspects included: a handsome canon from the Washington Cathedral; Caroline's beau, a United States Navy Lt. Commander; a Congressman mentioned for a cabinet post; his ambitious wife, a feline television reporter, and a handsome young Italian stonecutter. Interesting characterizations.

Sgt. Molly Flanagan

Author: David Nighbert

Emily Louise "Molly" Flanagan left her wealthy family and expensive college education behind to become a police officer. Her first job with the Houston Police Department became untenable after she won a sexual harassment suit. She relocated to Galveston, where she achieved promotion to sergeant. Like many other female sleuths, her mother had died when she was young. Her father, who was now in ill health in California, had raised her. A green-eyed redhead about forty, she had never married, but maintained a relationship with officer "Bull" Cochran, the major protagonist of the series. Cochran had been a baseball pitcher until he killed a man with his fastball.

Molly and "Bull" met in *Strikezone* (St. Martin, 1989), when he was a suspect in the death of his partner in a transfer business. Bull evaded two sets of gangsters, while seeking a missing suitcase of money. Molly remained on the fringes. Twice however she arrived just in time to rescue him.

Although she was referred to on occasion, and helped Bull by finding a retired cop to back him up, Molly played no significant role in *Squeezeplay* (St. Martin, 1992). On his own, Bull defended the reputation of "Holy Joe" Ahern, a born-again Christian who was found dead beside the body of a call girl.

In *Shutout* (St. Martin, 1995), Molly took time from work to deal with family problems. Uncle Dewey had managed the Flanagan business, Shamrock Coffee, but his recent behavior had caused him to be hospitalized. The four Flanagan brothers disputed whether to keep the languishing business going or to sell the factory site to developers. Before the matter could be settled, Dewey died in the nursing home. Molly and Bull rejected the official decision that his death was suicide.

Enough sports for the jocks; enough romance for the tender hearted; enough mystery for both.

Dixie Flannigan

Author: L. V. Sims

See: Dixie Flannigan Struthers, Page 276

Sgt. Carollee Fleetwood

Author: Michael Z. Lewin

Carollee Fleetwood was a female police officer, so seriously injured on duty that she was confined to a wheelchair in *Hard Line* (Morrow, 1982), a part of the Lt. LeRoy Powder series set in Indianapolis. Although Carollee expected to be on crutches soon, she was unfit for regular duty and assigned to the Missing Persons Bureau. Powder, old enough to be her father, not only resented her presence in his office, but also considered it a ploy to obtain favorable publicity for the department's disability policy. They worked on several cases—a suicidal woman found burning her clothes in an alley; a seven-year-old murder which Carollee solved; a suspect who killed his wife and her female lover. After Powder was seriously injured, he began a sexual relationship with Carollee.

Although he was crude, insulting, and moody, they continued to spend their leisure time together in *Late Payments* (Morrow, 1986). It was Carollee who turned up Jules Mencelli, an unemployed disabled worker. Mancelli's statistics indicated the handicapped people in Indiana were dying at a considerably higher rate than in nearby states. Powder had problems of his own with a former sweetheart, whose overtures he could not trust, and a twelve-year-old boy whose father had disappeared. Powder's inheritance from an aunt made him vulnerable to pressure from his superiors to resign.

Carollee and Powder also made brief appearances in *And Baby Will Fall* (Morrow, 1988), in which social worker Adele Buffington had the lead role.

Jessica Fletcher

Authors: 1 – James Anderson; 2 – David Deutsch;
3 – Jessica Fletcher/Donald Bain

The success of the television series, *Murder, She Wrote*, led first to the novelization of popular episodes by Anderson; a fourth paperback by David Deutsch; and then to a hardcover edition *Gin & Daggers*, purportedly written by the fictional detective herself "with Donald Bain." This latest series returned to paperback form eventually but went on and on and on. There was no need to describe Jessica except to say that she looked just like Angela Lansbury, sexagenarian, still blonde, tall, retaining an excellent figure. She spoke frequently of her deep attachment to Cabot Cove, but seemed to spend an inordinate amount of time elsewhere.

Jessica had been substituting as an English teacher since the death of her husband when, in *The Murder of Sherlock Holmes* (Anderson, Avon 1985), Grady, her husband's nephew, forwarded a draft of her mystery novel to a New York publisher. She returned the favor when publisher Preston Giles invited them to a costume weekend at his estate and Grady was suspected of murder.

Hooray for Homicide (Anderson, Avon, 1985) contained two episodes:

- Amos Tupper, the Cabot Cove sheriff, asked Jessica to question the four daughters of a millionaire who supposedly disappeared from his yacht; and

- Jessica went to Hollywood to express her disapproval of a script based on her book. The producer was unsympathetic so Jessica became one of a half-dozen suspects when he was killed.

Lovers and Other Killers (Anderson, Avon, 1986) consisted of two novelettes:

- While lecturing at Sequoia College, Jessica not only solved two murders, but also learned to beware of handsome young men;

- During a visit in the Virginia hunt country, she appeared in court as "Amicus Curiae" to defend her hostess against an accusation of murder.

Murder in Two Acts (Deutsch, W. H. Allen, 1986) was adapted from two television episodes (*Sing a Song of Murder* by Peter S. Fischer and *Death in the Afternoon*, teleplay by Paul Savage, story by Paul Cooper). Jessica was called to London in the first episode to attend the funeral of her cousin Emma Macgill, an English music hall performer. Fortunately, Emma was still alive. Unfortunately, the killer knew she was and intended to keep trying. Once Emma was safe, the story segued into a New York City background. Although Jessica had business matters to attend to in Manhattan, she also made time to visit her niece, Nita. Nita was a member of the cast of the television soap opera, *Our Secret Lives*. With few exceptions those involved in the series were fearful of Joyce Holleran, the domineering writer/producer. Nita was framed when Joyce was murdered. Jessica convinced a stubborn police inspector to look further.

In *Gin & Daggers* (Fletcher/Bain, McGraw 1989), Jessica, who seemingly spent scant time writing mysteries, was in London attending an International Society of Mystery Writer's Conference. The mental deterioration of an old friend substantiated rumors that someone had ghosted her latest book. When the woman was murdered, Jessica was a suspect. Old friends, Dr. Seth Hazlett and Sheriff Amos Tupper of Cabot Cover, flew over to help.

The next several books, all listing as authors Fletcher and Bain, linked alcohol and crime in their titles:

- *Manhattans & Murder* (Signet, 1994), during which a chance encounter while Christmas shopping in New York City put Jessica at odds with the witness relocation program
- *Rum & Razors* (Signet, 1995), when tired from her exertions, Jessica visited friends who owned a tropical inn, where infidelity, political corruption, and competition for an ideal site led to murder
- *Brandy & Bullets* (Signet, 1995), in which Jessica returned to Cabot Cove, then suffering from the loss of its recreational area to an Institute for Creativity;
- *Martinis & Mayhem* (Signet, 1995), where, during a book tour, Jessica met old friend, Inspector George Sutherland, in San Francisco. George and Jessica worked together when her contact with a convicted murderess convinced her to reopen the case.

The liquor references were dropped. Other paperbacks by Bain and the fictional Jessica Fletcher continued to arrive regularly:

- During *A Deadly Judgment* (Signet, 1996), Jessica, prodded by her publisher, served as a jury consultant on a highly publicized murder case.
- *A Palette for Murder* (Signet, 1996) took Jessica to the Hamptons where amidst the rich and famous, she attended an art course. Suspicious deaths within the art colony made Jessica concerned that there was a market for murder and art forgery.
- *Murder on the QE2* (Signet, 1997) provided Jessica with an opportunity to sail again on the ship that she and her deceased husband Frank had so enjoyed. Her task was initially to lecture to the passengers and write a play to be performed by fellow lecturers and professional actors. The deaths of a once famous actress and a dying explorer led to disclosures about several suspects. Jessica and her octogenarian friend, Mary Ward, inserted the material into a play to unmask the killers. Novel idea. Wonder why Shakespeare never thought of that?

■ *The Highland Fling Murders* (Signet, 1998), during which Jessica and eleven friends from Cabot Cove visited the "haunted" castle of George Sutherland, and exorcised the ghosts who were more concerned with money than revenge.

■ *In Murder in Moscow* (Signet, 1998), Jessica was included in a delegation representing the publishing industry in Russia. A confusing plot had her carrying signals to a young writer who had been providing the United States with information. The death of her Russian publisher was unsolved until a similar crime was committed in London.

■ *A Little Yuletide Murder* (Signet, 1998) was set in Cabot Cove for a change. The murder of local farmer Rory Brent received publicity far beyond the confines of the local paper, because Brent had served as the "Santa Claus" at annual Christmas festivals. With the assistance of serious breaches of confidentiality by Dr. Seth Hazlitt and the administrator of a social services agency, Jessica brought about the release of an unpopular suspect.

■ *In Murder at the Powderhorn Ranch* (Signet, 1999), Jessica and Seth visited old friends at their dude ranch in Colorado. Among their fellow guests were arms dealers, killers, and unfaithful spouses. Murder was to be expected. Jessica, who did not drive a car, took flying lessons and made her solo flight under pressure.

■ Although several of Jessica's books had been made into movies, *Knock 'Em Dead* (Signet, 1999) was the first brought to the Broadway stage. Jessica spent considerable time in New York City, acting as an advisor,

■ Halloween in Cabot Cove was spookier then usual in *Trick or Treachery* (Signet, 2000). Part of the local hysteria was generated by the eerie prophecies of a paranormal investigator; part, by the presence of a strange witch-like newcomer. In the background was the tradition of the ghost of Hezibah Cabot, who had hacked off her unfaithful husband's head. Murder in the present was connected to murder in the past by Jessica's assistance to Sheriff Mort Metzger in identifying a serial killer and a pair of opportunistic copycats.

■ *Blood on the Vine* (Signet, 2001) was one of the better Fletchers. Jessica and Scotland Yard Inspector George Sutherland helped a Napa Valley, California sheriff solve several crimes. Successful vintner Bill Ladington was cruel and manipulative in both his personal and professional lives. His decision to invite Jessica to assist in writing his autobiography was contrived to involve her when he was murdered.

Although they must sell well to continue the series for such a long time, these were simplistic narratives.

Fiora Flynn
Authors: A. E. Maxwell, pseudonym for Ann and Evan Maxwell

Perhaps Fiddler, the footloose and unscrupulous hero-narrator of the series should have selected a more passive wife. Fiora Flynn was intolerant of the lifestyle Fiddler chose for himself and into which he thrust her. She did not depend on Fiddler for her subsistence. A tiny blonde with hazel-green eyes, she had accumulated degrees from Pomona College, Harvard Business School, the London School of Economics, and the University of Tokyo. Of Irish derivation, her name was meant to be Fiona, but the nurse misspelled it. She and Fiddler had begun as lovers, married, then separated. In the course of the series, they met and mated and parted again. Fiddler, so called because he ended a career as a violinist when unable to achieve the level of expertise he demanded of himself, was a private investigator. The drug money Fiddler inherited from his Uncle Jake multiplied under Fiora's management. They could not stay married because she could not handle the risk-taking he found so necessary, but they could not forget or replace one another.

In *Just Another Day in Paradise* (Doubleday, 1985), Danny, Fiora's twin brother, was in trouble and she knew it. Although she and Fiddler were separated, she needed his skills. Fiddler challenged the FBI, the Customs and Volker, Fiora's former lover, to help, but she left him again. Fiddler had a solo adventure in *The Frog and the Scorpion* (Doubleday, 1985) while Fiora attended a summer seminar at Harvard.

Fiddler's loyalty to former lover Sandra Autry sent him to the Napa Valley in *Gatsby's Vineyard* (Doubleday, 1987). Fiora, then reunited with Fiddler, provided financial advice while Fiddler determined who was sabotaging Sandra's vineyard. Although Fiora saved Fiddler's life, she could not cope with his constant need for danger, and left again.

Customs agent Aaron Sharp had been killed when *Just Enough Light to Kill* (Doubleday, 1988) began. Before Fiddler headed for Mexico to probe the death, Fiora issued a twenty-four hour ultimatum. The relationship between Fiora and Fiddler was seriously damaged by what he considered a betrayal.

When, in *The Art of Survival* (Doubleday, 1989), Fiddler intervened in the problems of Santa Fe artist Maggie Tenorio, he and Fiora had a common adversary, IRS investigator Harvey Durham. Their reconciliation lasted through *Money Burns* (Villard, 1991) even though there was tension. Fiora's old friend Marianne Bradford Simms was concerned that her son might be abusing his authority as head of the family bank. Fiora, burned out as an investment banker, joined Fiddler in the investigation.

While visiting old friend Rory Cairns in Washington state during *The King of Nothing* (Villard, 1992) Fiddler learned that he had been named executor of Cairns's estate. Fiora was a beneficiary. Fiddler and Fiora connected Cairns' subsequent death (for which Fiddler was a suspect) to an antique Japanese family sword.

Murder Hurts (Villard, 1993) sent Fiddler on the trail of Uncle Jake's killer regardless of Fiora's opposition. Fiddler knew the hired gun, but wanted the person who paid Jake's killer. Fiora paid an unintended price for Fiddler's persistence in revenging Jake's death.

She was second fiddle, all the way.

Theresa Fortunato

Author: Kate Green

Over the years, there have been a considerable number of female investigators or criminals who utilized non-traditional skills, e.g. Hilda Wade, Solange Fontaine, Jane Carberry, Myra Savage, Edwina Charles, and Maddie Phillips.

Theresa Fortunato suffered from her psychic powers. They doomed her marriage to funeral director Michael Fortunato. Appalled by her powers, Michael had her placed temporarily in a mental institution. After their divorce, Theresa, still in her twenties, worked on a master's degree in "consciousness" psychology. Isolated by her gift, already finding gray in her curly black hair, she lived alone with her cat Osiris.

When consulted by a client desperate at her daughter's disappearance in *Shattered Moon* (Dell, 1986), Theresa experienced terrifying dreams and impressions. Surprisingly, Lt. Oliver Jardine did not dismiss her reactions as neurotic or fakery, particularly after she directed him to a buried corpse. Later she sent him to a location where murder had not yet occurred but would.

In *Black Dreams* (HarperCollins, 1993) Theresa, awakened by images of a child being forcibly removed by a man, contacted Jardine. Ellen Carlin was sent to Theresa because the dream child resembled her missing daughter.

Theresa's search connected with Jardine's investigation of the death of a wealthy antique dealer.

Spooky, but well written.

Sarah Fortune

Author: Frances Fyfield (Hegarty)

Attorney Sarah Fortune had survived an unhappy marriage during which her husband had been unfaithful with her sister. His death was followed by the miscarriage of their child, leaving her seriously disturbed. As portrayed in *Shadows on the Mirror* (Heinemann, 1989), Sarah hated her job. Her primary satisfaction was the joy that her sexual encounters brought to lonely men, including overweight prosecutor Malcolm Cook. She had an ominous suitor, Charles Tysall, a perfectionist who destroyed the women he loved when they failed to measure up to his standards.

Although Tysall had been presumed to be dead, he returned to destroy the delicate relationship between Sarah and Malcolm in *Perfectly Pure and Good* (Pantheon, 1994). Sarah's probe of the past to discover what had happened to Tysall and his dead wife Elizabeth was triggered by what seemed a routine probate matter.

Staring at the Light (Bantam, GB 1999), a terrifying introspective narrative, will tax even the most devoted Fyfield fan. William Dalrymple, a dentist devastated by his divorce, had replaced Malcolm as Sarah's lover. She still worked in the law firm headed by Malcolm's father. They would never make her a partner, but they could not manage without her. She took on the weird and dysfunctional clients that no one else would consider. One such client, Cannon Smith, whom she had befriended personally, brought disaster. In his frantic escape from the domination (sexual and emotional) of his twin brother John, Cannon endangered his wife Julie and his friends, Sarah and William.

Fyfield is a haunting writer, forcing even those readers who might find Sarah distasteful to persist until the outcome is determined.

Kit Franklyn

Author: D. (Donald) J. Donaldson

Kit Franklyn lived in New Orleans, a city with a history of voodoo and witchcraft. She was a young auburn haired import from a middle class family in Speculator, New York. Kit was employed as a suicide researcher attached to the office of Medical Examiner Andrew Broussard. There was no romance between Kit and Broussard, a single overweight gourmet, native to the area and a member of New Orleans's exclusive society.

Cajun Nights (St. Martin, 1988) opened with the Eighteenth Century execution of a vengeful murderer/witch. Years later, Kit, whose Ph.D. in psychology should have prepared her to deal realistically with superstition, investigated a series of motiveless suicides and murders. Broussard was a worthy mentor and partner. They blended their psychological and physiological skills to establish a credible cause for the increase in murder-suicides. Kit, and her life saving dachshund, moved in with Asst. District Attorney David Andropoulas, even though she rejected his proposal.

By *Blood on the Bayou* (St. Martin, 1991) Kit's relationship with Andropoulas had ended with his move to Shreveport. En route from a visit, Kit delivered a gift from Broussard to old friends in Bayou Coteau. While there, she was attracted to a handsome alligator trapper and breeder. Connections emerged between the residents of Bayou Coteau and a serial killer terrifying New Orleans.

During *No Mardi Gras for the Dead* (St. Martin, 1992), Kit maintained a relationship with alligator man Teddy La Biche. She was settling into her New Orleans home when she discovered a human jawbone on the property. Kit recruited not only Broussard to solve this one, but also other allies: Bubba Oustellette, a colorful African-American police department employee whose grandmother ran a Creole restaurant; and tough guy, Lt. Phil Gatlin of the NOPD.

The motives for murder became more personal for Broussard and Franklyn in *New Orleans Requiem* (St. Martin, 1994), when serial killings were linked to a conference of medical examiners in New Orleans. The motivation for the random deaths was weak, unworthy of the series. Teddy La Biche continued as Kit's occasional lover, but had to compete with an unorthodox crime reporter, Nick Lawson.

Kit was in so much trouble in *Louisiana Fever* (St. Martin, 1996) that it took Lawson, Teddy, Andy Broussard, Bubba and Phil Gatlin to rescue her. Smugglers, headed by a man with a special interest in Kit, brought a deadly virus into New Orleans. Before the virus carrier was located and the thieves dealt with, Kit received a shock that threatened her well-being.

Sleeping with the Crawfish (St. Martin, 1997) found Kit so traumatized by her experience with a brutal kidnapper that she resigned her position at the Medical Examiner's office. Broussard was deeply affected, but found no way to communicate his sense of loss until he needed her services. He had a corpse on the table in his laboratory that resembled Ronald Cicero. Cicero, who had been sent to prison for armed robbery and murder, was still in the facility according to the warden. Kit's willingness to travel to the prison, fingerprint, and photograph the institutionalized Cicero put her at risk. She was determined not to be manipulated, even as she came to believe that major state government officials were involved in a scam.

Frequently Donaldson relied for tension on Franklyn's tendency to be trapped by murderers of whom she should have been suspicious.

Cynthia Frost
Author: Haughton Murphy, pseudonym for James H. Duffy

Reuben Frost, a retired corporate attorney from a mid-sized New York City law firm, had many of the characteristics of John Thatcher Putnam (Emma Lathen) as a high finance detective. He had an additional advantage in his attractive wife, Cynthia. Cynthia, age sixty-three as the series began, was originally from Kansas City, Missouri. She moved to New York City where she became a successful ballet dancer. When she met Reuben on a double date, he was very attracted to her. While Reuben served in World War II, Cynthia prospered in her career. They married on his return. She remained with the ballet company in other capacities after she retired as a dancer. When the series began, she was serving as head of the Performing Arts Activities section of the Brigham Foundation, requiring her to do lobbying, publicity, and public relations. Reuben and Cynthia had a happy, although childless, marriage. She stayed petite and slim, maintaining her figure and agility by regular workouts at the National Ballet. The Frosts lived in the rarified atmosphere of upper class New York City, but maintained a personal friendship with Luis and Francesca Bautista.

Reuben's involvement with the police department, and particularly with Detective Bautista, came naturally when his law partner was murdered in *Murder for Lunch* (Simon & Schuster, 1986) during which Cynthia had no meaningful participation.

Reuben's second entry into crime investigation came through Cynthia in *Murder Takes a Partner* (Simon & Schuster, 1987). She convinced Reuben to serve as Chairman of the Board of Trustees of the National Ballet. When Clifton Holt, artistic director of the ballet, was murdered, Reuben, Cynthia and Luis pooled their insights to identify the killer.

Reuben had handled the legal business for Anderson Foods when he worked at Chase & Ward, but in *Murders and Acquisitions* (Simon & Schuster, 1988), the business was murder. Flemming Anderson, Chairman of the Board, invited Reuben and Cynthia to a family gathering. The social aspects of the evening were disrupted by anger when it was revealed that there might be a forced takeover of the corporation. Flemming who was determined to fight such action was murdered, leaving squabbles and suspicion among the members of his family. Cynthia had no part in the action, but counseled with Reuben on the interactions among family members.

Reuben and Luis carried the lion's share of the action in *Murder Keeps a Secret* (Simon & Schuster, 1989). Cynthia and Francesca provided useful information when David Rowan, Reuben's godson and a Pulitzer Prize winning author, leapt (or was thrown) from his office window.

Murder Times Two (Simon & Schuster, 1990) focused on murder within the couple's social and literary circles, specifically the familial and financial problems of the Vandermeer family.

Although *Murder Saves Face* (Simon & Schuster, 1991) was subtitled "A Reuben and Cynthia Frost Mystery," her role was minimal. Reuben had returned to his law firm when an ambitious female attorney was murdered in the final stages of a major financial takeover.

During *A Very Venetian Murder* (Simon & Schuster, 1992), the Frosts were included in an elite gathering at a Venice hotel. Their host, a prominent American fashion designer invited them because of Cynthia's connection with the ballet. However, it was Reuben who was called upon when the designer suspected that someone had tampered with his insulin. The man's subsequent death drew Reuben into conflict with the Italian police as to who had committed the murder.

Clara Dawson Gamadge

Authors: Elizabeth Daly/Eleanor Boylan

Henry Gamadge, Elizabeth Daly's sleuth during the Forties, was a New York City investigator with expertise in antiquarian books and documents. In his fourth appearance, *Murders in Volume 2* (Farrar & Rinehart, 1941) he met Clara Dawson, the orphaned niece of an impoverished society woman.

Gamadge was attracted to and married Clara, a young woman with dark brown hair, gray eyes and a "rangy" figure.

During *Evidence of Things Seen* (Holt, Rinehart, Winston, 1943), Clara stayed at a secluded mountain cottage while Henry served overseas. When her landlady was murdered, Clara's testimony was so incredible that the local police considered her unstable. On his return, Henry restored Clara's confidence in her own perceptions.

Clara appeared occasionally in the post-war Daly books. In some cases he explained her absences; in others, she provided Henry with access to exclusive society homes (*Murder Listens In*, Murray Hill, 1944). However, in *Death and Letters* (Rinehart, 1950), Henry commented that he rarely involved his wife in his investigations.

Twenty years after Daly's death, her niece Eleanor Boylan revitalized the widowed Clara, included supportive children and put them to work solving mysteries. As *Working Murder* (Holt, 1989) began, Clara was sixty-eight, spending her spare time gardening and painting. Aunt May Dawson summoned her from Florida to attend a family funeral. Accompanied by cousin Charles "Sadd" Saddlier, she arrived in New York to learn that Aunt May had died. Clara, Sadd, Henry Jr. and his attorney-wife Tina uncovered the family secrets and the booty to be found in a mausoleum.

In *Murder Observed* (Holt, 1990), while attending the funeral of friend Anna Pitman, Sadd and Clara became re-acquainted with Anna's former husband Barry Lockwood. Her conviction that Anna had not died a natural death caused Clara to investigate Barry's relationship with a young woman.

Clara and her extended family vacationed on Cape Cod in *Murder Machree* (Holt, 1992). Old friend Armand Evers wanted Clara to verify the parentage of his sister Rachel, now living in Ireland; or was it unscrupulous cousin Boyd Evers III, a "double" for Armand, who had asked the favor? Which man had been found dead in a New York City hotel?

Clara did her sleuthing from a hospital bed in *Pushing Murder* (Holt, 1993). Murder visited through Janet Folsom who had recognized a scoundrel from her past as the current husband of a mutual friend.

Her loyalty caused problems for Clara in *Murder Crossed* (Holt, 1995), when her ties to Woolcott Academy connected her with the death of a younger alumna and the welfare of three small girls. Against her family's advice, she accepted responsibilities that impelled her to investigate a murder and a disappearance.

These were low-key mysteries with light humor, charm, and a modicum of violence.

Ingrid Langley Gilliard

Author: Margaret Duffy

Ingrid and Patrick Gilliard were intelligence agents, unconnected to the MI5 or MI6, and therefore unfettered by political (or literary constraints). Ingrid was a slim green-eyed woman with black bobbed hair. Her father, a stockbroker to whom she was deeply attached, had died when she was twenty; her mother was portrayed as self-centered and irresponsible. Ingrid married, and then divorced Patrick Gilliard, a British Army officer. Her second husband Peter Clyde, a childhood friend, was murdered. Patrick, who had been seriously injured in the Falkland Islands, left the military for Department 12, a maverick intelligence group headed by Col. Richard Daws.

A Murder of Crows (St. Martin, 1988) provided action so swift that only on reflection would the reader confront its improbabilities. Patrick and Ingrid remarried during an assignment to uncover moles in the British government.

Daws sent Ingrid, Patrick and his assistant Terry to Canada in *Death of a Raven* (St. Martin, 1989) to monitor intrigue in a joint British/Canadian research center. Terry posed as an engineer; Patrick, as a scruffy gardener while Ingrid, a novelist, used her own identity. She managed, although pregnant, to survive brutality, mayhem, murder and the Canadian wilderness. Only an act of heroism by Patrick saved him from official disgrace.

Son Justin had arrived by *Brass Eagle* (St. Martin, 1989). Patrick, son of an Episcopalian priest, was drawn to a clerical vocation during their investigation of suicides among British scientists.

Ingrid had a reduced role in *Who Killed Cock Robin?* (St. Martin, 1990). Patrick and Ingrid, devastated by the news that Terry had been killed, found it difficult to work with his replacement. They surmounted drugs, kidnapping and espionage only to decide that maybe they were in the wrong line of work.

Patrick and Ingrid had been granted indefinite leave in *Rook Shoot* (St. Martin, 1991). Not for them, the comfortable weekend at the seashore or the cruise in the Mediterranean. They investigated sabotage of an "Outward Bound" type course supervised by Patrick's brother Larry, culminating in confrontation with a training school for terrorists.

Patrick who had been forced into retirement from D12, the secret agency within British Intelligence, was acting as Ingrid's literary agent when *Gallow's Bird* (Piatkus, 1993) began. Her books were selling well, although she was shocked to learn that her publisher had expanded into soft pornography; and further embarrassed when a corpse, discovered at a literary gathering, was attributed by some to a publicity stunt! Terry Meadows, who had ascended to Patrick's position, was so disturbed by his new supervisor that he was ready to resign. The former director Colonel Richard Daws was ill; Nicholas Haldane, his replacement, was a cold and malevolent man, determined to destroy Patrick personally and professionally. The complexities of rescuing Daws and restoring him to power would have been a joyful adventure had not their son Justin, been endangered. Patrick and Ingrid's wings would be further clipped by a new addition to the family, daughter Victoria Louise.

Although Patrick played a significant role in another Duffy series (see Joanna MacKenzie in Volume 3), Ingrid merely had bit parts.

The series will work best for those who enjoy intrigue, physical violence and have a limited need for credibility.

Paula Glenning

Author: Anna Clarke

Divorcee Paula Glenning's Ph.D. in literature had earned her a post as an English lecturer at the University of London. She was slim, slight, and fair-haired.

In *Last Judgement* (Doubleday, 1985), Paula's lover James Goff coveted the documents of his author/grandfather as the old man lay dying. Paula made some deductions, but her role was supportive to James'. Her interest was a literary biography of the elder Goff.

While at sea in *Cabin 3033* (Doubleday, 1986), Paula met Louis Hillman, a fading mystery writer, and his agent/wife Josephine Black. Paula's interest in Josephine's death was increased by Hillman's attentions to her.

Paula's biography of G. E. Goff (James's grandfather) having been well received, she planned a book about Rosie O'Grady, a reclusive romance writer in *The Mystery Lady* (Doubleday, 1986). She and James sought the "real" Rosie O'Grady, unaware that they were being manipulated.

James and Paula maintained their comfortable relationship in *Last Seen in London* (Doubleday, 1987) during which Cathy Bradshaw, an American graduate student, interested Paula in Mrs. Merton, an elderly woman who subsequently died. Although the characters dashed about frantically, they failed to generate much suspense.

In *Murder in Writing* (Doubleday, 1988), Paula substituted as leader of a creative writing group, which met at a country estate. The death of their hostess, who encouraged the class members to reveal intimate personal details in their writings, came as no surprise and neither did the conclusion.

James convinced Paula to spend a weekend with dysfunctional friends in *The Whitelands Affair* (Doubleday, 1989). When the host was murdered, Paula's suspicions as to the killer were confirmed, but she took no action.

The Case of the Paranoid Patient (Doubleday, 1991) focused on James while Paula was ill in the hospital. After she made him aware of a patient who seemed over-medicated, James rescued the young woman. More action than usual but with an inconclusive ending.

The Case of the Ludicrous Letters (Berkley, 1994) found James and Paula in a Hampstead village, having sold their apartments to buy a home together. Someone in Heathview Villas was sending anonymous letters commenting on the sexual and personal peccadilloes of the residents. After one recipient died in an accident, getting to know the neighbors took on a new dimension.

The Case of the Anxious Aunt (Berkley, 1996) continued the low-key paperback series. Paula had avoided James's relatives since the death of his grandfather, G. E. Goff, a prominent English novelist. She could not ignore the pleas of Isobel Macgregor, G. E.'s sister, whose household contained all the ingredients for murder.

Glad Gold

Author: Theodora (Dorothea) Wender

Like many academic sleuths, Glad Gold enjoyed unconventional behavior. A tall, thin brunette Ph.D., who shunned her birth name, "Gladiola", she taught English at Turnbull College in Massachusetts.

As *Knight Must Fall* (Avon, 1985) began, the faculty of the female college enjoyed a party at the home of Professor Howard Disher, about to be dismissed by President Henderson Neville Knight. The party ended at the college pool, where Knight's body was discovered the next morning. Police Chief Alden Chase was a fast worker. He bedded Glad the first time they were together, but took longer to identify who had most to fear from Knight.

Glad and Alden returned in *Murder Gets a Degree* (Avon, 1986). Elderly Adah Storm, a Turnbull alumna, asserted a right to property gained by her ancestor Jabez Storm. After her death, other claimants stepped forward. At Alden's request, Glad investigated the suspects, including members of a student witch's coven. Although Alden found the correct solution, he had to be rescued by Glad.

An average buy at paperback prices.

Norma Gold

Author: Herbert Resnicow

Alexander and Norma Gold came to criminal investigations late in life. They were an unusual pair. Alexander was a short, stocky, but powerful man who had been a successful financial consultant. His partner in a tempestuous and childless marriage was Norma, who towered over him at a well-built 6' 1" but deferred to his intellectual capacities. Norma, no dumb brunette, had a twelve-year career as an industrial research librarian. Forced to lose weight and restructure his life after a serious heart attack, Alex needed a consuming interest. Norma and her friend Pearl Hanslik thought murder investigations might provide one. Norma and Pearl (a Ph.D. in comparative literature) played high I. Q. "Lucy Ricardo and Ethel Mertz" while Alexander enjoyed Nero Wolfe seclusion. He was the resident genius, assisted by their research and organizational skills.

Pearl's attorney/husband Burt represented suspect Jonathan Cancell in *The Gold Solution* (St. Martin, 1983), a locked room mystery. Although Norma had her own theory as to "whodunit", Alexander topped her by identifying the killer.

In *The Gold Deadline* (St. Martin, 1984), Alexander accepted a million-dollar bet that he could identify the killer of producer Viktor Boguslav within three days.

During *The Gold Frame* (St. Martin, 1984) subtitled "A Norma and Alexander Gold Mystery," they and the Hansliks purchased Arthur Kaplan's licensed detective agency. The murder of museum director Orville Pembroke complicated the question of whether a major painting was a forgery. Although Alexander played Solomon with a real Vermeer to find the killer, the ending depended upon tax considerations.

The Golds and Hansliks supported the Tay-Sachs benefit at the Opera in *The Gold Curse* (St. Martin, 1986). When singer Thea Malabar was killed during the performance, her billionaire ex-lover Minos Zacharias hired the agency to solve the crime with a fee contingent upon quick results. Norma used her gun in a reenactment of Thea's death; then had a difficult time adjusting to the fact that she had killed someone.

Pearl and Alexander provided a new mystery to divert Norma in *The Gold Gamble* (St. Martin, 1988). Former classmate Carol Sands played a leading role in a revival of *Guys and Dolls*, which Norma helped to produce. When Carol's rival and understudy Lisa Terrane was murdered, Carol was arrested.

The brittle badinage between Norma and Alexander wore thin, as did the emphasis on solving the murders within a short time frame. Readers are encouraged to begin with the first and best of the series.

Rachel Gold

Author: Michael A. Kahn

Attorney Rachel Gold had an auspicious start. After graduation from Harvard Law School, she was hired as a litigator by the prestigious Chicago law firm, Abbott & Windsor. By *Grave Designs* (Signet, 1992, previously published in hardcover by Lynx in 1988 as *The Canaan Legacy*), Rachel had left the firm, but was not forgotten. When attorney Graham A. Marshall III died in a young woman's condo while wearing a scuba suit, his will established a substantial trust for the maintenance of a pet's grave. The firm hired Rachel to resolve this matter. The rollicking good action was tainted by an overabundance of foul language.

Rachel's pal, financial expert Benny Goldberg, had left A&W for a position as a law professor by *Death Benefits* (Dutton, 1992) but shared office space with Rachel. The firm called on Rachel again when managing partner Stoddard Anderson was found dead at an airport hotel. The designation of possible suicide could have serious financial impact for Anderson's widow and handicapped child. Rachel's car was smashed; her briefcase, searched; a warning note received; and an attractive new friend turned out to be treacherous.

After her father's death, Rachel returned to St. Louis to live with her mother. By *Firm Ambitions* (Dutton, 1994), Benny had left Chicago to teach law at a St. Louis university. When Rachel agreed to handle high school classmate Eileen Landau's divorce, she did not expect to be drawn into a tawdry murder. While Rachel's mom found new meaning to her life through a flamboyant judge, Rachel fought the Mafia with the help of a man whom she had once idolized.

Three murders tied to an industrial takeover claimed Rachel's attention in *Due Diligence* (Dutton, 1995). One victim was a man she had come to love; a major suspect was a man she planned to endorse for the Senate.

During *Sheer Gall* (Dutton, 1996), Rachel realized that she had been manipulated. The woman who came to her office, claiming to have been battered by her husband, was not Attorney Sally Wade. When the real Sally was murdered and her husband arrested, Rachel reluctantly assisted his attorney in proving his innocence. There was a positive aspect to the narrative in that Rachel met a man who not only interested her, but also was acceptable to her mother.

Kahn provided credible legal background, but the supporting cast was stealing the show.

Peg Goodenough

Author: Liza Bennett

Peg Goodenough, the assistant art director at Peabody & Quinlan, came by her creative skills the old fashioned way. She inherited them. Her mother was a recognized artist. Her father had been an art dealer. Peg was educated in Switzerland and Germany, moving from one school to another as her widowed mother traveled around Europe. She was described as having coal black hair with gray eyes, and an over-emphasized Triple C bra size.

Gay art director Ramsey Farnsworth, her mentor/employer at P&Q in *Madison Avenue Murder* (Worldwide, 1989), had seemed preoccupied for several weeks. When Ramsey missed an important shooting date, and was then discovered dead, it could mean a promotion for Peg. Detective Dante Cursio, who qualified as an expert with an MFA (Master in Fine Arts) from Columbia, rescued Peg when she pushed too hard.

By *Seventh Avenue Murder* (Worldwide, 1990), Peg had been promoted to art director. Not only did P&Q keep the Merriweather account when Beryl Merriweather sold out, but they also hoped to gather new accounts from the purchaser, Tantamount. At the last minute, Beryl cancelled the deal; then was murdered. Although their romance was on hold, Cursio expected Peg to entertain his visiting eight-year-old daughter, and not be preoccupied with murder. She was shot while trying to solve the case. Peg must have done something right. Cursio proposed. Since there were no additional books, she must have decided to keep out of his business.

Ellie Gordon

Author: Karin Berne, pseudonym for Sue Bernell and Michaela Karni.

Ellie Gordon was a forty-year old woman trying to make a life for herself after a traumatic divorce. She was short and plump, brown haired and eyed, and addicted to mystery stories and chocolate—a great combination. Ellie had finished high school at sixteen, then graduated summa cum laude from Stanford, but hit a snag in her career when she married. As the series began she and eighteen year old son Michael were starting over in Casa Grande, California, where she was underemployed as office manager for a law firm.

Ellie's participation in Philip Abbott's political campaign led to a job in *Bare Acquaintances* (Popular Library, 1985). She had slimmed down, bought new clothes, and begun a relationship with Mark, a disabled attorney in Abbott's firm. The discovery of a militant feminist dead on the job put Ellie and Mark in danger.

Ellie's membership in a group of single professional women during *Shock Value* (Popular Library, 1985) made her aware of the electrocution of an unpleasant supervisor whose death was blamed on another member of the group.

False Impressions (Popular Library, 1986) took Ellie to the art world of Santa Fe, New Mexico at the invitation of gallery owner Nessa Harper. Nessa had a beau lined up for Ellie, but she spent her time investigating the shooting of a sharp-tongued art critic. Above average.

Lindsay Gordon

Author: Val McDermid

Lesbian photojournalist Lindsay Gordon was a Scotswoman with brown hair and dark blue eyes. After graduating from a comprehensive school in Glasgow, she attended Oxford University; then worked first in Glasgow, later in London. A socialist feminist, Lindsay was dedicated to her career. Her personal life had been erratic. An early lover died. Her relationship with playwright/television hostess Cordelia Brown did not survive the intimacy of living together.

In *Report for Murder* (Women's Press, 1987), Lindsay promoted fund-raising events at Derbyshire House Girl's school out of friendship for drama teacher Paddy Callaghan. One performance was to include a concert by cellist Lorna Smith-Couper, and a play by Cordelia, both graduates. Lorna's murder frightened more than a few whose secrets she had shared.

In *Common Murder* (Women's Press, 1989), Lindsay moved into Cordelia's London home, but the arrangement failed. Lindsay then reunited with anti-nuclear protester Deborah Patterson, mother of a four-year-old girl. When Deborah was arrested for the murder of Rupert Crabtree, Lindsay confronted British intelligence agents. Aware that Crabtree's death was tied to the traitorous activities of his son, Lindsay traveled to Germany to expose the intelligence secrets.

When she returned in *Final Edition* a.k.a. *Open and Shut* (St. Martin, 1991; reprinted by Spinsters Ink, 1997), Lindsay was unaware of the murder of bisexual reporter Alison Maxwell and the conviction of her own friend, Jackie Mitchell. Cordelia had formed a liaison with Claire Ogilvie, a wealthy attorney and Jackie's ex-lover.

Union Jack (Women's Press, 1993) a.k.a. *Conferences Are Murder* (Spinster's Ink, 1999) returned Lindsay to England after three years teaching journalism in California. She had been active in the newspaper guilds as a working reporter, and her current lover, Sophie Hartley, was a presenter at a union conference. Once there, Lindsay found that old feuds and resentments were still tearing the group apart. She was jailed on suspicion of murdering a union official with whom she quarreled before he fell or was pushed out her window.

By 1996, Lindsay had earned her Ph.D. and was well established as a teacher at Santa Cruz College's School of Journalism. She was writing a commentary on the sad state of British tabloids. Author Penny Varnavides and her computer expert lover Meredith had been dear friends of Lindsay and Sophie for years. When Penny was murdered in England during *Booked for Murder* (Women's Press, 1996), Lindsay returned there to discover the killer before Meredith could be tried by the courts. Her reckless behavior resulted in multiple injuries. At the conclusion she considered remaining in England, but decided against it to spare her dog six months of quarantine.

Davina Graham

Author: Evelyn Anthony, pseudonym for
Evelyn Bridget Patricia Ward-Thomas

Davina was tall, slim with reddish hair and green eyes. She had always known that her sister "Charley" was her father's favorite child. Davina attended St. Hilda's, earning a first class honors degree, began her career with the British Intelligence as a secretary and worked her way through the ranks.

During *The Defector* (Coward, 1981), Davina, assigned to monitor Russian defector Ivan Sasanov, fell in love with him. Sasanov refused to release information to the British until his wife and daughter were brought to England. Davina and two fellow agents, one a mole, arranged their escape. After the death of his wife, Davina married Sasanov but he was killed in Australia. When Davina subsequently miscarried, she returned to England to immerse herself in work.

In *The Avenue of the Dead* (Coward, 1982), she evaluated charges that Edward Fleming, a close friend of the U. S. president, was a Russian agent. After his wife (and accuser) was murdered, Davina uncovered a plot to create ill feeling between the U.S. and British governments. Davina realized that her own loyalty, questioned because of Sasanov, had been tested.

The agency director neared retirement in *Albatross* (Putnam, 1983) but could not be replaced until a suspected mole was identified. Davina had ostensibly resigned, but her assignment was to find the traitor. She did so at a serious cost in personal relationships.

Davina switched her affections from fellow agent Colin Lomax to advertising tycoon Tony Walden. In *The Company of Saints* (Putnam, 1984), while she and Tony vacationed in Italy, their relationship ended abruptly. A subversive group was assassinating major political figures during a power struggle in the USSR.

The narratives lacked the icy tension and stark realism that Le Carre and Deighton infused into their books. Anthony had the difficult task of creating a sympathetic female character capable of the choices and activities of an espionage agent. In 1981, even with a history of reigning queens and Margaret Thatcher as prime minister in England, it seemed unlikely that a woman would be chosen to head British Intelligence. However, in March 1992, Stella Rimington was named director-general of MI5, responsible for the internal security of England.

Celia Grant
Author: John Sherwood, pseudonym for Herman Mulso

Gardening may be a "feminine" pursuit, acceptable in a mystery heroine, but Celia Grant was not the stereotypical elderly woman tending flowers while spying on the neighbors. Celia was a professional, widowed in her forties when her husband, a Kew Garden horticulturist, died. A diminutive woman with silver hair, she remained physically active, still attracted to, and by, the opposite sex. Celia utilized her investments to buy a small nursery in the village of Westfield. Although she had children, the young person most important in her life was Bill Wilkins, who became her business partner.

In *Green Trigger Fingers* (Scribners, 1985), Celia upset the locals by defending a teenager accused of murdering two "weekenders." She was denounced as a lesbian, perceived as unstable when she found a corpse that disappeared, and an attempt was made to poison her.

Feeling unwelcome, Celia had relocated her business when her pregnant daughter convinced her to visit New Zealand in *A Botanist at Bay* (Scribners, 1985). While there, Celia searched for a British horticulturist who had left England hurriedly. Her interest in rare plants enabled Celia to identify a hoax, meant to delay construction of a dam. She solved a murder, kidnapping and political chicanery amid the racial tensions of New Zealand.

Back in England in *The Mantrap Garden* (Scribners, 1986) an old friend convinced Celia to explore the deterioration of a Gertrude Jekyll designed garden. The roots of the problem went deep into the history of the Monk's Mead owners. The solution lay, not in horticulture, but in poetry and War Office records.

Celia diagnosed the bizarre behavior of an ambitious businessman through her knowledge of the medicinal aspects of plants in *Flowers of Evil* (Scribners, 1987). Further investigations into fashion designs, South American revolutionaries, and the Glyndebourne Opera Festival ended in tragedy for Bill Wilkins.

In *Menacing Groves* (Scribners, 1989), Celia posed as her sister-in-law on a tour of Italian gardens, traveling with two annoying suitors and actors posing as wealthy South Africans.

It was "back to business" in *A Bouquet of Thorns* (Scribners, 1989). The language of flowers enabled Celia to rescue Bill Wilkins from unrequited love and a murder charge. After gallivanting around solving mysteries, Celia discovered that her business needed attention in *The Sunflower Plot* (Scribners, 1991). She reluctantly created an Elizabethan garden for a wealthy businessman. Her presence on the estate drew Celia into a purported drug ring, art thefts and the kidnapping of a child.

The Hanging Garden (Scribners, 1992) brought Celia to Funchal, Madeira as the executor of the estate of Antonia Hanbury. Antonia's death left behind her paralyzed father, Sir Adrian Morton, and two children, Sarah and Peter. Although Celia wanted no part in raising children at her age, she was concerned that their father might not be a suitable guardian—certainly not if he were a killer.

Admiral Bond, head of the Garden Society, had become a thorn in Celia's existence by *Creeping Jenny* (Scribners, 1993). He rejected newcomer Margaret Fortescue, and interfered with Celia's entry in the Chelsea Exposition. Jenny Watson, ostensibly shy and demure, was a different problem, insinuating herself into Bill Wilkins' affections, then disappearing in an apparent kidnapping to lure him and Celia into a terrorist scheme.

Celia recommended botanist Jane Greenwood as editor for a memorial volume planned by matriarch Adrienne de Fleury, in *Bones Gather No*

Moss (Scribners, 1994). When Jane disappeared, Celia's conscience and her curiosity sent her to France where she entangled herself in the haughty de Fleury family affairs. Fortunately two left-wing police officers were willing to risk official censure when Jane's body was discovered and clues led back to the Chateau Fleury.

It was refreshing to have a mystery heroine who managed a business. Celia's expertise provided her with access to the great homes and mansions of England and insights that might be meaningless to a layperson.

Jennifer Grey

Author: Jerry Jenkins

Jennifer Grey, a 31-year-old widow, worked as reporter and columnist on "Chicago Day," a general circulation newspaper. She was a devout Christian whose decisions were based on religious principles.

In *Heartbeat* (Victor, 1983), Jennifer reported charges by the Internal Affairs Unit of the Chicago Police Department against her fiancé, Sgt. Jim Purcell. Her failure to reveal this conflict of interest caused her suspension, but did not deter her from clearing Jim's name.

Three Days in Winter (Victor, 1983) entangled Jennifer with the disappearance, abuse, and death of four-year-old Heather. Her denunciation of the man suspected of the abuse put her under suspicion when he was killed. In *Gateway* (Victor, 1983) Samantha, the diabetic wife of managing editor Leo Stanton, died. Jennifer found euthanasia pamphlets in Samantha's room but remained unconvinced that the woman had committed suicide.

During *Too Late to Tell* (Victor, 1984), Jennifer wrestled with her dislike of former co-worker Bobby Black. He had been trying to contact her before he was murdered. Her conscience was more supple when she tricked a suspect into releasing a notebook that explained the death.

Jim and Jennifer encountered international politics in *The Calling* (Victor, 1984) when he guarded two Russian defectors. Jim's decision to leave the police force and enter the foreign missions was in conflict with Jennifer's professional career.

In *Veiled Threat* (Victor, 1985), just as they were to be married, Jennifer was decoyed out of the church by kidnappers who wanted a ransom and access to Jennifer's column.

Moody Press published a collection of the Jennifer Grey books in a single volume, *The Jennifer Grey Mysteries*. She was a more independent heroine than Margo Franklin, but continued Jenkins' emphasis on moral and religious values.

Lonia Guiu

Author: Maria-Antonia Oliver,
as translated from Catalan by Kathleen McNerney

Seal Press introduced Lonia Guiu to English speaking readers as part of their International Women's Crime Series. Lonia (short for Apollonia) was a Majorcan who had lived in Barcelona, Spain for ten years. A former employee of the Mari Credit Agency, she worked as a private investigator. Lonia was a defiantly independent feminist, concerned with crimes against women. Although she disliked guns, she studied self-defense and used a repellant spray for protection. A vegetarian who occasionally ate meat, she loved to drive but could not tell one brand of car from another. Her gay male assistant was Quimet, but two fictional detectives (Pepe Carvalho by Manuel Vasquez Montalban and Luis Arquer by Jaime Fuster) appeared briefly in the narratives.

In *Study in Lilac* (Seal, 1987), Lonia shared a residence with college students, taking classes in her spare time. Antique dealer Elena Gaudi hired her to trace three men by way of an automobile license, but Lonia suspected a hidden agenda. A frantic Majorcan mother wanted Lonia to find her runaway daughter, Sebastiana. In the end, Lonia found it necessary to bargain for two tickets to Australia and leave Spain burdened with a sense of guilt.

In *Antipodes* (Seal, 1989), Lonia found part time work with friends Lida and Jem on their Australian charter boat. After recognizing a young Majorcan girl as a bordello resident, Lonia investigated the facility until balked by local authorities. Her return to Majorca brought more problems and a greater sense of rejection even though she uncovered a local exploiter.

Lonia's cases centered on the abuse of women and the failure of the justice system to provide protection. The translation from Catalan must have been very difficult, at times it read clumsily, but the intense Lonia and her cases were worth the trouble.

Jane Winfield Hall

Author: Audrey Peterson

See: Jane Winfield, Page 310

Meg Halloran

Author: Janet LaPierre

High school teacher Meg Halloran, a tall brown haired widow, had moved from Arizona to Port Silva, California with her ten-year-old daughter Katy. Meg made a brief appearance in *Unquiet Grave* (St. Martin, 1987) providing information about a missing witness to Police Chief Vince Guiterrez.

In *Children's Games* (Scribners, 1989), Meg, raised by an atheist father, considered the local emphasis on fundamentalist beliefs to be rigid and unhealthy. Student Dave Tucker harassed Meg when he earned a flunking grade in her class. Although Meg and Katy were camping in the Mendecino National Forest when Dave was murdered, she was accused of having made sexual advances to the youth, and considered responsible for his death.

By *The Cruel Mother* (Scribners, 1990), Guiterrez was Meg's lover. Ex-radical Michael Tannenbaum, dying of cancer at his parents' home, sought a reunion with his wife Elizabeth, who managed a shelter for battered women. While seeking Elizabeth, Meg and Cass, Vince's rebellious niece, shared a brutal abduction until rescued.

Meg and Vince had married by *Grandmother's House* (Scribners, 1991), but played only peripheral roles in young Petey Birdsong's fight against real estate developers.

Leaving Vince behind in *Old Enemies* (Scribners, 1993), Meg visited a former student and her family just as new and old murders tore the household apart. Meg, always a complex character, exhibited generosity of spirit but lacked common sense in dealing with family feuds.

Port Silva had changed since Meg moved there. There was a new university but fewer jobs for the average worker. The population had risen but there was evidence of more ethnic hostility. Meg's students were harder to reach, often tired from working nights to help their families. In *Baby Mine* (Perseverance Press, 1999), youth gangs robbed, assaulted, and even raped young women. This became very personal when Meg was attacked, her daughter threatened, and finally, Vince's niece Cass disappeared. These matters were not the only problem Vince had to face at work. The fertility clinic, run by Dr. James Ferrar was besieged by protestors, and then burned down resulting in the death of Dr. Gabe Ferrar, who had been closer to Vince than to his own son.

Absorbing characters and tense plots produced narratives of above average interest.

Neil Hamel

Author: Judith Van Gieson

Neil Hamel's unconventional behavior extended to her personal life. A divorced female attorney in Albuquerque, New Mexico, she chose for a lover, "The Kid", a young Chilean-Mexican-American mechanic. Totally unimpressed by social or financial status, Neil had left a large firm practice for a small partnership. She was anti-establishment, smoked, gorged on Cuervo Gold, Tecate beer and Mexican food one day and ate Lean Cuisine the next. Her language could be charitably described as colorful. Neil drove a decrepit Volkswagen that "The Kid" kept functional. She studied tai chi but carried a gun, and was a risk taker, except when "The Kid" suggested unprotected sex.

In *North of the Border* (Walker, 1988), Carl Roberts, Neil's former employer and lover had a problem. The legality of the Roberts' Mexican adoption was in question. Neil investigated, even after the attorney who arranged the adoption was murdered.

In *Raptor* (Harper, 1990), Neil went bird watching in Montana. Group leader March Augusta hired Neil when he was accused of killing a poacher, who was working in a government sting.

During *The Other Side of Death* (Harper, 1991), Neil indulged in nostalgia, traveling to the Santa Fe reunion of a group that had spent a year together in Mexico. Lonie Darner, vehemently opposed to the construction of a building designed by her ex-husband, was killed while Neil was her houseguest.

Neil's love for nature motivated her in *The Wolf Path* (HarperCollins, 1992) when the reintroduction of wolves into New Mexico provoked murder. Neil and a young pro-wolf advocate challenged local ranchers and corrupt officials to uncover the truth.

In *The Lies That Bind* (HarperCollins, 1993), Neil defended a woman who was suspected of the hit-and-run death of a person she hated. Other suspects had secrets that Neil uncovered but protected. In doing so, Neil worked her way through troubled memories of her own mother.

Wildlife remained a concern for Neil. During *Parrot Blues* (Harper-Collins, 1995), Terrance Lewellen, a wealthy businessman, hired Neil to negotiate with the kidnapper who stole his wife and a valuable indigo macaw. Lewellen, who was comforting himself with his wife's half-sister, showed more concern for the macaw whose mate was molting with grief. Neil, with the Kid for protection, went into the desert for the ransom transaction. Unable to locate her contact, she returned to find her client dead.

Neil felt glimmerings of maturity in *Hotshots* (HarperCollins, 1996). Could it be she who was buying a house; sharing it regularly with The Kid, now a moderately prosperous businessman? Whatever her personal life, Neil's love for adventure and risk served her well when the parents of a dead "hotshot" fire fighter hired her to investigate the Forest Service's handling of a major conflagration.

The Kid and Neil had eased into a comfortable relationship. They shared a home and had adapted to one another's household regimens. He became angry when she courted needless danger, but enjoyed going along on risky enterprises. Neither pushed for more; i.e. marriage or children. Neil respected The Kid's adjustment to the United States. He was a more than competent workman. She had no sense of superiority in that her profession was at a different social level than his. When in *Ditch Rider* (HarperCollins, 1998), Neil became personally and professionally connected to a thirteen-year-old girl who insisted that she had killed a youth gang member, the Kid provided sage advice and physical support.

This has been a high-tension series with excellent physical descriptions and a provocative heroine.

Blanche Hampton

Author: Trevor Barnes

Blanche Hampton, a tall brown-haired woman in her thirties, earned her rank as a London detective superintendent. A Cambridge degree made it possible for her to enter the police system at a higher level, but created hostility that Blanche countered with extra dedication. Her incompetent supervisor Commander Brian Spittal resented Blanche, but used her successes to build his own reputation.

In *A Midsummer Killing* (NEL, GB 1989; Morrow, US 1992) Blanche was assigned a politically significant case, the murder of a British Intelligence employee. Special Branch investigators and the lack of support from Spittal hampered her investigation.

By *A Pound of Flesh* a.k.a. *Dead Meat*, (Morrow, 1993) Blanche's sense of isolation was increased by her divorce. Her encouragement came from her gay African-American assistant, Dexter Bazalgette. The death of Patricia Hoskin, daughter of a government official, was bloody and vicious. Blanche's resistance to pressure for a quick solution was juxtaposed with the killer's descent into cannibalism and an increased appetite for murder.

In *Taped* (Coronet, 1993), ambitious reporter Nicola Sharpe was stabbed to death while dozens of television celebrities and their spouses attended a retirement party in a nearby room. Blanche and Dexter focused on Nicola's probes into drug smuggling and child pornography as motives for her death.

Blanche was a worthy complement to American policewoman heroines, although her personal life was less developed.

Arly Hanks

Author: Joan Hess, who also wrote as Joan Hadley

Arly Hanks, originally named Ariel, returned to her Arkansas hometown from Manhattan after a failed marriage. Dark haired, about 5' 10" and thirty-four years old, she had a short-term relationship with a state police officer, but romance for Arly was never a major element of the series. When the position of police chief was vacant, she was hired under the general supervision and constant nagging of Mayor Jim-Bob Buchanon (of the dim-witted, nefarious, and ubiquitous Buchanon clan). It helped that she had police training and that nobody else wanted the job. This should not be considered a police procedural however. The cast of characters was a cross between *The Dukes of Hazard* and *Tobacco Row*, even as the narratives confronted incest, child abuse, and casual violence. Part of Arly's reason to return was to be near her mother, Ruby Bee, owner of the local restaurant (where Arly cadged meals) and a third rate motel.

During *Malice in Maggody* (St. Martin, 1987), Arly encountered political corruption in pollution control, leading to the death by crossbow of a would-be beautician. Then came *Mischief in Maggody* (St. Martin, 1988), wherein hippies and a psychic invaded the community, and a well-known prostitute disappeared, leaving her five children behind. *Much Ado in Maggody* (St. Martin, 1989) examined the state of women's rights in rural Arkansas, and found them wanting. *Madness in Maggody* (St. Martin, 1991) traced the effect of progress, in the form of a supermarket, on local merchants, and the impact of food poisoning on its customers.

Mortal Remains in Maggody (Dutton, 1991) highlighted a sleazy film company that used the naive locals for an XXX rated film. The newcomers had problems of their own that included murder. Hess explored the "rustic in the big city" theme in *Maggody in Manhattan* (Dutton, 1992), during which a substantial portion of the supporting characters found reasons to vacation and to need Arly to get them safely back home. The sex was raunchier and the humor more caustic, unrelieved by Hess's usual light touches. Even Arly's new romance turned out to be a dud.

In *O Little Town of Maggody* (Dutton, 1993), the regulars were joined by country singer Matt Montana. Matt returned to his Ozark roots but his entourage included a killer. In *Martians in Maggody* (Dutton, 1994), Hess took on new targets—the pseudo-scientists of the extra-terrestrials (ET) and their rivals for publicity, the Intra-territorials (IT). Arly was overwhelmed by the attention given when three mysterious circles appeared in Raz Buchanon's cornfield. There was no simple explanation, even in Maggody where almost everything and everyone was simple. When members of the rival groups of scientists were found dead, and the local beauty parlor operator kidnapped, Arly brought the proceedings to a halt.

Arly's next encounter with the outer world came when evangelist Malachi Hope and his entourage arrived in *Miracles in Maggody* (Dutton, 1995). Malachi had visions of creating a religious theme park on nearby acreage but he failed to foresee the ensuing murders. The shenanigans of Ruby Bee, Arly's mother, and religious rivalries enlivened the narrative.

It was not to be expected that the anti-government hysteria would pass over Maggody, so in *The Maggody Militia* (Dutton, 1997), Arly contended with bellicose bumpkins roaming the woods during deer season while she assisted the sheriff with a series of burglaries. While Ruby Bee and her dearest friend Estelle chased ostriches, the stork arrived for Dahlia and Kevin Buchanon.

Ruby Bee and Estelle were unable to convince Arly to join them on an economy style tour to Elvis Presley's Graceland in *Maggody Loves Misery* (Simon & Schuster, 1999). Within days however she was on their trail, and ended up sitting by Ruby Bee's bed in a small town Mississippi hospital, and finally solving a trio of murders that led back to Maggody. Author Hess took a wry look at the lure of gambling, the Elvis watchers, and the paucity of health care in rural Mississippi.

Another external influence, the Internet, appeared on the screen in *Murder@Maggody.com* (Simon & Schuster, 2000). Teacher Lottie Estes was awarded a grant for computers to be used to train both high school students and adults. An out-of-town expert, his dissatisfied wife, and a teenage delinquent created havoc amongst the slow learning but good-hearted residents.

All the news in Maggody was bad news in *Maggody and the Moonbeams* (Simon & Schuster, 2001). Ruby Bee's Bar and Grill was shut down due to a grease fire, leaving Ruby in a foul mood. Duluth Buchanon's wife Norella had taken off with the kids. Arly couldn't get out of serving as chaperone for ten teenagers at Mrs. Jim Bob's insistence when the group went to Camp Pearly Gates. Then it got worse: too little food and too much sanctity at the camp, the presence of a nearby female cult, Duluth in jail for being drunk and disorderly, and Norella dead in the woods. Hess had great names for her characters.

Beneath the crudities of language and behavior, echoed the frustration of under-educated, under-employed rural poor who knew they would never achieve the lifestyles they watched on television. Ruby Bee and her pal Estelle, local beauty parlor operator, insinuated themselves into Arly's investigations, risking life and limb. They were not stupid women, limited rather by their environment and opportunities. The denizens of Maggody, Arkansas (population circa 755) were inbred, sexually promiscuous, influenced by fundamental religion and violence. The series carried a bite that differed from contempt for the locals, instead creating a level of affection. The narratives targeted right-wing militants, UFO believers, bogus religious fundamentalism, and other worthy opponents. Hess slipped easily from Arly's first person narration to third person when describing the Maggody ensemble.

Lt. Sigrid Harald

Author: Margaret Maron

Sigrid Harald, a policewoman, was tall and thin with her dark hair worn as a braid. Initially, she took little pride in her appearance, considering herself the unattractive daughter of a beautiful woman. Anne, her mother, a renowned photojournalist, had been a Southern beauty. Police officer Leif Harald, Sigrid's father, was killed in action when she was young. She spent her youth in boarding schools but acquired few of the social graces they promoted; remaining shy, unsure of herself, naive and virginal.

There were no special favors for Sigrid in the New York City Police Department. She rose from the ranks, and earned appointment as a Lieutenant in the Detective Bureau. She served under Captain McKinnon, her father's former patrol partner, blamed by Anne for contributing to his death.

One Coffee With (Raven, 1981) blended police procedural and academic mystery. The art department at Vanderlyn College was split by antipathy between the staff artists and the art historians. When the unpopular department chairman was poisoned at break time, the suspects included painter Oscar Naumann, an attractive older man who awakened Sigrid's dormant sexuality. *Death of a Butterfly* (Doubleday, 1984) revolved around the murder of a socialite who had fought for custody of her son.

Attorney Clayton Gladwell's files became significant when he was murdered and his office ransacked in *Death in Blue Folders* (Doubleday, 1985). Sigrid's assistant, Charles Tildon a.k.a. Tillie reluctantly entered a cribbage tournament at the Maintenon Hotel in *The Right Jack* (Bantam, 1987), but was injured when a bomb exploded in a narrative that centered on radicals from the Sixties. Because Tillie could not return to full time work in *Baby Doll Games* (Bantam, 1988), Sigrid relied on an inadequate substitute while she investigated the murder of dancer Emmy Mion during a stage performance.

Maron mixed a variety of subplots in *Corpus Christmas* (Doubleday, 1989): the murder of an art historian at a party honoring Oscar, the deaths of four infants, and potential side romances for both Oscar and Sigrid. Unresolved questions about her father's death and her mother's involvement with McKinnon surfaced in *Past Imperfect* (Doubleday, 1991), when Officer Mick Cluett was killed just short of retirement.

In *Fugitive Colors* (Mysterious Press, 1995), Harald returned emotionally drained by Oscar's death. She was aroused from her depression by the murder of an art dealer in Oscar's vacant apartment, and by pressure from Oscar's friends to mount a retrospective of his work. The investigation left her as changed by his death as she had been by his life. The series, which appeared over a decade, covered a much shorter period in time. In 1997, Maron published a collection of short stories, *Shoveling Smoke* (Crippen & Landru) that included two featuring Sigrid.

Maron's books were complex, but enjoyable reading, her skills improving as the series progressed. Deborah Knott, Maron's heroine yet to come in the 1990's, displayed the author's warmth and skill in depicting the South.

Ellie Simon Haskell

Author: Dorothy Cannell

Ellie's Simon's mother had been a movie extra. Her father had taken leave of his senses after his wife died. He became first a rainmaker in the Sahara, then an organizer of beauty pageants on tropical islands. Feeling abandoned, Ellie lost control over her weight.

Ellie (Giselle), who worked as an interior decorator, was willing to give her age (27), her height (5' 6") but not her weight in *The Thin Woman* (St. Martin, 1984). When she was desperate for a date to a family weekend, Eligibility Escorts provided Bentley T. Haskell, a chef and author of pornographic literature. Ellie's reclusive "Uncle Merlin" was so impressed by the couple that he willed them his estate under three conditions: Ellie must lose 63 pounds, Ben must write a "clean" book, and they must find the hidden treasure at Merlin's Court, all within six months. The contingent heirs hoped for none of the above. *Down the Garden Path* was not part of the series, but featured the Tramwell sisters.

Ben and Ellie married and took up residence in Chitterton Falls, England in *The Widow's Club* (Bantam, 1988), but did not necessarily live happily ever after. A diner at their restaurant died after eating food prepared by Ellie. Tipped off by the eccentric Tramwell sisters, Ellie infiltrated the Widows Club, dedicated to the extinction of unfaithful husbands.

In *Mum's the Word* (Bantam, 1990), the pregnant Ellie accompanied Ben to the U. S. where he would compete for membership in an exclusive chef's society. Ellie solved the mysterious death of an aging movie comedienne in time for the birth of their twins.

She could have been suffering from post-partum depression in *Femmes Fatale* (Bantam, 1992). She felt listless, had lost her sense of "true love", and regained weight. Together with her equally depressed cleaning woman, Ellie joined Femmes Fatale for diet and exercise. Several of her fellow students or members of their families had died mysteriously. Only the cupidity of a killer saved Ellie from a toasty death.

Twins, Tam and Abbey, were eighteen months old when Ellie invited her in-laws to spend their wedding anniversary at her home in *How to Murder Your Mother-in-Law* (Bantam, 1994). When the senior Haskell's marriage was ruptured by the intrusion of an old girlfriend, Ben's mother stayed on in their household. Misery loves company and Ellie learned that she was not the only local woman suffering from a surfeit of her mother-in-law. When the seniors experienced deadly accidents, mirroring some light hearted jests made by the daughters-in-law, Ellie made peace with the senior Mrs. Haskell. She learned who did not think mothers-in-law were funny.

Weight resurfaced as a problem for Ellie in *How to Murder the Man of Your Dreams* (Bantam, 1995), but that was minor compared to her infatuation for Karisma, male model for the dust jackets of romantic novels. In her confusion she adopted an ungovernable dog, unfairly suspected a friend of a sex change, but identified the killer of a meticulous librarian.

Ellie, Ben and the twins were very dependent upon their cleaning woman, so in *The Spring Cleaning Murders* (Viking, 1998), Mrs. Roxie Malloy's decision to turn in her mop created a crisis. The tension increased when three other members of the Chitterton Fells Charwomen's Association died suddenly. Ellie checked out the chars' clients, particularly those new in town, because her friend Bunty Wiseman was a major suspect.

Careers and family were to take a backseat while Ellie and Ben went on a Parisian vacation in *The Trouble with Harriet* (Viking, 1999). The children had been sent to Ben's parents. They were packing their bags, when who appeared upon the scene, but Ellie's father, Morley Simon. Morley had stolen Ellie's bike and ridden out of the seventeen-year-old girl's life when his wife died. Now he visited Chittenden Falls, not just to see her again, but also to deliver the ashes of the "great love of his life"—Harriet. Postponing their trip, Ben and Ellie took a sharp look at the urn of ashes, which so many people wanted to acquire. They were sure "dear old Dad" had been conned and that something of value had been smuggled into England. Only the fertile mind of Dorothy Cannell could devise the motivation behind the scam.

While Ben and the children were attending a summer camp in *Bridesmaids Revisited* (Viking, 2000), Ellie had an adventure of her own. Three elderly friends of her grandmother Sophia, who were known collectively as "the bridesmaids", invited her to their home to "receive a message". Ellie learned a lot during her visit: that her mother had been murdered, that she might be killed, and that she had relatives of whom she was unaware.

Cannell used Roxie, Ellie's cleaning woman and friend, to provide humorous touches.

Vejay Haskell

Author: Susan Dunlap

Vejay (Veronica Joan) Haskell, a thirty-two-year old California divorcee, left a high profile job in public relations to build a new life as a Henderson, California meter-reader. Now she could wear casual clothes, let her brown hair hang, and drive a pick-up. She became aware that the locals resented changes; i.e. newcomers, a rise in property values, and increasing thefts.

Vejay contacted bar owner Frank Gaulet about a possible problem with his electrical system in *An Equal Opportunity Death* (St. Martin, 1984). Her presence on the property made her a suspect when Frank was murdered.

Vejay was drawn into a Henderson festival week in *The Bohemian Connection* (St. Martin, 1985) while searching for an activist housewife who had disappeared. Vejay suspected a connection between the housewife's death and the hookers provided for tourists during the weekend.

Another quaint California attraction, the slug festival, provided background for *The Last Annual Slugfest* (St. Martin, 1986) when the gastropods were featured in races, contests, and menus. Edwina Henderson, local social leader, died during the slug-eating contest. Although all the right ingredients were there, this series ended when author Susan Dunlap concentrated on other female sleuths; i.e. Kieran O'Shaughnessy and policewoman Jill Smith.

Barbara Havers

Author: Elizabeth George

Detective Sgt. Barbara Havers was the "odd woman out" of the ensemble featured in Elizabeth George's mystery series. She lacked the beauty and distinction of Lady Helen Clyde or the noble heritage of Scotland Yard Inspector Thomas Lynley, the special skills of handicapped forensic scientist Simon Allcourt-Jones or his photographer wife, Deborah. Barbara was a dowdy working class policewoman, serving her time in the company of the elite. Lynley, a dedicated police officer, had accepted the dour Barbara as his assistant. She had good reason to be difficult, living in a stuffy home with an invalid father and a grieving mother. Barbara had not sought the assignment with Lynley, whom she considered a dilettante. Once past their first impressions, they developed mutual respect, heavily tested at times.

A Great Deliverance (Bantam, 1988) teamed Lynley and Barbara when Scotland Yard sent them north to solve an ax murder. Roberta Teys had been found standing over her father's body but the locals doubted that she had killed him. In *Payment in Blood* (Bantam, 1989) Lynley and Barbara journeyed to Scotland where Lady Helen Clyde, a woman with whom both Allcourt-Jones and Lynley once had a relationship, was the obvious suspect in a murder.

Well-Schooled in Murder (Bantam, 1990) touched on the problems in the Allcourt-Jones marriage, stemming from a prior relationship between Lynley and Deborah. Deborah found the body of a thirteen-year-old boy in a graveyard when she was taking photographs. In another complex narrative Lynley was forced by Barbara to become objective about the motives for murder.

After Barbara's father died, her mother faded deeper into incompetence. *A Suitable Vengeance* (Bantam, 1991) was a retrospective of the relationships among Thomas, Helen, Deborah, and Simon. Barbara played a minor role when murder occurred on the Lynley estate where Deborah and Lynley had once celebrated their engagement.

For the Sake of Elena (Bantam, 1992) took Lynley to Cambridge to investigate the murder of a young deaf student. Barbara made occasional appearances, assisting Lynley in his investigation, but her work was usually described by others. She searched for an appropriate place for her mother to live. Barbara, once set free by her mother's placement in a nursing home, had a minor role in *Missing Joseph* (Bantam, 1993), a powerful exploration of mother love, centering on a woman's obsessive love for a child that was hers in every sense but one.

Playing for the Ashes (Bantam, 1994) found Barbara in her own small home, Chalk Farm, showing some interest in her neighbors, an Indian immigrant and his small daughter. Lynley had proposed and been accepted by Lady Helen. The narrative focused on Jean, the lower class wife of a famous cricket player, who could not believe he would leave her and the children for another man's wife, and Olivia, the daughter of the cricket player's benefactress, who had countered rejection with rebellion.

The first third of *In the Presence of the Enemy* (Bantam, 1996) narrated the involvement of Helen, Deborah, and Simon in the disappearance of young Charlotte Bowen. Charlotte's birth was the result of a sexual encounter between an ambitious British governmental official and a scurrilous newspaper editor. When the child's corpse was discovered, Scotland Yard took over. Barbara's efforts to control Thomas's rage that the kidnapping had not been reported to the authorities were unsuccessful. His reaction to what he perceived as Helen's treachery and Simon and Deborah's stupidity damaged their relationships. He took charge of the London aspects of the case, sending Barbara to Wiltshire, where the body had been discovered. She was well aware that the independent assignment enhanced her status. She did not expect to meet a man who courted her attentions. The interplay among a variety of well-drawn suspects kept a reader's attention through an unusually long narrative.

Deception on His Mind (Bantam, 1997) concentrated on Barbara's involvement in the affairs of her neighbor, Taymullah Azhar and his daughter Khalidah Hadiyyah. Lynley and Lady Helen were honeymooning. Barbara was still recovering from injuries. During this time, Azhar was acting as negotiator for Pakistanis in Balford-le-Nez. The Pakistanis who were led by Azhar's cousin, Muhammad, distrusted the local police department's investigation of the death of a recent immigrant who was to marry Muhammad's sister. Barbara's acquaintanceship with DCI Emily Barlow gave her access to the probe, but her failure to acquaint both sides with her conflict of interest created problems. Barbara was in real trouble.

Tommy did little to make things easier for Barbara during *In Pursuit of the Proper Sinner* (Bantam, 1999) when he supported her demotion to constable and denied her a role in his next big case, the murder of Nicola Maiden, daughter of a retired colleague. Only when Tommy recognized how controlling he had become, was he able to accept that Barbara had not only solved his current case, but had acted correctly in the prior one—*Deception on His Mind*.

In the long (over 700 pages) but engrossing *A Traitor to Memory* (Bantam, 2001), George gave limited attention to Havers or Lynley as she explored parent-child relationships, particularly those where there were special needs—as for a musical genius or a Downs Syndrome child. Eugenie Davis, the mother of both such children, had left her husband Richard and talented violinist Gideon when little Sonia was drowned in the bathtub. Katja, the German "nanny" held responsible for the death, spent twenty years in prison. The current story of the investigation of Eugenie's hit and run death was interspersed with a journal kept by Gideon on the advice of his therapist. Although Tommy and Barbara protected a police official who had been involved with Eugenie, Winston Nkata had a broader role interacting with Katja who was "owed" by the Davis family. Helen's pregnancy added a personal note, but Gideon and his narcissistic reminiscences dominated the narrative.

George created complex characters and played them off against one another for dramatic tension. She shifted the spotlight from one to another, juggling their personal problems. George, an American writing in an English setting, left her readers moved, disturbed, and wanting more – but perhaps not longer.

Judith Hayes

Author: Anna Porter

Canadian writer Judith Hayes supported a household that included two teenagers, so solving mysteries did not come easily. James, her ex-husband, visited Toronto occasionally to spend time with the children if not with Judith.

In *Hidden Agenda* (Dutton, 1986), Judith was convinced that her friend George Harris had not thrown himself in front of a Toronto subway train. One reason that suicide was unlikely, George had been excited about a new publishing venture with American Max Grafstein. By *Mortal Sins* (New American Library, 1988), Detective Inspector David Parr had become the man in Judith's life, even though his wife had not consented to a divorce. Judith interviewed Hungarian refugee Paul Zimmerman, then attended the dinner where he died. She accompanied Parr to Hungary, where they uncovered a story of past wrongs and more recent efforts to protect the future.

Porter made Judith a credible character, difficult to do in an espionage narrative featuring a female.

Jennifer Heath

Author: Alison Tyler, pseudonym for Elise Title

The Dell trilogy featuring Jennifer Heath could be better categorized as a romantic thriller than as a mystery. Her partner Laura Cole managed their antique store while Jennifer ranged the world looking for bargains. She was a tall brown-haired woman in her mid-twenties, not ready to settle down. She was the daughter of enlightened parents. Her father wrote cookbooks and her mother had a lovelorn column.

Jennifer found what had been missing in her life during *Chase the Wind* (Dell, 1987)—the excitement of international espionage. She and handsome agent Alex Perry traveled by foot, Jeep, and helicopter through Italy in possession of a silver pillbox containing a microdot. On their trail were Italian terrorists, criminals and KGB agents. During their tribulations, Jennifer displayed her karate expertise, driving skills, and the ability to fly a helicopter (all of which she had learned from prior boyfriends).

Exhilarated by her initial adventure in international espionage, Jenny agreed to make a pickup at the Louvre Museum for CIA chief George Abraham in *Chase the Storm* (Dell 1987). Not only was the courier dying when she met him, but when she later returned to her hotel bedroom, his body had been moved there. George sent Alex Perry to help. He was attracted to Jenny, enjoyed intimacy with her but had no plans to marry. As before Jenny called on her hidden talents; i.e. diving and modeling to get into and out of trouble. They uncovered weapons dealers operating out of the fashion business. She and Alex came together long enough for some steamy sex as the narrative progressed. Her hopes for a more permanent arrangement blew up at the conclusion.

Other: *Chase the Sun* (Dell), the last of the trilogy can hopefully be depended upon to provide a happy ending.

Dittany Henbit

Author: Alisa Craig, pseudonym for Charlotte MacLeod

Dittany Henbit was a small, slim ash-blonde with green/blue eyes. She lived in Lobelia Falls, Ontario, Canada where she ran a secretarial service. When her widowed mother remarried and moved to Vancouver, Dittany remained in the community where her family had lived for three generations.

She was introduced in *The Grub-and-Stakers Move a Mountain* (Doubleday, 1981) as a member of a group dedicated to archery, conservation, and gardening. While walking, Dittany observed the murder of an employee of the water department who was working on a wild flower preserve. He had been shot by an arrow. The Grub-and-Stakers rallied to win a crucial election, save a mountain, and unmask a killer. One of Dittany's allies was Osbert Monk, an author of westerns under the name Lex Laramie and nephew of local Gothic novelist Arethusa Monk.

The home of a distinguished local family had been left to the Grub-and-Stakers as a museum. Dittany, now Mrs. Osbert Monk, was a trustee in *The Grub-and-Stakers Quilt a Bee* (Doubleday, 1985). After the museum curator died, possibly in a fall from the roof or attic of the museum, Osbert and Dittany discovered a hidden treasure and the curator's killer. *The Grub-and-Stakers Pinch a Poke* (Doubleday, 1988) was heavily dependent upon knowledge of characters from prior books. Someone intended to kill or injure attorney Carolus Bledsoe, but a solution was delayed until the Lobelia Falls theatre group won an invitation to a regional play contest.

Dittany, expecting twins, was in no condition to pursue evildoers in *The Grub-and-Stakers Spin a Yarn* (Avon, 1990). Charles McCorquendale, husband of Mother Matilda whose secret mincemeat recipe founded an industry, was kidnapped and murdered. Osbert and Dittany realized that the killers were after Charles' portion of the recipe.

Reality was the first victim in *The Grub-and-Stakers House a Haunt* (Morrow, 1993). Widow Zilla Trott confided to Dittany and Osbert that the deceased Hiram Jellaby had visited her. He was determined to uncover the gold he had buried and identify his own killer.

A reader may enjoy humor in the mystery novel or find it distracting. There is no halfway with MacLeod, laugh at it or leave it. A reader can expect humor, action and warmth, quaint characters possessing names that only a genealogist could love, and a frantic interplay of sub-plots.

Rachel Hennings

Author: Jon Breen

Rachel Hennings, a part-time college student in Tempe, Arizona, learned that her Uncle Oscar had bequeathed his used book store, not to his son Daniel, but to her. Although she dabbled in automatic writing, Rachel had not been considered psychic in the Arizona State extra-sensory perception tests. So why was she autographing the books of dead authors in their handwriting? Why did she autograph Arlen Kitchener's book with the name "Ransom Blaisdell"? In *The Gathering Place* (Walker, 1984) she had shared these incidents with book review editor Stu Wellman even before they found a corpse in the shop.

In *Touch of the Past* (Walker, 1988), Rachel was commissioned by steady customer Gil Franklin to purchase the mystery collection of reclusive Wilbur DeMarco. She and Stu attended the auction of DeMarco's 1937 era possessions, marred by the discovery of his corpse. Rachel moved into DeMarco's home to soak up psychic atmosphere, and interview those who had known him in 1937 so she could reconstruct the trauma which held him in that time period.

A touch of the occult in a bibliographic mystery.

Kate Henry

Author: Alison Gordon

Kate Henry covered the fictional Toronto Titans baseball team, a controversial assignment for a woman even today. She was single and in her forties as the series began. Although she was the daughter of a small town minister, she was intolerant of religion, giving her devotion to Canada and to baseball. Kate had trained for ballet but was too tall (5' 9"). Accepting this, she attended the University of Saskatchewan, then found success as a sports reporter for the Toronto Planet. She rented half of her duplex to Sally Parker, whose twelve-year-old son, T. C., was featured in the series.

The Titans were in the final stretch before the playoffs when *The Dead Pull Hitter* (St. Martin, 1989) began. The tensions among the players jeopardized the team's ability to win important games. Just as the team clinched a spot in the playoffs, a disgruntled veteran player was murdered in his apartment. Pitcher Steve Thorson was found dead at the Stadium. Henry, who enjoyed a working relationship with Sgt. Andrew Munro of the Royal Canadian Mounted Police, passed along rumors about blackmail and drug dealing on the squad. Her twenty-pound cat Elway was the hero of the narrative.

In *Safe at Home* (St. Martin, 1991), Kate accompanied the Titans to spring training in Florida. Munro remained in Toronto investigating homosexual rape and murders of young boys. On the team's return to Canada, a gay baseball player and Kate rescued a child from the molester before Munro could make an inappropriate arrest, straining their relationship.

Night Game (St. Martin, 1994) returned the Titans to Florida for spring training. Kate, alone on her birthday, almost surrendered to a romantic interlude with a fellow writer, but the discovery of a corpse interrupted their moonlight walk. The victim was an eager young local reporter whose sexuality had created tension in the marriages of several players.

There was something missing in *Striking Out* (St. Martin, 1995). Baseball was on strike! That left Kate as just another female sleuth solving the problems of her friends and neighbors. The neighbor in this case was a street person, suspected when the husband she had fled for years was found dead in Kate's alley. Andy, recovering from a bullet wound, kept Kate on edge, balancing her feelings about the police department and racial discrimination.

Kate had little awareness of her mother's athletic past until *Prairie Hardball* (McClelland & Stewart, 1997), when she returned to rural Saskatchewan. Helen, Kate's mother, was to be inducted into the Saskatchewan Baseball Hall of Fame for her play on the Racine (Wisconsin) Belles during World War II. She and other team members had been warned not to attend, but did so anyway. Kate's involvement opened the door to a chapter of Helen's life that contained a major surprise. This was the most revealing of the series in terms of Kate's character.

Gordon's books provided inside touches about baseball and Canada's new interest in the sport. Baseball players, their wives and lovers created lengthy casts of characters.

Susan Henshaw

Author: Valerie Wolzien

Initially Susan Henshaw seemed to be a materialistic, self-centered character in comparison to her friend and fellow investigator, Kathleen Somerville Gordon. Susan, an attractive brunette, had a successful marriage and two teenage children. She and Kathleen, then a police officer, met in *Murder at the PTA Luncheon* (St. Martin, 1988), when the president of the Hancock, Connecticut group, was poisoned by an appetizer. As part of the investigation, Kathleen met advertising executive Jerry Gordon, whom she married. She resigned from the police department to set up a security agency. During *The Fortieth Birthday Party* (St. Martin, 1989), the two women became close friends. It was Susan's fortieth birthday, but her husband Jed had not placed the corpse in the new Volvo he was giving her.

We Wish You a Merry Murder (Fawcett Gold Medal, 1991) was a change from hardcover. The discovery of a dead investor in his ex-wife's living room and the subsequent disappearance of his corpse formed the core of the book. However there were too-frequent diversions into marital discord, selfish teenagers, interfering mothers and mothers-in-law. In *An Old Faithful Murder* (Fawcett, 1992), the Henshaw and Gordon families, vacationing at Yellowstone Park, were drawn by isolation into the tangled affairs of the extended Erickson family that included murder.

Next was *All Hallows' Evil* (Fawcett, 1992) where Susan befriended TV anchorwoman Rebecca Armstrong when her husband was found dead. The Fourth of July was the next holiday in *A Star-Spangled Murder* (Fawcett, 1993), when Kathleen and Susan prepared the family cottage on a Maine coastal island. Obviously someone had been using the Henshaw cottage, and even more obviously, they had left a corpse behind. The solution was contrived and insensitive to the needs of the children involved.

A Good Year for a Corpse (Fawcett, 1994) was reminiscent of Mark Twain's *The Man Who Corrupted Hadleyburg*. Horace Harvey, an alumnus of the Hancock high school, returned, convincing individuals and organizations that he would bequeath them a substantial fortune…until someone killed him.

Susan had always prepared the food for her traditional New Year's Eve party, but in *'Tis the Season to Be Murdered* (Fawcett, 1994), she hired a catering firm, (The Holly and Ms. Ivy). She considered herself fortunate until a series of bungled assignments and the death of Zeke Holly, the charming front man for the business, damaged the firm's reputation. Susan could not understand why her friend, Kathleen, and Police Chief Brett Fortescue had frozen her out of the investigation, so she worked this one alone.

By *Remodeled to Death* (Fawcett, 1995), Susan had assumed a semi-official role as investigator for the local police department. She combined her probe into the death of the building inspector with a *Mrs. Blandings Builds Her Dream Bathroom* fling.

Jed's decision to run for the town council placed Susan in the midst of local politics in *Elected to Death* (Fawcett, 1996). The death of a mayoral candidate complicated a campaign focused on the preservation of local buildings. Susan's comfortable working relationship with Police Chief Brett Fortescue was disrupted by his personal interest in a murder suspect.

During *Weddings Are Murder* (Fawcett, 1998), her anxieties about the forthcoming wedding of her daughter, Chrissy, took precedence over the death of an unknown woman (whose corpse she treated as unwelcome refuse). Instead of a second honeymoon, Susan and Jed should have had a year in the county jail for obstruction of justice and tampering with evidence at a level that might prevent the conviction of a killer.

With both children leading independent lives as *The Student Body* (Fawcett, 1999) began, Susan returned to college. In a less adventurous woman, this might have kept her too busy to meddle in murders but she had no choice when her lab partner was murdered. Although the setting had potential, the narrative was predictable.

Even in the haute couture community of Hancock, Connecticut, the introduction of an up-market outlet mall called "Once in a Blue Moon" was a matter of interest. In *Death at a Discount* (Fawcett, 2000), the least likely person to be present at the grand opening was Amanda Worth, whose designer clothes and boasting husband proclaimed her a shopaholic at full price. After Susan found Amanda dead in a mall dressing room, she spent the next few days seeking her killer. Readers may accept the intelligence of the killer in diverting Susan, but find it difficult to attribute the physical capacity to carry out two deaths. Susan gained some insights into the value system of Hancock and the difficulties it created for those unwilling or unable to keep up with the Joneses.

On the whole, Susan still seemed a materialistic, self-centered character.

Lady Jane Hildreth

Author: Michael Spicer

Lady Jane was an espionage agent contending against Irish insurgents, right wing Pan-Europeans, and Russians. A fair-haired beauty, she boasted her physical fitness, an upper class education (Roedean, Girton at Cambridge University), and legal training. Her early employment was in the Metropolitan Police, but she was neither well received by her fellow officers, nor willing to make the sacrifices necessary to succeed there. It was during her police training when she met Patricia Huntington who served as an instructor.

Her divorced husband was killed during *Cotswold Manners* (St. Martin, 1989). Lord John, who had remarried, invited Jane to Greysham Park because he suspected that a guest had murdered Argentine polo player Antonio Alba. Lady Jane did not seem overly sentimental when Sir John died. She stuffed him in a cupboard and called British Intelligence. "Manners" were in short supply in the Cotswolds.

Lady Jane did not work alone in *Cotswold Murders* (St. Martin, 1990). Septuagenarian neighbor Patricia Huntington, a tough retired Special Services agent, served as her bodyguard. During a shared train trip, a young Irishwoman confessed her involvement in a political murder. After Jane passed along this information to the authorities, the young woman was brutally murdered and Jane was assigned the case.

Lady Jane took a Florida vacation in *Cotswold Mistress* (St. Martin, 1992) where she met aviation entrepreneur Marvin Lockhart, and agreed to investigate the deaths of military scientists. The book was initially interesting, but lost its focus. *Cotswold Moles* (St. Martin, 1993) sent Lady Jane to investigate the death of Veronica Langhorn, and the apparent suicide of her "handyman" Jack Swinton. The "Chief", head of MI5, who held a mysterious attraction for Jane, had more than a professional interest in the case. Jane and Patricia Huntington visited Australia in search of connections among the victims, her Chief, and a mid-eastern oil businessman.

Jane exhibited contempt for other nationalities and approval of police brutality against those who rejected English colonialism.

Inspector Judy Hill

Author: Jill McGown

Then married Chief Inspector Lloyd (who withheld his first name) and Judy met when both worked in London. Although they were aware of their mutual interest, Lloyd's divorce occurred later. Judy, an attractive young woman with dark curly hair and brown eyes, married Michael Hill, a computer salesman. Judy's decision to remain childless furthered her career but presented a problem in the marriage.

In *A Perfect Match* (St. Martin, 1983), Judy and Lloyd were reunited by their assignments to the regional police department in Stansfield. Widower Chris Wade, who escorted newcomer Julia Mitchell home from a party, became the primary suspect when her corpse was found. At first, Hill and Lloyd agreed that Chris was the killer, but his continued protestations of innocence forced them to look further. Close cooperation brought them into an intimate relationship.

Although Judy and Lloyd had become lovers, she lived with her husband in *Murder at the Old Vicarage* (St. Martin, 1989) a.k.a. *Redemption*. She was unwilling to end her marriage even though Lloyd insisted that she do so. When Graham Elstow, abusive husband of Joanna Wheeler, was found dead, Judy, the more intuitive of the pair, picked up on nuances that refocused the inquiry and disclosed the truth.

Michael admitted that he had been unfaithful in *Gone to Her Death* (St. Martin, 1990) a.k.a. *Death of a Dancer*. Judy was assigned to investigate thefts at a nearby preparatory school. Lloyd was brought in when the deputy headmaster's promiscuous wife was murdered. Judy's incisive questioning, including her ability to use silence to pressure the suspect to talk, brought out the motive for murder.

Judy's promotion to Detective Inspector necessitated her move to Malworth in *The Murders of Mrs. Austin and Mrs. Beale* (St. Martin, 1991). She and Lloyd assumed that their professional collaboration would end, but they were soon working on murders connected by a telephone line. Lloyd prevented Judy from making a serious error.

In *The Other Woman* (St. Martin, 1993) Melissa Whitworth, using her professional name, interviewed her husband Simon's secretary, Sharon Smith, and learned that she was his mistress. The night that Sharon's dead body was discovered, a young woman was raped in Malworth. McGown's plot was as complex as usual, but the solution depended upon an unlikely possibility. Judy's strong response to misconduct on her staff prompted her reassignment.

Judy and Lloyd probed a death together in Stansfield in *Murder...Now and Then* (St. Martin, 1993), which could only be understood when the past history of the characters was explored. While Lloyd attended computer training, Judy was Acting Chief Inspector in *A Shred of Evidence* (Fawcett-Columbine, 1996). A potential Olympic runner became the prime suspect when an attractive young woman was murdered in the park. As always, McGown developed the suspects with fascinating detail and layers of intrigue. Lloyd returned from the training to take part in the investigation, careful not to offend Judy. He wanted a real commitment. She agreed to marriage, but would not set a date.

Judy's response to police abuse of a suspect during a prior book returned to center stage during *Verdict Unsafe* (Macmillan, 1997) when the suspect was released from prison and sued the department. If Colin Drummond had not been the serial killer who had terrorized women in the area, who was? Lloyd's potential conflict of interest and threats against Judy created tensions between them and their new supervisor, but may have drawn the couple closer together.

The decision of a real estate developer to purchase the land of Bernard Bailey, a reclusive farmer, might have triggered death threats in *Picture of Innocence* (FawcettColumbine, 1998), but Judy did not take the matter seriously. Bailey's death was a serious failure for both Judy and Lloyd, who had assigned her to the case. Judy had a major decision of her own to make, balancing her independence and strong professional ambitions against a new responsibility in her personal life.

Plots and Errors (Ballantine, 1999 in US) utilized a Dramatis Personae and was structured as a play script, yet its twists and turns would have been difficult to achieve in a visual art. Judy's pregnancy and reassignment to a staff job gave Lloyd hope that they could live together, and perhaps marry. The bigamous relationships of an industrialist and the controlling will provisions he left behind spawned death and deceit to his spouses and their children.

In the eighth month of her pregnancy, Judy—now equal to Lloyd in rank as a Detective Chief Inspector—worked primarily from her home. She was assigned in *Scene of Crime* (Ballantine, 2000) to LINKS, a computerized system that sought patterns in crime over multiple districts. Her interest in the local dramatic society introduced Judy and Lloyd to Dr. Carl Bignall, whose wife Estelle died in what seemed to be a routine burglary. There were enough details that indicated Estelle's suffocation might have been murder to keep both Lloyd and his newly shorn sergeant, Tom Finch, busy. Judy was the pipeline for community gossip about the Bignalls and, as always, raised pertinent questions that clarified Lloyd's premises. On a personal level, their relationship continued to inch forward. Judy accepted an engagement ring, tacitly approving plans for a wedding.

McGown's books have been among the best English procedurals. Judy was professional, a dedicated career woman coping with her personal life. She and Lloyd realized that she might eventually outrank him. Their intimacy was sensitively described with occasional touches of humor. They, and other characters in the narratives, developed into three-dimensional figures, gradually revealing themselves.

Maggie Hill

Author: Melodie Johnson Howe

Divorced writer Maggie Hill supported herself as a typist as *The Mother Shadow* (Viking, 1989) opened. She witnessed the codicil to coin collector Ellis Kenilworth's will. In quick succession, Kenilworth died, his lawyer repudiated the codicil, and the document was removed from Maggie's purse. She remembered the name of the beneficiary, Pasadena private investigator Claire Conrad. Once Maggie made the contact, Claire took command of the subsequent investigation. An older (50) taller, wealthier, and more sophisticated woman, Claire had been depressed, perhaps by a recent hysterectomy. An investigation was what she needed. Assisted by her handsome chauffeur Boulton and Maggie, Claire researched the eccentric, but recently impoverished Kenilworth.

By *Beauty Dies* (Viking, 1994), Maggie had become part of the Conrad household and was definitely attracted to Boulton. The trio was visiting Boston when Maggie was approached by a young woman who declared that the death of fashion model Cybella had been murder. After the informant was murdered, Maggie and Claire took on an investigation that had not interested the Boston police. Maggie and Boulton ventured into the world of peep shows, pornographic films, and sleazy hotels to locate Cybella's daughter and the killer who resented her.

Nikki Holden

Author: Elaine Raco Chase

Nikki Holden, tall and trim, just short of thirty, was single. She had a troubled childhood: an abusive mother, teenage years marked by truancy, theft, and detention in a youth center. The cycle ended unrealistically with her parole to magazine publisher Matthew Cortlund. Scars remained on her back, in a broken nose, and in her mind.

When, in *Dangerous Places* (Bantam, 1987), teenager Marcy Nathan sought refuge from her mother, Nikki made it available, judging that Leonora Reichman had no more maternal instinct than her own mother. Ex-mercenary Roman Cantrell was hired to bring Marcy home. The romantic/humorous, but incendiary conflict between Cantrell and Holden read like a television script with short takes, mistakes, and magnetic physical attraction. Roman restored Nikki's interest in love and sex, although he could not prevent his client from being murdered. Nikki was a victim, past and present, leaving the investigation to Cantrell.

Nikki's injuries forced her to take several months off from work, living at Cantrell's place as *Dark Corners* (Bantam, 1988) began. Matt Cortlund recalled her to research a story of UFO (Unidentified Flying Object) sightings, while Cantrell investigated an armored car heist. Nikki not only solved both cases but also had matters well in hand when Cantrell came to rescue her. In a turnabout, she was sensitized to the post-Vietnam trauma from which Cantrell suffered.

Although the books were composites of mystery, pop psychology, and science fiction, they were interesting.

Roz Howard

Author: Susan Kenney

Roz Howard, one of many recent sleuths with doctorates, was a tall New Englander with brown hair. She began the series as a college professor but switched to crime writing.

In *Garden of Malice* (Scribners, 1983), while Roz was in England editing the diaries of a famous gardener, someone sought to prevent the publication by vandalism and murder. Roz, a trifle Gothic in her naivete, risked death in her investigation.

Graves in Academe (Viking, 1985) set Roz in a traditional academic mystery in Canterbury College, Maine. An unorthodox Dean had the English faculty in an uproar, and a series of "accidents" were depleting its ranks.

During *One Fell Sloop* (Viking, 1990), Roz and Alan Stewart, her British artist/scientist lover, celebrated their reunion with a cruise along the New England coast, jealously comparing their nautical skills. When they were diverted by a corpse and a family struggle involving the environment and business strategy, their relationship improved.

Roz did not carve out a special niche for herself, although the books were enjoyable reads.

Tamara Hoyland

Author: Jessica Mann

Tamara Hoyland was an appealing mystery heroine with an emotional depth that was not shown by Mann's prior sleuth Thea Crawford. She became deeply affected by the death of Ian Barnes, a British Intelligence agent, and later by the disclosure that another lover was a criminal. An attractive blonde, the daughter of an attorney and a BBC programmer, Tamara had trained as an archeologist. After Ian's death, she joined British Intelligence. With her command of languages, photographic memory, and organizational skills, she was well suited for the work. Her mother was the daughter of exiled Russian nobility, the Count and Countess Losinsky. Tamara was the youngest of four children, three daughters and a son.

In *Funeral Sites* (Doubleday, 1982), Rosamund Shatto, who suspected that her brother-in-law, a potential Prime Minister, had murdered her sister, fled in fear of her life. Tamara helped her avoid discovery; then, she and Ian unmasked a Soviet mole.

By *No Man's Island* (Doubleday, 1983), Tamara had been recruited into Dept E., trained in the use of weapons, and given a cover job on the Royal Commission on Historical Monuments. She was assigned to Forway, the island where Ian's widowed mother still lived. A planned royal visit encouraged local insurgents to declare independence from England. Her activities uncovered Ian's killer.

In *Grave Goods* (Doubleday, 1985), Tamara aided a family friend who was writing a book about the Crown Jewels of Charlemagne. The regalia was reputedly in the possession of the East German government, but found in unexpectedly humble surroundings. *A Kind of Healthy Grave* (St. Martin, 1986) wove the past into the present. In 1929 a mysterious fire had been blamed for the death of an iconoclastic artist whose drawings and other artistic obscenities were regarded as commonplace at a later period. Tamara linked the earlier incident to the recent murder of a society dilettante.

During *Death Beyond the Nile* (St. Martin, 1988), reminiscent of the Agatha Christie book, Tamara chaperoned a Royal princess, and monitored the contacts of an unhappy female scientist whose medical discovery had military implications. Tamara's personal life was significant in *Faith, Hope and Homicide* (St. Martin, 1991) when she fell in love with a scientist suspected of murder. Although her previous relationships had left Tamara suspicious, she focused on saving her lover's reputation and his life. Tamara, hearing her biological clock ticking, resigned from the Service.

Thea Crawford was involved in several of the Hoyland books as mentor and friend. Mann's books were complex, shifting time periods, employing different narrators and journals. She provided balance between characterization and plotting.

Bonnie Indermill

Author: Carole Berry (Summerlin)

To a person who categorizes individuals by occupations, a "temp" (short-term employee) might resemble a chameleon; e.g. a legal assistant; then, an exercise instructor or a fund-raiser. Bonnie Indermill had been all of the above, plus kindergarten teacher and professional dancer. She had reddish blonde hair and blue eyes, and kept fit through her dancing. Divorced in her late thirties after a childless marriage, Bonnie moved at whim from one job to another, unconcerned about such prosaic matters as health insurance and retirement benefits. Even her cat, Moses, could be boarded out if she wished to travel. A self-reliant woman from a blue-collar liberal background, she had been active in the anti-war movement. Her close ties were to her parents and a married brother, all of whom hoped she would settle down and marry.

In *The Letter of the Law* (St. Martin, 1987), Bonnie was the office manager for a second-rate New York City law firm. When attorney Albert

Janowski missed his appointments, the police department was notified. At their request, Bonnie identified his corpse in a sleazy hotel. Unable to resist a $30,000 reward for information leading to the arrest of Janowski's killer, Bonnie earned the money and spent it on travel. After a short vacation, Bonnie hired on at Creative Financial Ventures in *The Year of the Monkey* (St. Martin, 1988). Already an unhappy work site, the staff became even less congenial when the manager was murdered after the office Christmas party.

Bonnie had several romantic relationships: Detective Tony La Marca (Book #1) whose wife later became a friend; artist Derek Thorensen (Book #2), and business man Sam Finkelstein later in the series.

She focused on her first love, the world of dance in *Good Night, Sweet Prince* (St. Martin, 1990) when hired by the fund raising section of the Gotham Ballet. When Nikolai Koslov defected from the USSR, he chose Bonnie as his conduit to the authorities. His "accidental" death brought La Marca and Bonnie into conflict.

Her relationships floundering, a trip to the Caribbean sounded ideal. So, in *Island Girl* (St. Martin, 1991), Bonnie substituted as an aerobics instructor at a struggling hotel. When her beautiful but opportunistic roommate was drowned on an evening diving excursion, Bonnie sought the motive for the death.

She had decided never to work for a law firm again, but relented in *The Death of a Difficult Woman* (Berkley Prime Crime, 1994) because the money was good. She coordinated the firm's move to a new building. The "difficult woman" was murdered during the chaos of the move and the rivalry for advancement within the firm. Bonnie, unusually guileless for one who has encountered so many killers, saved herself from a classic "Had I But Known" situation.

Fast Eddie Fong had taken advantage of Bonnie's good nature before, but in *The Death of a Dancing Fool* (Berkley, 1996) he stepped over the line. His new nightclub, financed by mob money, caught the attention of the local police. Restless, uncertain as to whether or not she should give up her own apartment and move in with her lover, Sam Finkelstein, Bonnie went undercover at "The Dancing Fool", found and then lost a new dancing partner, and saved Eddie from disaster.

Although she had no immediate intention of adding a wedding ring to the engagement ring Sam had given her, in *Death of a Dimpled Darling* (Berkley, 1997), Bonnie spent a lot of time at a bridal salon. Her dear friend, Amanda La Marca, a novice bridal consultant, needed Bonnie to fill in during bouts of morning sickness. The nouveau riche Dunn family intended to have a memorable wedding for their daughter, Courtney. The reception would be held at the aging Ambassador Hotel, currently being renovated by Dunn Construction Corporation. The assignment eventually included two murders and corporate theft.

The plush rugs, spacious rooms, and formal atmosphere at Bonnie's new place of employment seemed too good to be true in *Death of a Downsizer* (Berkley, 1999). It was. Carl Dorfmeyer, the "hatchet man" appointed to cut back on expenses, was murdered. Clues at the scene of the crime pointed to Bonnie. She solved this one "on the run." For all her exposure to crime, Bonnie remained credulous, and easily deceived.

Carole Berry conjured up intriguing plots, placing Bonnie in one dysfunctional work setting after another.

Zee Madeiras Jackson

Author: Philip R. Craig

J. W. Jackson, a police officer who retired on disability and did assorted part-time security and investigative work, was the primary in the series. His second marriage was to Zee Madeiras, a registered nurse at the hospital on Martha's Vineyard, a setting that was an essential element of the narratives. (The series was subtitled *A Martha's Vineyard Mystery.*)

Zee was the daughter of immigrant parents, who had worked at low-level jobs until they had the money to open a small grocery store. Uneducated themselves, they were ambitious for their children. When Zee, then an undergraduate in college, met and dated Paul Madeiras, her parents were delighted. Their daughter would be the wife of a doctor! To this end, Zee studied nursing. Once out of school, she subsidized Paul's education through medical school. He discarded Zee for a younger, more adoring wife shortly after he began practice. Zee's parents had assumed the divorce to be her fault; for a while, she did too. She stated later that J. W. and the aunt and uncle who offered her refuge at this time in her life made it possible for her to recover from the rejection and guilt she had experienced. Although Zee's mother, Maria, a devout Catholic, was dismayed at J. W.'s agnosticism and his propensity for exposing Zee to danger, she found him personally charming.

Over the series, Zee and J. W. had a son, Joshua, and a daughter, Diana, and kept a pair of cats (Oliver Underfoot and Velcro). In addition to raising children and working part-time at the hospital, Zee had a variety of interests—most shared with J. W. —fishing, target shooting on a competitive level, the Boston Red Sox, and vodka martinis. She was extremely attractive with blue-black hair, but not vain. Opportunities to capitalize on her appearance presented themselves but she was content with her current lifestyle. Her birthname Zeolinda came from a grandmother born in the Azores. Like Spenser and Susan Silverman, or Nick and Nora, the couple shared a light badinage that had overtones of sexuality and deep affection. Similarly, J. W. cooked, absorbed beatings, and had a sense of justice that overrode the law. Few of the perpetrators in the series were ever dealt with legally. Some killed themselves or were killed in the climax; a small number had their transgressions ignored by J. W.

The couple met on the beach in *A Beautiful Place to Die* (Scribners, 1989). As J. W. taught Zee the secrets of casting for bluefish, they saw a boat blow up under circumstances that could not be ignored.

Martha's Vineyard was a second home or vacation spot for many New England academics. During *The Woman Who Walked into the Sea* (Scribners, 1991) J. W.'s friend John Skye made his home available to two fellow professors. Handsome Ian McGregor earned J. W.'s enmity when he first romanced, and then affronted Zee. Acerbic Marjorie Summerharp insulted so many of the summertime residents that J. W. had difficulty in identifying her killer. He and Zee almost became victims before he figured it out.

In *The Double Minded Men* (Scribners, 1992), the petulant potentate of an oil producing Middle Eastern nation had a grudge against J. W. and Zee. It did not help that an emerald necklace, once stolen from his country but intended to be returned to him, was stolen again. The potentate failed to get his revenge thanks to quick action by Zee. She needed time, private and personal, to decide whether or not to apply to medical school and whether J. W. could be the husband and father for the children she desired.

During *Cliff Hanger* (Scribners, 1993), while Zee left the island for a month, J. W. was more than distracted. Several attempts were made on his life, causing him to seek out friend Professor John Skye in Colorado who was similarly threatened. A confused avenger was determined to destroy the man who had ruined his sister's life.

When the cold weather settled on Martha's Vineyard, the population dwindled. In *Off Season* (Scribners, 1994), this allowed the locals to focus on their internal disagreements. A proposed government purchase of fifty acres of woodland pitted the hunters against the animal rights activists, but the ensuing murder had a totally different motive. Zee had no role in the detecting although her insights and access to gossip helped J. W. to find the killer.

It would seem that Zee and J. W.'s forthcoming wedding would find both too busy for murder in *A Case of Vineyard Poison* (Scribners, 1995). The coordination of the event kept Zee and her mother Maria out of trouble, although there were mysterious discrepancies in her bank account.

J. W. was not only diverted by important guests, but by the death of a young college student on his property. He researched the worlds of computers and banking to locate a well-hidden killer.

It took urging by J. W. and the realization that she might be in danger to bring Zee to the Rod and Gun Club in *Death on a Vineyard Beach* (Scribners, 1996). She learned that not only did she enjoy target shooting, but that she was a "natural." On their honeymoon J. W. foiled an attempt to murder Luciano Marcus, a retired member of an organized crime family. Marcus hired J. W. to find his attackers whom he believed to be local Native Americans with a grudge. Although he had close friends among the Wampanoag tribe, J. W. took on the assignment because he and Zee, as witnesses to the shooting, were vulnerable.

Martha's Vineyard had become a haven for retired government officials including intelligence agents. Summer became more complicated in *A Deadly Vineyard Holiday* (Scribners, 1997) due to the visit of the presidential family. Cricket, the president's teenage daughter enjoyed the simplicity of island life, moving in with the Jacksons in the guise of a cousin. That not only met her needs, but also kept her safe from a vengeful attacker. Zee had a delightful surprise for J. W. at the conclusion.

In *A Shoot on Martha's Vineyard* (Scribners, 1998), J.W.'s hot temper made him the primary suspect when an over-zealous environmental official was murdered. He rallied his contacts to discover the less obvious motive for the victim's death. Both Zee and J. W. had their fidelity tested by amorous movie stars filming on the Island.

Zee had no meaningful role in *A Fatal Vineyard Season* (Scribners, 1999) during which she and the children visited her parents on the mainland. Left behind, J. W. embroiled himself in protecting two attractive African-American women against the racist attacks of gangster brothers.

The Krane brothers had few friends or admirers on Martha's Vineyard. Peter was a sadist; Ben, an attorney and slumlord. When, in *Vineyard Blues* (Scribners, 2000), an arsonist set fire to several of Ben's empty buildings no one was too upset. The discovery of a corpse in the third incident brought the attention of state and local authorities. So why, over Zee's objections, would J. W. work for Ben, seeking the arsonist? Maybe, because the latest victim had been an old friend.

It was Zee who bore the brunt of the first attack by Boston gangsters in *Vineyard Shadows* (Scribners, 2001). When she and Diana, their daughter, were threatened Zee put aside her reluctance to use a gun off the firing range, killing one attacker and wounding another. J. W. took over. Out of kindness to his former wife Carla, he helped Tom Rimini, the schoolteacher she had married. Quinn, a Boston Globe reporter, guided J. W. through the internicene battle to control Boston's rackets. As always, the narration ended with a final jolt for the reader. Zee was changed by her experience, and wondered if the woman she had become—a killer—was worthy of love. J. W. had no doubts as to his feelings for her, although he was surprised at his reaction to Carla's neediness.

J. W. narrated the rambling series, expressing the easygoing lifestyle he had adopted after years as a police officer.

Calista Jacobs

Author: Kathryn Lasky Knight

Calista Jacobs counted among her adversaries, the CIA, religious fundamentalists, cults, and land grabbers. She relished such challenges, because of her liberal ideology. In her forties, she was a distinguished artist and book illustrator, the widow of a Harvard astrophysicist, and the mother of Charlie, a precocious computer whiz. In her spare time she was an expert fly-fisherwoman and a great cook.

As *Trace Elements* (Norton, 1986) began, Calista's husband Tom and another researcher were killed by rattlesnakes while on a field trip. Tom had been testing his "Time Slicer", an invention that dated archeological material and detected nuclear explosions. His death devastated Calista and Charlie. A year later Charlie, using parts of a second Time Slicer and a computer, realized that his father's experiments had been distorted. He and Calista re-examined the death, uncovering a rogue CIA agent.

During *Mortal Words* (Summit, 1990), Calista and other liberal authors were maligned by religious fanatics. She recruited Charlie, his buddies, and her lover, archeologist Archie Baldwin, to expose a fundamentalist group who would falsify scientific results to bolster their theories.

When Archie and Charlie joined an archeological dig in Arizona, Calista visited them in *Mumbo Jumbo* (Summit, 1991). Their project was thwarted by a religious cult who considered the land to have special powers. Calista had inside information about the cult leader that enabled her to rescue an elderly man, protect an innocent young girl, and rally the citizenry against those who would control water rights.

Calista moved temporarily while her house was being renovated during *Dark Swan* (St. Martin, 1994). Her new neighbor Queenie Kingsley was killed with a pair of pruning shears. The prominent Kingsley clan was rife with reasons for the murder but Calista and young Charlie used computers and common sense to go beyond the obvious solution.

A prickly heroine in an imaginative series.

Cass Jameson

Author: Carolyn Wheat

Cass Jameson, of Chagrin Falls, Ohio, entered law school after the Kent State massacre. During her undergraduate years at Kent State, she had been active in anti-war activities, partly because her brother, a Vietnam veteran was a paraplegic. Cass, who had had an abortion, was resolutely pro-choice.

In *Dead Man's Thoughts* (St. Martin, 1983), it was not routine responsibility that motivated legal aid attorney Jameson to investigate the death of Nathan Wasserstein. He had been discovered in what appeared to be a homosexual murder, but he was Cass's lover, and she knew better.

Cass's caseload at Legal Aid included divorce and family law in *Where Nobody Dies* (St. Martin, 1986). She was assigned to the custody battle between tiny but vindictive Linda Ritchie and her ex-jock husband, Brad. Linda was murdered and Brad arrested. Busy with a full caseload, Cass managed to prove Brad innocent and work out a reasonable custody arrangement. Cass reappeared in *Fresh Kills* (Berkley, 1995) acting on behalf of a young mother who was placing her child for adoption. The woman reneged on her contract with the prospective parents, then disappeared, only to be found dead without the infant. Cass was determined to find the child and return her to a home where she would be loved.

She took personal and professional risks in *Mean Streak* (Berkley, 1996) defending her former lover, Attorney Matt Riordan from charges of bribery. Her feeling for Riordan, whose ties with the mob she had ignored during their relationship, distracted Cass when she challenged an ambitious attorney in court. A history of corruption came to light when the primary witness against Riordan was murdered. Once Cass discovered the killer, she had to know the whole story.

The involvement of Cass and her brother Ron in the migrant labor movement of the Sixties had disastrous consequences. An early arrest ended Ron's draft deferment, sending him to Vietnam where he incurred an injury that left him a paraplegic. His subsequent connection with radical movements, transporting political refugees to Canada, ended in murder. As *Troubled Waters* (Berkley, 1997) began, Jan, once Ron's lover, emerged from years of concealment to face charges for the death of a government agent. When Ron was named as a co-defendant, Cass put her professional responsibilities on hold to defend her brother by researching what really happened in 1969 and 1982.

Defense attorneys, to varying degrees, were concerned that they might have obtained the release of a guilty party who could continue to be a danger to society. Cass felt only a sense of accomplishment when she had Keith Jernigan's guilty verdict returned for a new trial in *Sworn to Defend* (Berkley, 1998). Keith became a part of her personal and professional life until disclosures about his past and his continued behaviors shattered her faith. The disillusionment was so great that Cass ignored a threat by a guilt-ridden killer.

Wheat shared her knowledge as a mystery buff, referring to classic detective novels and movies. Her experience as a public defender and advisor to the New York City police department provided realistic background. The narratives expanded Cass as a character over a period of time.

Willa Jansson

Author: Lia Matera

Willa Jansson was unwilling to base her future on the past. Her parents June Jansson and William Creel were political activists who married only when their child was born. Their experience of the legal system had been as victim or violator. Willa was more conventional, fascinated by Nancy Drew, Trixie Belden, and Annette Funicello, hardly heroines of the righteous left. Although Willa admired her parents' commitment, she was not inclined to emulate it. She coveted security, even luxury, but felt guilty about it. A tiny blonde, she was pro-choice, smoked pot, (but would like to give up tobacco), had herpes, but was sexually active. After a degree in Latin American literature, Willa entered Malhousie Law School in San Francisco. Her high grades qualified her for the Law Review, a scholarly journal published by law students.

Where Lawyers Fear to Tread (Bantam, 1987) began when Malhousie Law Review editors were an endangered species; two killed and one missing. The law school was provided with police protection, but Willa pursued her own investigation She uncovered students, faculty, and alumni enmeshed in sexual dalliance, possible plagiarism, and blackmail.

In her mid-thirties when she graduated, Willa was hired by activist attorney Julian Warneke, a friend of her parents. During *A Radical Departure* (Bantam, 1988), Julian was poisoned as he and Willa shared a power lunch. June Jansson was a major beneficiary under his will. Her status as a suspect was enhanced when Julian's ex-wife was murdered in June's presence. After the killer was identified, the Warneke firm was in shambles.

Willa moved to another law firm in *Hidden Agenda* (Bantam, 1988). Her relationship with Police Lt. Don Surgelato had not survived a crisis during which he killed a murder suspect. Willa was assigned to a corporate law unit, but became suspicious that she was being manipulated.

In *Prior Convictions* (Simon, 1991), Willa returned to San Francisco for a judicial clerkship. A major factor in the narrative was a group of former Vietnam activists working out their conflicts. The complex but terse narrative ended with more questions than answers, leaving Willa unsure about the principles that guided her parents' lives and her own.

In *Last Chants* (Simon & Schuster, 1996), Willa left the courtrooms and the law libraries behind for the intersection of Shamanism and virtual reality. She took time from her new job to rescue an elderly friend, joining him on a journey into the hills. She pitted the inner sources of her spirit against the madness of a killer. Readers may find the computer language and mythical references more complex than the workings of the legal system.

Willa continued to involve herself with the unknown in *Star Witness* (Simon & Schuster, 1997) wherein she represented a man accused of vehicular homicide. She had reservations about a defense based upon extra-terrestrials, but then this was California.

June, Willa's mother, had an unrelenting commitment to left-wing causes, including the Castro regime. Although Willa might not share her political ideology, she could not ignore her mother's disappearance while visiting Cuba in *Havana Twist* (Simon & Schuster, 1998). "Twist" was an appropriate word in the title as the narrative worked its way through false identities and political deceit. Willa, called on a former resource, her friend Don Surgelato, who risked his career to help.

Matera carried no brief for happy endings, accepting that one, often both parties, lost in the legal system. Her reflections on the clash between idealistic parents and pragmatic offspring were interesting.

Selena Jardine
Author: Sarah Caudwell, pseudonym for Sarah Cockburn

See: Julia Larmore, Page 159

Harriet Jeffries

Author: Medora Sale, who also writes as Caroline Roe

Harriet Jeffries, a commercial photographer, assisted Canadian police inspector, John Sanders. Dark haired and green-eyed, Harriet specialized in photographing architecture. Although Sanders was identified as appearing in *Murder on the Run* (PaperJacks, Canada 1986), Harriet was not.

During *Murder in Focus* (Scribners, 1989), the Royal Canadian Mounted Police had the unenviable task of guarding foreign delegates to a Toronto conference. The guests were offered optional tours and trips throughout Canada as part of their visit. Sanders had been detailed to assist the CSIS (Canadian Secret Intelligence Service) unit of the RCMP. Harriet was photographing the Canadian Supreme Court when a murder occurred, and her pictures became evidence. Recently jilted, she found the contacts with Sanders stimulating.

Harriet's involvement was more tenuous in *Murder in a Good Cause* (Scribners, 1990). The relationship with Sanders had stalled until he investigated the death of a friend of Harriet's. The contact rekindled their affair.

During *Sleep of the Innocent* (Scribners, 1991), Inspector Matt Baldwin assumed Sanders' caseload while he and Harriet vacationed at Martha's Vineyard. When Baldwin cracked under pressure during a murder investigation and his substitute became personally involved, Sanders was recalled. Harriet accompanied him.

Sanders and Harriet's relationship remained prickly in *Pursued by Shadows* (Scribners, 1992). Fearful because she had been involved in theft and aware that she was targeted for murder, Harriet's friend Jane Sinclair returned to Canada. Guy Beaumont, Harriet's former lover, followed her there. When Guy's corpse surfaced in Harriet's apartment, John and Harriet were both suspected.

Harriet had a stronger role in *Short Cut to Santa Fe* (Scribners, 1994), an absorbing tale of Harriet's and Sanders' adventure in a hijacked tour bus. Besides giving Harriet an opportunity to shine, the narrative focused on her friend Kate Grosvenor, who fought her way back from alcoholism and depression.

The limitations of Harriet's role illustrated the problem of keeping a non-professional female relevant over a mystery series.

Jane Jeffry

Author: Jill Churchill, pseudonym for Janice Young Brooks

Jane was a short blonde widow in her late thirties, managing a suburban Chicago household of three teenage children, two cats and a dog. She had controlled her grief for the death of a husband, who died en route to a tryst with a married woman. Although the child of a career diplomat and his sophisticated hostess wife, Jane was vulnerable, and overwhelmed by the changes in her life. In her spare time, she worked on her "story" of Priscilla, an Eighteenth Century heroine, as a first step toward a writing career.

Jane met detective Mel VanDyne in *Grime and Punishment* (Bantam, 1989), when a substitute cleaning woman was killed in neighbor Shelley Nowack's house. Shelley and Jane investigated a blackmailing domestic. The Jeffry household expanded in *A Farewell to Yarns* (Avon, 1991), when former neighbor Phyllis Wagner visited. Phyllis's efforts to re-establish a relationship with a child she had placed for adoption threatened the stability of her current marriage and perhaps led to her death.

A Quiche Before Dying (Avon, 1993) featured a writing class in which participants were encouraged to share biographical details, one of which precipitated murder at a group potluck. *The Class Menagerie* (Avon, 1994) described a high school class reunion. Memories of the death of a classmate during graduation week stirred revelations and murder.

Jane's children were maturing by *A Knife to Remember* (Avon, 1994) when she leased adjacent property to a movie company, only to find her older son enamored of an actress. The fact that the woman once had an affair with Jane's deceased husband did not improve the atmosphere on set. The actress's murder interfered with Jane's plans for a weekend getaway with Mel.

Mel, Jane and the children trekked to a Colorado ski resort in *From Here to Paternity* (Avon, 1995). They entangled themselves in the rivalries of a middle European genealogical society who were seeking a descendant of the Czar, and the claims of Native Americans for land in which the resort had an interest. *Silence of the Hams* (Avon, 1996) put Jane and Shelley on site at a newly opened delicatessen when a local attorney died. Unwilling to miss a chance to detect, the duo uncovered an accident that looked like murder and a real homicide.

Shelley and Jane frequently involved one another in community activities. In *War and Peas* (Avon, 1996), Jane assisted the Snellen Pea Museum in organizing stored material for the move to a new building. Although there was a genetic secret hidden in the museum, the murder of the director was motivated by a personal relationship.

Jane and Shelley joined a group of parents and officials in assessing a Wisconsin resort as the potential summer site for children in their school system in *Fear of Frying* (Avon, 1997). When they discovered a corpse that did not stay around long enough for the authorities to arrive, they were perceived as hysterics. A returned "victim" was met with warmth by his spouse, but skepticism by the sleuths.

The Merchants of Menace (Avon, 1998) expected loyal readers of the series to believe that Mel would foist his sophisticated mother upon Jane's hospitality at a time when she was already overburdened with neighborhood activities. A vindictive television reporter, dressed as Santa, intruded long enough to get murdered.

With her own wedding plans on hold, Jane was hired to plan one for a reluctant bride in *A Groom with a View* (Avon, 1999). The setting, an isolated hunting lodge, provided a small circle of suspects when first a seamstress, then the groom, were murdered. Jane seemed less frantic this time out.

Mulch Ado About Nothing (William Morrow, 2000) failed to meet the standards of prior books. The plot was thin stretched out by domestic details. Jane and Shelley were disappointed to learn that the instructor for their gardening class had been attacked. They were drawn further into the case when the replacement expert was murdered. Jane convinced Mel to investigate the backgrounds of students in the gardening class. Although she was shocked by the identification of the killer, readers should not be.

Give the series credit for a kindly heroine and a special award for titles.

Gwen Jones

Author: Jayne Castle, pseudonym for Jayne Krentz

Four Dell paperbacks were published in 1986 featuring Gwen Jones, operator of a temporary clerical service, and private investigator Zac Justis. The relationship between Gwen and Zac was initially adversarial. In *The Desperate Games,* Zac forced her to return to Starr Tech. He was aware that, while working at Starr, she had tinkered with the benefits program to help her sister. Still he needed Gwen to find the manipulator of the company records and killer of a systems analyst.

After they became lovers, Zac was assigned to guard Gwen's boss during his stay on islands off the Washington coast in *The Chilling Deception.* What had seemed a pleasant assignment became a dangerous joust with drug smugglers. *The Sinister Touch* involved Gwen and Zac with Mason Adair, a young artist who dabbled in witchcraft. In *The Fatal Fortune,* Sally Evanson, Gwen's employee at Camelot Services, consulted a psychic, Madame Zoltana. When Gwen investigated, the medium disappeared, probably because someone was blackmailing her clients.

The series may have appeal for young adults, conditioned to television formulas, less so to serious mystery fans.

Sara Joslyn

Author: Donald E. Westlake, who also writes as
Timothy Culver, Richard Stark, Curt Clark, and Tucker Coe.

Sara Joslyn, an attractive young journalism school graduate, had tired of her job at a small New Hampshire newspaper even before it succumbed to a takeover. She was ready for something totally different. She did not need the pressure of a daily paper because, after all, she wanted to be a novelist. Florida was copacetic because those New Hampshire winters had worn her down. The salary offered by *Weekly Galaxy* was terrific. There had to be something wrong with the checkout counter tabloid.

Author Westlake's irreverent (but possibly accurate) send-up of tabloid magazines in *Trust Me on This* (Mysterious Press, 1988) had Sara assigned to Jack Ingersoll's team. He, too, had once been an idealist, but had accepted the big bucks, and unlike his fellow reporters, salted it away. After that first exciting day Sara was busy learning the tricks of the trade—lying, impersonating, putting words into people's mouths, and misquoting them. She almost forgot about the dead man she had noted in the Buick on the way to work. Jack considered himself inured to the treachery required of staff, but it bothered him to see Sara become so good at it. Only the revelation of how relentless a *Galaxy* reporter could become, made it possible for Jack and Sara to solve a murder and regain some portion of their integrity. Not too much, though. They used blackmail to get new jobs.

The trial of country singer Ray Jones for murder in *Baby, Would I Lie?* (Mysterious Press, 1994) was just one of Jones's problems. The IRS was ready to attach his assets and earnings for the rest of his life. *Trend* magazine, where Sara and Jack now worked, sent her to Branson, Missouri to cover the trial. Later Jack joined her, working on an expose of the unethical and illegal methods used by their former employer, *Weekly Galaxy*. Sara gained entry into the innermost circles of the defense team with surprising ease, only to watch its strategy blow up in the courtroom. A too blatant device made her aware that a master schemer was manipulating her.

Westlake has a wicked wit. Enjoy it.

Helena Justina

Author: Lindsey Davis

A heroine set in the Rome of 70 A.D., even one of noble origin, would receive her status from the males in her family. Marcus Didius Falco, a scruffy spy and informer, could offer little but excitement to a woman of spirit. Yet, perhaps that was what she wanted. Regardless of their personal relationship, Helena, the daughter of a rich Roman Senator and wife of a prominent man, ranked far above Marcus in Roman society.

In *The Silver Pigs* (Crown, 1989), when Marcus escorted Helena home from Britain, proximity overcame propriety and they fell in love. Marcus, a paid informant, who did not know where his next toga was coming from, sought Helena's love when her husband was presumed dead.

By *Shadows in Bronze* (Crown, 1990), they had consummated their relationship, but Marcus was preoccupied with plots against the Emperor. Helena had a problem of her own. Her husband had resurfaced, but she was pregnant by Marcus.

The loss of the expected child left Helena depressed in *Venus in Copper* (Crown, 1991). Marcus was in prison accused by a jealous rival. Fortunately his mother bribed his way out of prison. He worked through a complex case in which a Roman matron had been accused of killing a series of husbands. Helena needed personal time in *The Iron Hand of Mars* (Crown, 1992). Titus, the Emperor's son, wanted her in Rome for his own purposes. When Emperor Vespasian sent Marcus to Germany to check out problems with Germanic tribes, he discovered Helena was already there, visiting her brother.

Although Helena acted as a peacemaker with Marcus's estranged father in *Poseidon's Gold* (Crown, 1994), she played only a minor role in Marcus' search for the treasure left behind by his soldier-brother Festus. Helena did not even have the satisfaction of marrying Marcus because his efforts to achieve middle class status were blocked.

Since Marcus was currently unable to rise to her social level, in *Last Act in Palmyra* (Mysterious Press, 1996), she descended to his, following him across the Mideast, searching for information for the Emperor and seeking a young musician. Marcus and Helena joined a group of traveling players, adding another task, finding the killer of a third rate playwright. Readers may find the journey almost as arduous as did the actors.

On their return to Rome in *Time to Depart* (Century, London, 1995) Marcus and his friend Petronius absorbed themselves in a search for a master criminal. Helena, again pregnant, kept busy by caring for an abandoned infant, assisting Marcus in his search for a stolen shipment of goods, and investigating a rash of kidnappings, which included Marcus's niece.

The pregnant Helena insisted on accompanying Marcus Didius Falco to the olive-growing portion of Spain then known as Baeticia in *A Dying Light in Corduba* (Century, 1996). She played only a minor role in his search for a murderous dancing girl, but delayed her delivery until Marcus could be at her side to assist in the process. Nothing had been resolved as to the child's status or to Marcus's elevation to equestrian so that the couple could marry.

Motherhood provided Helena with even less opportunity to share in Falco's investigations during *Three Hands in the Fountain* (Mysterious Press, 1999). Some elements of conventionality had permeated Falco's lifestyle—a new and larger apartment, and a partnership with his friend Petronius Longus. Petronius was at leisure because his romance with a member of a criminal family had caused his suspension from the Vigeles. Falco and Helena had both a professional and personal interest in the body parts surfacing in Rome's water supply: they and their beloved daughter Julia were drinking it, and Falco needed the business.

While Falco and a new ally, historical character Julius Frontinus followed the trail of a serial killer, Helena was preoccupied with familial duties. She had concerns about young Claudia Rufina, whom they had brought back with them from Spain. The young heiress was now engaged to Helena's brother, Aelianus. *Two for the Lions* (Century, 1998) had Falco and his former rival and enemy Anacrites, the Chief Spy, evaluating the assets of businessmen who provided the Circus games with animals and gladiators. The evaluation was to be the basis for taxes with the partners receiving a percentage of the collections. Falco was diverted by the death of a man-eating lion, and the murder of a dimwitted gladiator. Helena was concerned for her brother Justinus, who had run off with the bride designated for Aelianus. Although the ability of women to manipulate, to influence, and even to enter the deadly games was a factor, Helena's role was minor.

The tax collections had not only made Falco financially independent but resulted in his rise to the middle class and an appointment as Procurator of Poultry in *One Virgin Too Many* (Century, 1999). This affected his sense of freedom from societal pressures, but was too recent to keep him from invading the hallowed residences of the Vestal Virgins in search of a lost child whose family had a secret to keep. Helena had her moments, but it was Falco who risked his life and earned the plaudits of a trio of partners and ex-partners.

Falco's entry into Roman literary society in *Ode to a Banker* (Century 2000) brought him limited fame. Cleared as a potential suspect in the murder of publisher-banker Aurelius Chrysippus, he agreed to find the killer for his overburdened vigiles friend Petronius. Despite numerous upheavals in his own family, Falco questioned dissatisfied authors, unfortunate debtors of the Aurelian Bank, a disgruntled first wife, her restless replacement, and a son with aspirations. Helena, experiencing symptoms of another pregnancy, possessed the literary skills needed to pinpoint the killer. She and Marcus's sisters dealt with the problems arising from the death of his father's companion.

Davis's novels were replete with history and politics, enlivened by the witty self-deprecatory narrations by Marcus.

Jennifer Terry Kaine

Author: B. J. (Brenda Jane) Hoff

Jennifer Terry, a tall auburn-haired woman in her late twenties, had struggled with her religious faith. Her grandfather had been a minister. She had been raised as a devout Christian, but twin personal tragedies had challenged his beliefs. Her younger brother Loren was born with cerebral palsy. Her mother had died young of cancer. She was unwilling to make a personal commitment, but chose employment at a Christian radio station in West Virginia.

Jennifer's original goal had been to become an opera singer. To that purpose she had studied music in Rome, but, once told that her voice was not of operatic quality, gave up singing. She returned to Ohio, took a degree in broadcast communications at the state university, and went to work. Jennifer's first glance at the tall handsome man who was to become first her employer and then her husband revealed that Daniel Kaine was blind. That never mattered to her

Daniel restored Jennifer's faith during *Storm at Daybreak* (Tyndale House, 1986), partly by his patience with his blindness. The automobile accident caused by a drunken driver, which ended his athletic career, had brought short-term anger and depression, but Daniel had turned to religion to understand what had occurred. The persecutions of a deranged man helped Jennifer to restore her faith and Daniel to test his.

On their honeymoon during *The Captive Voice* (Tyndale, 1987) Jenifer and Daniel met Vali Tremayne, Christian singer who had retired after the death of her fiance, Paul Alexander. She and her close friend, David Keye, a young composer, became friends, going to an amusement park, sharing meals, and problems. During their meetings several accidents occurred. Jennifer and Vali both noticed that a bald man was present each time there was a mishap. Vali was considering a return to her career, featuring songs composed by David, but her terrible headaches made it difficult. Daniel's counsel to Vali made him a target of those who feared what Vali might remember.

By *The Tangled Web* (Accent/David C. Cook, 1988), not only had Jennifer and Daniel married, but his sister, Lyss and best friend, Gabe Denton had too. The four were prepaing the facilities of the Helping Hand Farm used as a vacation site for disabled children when three strangers came seeking refuge. Although they knew the young man and two children brought trouble, they could not turn them away. Their courage brought safety and a new sense of Christianity to those they helped. One aspect of Jennifer and Daniel's feeling for others was their decision to adopt Jason, a developmentally disabled boy, who had been living in an institutional setting.

Jennifer was sensitive to the needs of the vulnerable. In *Vow of Silence* (Accent/David C. Cook, 1988), she was concerned about Whitney Sharyn, director of the Friend-to-Friend Program which matched disabled children and adults. Not only had a man dressed in a Pierrot costume attacked Whitney, but she was spending her leisure time with Michael Devlin, a mysterious photojournalist. Whitney knew who had attacked her and why, but was reluctant to share her fears with Jennifer and Daniel, lest they too become victims of an obsessive and brutal stalker.

An opportunity to present a workshop at a music festival brought Jennifer and Daniel to Derry Ridge, Kentucky in *Dark River Legacy* (Accent/David C. Cook, 1990). New friends Mitch and Freddi were dealing with memories of the close relationship they shared before she left Derry Ridge to become a famous novelist. Abby, an elderly woman whose past had been obliterated, had no such memories, only a vague terror.

The series may not appeal to everyone, but provided competent mysteries based upon a Christian set of values.

Marlene Ciampi Karp

Author: Robert K. Tanenbaum

See: Marlene Ciampi, Page 57

Kyra Keaton

Author: Teona Tone

Kyra Keaton, an early Twentieth Century sleuth, was an attractive red-blonde with hazel eyes. She had lost her mother at age 11 and her father at 17. A rebellious young woman, she was dismissed from medical school after an affair with a faculty member. While in Paris, she lived with an artist, but eventually returned to America to become a private investigator.

In *Lady on the Line* (Fawcett, 1983), while researching the merits of nationalizing the telephone system, Kyra uncovered the mystery behind her father's death. During her investigation, she met and fell in love with U. S. Senator Gerald McMasters.

By *Full Cry* (Fawcett, 1985), Kyra had married McMasters, who had been intrigued by her independent spirit. Kyra had abandoned her career to preside over the McMasters' estate, but when Nathaniel Howard, Master of the Daisy Hill Hunt, died in a suspicious riding accident, she could not resist.

An early version of the light historical mystery; perhaps ahead of its time.

Charlotte Kent

Author: Mary Kittredge

Charlotte Kent wrote, not mysteries or romance novels, but "how-to" books. Actually she wrote whatever her agent Bernie Holloway told her to because she needed the money.

In *Murder in Mendocino* (Walker, 1987), faced with the prospect of writing "A Hundred and One Perfect Plywood Projects", Charlotte rebelled. She turned her attention to a history of Pelican Rock, California, her adoptive home, to rescuing Joey, a neglected twelve-year-old neighbor, and to murder.

Joey became Charlotte's foster son by the time *Dead and Gone* (Walker, 1989) began. While Charlotte monitored major surgery for the boy in a New Haven, Connecticut hospital, she wrote a book about how to protect yourself when a patient. Helen Terrell, Charlotte's friend and New Haven hostess, was suspected when her lover, a medical student, was murdered.

Putting freelance writing aside temporarily, Charlotte accepted a position as editor of a writer's magazine in *Poison Pen* (Walker, 1990). Wesley Bell, her most productive writer, was found dead in Charlotte's desk chair. Joey, who wanted to prove his right to be independent, joined the investigation with a bang. Competent.

Fiona Kimber-Hutchinson

Author: Len Deighton

See: Fiona Kimber-Hutchinson Samson, Page 258

Viera Kolarova

Author: Elizabeth Powers

Because many people read mysteries to escape from the drabness or pressures of their lives, immigrant domestics make unlikely sleuths. Viera Kolarova was a Czechoslovakian refugee who had been denied access to college in her own country. Her mother, the daughter of an industrialist and her doctor father remained in Prague. When Viera entered the United States in her early thirties, hoping to build a new life, she had limited skills. Over the years, she ushered in a theatre, worked in a fast food restaurant and a child care center, as a hotel maid, and pastry chef. She was gifted with total recall, high-spirited, and loved to dance and drink wine, but did not handle authority figures well. She described herself as 5' 7", sloe-eyed, having a Slavic face with high cheekbones and reddish curly hair.

In *All that Glitters* (Doubleday, 1981), Viera worked part time for the Orthodox Jewish family of Martin and Myra Heckle. One Friday evening she discovered Myra killed by an ice pick. Although the Heckler family was connected with the diamond market, Viera assumed it had been a domestic murder. She investigated with disastrous results, getting into trouble with the police and breaking her leg, but persisting.

Viera had a change of pace in *On Account of Murder* (Avon, 1984), working as a temporary secretary for Liliana Lukas, a cruel blackmailer. When Viera returned from an errand to find her employer dead, there were suspects in the office and in the Lukas family.

Viera was a quirky, unpredictable heroine, who received little attention.

Karen Kovacs

Author: Bill Granger wrote all books but some were published under the name Joe Gash

Karen was a slender blonde divorcee, raising a son from her marriage to an advertising executive who did not approve of her career as a police officer in Chicago.

In *Public Murders* (Granger, Jove, 1980), Sgt. Terry Flynn was an embittered man, investigating the rape and murder of a Swedish tourist in Grant Park. Chicago authorities, protective of the city's image as a tourist attraction, wanted the case, the latest in a series of killings, cleared. A wino found on the premises was a convenient suspect. The investigation by Flynn and Kovacs, whom he reluctantly accepted as his partner, was interspersed with reflections by the killer.

By *Priestly Murders* (Gash, Holt, 1984) Karen and Flynn had become intimate. A man wearing the uniform of a motorcycle policeman shot down Father Michael Doherty. Flynn was assigned the case but it was Karen who deduced that Doherty had been mistaken for a different priest.

Murder victims and suspects in this series came from powerful interest groups capable of exerting pressure on the police department—the tourist industry, the Catholic church, and in *Newspaper Murders* (Gash, Holt, 1985) the press and African-American civil rights groups. Reporter Francis X. Sweeney had been investigating the Brotherhood of Mecca when he was beaten to death. Pressure built for an early arrest, a scapegoat. Karen came up with a lead, but Flynn found the killer.

By *The El Murders* (Holt, 1987), Granger had dropped the "Joe Gash" pseudonym and used his own name. Karen had transferred out of the Special Squad to a precinct so she and Terry had less contact. When Flynn was assigned the murder of a white homosexual, the assailants were African-American. The precinct officers were content to write the death off as fag bashing. Karen thought otherwise. She and Terry were at odds with their assignments. Their relationship resumed only after he transferred to the airport police and she decided to go to law school.

The series was not for the tender minded. Granger's prose was raw and realistic, his murders messy, and his relationships troubled.

Meg Lacey

Author: Elizabeth Bowers

Meg Lacey, a Canadian sleuth, was brought to the attention of American mystery fans by Seal Press's International Women's Crime Series, along with Lonia Guiu by Maria-Antonia Oliver (Spain) and Katrin Skafte by Elizabet Peterzen (Sweden).

After her divorce, Meg shared her home with daughter Katie and son Ben. Her lover Tom, a biologist, spent time in the household, but was often away on field trips. Meg had learned to protect herself after having been raped. After ten years as an investigator, Meg was comfortable in the Vancouver area, the establishment and the underworld. She described herself as brown haired, of average height and weight.

In *Ladies' Night* (Seal, 1988), Fred and Gloria Chase hired Meg to find their nineteen-year-old daughter, Alison. Alison was engaged to Danny Haswell, the owner of a raunchy nightclub where Ladies' Nights were held. The promotion offered free alcohol and erotic stimulation to young (even teenage) females, followed by paid admissions for males, who could reap the rewards of the over-indulgence.

As *No Forwarding Address* (Seal, 1991) began, Sherry Hovey, who had been unsuccessfully dealing with postpartum depression, left her husband Glen, taking their four-year-old son. Meg found Sherry, but within 24 hours, the woman had been beaten to death. Meg used her connections and her aikido to find the killer and protect the boy. This was a subtle and complex narrative, which involved Meg's family and developed her character.

Elizabeth Lamb

Author: B. J. Morison

See: Elizabeth Lamb Worthington, Page 313

Raina Lambert

Author: Lloyd Biggle, Jr.

A tiny redhead, more than able to take care of herself, and head of the Lambert & Associates agency, Raina Lambert had only limited opportunities to display her talents. Jay Pletcher, staff detective, narrated and dominated the series, Raina appearing primarily by reference. She maintained offices in

Los Angeles and New York City, had a wide circle of friends and business acquaintances, so served as a "rainmaker" for the agency. In each case, she came on scene in some capacity.

During *Interface for Murder* (Doubleday, 1987), Raina and Jay flew independently to Sparta, Ohio to investigate a stalker who had injured one woman and terrorized others; and the death of a young computer expert who had developed a profile of the stalker. Raina appeared first as a guest of the industrialist whose employees were threatened, and later as a union organizer probing for drug suppliers.

During *A Hazard of Losers* (Council Oak Books, 1991), Jay probed a Los Vegas casino (the Diamond D) where too many winners had occurred in the keno games. Raina made appearances at the casino as a party girl at the gambling tables, a college student, and a drab secretary. She kept in regular contact with Jay by phone. Raina investigated a neo-Nazi group that might be involved in the scam, working in liaison with local and state authorities, but also shot an attacker who tried to kill Jay.

Jay was sent to Napoleon Corners, Georgia as *Where Dead Soldiers Walk* (St. Martin, 1994) began. General Bramwell Johnston, a born Northerner, had immersed himself in Confederate history and modern reenactments. His complex will left the bulk of his fortune to any grandchildren whom he had known in his lifetime. As he had been estranged from most of his children, the identity of grandchildren was a missing piece of the puzzle. Jay's concern for potential heirs was expanded when Raina came on scene as a granddaughter seeking to be reunited with the General. Complications arose from neighboring witches and monastic organizations that rehabilitated alcohol and drug abusers. Raina and Jay muddled through an incredible plot, playing Cupid in their spare time.

Marian Larch

Author: Barbara Paul

In her work as a New York City police detective, Marian Larch was a stolid perfectionist, scrupulously honest, and intolerant of inadequacies in fellow officers. After each arrest, she suffered from depression. On a personal level, she was a sexually active single woman in her thirties,

In *The Renewable Virgin* (Scribners, 1985), Marion appeared in a minor role investigating the death of a second-rate television writer. Actress Kelly Ingram, who narrated portions of the story, lent a hand, not only in trapping the killer, but also with Marian's post-investigation depression.

Good King Sauerkraut (Scribners, 1989), reissued as *King of Misrule*, concerned itself primarily with the metamorphosis of computer fanatic King Sarcowicz into a more empathetic person. The change came too late to avoid a series of deaths that might have been accidents or murders.

Marian appeared belatedly in *He Huffed and He Puffed* (Scribners, 1989) wherein a corrupt businessman pressured stockholders to sell their holdings. When the businessman was murdered, Marian and her partner Ivan Malecki identified which of several ex-killers had murdered again.

In *You Have the Right To Remain Silent* (Scribners, 1992), Marian found it traumatic to arrest a young girl for the murder of her mother. She had little time for remorse because her new assignment was to a multiple murder with national defense implications. With an irresponsible partner, Marian depended on Jake Holland, an unlikely FBI agent with whom she made an unusual bargain.

Holland, although he left the FBI, remained a part of Marian's life in *The Apostrophe Thief* (Scribners, 1993). Suffering from burnout and a hostile supervisor, Marian was ready to resign when handed an interesting assignment. Actress Kelly Ingram alerted her to theatrical theft, which led to murder. Success coupled with Jake Holland's affection restored Marian's equanimity.

Holland's and Larch's professional lives crossed again in *Fare Play* (Scribners, 1995) when Zoe Esterhaus, an operative in Jake's agency, witnessed the death of a man she had been following. The victim was finally identified as an ostensibly beloved businessman. Why would he be the target of a professional hit man?

By *Full Frontal Murder* (Scribners, 1997), Marian was a lieutenant, working to gain the confidence of her subordinates. Her fictional persona had changed from the stolid, rather depressed woman of the early books into a self-assured, sensual lover, who showed surprising touches of humor. Some credit for the change was due to Jake Holland's affection. She needed the humor and the self-assurance, when a crazed child kidnapper chose Holland as a victim to intimidate Marian. The tenor of this book was more personal, and more imaginative than earlier narratives.

Julia Larmore
Author: Sarah Caudwell, pseudonym for Sarah Cockburn

Although Julia Larmore and Selena Jardine were English women barristers, author Caudwell described their co-protagonist Hilary Tamar in such androgynous fashion that his/her gender could not be determined. Hilary was a professor on the Oxford law faculty and mentor to Selena and Julia's firm. Selena was a blonde in her mid-twenties, distinguished by a voice that was "unmistakable, smooth, and persuasive." She enjoyed sailing, often with her lover, Oxford Greek professor Sebastian Verity. Julia, an Oxford graduate who practiced tax law, was characterized as scatterbrained.

In *Thus Was Adonis Murdered* (Scribners, 1981), narrated by Tamar, Julia vacationed in Venice. Members of the firm shared her letters. When she was detained on suspicion of murder, the attorneys led by Tamar rallied to rescue her.

Caudwell's eagerly awaited second book, *The Shortest Way to Hades* (Scribners, 1985) found Julia as guardian ad litem for potential heiress Deirdre Robinson, whose interest in a trust was being challenged. After Deirdre was killed in a fall, Selena and Julia believed it was no accident. Subsequent letters from Selena to Tamar kept her/him apprised of the activities of other heirs and provided the clues that warned Tamar of danger and identified the killer.

In *The Sirens Sang of Murder* (Delacorte, 1989), the identity of the grantor for the Daffodil Trust could not be determined and the instructions for distribution of the assets were missing. Attorney Michael Cantrip went to the Isle of Jersey to investigate. His letters involved Selena, Julia, and Hilary, who had been hired to find the descendants of the alternate beneficiaries. Julia and an aging World War II hero rescued Cantrip and a suspect from drowning.

The long awaited fourth novel, *The Sibyl in Her Grave* (Delacorte, 2000) was published after Caudwell's death in January 2000. The delight that her fans felt to learn of the new narrative featuring the still androgynous Hilary Tamar and the legal practitioners at 62 and 63 New Square in London might be tempered on reading the book. There were many questions arising from the investment gains of Regina, Julia's aunt, and the possibility that insider information might have come from the reputable Renfrew Bank, a client of Selena. The subsequent deaths of a psychic, a vicar, and an annoying young woman left too many questions. A lesser Caudwell was, however, better than no Caudwell at all.

Caudwell's plots featured twists and turns that rivaled those of Agatha Christie. Developments often arose as the contents of letters were analyzed by those not on the scene of the crime. The technical background was well explained to keep the reader aware of the legal issues.

Mavis Lashley

Author: Robert Nordan

Mavis Lashley was kind and thoughtful, occasionally censorious, judgmental, and frequently tedious. Her nephew Dale, who worked as a police and newspaper photographer, shared information about crimes with her. The closeness between Mavis and her nephew seemed excessive at times, but she needed someone to love. Her only child, a daughter, had been killed in a car-bicycle accident. Her dedication to her deceased husband, John, caused Mavis to reject romantic overtures from a prosperous lonely widower. Mavis' affiliation with a Southern Baptist church dominated her existence. She practiced charity as a way of life. Her genuine interest in others often caused persons to share their intimate secrets.

Mavis was only being neighborly in *All Dressed Up to Die* (Fawcett Gold Medal, 1989), when she brought a covered dish to a bereaved home, only to learn that widow Theda Hedrick had disappeared. When Theda's corpse was found, Mavis located her daughter, missing since high school, and freed her from a vicious killer. In *Death Beneath the Christmas Tree* (Fawcett, 1991), Mavis sewed choir robes for the Christmas program, during which demure, but pregnant Frances Sedbury was shot. Mavis identified Frances's killer and turned her over to the police, but concealed other information.

In *Death on Wheels* (Fawcett, 1993), Officer Morgan, her former Sunday school pupil, convinced Mavis to go undercover in Lakeview Nursing Home as a temporarily disabled patient. Several residents had died unexpectedly and Mavis was to discover the killer. Encumbered by a cast on her leg, she wheeled and dealed through the institution making friends, confusing enemies and uncovering sexual improprieties.

Annie Laurance

Author: Carolyn G. Hart

See: Annie Laurance Darling, Page 66

Jane Lawless

Author: Ellen Hart, pseudonym for Patricia Boehnhardt

Jane Lawless was a successful Minneapolis restaurateur whose family accepted her lesbian orientation. Her circle of friends included those who were gay or straight, male or female, single, divorced, married or widowed. She was portrayed in a broad social context with limited explicit sex, and well balanced plots. Jane was tall, chestnut haired with violet eyes. Because her deceased mother had been from England, she spent several years there with her Aunt Beryl. Her father, Raymond, a Twin Cities defense attorney, had never remarried but had a long standing heterosexual live-in lover who was accepted by Jane and brother Peter, a television cameraman. As the series began Jane was in her thirties, still mourning the cancer death of Christine, her lover for ten years. She managed the Lyme House Restaurant in South Minneapolis, served as an alumnae advisor to the University of Minnesota chapter of Kappa Alpha Sorority, and shared the theatrical interests of friend, Cordelia Thorn, also a lesbian.

Kappa Alpha was the focus in *Hallowed Murder* (Seal, 1989). While walking her dogs, Jane discovered the body of Alison Lord, an undergraduate member. Police assumed the death to be a suicide, triggered by a lesbian relationship. Jane uncovered the motive for the murder; then, set a trap for the killer. In *Vital Lies* (Seal, 1991), Leigh Elstad needed help when her rural inn was vandalized and prospective guests discouraged by a planted news story. The romantic and inter-familial ties were complex.

Stage Fright (Seal, 1992) took Jane into Cordelia's world of live theatre where she encountered the complex Werness family. The decision as to who would inherit playwright Gaylord's copyrights was clouded when a previously unknown member of the family made his presence felt.

Cordelia was delighted to join the exclusive Gower Woman's Club of Minneapolis in *A Killing Cure* (Seal, 1993). She invited Jane there for dinner shortly after young Emery Gower was accused of killing his Aunt Rose. Rose Gower, German professor Charlotte Fortnum, poetess Mae Williams, and art curator Miriam Cipriani were the members of an inner circle that controlled the Gower Foundation. When Charlotte also died in an "accident", Jane investigated both deaths. She risked rape at the hands of an arrogant male, but suffered more from her friends than her enemies.

A Small Sacrifice (Seal, 1994) centered on Cordelia. While in college during the early 1970's, she had belonged to a tightly bonded group in the Drama Department, the "Shevlin Underground." The members met rarely over later years as imprisonment, marriage, success and failure separated them. They were reunited in the small Wisconsin town where alcoholic actress Diana Stanwood operated a theater. Their intent was to convince Diana to enter a treatment center. They were diverted when a member of the group died and the others were suspected.

Faint Praise (Seal, 1995) involved Jane with the residents of Linden Lofts, a warehouse converted into apartments. The owner, Arno Heywood, had rented to family and close friends, but one was too close for comfort. After Arno committed suicide and Jane's friend Roz Barrie felt threatened, Jane rented Arno's apartment. She persevered through an additional murder, but found someone she might be able to love.

Misunderstood words during childhood provided one aspect of the mystery in *Robber's Wine* (Seal, 1996). All three Dumont children became suspects in the death of their mother. Jane and Cordelia were guests of the family but wore out their welcome when their investigation came too close to home.

By *Wicked Games* (1998), Hart had a mainstream publisher, St. Martin's Press. Initially Jane had no idea that the house she purchased had been the scene, a decade before, of a fatal accident to a ten-year-old boy. Nor did she realize that her new tenant and an aggressive neighbor were related to the child. Bothered by suspicions of her lover (Dr. Julia Martinsen), who had recently relocated in Northern Minnesota, and the absence of her aunt and uncle who were visiting England, Jane was vulnerable to manipulation. The discovery of a child's bones under the tile of her patio, and the death of a private investigator propelled Jane into an interfamilial struggle that had no winners, and left her seriously injured.

Jane's physical and emotional condition was so pronounced that she moved to Julia's rural home and office to recover. In *Hunting the Witch* (St. Martin, 1999), her troubles followed her. The murders of a retired Marine colonel and a Catholic priest exposed not only Julia's connections with ailing homosexuals, but also the greed of others who preyed upon them.

In *The Merchant of Venus* (St. Martin, 2001), Hart expanded her series beyond Minnesota to encompass the dilemma of lesbians and gays who concealed their sexuality to protect careers, particularly in the entertainment industry. Cordelia's estranged sister, Octavia, invited her to take part in her marriage to an elderly but distinguished film director. Jane, still bruised physically and emotionally, agreed to accompany Cordelia to Connecticut. The reason for Octavia's unusual marriage, the consternation it brought to the groom's friends and family, and the deaths that followed were explored in the narrative. In the process Cordelia learned the truth about her mother's death, and the reader learned a great deal about the movie industry.

Loretta Lawson

Author: Joan Smith

Loretta Lawson, a blonde Ph.D. in English Literature, was employed at London University. Her marriage to newspaperman John Tracey ended in separation, although not initially divorce. Loretta, a militant feminist who viewed marriage as a patriarchal system, had short-term physical relationships outside of marriage, but was disturbed when Tracey wanted a divorce.

In *A Masculine Ending* (Scribners, 1988), she traveled to a Paris conference for a feminist literary magazine. Free occupancy of a friend's apartment seemed a boon, until Loretta realized that murder might have been committed on the premises. Even though she eventually learned the identity of the victim and his killer, she felt no need to share her discovery with the police.

Loretta (birth name Laura) was thirty-two and recovering from glandular fever when *Why Aren't They Screaming?* (Scribners, 1989) began. Her visit to the countryside engaged her in confrontations between peace demonstrators and the supporters of the American Air Force base. When her hostess was murdered, Loretta uncharacteristically responded like a heroine of the 1930's.

In *Don't Leave Me This Way* (Scribners, 1990), Loretta offered Sandra, a casual acquaintance from a support group, a place to stay in an emergency; then, could not get rid of her. Sandra's later disappearance was solved when she was killed in a car accident. Loretta reconvened the support group to investigate whether it had been murder.

Loretta found it difficult to deal with the marriage and pregnancy of her friend Bridget in *What Men Say* (FawcettColumbine, 1994). She did not approve of Sam Becker, the American who had swept Bridget off her feet. When a corpse was discovered on the Becker property during a housewarming party, both Sam and Bridget were suspected. Despite its polemical tone, the narrative was interesting.

Full Stop (FawcettColumbine, 1996) lacked the bite or bravado of prior books. During a stopover in New York City, Loretta ruminated on scenery, food, cab drivers, and theatre. There was a murder, even a plot, in there somewhere, but it took attention to find it.

Although extremely intelligent, Loretta was self-absorbed.

Rina Lazarus

Author: Faye Kellerman

Rina Lazarus, the daughter of Hungarian Jews who had survived Nazi concentration camps, had sapphire eyes and long ebony hair. Her husband Yitzchak, an Orthodox scholar, died of a brain tumor, leaving her with two young sons. She lived in the conservative, highly structured world of a Yeshiva.

Rina met Los Angeles Police detective Peter Decker in *The Ritual Bath* (Arbor House, 1986). A woman had been assaulted in the bath managed by Rina, so it was appropriate for her to serve as the liaison between the shy victim and the investigating officer. Only when Decker became convinced that Rina was the intended victim and rescued her was the murderer identified. Decker came to love Rina and understand her faith. Later, learning that he was Jewish, he joined joyfully in its practice.

Rina became Decker's wife, but in the next few books: *Sacred and Profane* (Arbor House, 1987); *Milk and Honey* (Morrow, 1990); *Day of Atonement* (Morrow, 1992); and *False Prophet* (Morrow, 1992), she faded into the background.

Although Peter had a teenage daughter from a prior marriage, and took a parental role with Rina's sons, he was delighted when Rina became pregnant. However, in *Grievous Sin* (Morrow, 1993) the baby's birth was difficult, requiring a hysterectomy. Peter realized the physical impact of barrenness for Rina, but could not relate to her psychological reaction.

Rina could not understand why Honey Klein, a casual friend in high school, chose to visit her in California during *Sanctuary* (Morrow, 1994). When Honey's husband Gershon, a diamond merchant, was found murdered, she and her children disappeared. The New York City murder connected with a California case and the disappearance of two boys. Peter and Rina worked together (he, as the assigned detective; she, as interpreter), journeying to Israel to find the "lost boys" and Rina's friend.

Later books, such as *Justice* (Morrow, 1995) were subtitled as "Peter Decker/Rina Lazarus", but this could be misleading. Rina was background again while Peter balanced his concerns about his daughter, Cindy, now in New York City, with the murder of a high school student. In *Prayers for the Dead* (Morrow, 1996), a major suspect in the murder of a prominent heart surgeon had played an important role in Rina's life before she met Peter, causing a conflict of interest. However, the narrative was a police procedural in which she had no significant role.

Peter's relationship with Rina, his daughter Cindy, and the members of his squad were tested in *Serpent's Tooth* (Morrow, 1997) when he was accused of sexually harassing the daughter of two murder victims. Jeanine Garrison's parents had been among those assassinated in what seemed to be the insane act of a disgruntled restaurant employee. Peter's gut instinct that there were two "shooters" was supplemented by physical evidence, but Jeanine had powerful friends in the community. Rina, although she rarely opposed the volatile Peter, secretly recruited an ally who provided valuable evidence.

Rina played a minor role in *Jupiter's Bones* (Morrow, 1999), during which Peter, Detective Marge Dunn, and an assortment of public officials coped with murder (single and mass) in a cult compound. *Stalker* (Morrow, 2000), had even less room for Rina, as the focus shifted to her stepdaughter. Cindy, who joined the Los Angeles police force, had found difficulty stepping out of her father's shadow.

The horrors of Treblinka, a Polish concentration camp during World War II, hung over *The Forgotten* (Morrow, 2001). The power of the past motivated a high school student to vandalize the synagogue where Rina, Peter and their family attended. Peter's unit investigated prep schools and adult hate groups in search of the intruders. The focus moved from that single incident to a series of four murders related to greed and parental need for achieving children. Amid the bigotry and sexual excess, Rina found consolation for a bereaved father.

The series provided interesting information about the Orthodox Jewish faith, romance and action within a police procedural format.

Anna Lee

Author: Liza Cody, pseudonym for Liza Nassim

Anna Lee, a British equivalent to the hard-boiled American sleuth, worked within Brierly Security Agency, although she often chafed at her assignments. She was tiny with hazel eyes, a single woman who lived in a London apartment building. The downstairs tenants, Bea and Selwyn Price, were among her closest friends. She viewed her childhood as repressed. Although her mother and sister were alive, Anna's contacts with them were infrequent. She was knowledgeable about cars, took part in motor rallies, swam and played squash for recreation. After five years as a policewoman, she had become phobic about crowded public transportation. A career woman, with a strong work ethic who left school at sixteen, Anna lived modestly and avoided violence, particularly the use of guns.

Anna was introduced in *Dupe* (Scribners, 1981), when she investigated the motor accident in which Deirdre Jackson, an experienced driver, had been killed. Anna's boss wanted the case treated routinely, but Anna researched the last year of Deirdre's life. She literally took a beating on this case. *Bad Company* (Scribners, 1983) began with a child custody investigation, but Anna was taken prisoner when she intervened in the kidnapping of the daughter of a witness in a criminal case.

Stalker (Scribners, 1984) was a downer. Anna not only had a disappointing love affair with a married man, but both Brierly and the police department discouraged her inquiries into the disappearance of Edward Marshall, owner of a furniture reproduction business.

Gifted sixteen-year-old Thea Hahn was visiting a cousin when she disappeared in *Head Case* (Scribners, 1986). Anna eventually returned the frightened unresponsive girl to her parents, but needed to understand the two missing weeks.

The agency contracted Anna's services to J. W. Protection in *Under Contract* (Scribners, 1987). Anna was to escort Shona Una, a young rock star who traveled with an entourage. Anna was framed on a drug charge, and failed to prevent serious injury and heartbreak to Shona.

By *Backhand* (Doubleday, 1992), Brierlys had become too involved in electronic security to suit Anna. Her private life was unsettled by Selwyn's efforts to prevent their landlord from selling the building, and by her lover's wish to stabilize their relationship. An assignment to trace another missing teenage girl offered a trip to Florida with posh accommodations and a chance to play tennis, but there were layers of sexual and criminal intrigue involved. The narratives had short chapters, but expanded on Anna's character and her need to have both a career and a personal life.

Anna had "walk-on" roles in Cody's other series, *Bucket Nut* (Doubleday, 1993), *Monkey Wrench* (Mysterious Press, 1995), and *Musclebound* (Mysterious Press, 1997). The protagonist was Eva Wylie, a female wrestler, who resented Anna's involvement in her life. The Arts & Entertainment cable network has carried feature mystery movies based on the Anna Lee series.

Constance Leidl

Author: Kate Wilhelm

Constance Leidl and her husband, Charlie Meiklejohn, were partners. He was a retired New York City police detective, who took early retirement because of burnout. Constance was a Ph.D. level psychologist who had taught at Columbia University. They could have lived comfortably on their investments and pensions, but chose to work as investigators. Their adult daughter Jessica had moved away, but several cats shared their home. Constance was a tall graying blonde with blue eyes, proficient at aikido and willing to use it. The couple had a loving physical relationship that added warmth without diverting from the plot. Charlie's investigative skills predominated, but he relied on Constance's experience as an interviewer, her insights, and professional knowledge.

Constance and Charlie, without last names, were introduced in several short stories, which related more to science fiction than to murder; e.g. *With Thimbles, with Forks, and Hope* in Wilhelm's book *Listen, Listen* (Houghton Mifflin, 1981). They reappeared in *The Hamlet Trap* (St. Martin, 1987) as Charlie Meiklejohn and Constance Leidl who had relocated from their New York City apartment to rural New York State. After two murders occurred among members of a regional theatre group in small town Oregon, the estranged grandparents of a suspect hired Charlie and Constance to investigate.

The Dark Door (St. Martin, 1988) called on Charlie's skills as an arson expert. Local fire departments were unwilling or unable to control fires in abandoned buildings that were connected with outbreaks of unexplained violence. Constance's skills were vital when a pattern of bizarre behavior by people without a medical history of instability emerged.

Smart House (St. Martin, 1989) referred to a computerized home built in Oregon to showcase electronic systems developed by a brilliant young scientist. When he and the architect were killed during a computerized "Murder Game", Charlie investigated.

Sweet, Sweet Poison (St. Martin, 1990) returned to a more conventional mystery format. As in several prior books, the relationships among the characters were developed before Constance and Charlie came on scene. David, a young Ph.D. candidate, who believed a friend's dog had been poisoned, was murdered.

Charlie had never liked Tootles Olsen, Constance's college classmate. He was infuriated when, in *Seven Kinds of Death* (St. Martin, 1992), Constance visited Tootles. After he learned of the vandalism of art works in Tootles's spacious home, and the death of editor Victoria Leeds, Charlie joined his wife. The narrative dwelt on the theory that artists have a special gift for which they pay a price, usually in some personal unhappiness or tragedy.

A Flush of Shadows (St. Martin, 1995) was a collection of short stories; mysteries, science fiction, and some blends. St. Martin also published a two volume collection of the above narratives: *The Casebook of Constance and Charlie, Volume I* (1999) contained *The Hamlet Trap, Smart House,* and

Seven Kinds of Death; The Casebook of Constance and Charlie, Volume II (2000) included three novelettes along with *The Dark Door* and *Sweet, Sweet Poison.*

Wilhelm bridged the genres of science fiction and mystery.

Denise Lemoyne

Author: Joyce H. and John William Corrington

The New Orleans based series used a trio, with each taking dominant roles in different books. Wes Colvin, a redneck reporter in the big city, narrated *So Small a Carnival* (Viking, 1986). His investigations brought conflict with the powerful Lemoyne family. He made friends with Denise, a young attorney who challenged her father's political ambitions.

Captain "Rat" Trapp of the New Orleans Police Department, friend to both Wes and Denise, was the primary character in *A Project Named Desire* (Viking, 1987), a moving story about a woman Trapp loved and a son he never knew. *The White Zone* (Viking, 1990) took Trapp to Los Angeles where he traced the killer of the great love of his life.

Although Denise had an impact in the other narratives, her book was *A Civil Death* (Viking, 1987). She worked with Wes (by then her lover), and Trapp in her capacity as an assistant district attorney. A member of a socially distinguished family, she entered the seamiest and most dangerous parts of the community. Professionally aware of hit men, Denise suspected that one had been employed to kill Madeline Holman St. Juste, her godmother. Madeline's husband, Rene, a redneck who made good in New Orleans, was the obvious suspect to everyone but Denise. The insights she gained from her investigation helped to resolve her problems with Wes.

These were gripping books, difficult to put down, although the use of dashes, rather than quotation marks, was disconcerting.

Darina Lisle

Author: Janet Laurence

Darina Lisle, a caterer, was a tall single blonde whose first contact with the criminal justice system in *A Deepe Coffyn* (Macmillan, London 1989; Doubleday, 1990) came as a suspect. Cousin Digby Cary, chairman of the Society of Historical Gastronomics, appointed Darina to supervise arrangements for the annual Symposium. The gathering of culinary experts curdled when Digby was stabbed to death. Darina, who discovered the corpse and inherited Digby's substantial estate, attracted both the professional and personal interest of upper class Sgt. William Pigram.

The daughter of a rural doctor and his vivacious widow, Darina yearned to own a small hotel with quality food service. The sale of her catering business plus Digby's legacy made this possible. She postponed this project in *A Tasty Way to Die* (Doubleday, 1991) to help former fellow student Eve Tarrant. Eve, an ambitious businesswoman with a second career as a television chef, was seriously affected when a luncheon guest died of poisoned mushrooms.

Pigram and Darina had become lovers by *Hotel Morgue* (Doubleday, 1992) during which Pigram introduced Darina to the Hotel Morgan, its terrible chef, and desperate owner, recent widow Ulla Mason. Darina seriously considered a partnership, but had to clean up the murder of an unidentified pregnant female first. The excitement attracted Hon. Ann Lisle, Darina's dominating mother, both a help and hindrance.

Recipe for Death (Doubleday, 1993) returned Darina to London as a cookbook editor and food columnist, but without Sgt. Pigram whose proposal she had rejected. Verity Fry, winner of a cooking contest, invited Darina to the Somerset area where the Fry family ran an organic meat ranch. Cooking was relegated to the back burner when close family friend Natasha Quantrell was poisoned.

Darina and William decided to marry. *As Death and the Epicure* (St. Martin, 1993) opened, she prepared to meet his family. His mother disapproved of Darina's commitment to a cookbook she was writing for Finer Foods. The volatile personalities and alliances on the Finer Foods Board of Directors led to a shocking murder.

William's reaction to Darina's new television career was a significant factor in *Death at the Table* (St. Martin, 1997). The "Table For Four" panel included a charismatic Australian winegrower who alienated cast and crew. His death might have been considered normal had there not been two succeeding deaths among his family and co-workers. With William pre-occupied with his work and the London police unimpressed, Darina found the killer to avoid being the next victim.

Marriage to William was happiness beyond Darina's expectations in *Death a la Provencale* (Macmillan, 1995). On their honeymoon in southern France, they visited Darina's friend Helen, a culinary expert. Her husband Bernard was renovating a mill to begin an olive oil business. After Darina and William visited friends of his family, they returned to discover Bernard dead. Within the households they had visited, there were multiple suspects for his killer.

Diet for Death (Macmillan, 1996) returned Darina to England, a few pounds heavier and ready to accompany her widowed mother to a health spa. Among the other guests were a much younger widow and a half dozen people whom she had irritated to death. Darina, feeling left out when William allied himself with the rude and chauvinistic local inspector, pursued her own investigation.

In *Appetite for Death,* (Macmillan, 1998) there were problems in the marriage. William had more administrative responsibilities, a considerable commute because Darina did not want to move to his new post The stress caused a recurrence of his eczema. More significantly, Darina, having lost both her column and her television show, was "at liberty." Still she was unwilling to consider having a child, very important to William. Their personal problems were interwoven into Darina's investigation of the parentage of Rory, motherless nephew of Jemima Ealham, an old friend of Darina. Jemima wanted Rory's father identified because she felt her own family could not provide a wholesome upbringing. Darina's search intersected with an arson/murder investigation headed by William where her insight pointed him to the killer.

In exchange for advice to the chef and a program for the other passengers, Darina and William were offered a free cruise to the Norwegian fjords in *Mermaid's Feast* (Macmillan, 2000). William needed a respite from his responsibilities but within days he was drawn into an investigation when first a crewmember, then a passenger, were murdered. He was instrumental in exposing a drug smuggling ring, but it was Darina's careful observations of their fellow passengers and her gift for eliciting confidences that exposed an unrepentant killer. Darina's unexpected morning sickness and the motivation for the murders spotlighted the joys and perils of motherhood.

Interesting characters in complex plots.

Sgt. Hilary Lloyd
Author: Sheila Radley, pseudonym for Sheila Robinson

Chief Inspector Douglas Quantrill, the hero of the Radley series, had appeared in several prior books. The characterizations of his family were skillfully drawn, but his professional companion was Sgt. Hilary Lloyd, a former nurse. Hilary had been assigned to his station in *The Quiet Road to Death* (Scribners, 1984). Her presence fueled Molly Quantrill's taunts about women on the job; understandable because Hilary, despite a slight facial scar, was an attractive single in her early thirties.

In *Fair Game* (Constable, 1984), Martin Tait, Quantrill's assistant (soon to be promoted) was living with Alison, Quantrill's daughter. Quantrill was unhappy with Tait in general and with this connection in particular. Alison was not keen about taking part in a hunting party held by one of Tait's upper class acquaintances. The murder of Hope Meynell, lovely fiancée of Will Glaven whose father was hosting the event, might have been an accident. Having trained as a nurse before going into police work, Hilary's medical background enabled her to pinpoint the motive for the murder.

Although both Quantrill and Hilary appeared in *Fate Worse Than Death* (Scribners, 1985), Martin Tait, reassigned elsewhere, was the primary figure. He was still in love with Alison, Quantrill's daughter. His position was threatened when he was a suspect in his aunt's death.

In *Who Saw Him Die* (Scribners, 1988) Quantrill, coming to grips with his age and new status as a grandfather, was so immobilized by an accident to son Peter, that Hilary stepped in and solved a murder on her own.

Proximity to Quantrill continued to create problems for Hilary, leading to a short-term liaison that had ended by *This Way Out* (Scribners, 1989), which was a variant on the *Strangers in a Train* plot. As in *Cross My Heart and Hope to Die* (Scribners, 1992), Radley concentrated her narratives on the suspects, not on the police.

Hilary and Quantrill worked well as a team, spurred on at times by Tait's involvement, but her role was clearly subordinate. She was a skillful interviewer, and made significant discoveries in physical evidence.

Clarissa Lovelace

> Author: *Nathan Aldyne, pseudonym for*
> *Michael McDowell and Dennis Schuetz*

The series featured a couple—heterosexual Clarissa Lovelace and homosexual Dan Valentine.

In *Cobalt* (St. Martin, 1982), Clarissa was an independent young woman who had worked at a real estate office and a gift shop, but planned to enter law school. She visited Valentine, a friend and former lover in Provincetown, Rhode Island. The death of a drug dealer, the protegee of Clarissa's gay Uncle Noah, involved Clarissa and Dan in detection.

In *Slate* (Villard, 1984), Clarissa had returned to Boston and entered law school. In addition she co-owned (with Dan) a gay bar financed by Uncle Noah. A corpse discovered in Clarissa's bed brought in authorities who were not always sympathetic to gay bars.

During *Canary* (Ballantine, 1986) Clarissa and Dan investigated a serial killer who strangled gay men. Clarissa was listed in Hubin as having made one other appearance: *Vermillion*, (Avon, 1980)

LuEllen

Author: John Sandford, who initially wrote the first two books under his real name, John Camp

The primary figure in the series was Kidd, an unscrupulous computer hacker, who sold his skills to the highest bidder. Occasional attacks of guilt were shrugged off or overcome by a sense of vendetta justice. Kidd killed when needed to defend himself, but also out of revenge. When not working, Kidd's passion was fishing. He owned an apartment in St. Paul, Minnesota and eventually acquired one in New Orleans. His cat (Cat) was deposited with an elderly neighbor when he worked. He had a fascination with Tarot cards. This was not a belief that they could predict the future as much as a sense that their use helped him to see beyond the obvious.

Kidd had no close attachments. His longest standing relationship was probably that with LuEllen but it was periodic and never reached the level of commitment. In specific assignments, Kidd often needed access to the homes and offices of company officials. Lacking the necessary skills he turned to LuEllen. Their association had begun when he caught her robbing an apartment in his building. He insisted that she disrobe before releasing her but there was never any force between them. They had sex when and where it was convenient; each knowing that monogamy was not part of the arrangement. Kidd was aware that LuEllen had come to depend on cocaine to sustain her when she was under stress. Although he was displeased and unwilling to join her, he made no demands. She tried to quit several times. At times she could get high on the expectation of risk.

LuEllen was a tiny woman with dark hair who never revealed her last name, even to Kidd. Although she generally wore western garb, she could dress appropriately when the occasion demanded. She had grown up in a small town, dropped out of high school, but gave little other background information.

LuEllen could be reached only through a contact in Duluth. When called to action, she would appear entering his apartment silently, sometimes when he was asleep. Her skills went beyond the mechanical. She could size up the potential of a target, knowing which buildings were worth the risk, what time of day or night the entry should be made, and what alarms would summon the police or security forces. Her initial goal had been to accumulate enough money to live comfortably, but she was unable to quit at that point. When an assignment ended, she disappeared from Kidd's life, going to warmer climates, playing golf or gambling although she always saved a percentage of each payoff.

Kidd accepted an offer of $2,000,000 from Rudolph Anshiser to ruin a competitor in the aviation business by disrupting computer systems in *The Fool's Run* (Henry Holt, 1989 by John Camp). He needed help so in addition to LuEllen, he recruited Bobby Duchamps, a young African-American computer hacker with a terminal disorder, and Dace Greeley, a discredited reporter. Each had specific assignments for which he/she would be well paid. Kidd failed to note that his Tarot cards warned him of betrayal, or that LuEllen and Dace had fallen in love. He had to shutdown major industries to save his life and hers.

Bobby Duchamps had been there for Kidd, so when he asked a favor in *The Empress File* (Henry Holt, 1991 by John Camp), there was no choice. This brought Kidd and LuEllen to a small Mississippi River town riddled by official corruption and bigotry. Kidd developed a plan that would not only turn the rascals out of office, but pay dividends to him and LuEllen. Unfortunately murder was part of the price that had to be paid.

It was neither greed nor loyalty to a friend that motivated Kidd in *The Devil's Code* (Putnam's, 2000). It was fear. Jack Morrison, who had worked with Kidd, LuEllen, and Bobby in earlier capers, had been murdered. Within days rumors floated that Firewall, a group of rogue hackers, had attacked government computers and become a danger to national security. Among those identified by their hacker nicknames were Bobby and Kidd. With help from Lane Ward (Jack's sister) and the regular cast of characters, Kidd protected himself and other hackers from undue harassment by federal agencies. His leverage came from the discovery of a scam by a major government contractor. Because her sense of justice differed from his, Kidd did not share with LuEllen the murders he committed along the way.

Isabel Macintosh
Author: Herbert Resnicow with puzzles by Henry Hook

Isabel Macintosh, an attractive older woman, began the series as an English professor at Windham University in Vermont, then moved up through administrative positions to become acting president. She frequently visited New York City, where her lover, retired attorney Giles Sullivan, lived. They had met shortly after the death of Giles' wife. There had been a time when she would have accepted a proposal, but he was still in mourning. When he was ready, their informal relationship had become enough for her.

She was visiting Giles in *Murder Across and Down* (Ballantine, 1985). Members of the Crossword Club competed for substantial prizes in a contest presided over by Giles as trustee for the Cornelius van Broek estate. Harvey Brundage, an obnoxious arbitrageur, was poisoned at a meeting of the competitors held at Giles's home. The suspects were quarantined until the guilty party was determined by (how else?) responses to a crossword puzzle.

Six assistant professors at Windham were utilizing material from crossword puzzles in an experiment on how to help children learn in *The Seventh Crossword* (Ballantine, 1985). Their domineering mentor was murdered. Giles, then visiting Isabel, developed a puzzle that would identify a killer, but Isabel conducted the interviews with the suspects. She risked her life, confronting a killer who had devised a way to combine phonics with puzzles.

The Crossword Code (Ballantine, 1986) brought Giles and Isabel into an even more select group than the crossword fanatics, the super secret Semiotics Institute. An elderly genius and his four brilliant daughters solved cipher and code problems that were beyond the skills of government officials. Someone close to the U. S. President was leaking significant information about his stance on demilitarization. Isabel, who had been displeased when told that she was sufficiently single-minded to risk danger to an associate, wondered if that analysis might be correct.

Conflicting van Broek heirs provided another puzzle murder in *The Crossword Legacy* (Ballantine, 1987). Isabel's unexpected arrival disrupted the quarrelsome sextet as they searched for hidden messages leading to a major inheritance. The premise had become formulaic by *The Crossword Hunt* (Ballantine, 1987). A wealthy benefactor to Windham, Abraham Hardwick considered a major donation to establish a school of "generalist studies." He would select the chairman based upon general knowledge as shown through skill at crossword puzzles. When Abe died before changing his will to set up the trust, Isabel's secretary Aggie, whom he had loved for forty years, inherited. Isabel carried responsibility for interviewing the candidates, but Giles was the major player.

Elizabeth MacPherson

Author: Sharyn McCrumb

See: Elizabeth MacPherson Dawson, Page 69

Kate Maddox

Author: Erica Quest, pseudonym for John and
Nancy Buckingham Sawyer

Kate Maddox, a widow whose husband had been killed in a hit and run accident, was a professional police officer. She began as a WPC (Woman Police Constable) in the British provincial system and was gradually promoted into administration.

By *Death Walk*, (Doubleday, 1988), Kate had become the first female Chief Inspector in the Cotswold Division. This promotion meant moving to a district that had never had a woman at command level. Kate coped while solving a prickly hit and run murder in which newspaper publisher Richard Gower was a suspect.

In *Cold Coffin* (Doubleday, 1990), Kate regarded the disappearance of Sir Noah Kimberley, head scientist at an agricultural chemical company, as "not police business." She changed her mind when his assistant was found dead.

Kate had become more comfortable in her job, in her own home, and in a relationship with Richard Gower by *Model Murder* (Doubleday, 1991). Then she learned that former model Corinne Saxon, victim of a vicious murder, was once Richard's mistress.

A chance encounter while Richard and Kate vacationed in Portugal led to her involvement in a murder during *Deadly Deceit* (Piatkus, 1992). After her return to England, a series of murders alerted Kate to the fact that she had been duped. Fortunately the pieces fell into place so that she could turn embarrassment into triumph. The usual conflict of interest between reporter/editor Richard and police official Kate was not a problem here.

Quest wrote well, kept the action flowing, but did not develop Kate as a character to the level of Charmian Daniels, Norah Mulcahaney, or Christie Opara.

Zee Madeiras

Author: Philip R. Craig

See: Zee Madeiras Jackson, Page 139

Claire Malloy

Author: Joan Hess a.k.a. Joan Hadley

Claire Malloy was a green-eyed, redheaded widow rebuilding a personal life, while running a marginally successful bookstore in Fayetteville, Arkansas. Her cynicism came from experience. Husband Carlton, a professor at the local college, had been notably unfaithful before he died in an automobile accident. She had a teenage daughter Caron whose problems occupied a substantial amount of her time. Claire shared a relationship with Detective Peter Rosen, but never hesitated to conceal information from him or challenge his conclusions.

In *Strangled Prose* (St. Martin, 1986), Claire finally agreed to have an autograph party for local author Mildred Twiller. After Mildred's murder, the fact that a major character in her new book was modeled on Carlton added Claire to the suspect list. On the plus side, this was how she met Rosen.

During *Murder at the Murder at the Mimosa Club* (St. Martin, 1986), the Mimosa Club staged an updated version of the "murder game" for weekend guests, including Claire and a reluctant Caron. Peter joined the party when real murder spoiled the fun.

Peter was adamant that Claire should stay out of criminal investigations so they clashed in *Dear Miss Demeanor* (St. Martin, 1987) one of the most amusing of the series. Claire served as a substitute teacher at Farberville High School, hoping to prove that senior teacher Emily Parchester had neither falsified her accounts nor murdered the principal and janitor.

Claire showed her vulnerability in *A Really Cute Corpse* (St. Martin, 1988). Local merchants sponsored a beauty pageant featuring the current "Miss Thurberfest", Cyndi Jay. When shots were fired, it was unclear whether Cyndi Jay or the handsome young politician escorting her was the target. Although she was a supportive mother, Claire did not express affection easily.

Caron's weight problem provided a humorous subplot in *A Diet to Die For* (St. Martin, 1989). Chronic dieter, Maribeth Galleston convinced the naturally indolent Claire to accompany her to exercise classes, but something terrible was happening to Maribeth.

Claire made it abundantly clear that she disliked pets. Then, why was she dog sitting, haunting animal shelters, and leading a Disney-like gang of pet lovers to rescue stolen animals in *Roll Over and Play Dead* (St. Martin, 1991)? Because underneath that brittle exterior beat a heart of mush.

Claire and Caron traveled south in *Death by the Light of the Moon* (St. Martin, 1992) to visit Carlton Malloy's Louisiana family. The narrative provided Southern mystery staples: a decaying mansion, a household of eccentrics, the death of a matriarch, and a disputable will to challenge Claire's skills.

The antics of coeds in the sorority house next door to Malloys kept Claire busy in *Poisoned Pins* (Dutton, 1993). Claire, who attended college in the Sixties when sororities were considered passe, was not surprised to learn the Kappas had a corpse in their chapter closet.

Claire's relationship with Peter Rosen was fragile in *Tickled to Death* (Dutton, 1994), just when she needed him to keep her out of jail. Her friend Luanne Bradshaw convinced Claire to probe the mysterious deaths of her new lover's prior wives. Pedodontist Dick Cissel did not appear to be a Bluebeard, but the authorities in the county where he resided were unconvinced.

Emily Parchester, Claire's elderly friend, called upon her in *Busy Bodies* (Dutton, 1995). Zeno Gorgias, the heir to nearby residential property, used his front yard for displays that offended local sensibilities. Unfortunately Caron and her best friend Iris played parts in the presentation. After a fire in which Zeno's estranged wife was killed, Claire played hide-and-go-seek with the primary suspect to the dismay of Peter Rosen.

Claire ventured far from Peter's sphere of influence when she and Caron sought a blackmailer in Mexico during *Closely Akin to Murder* (Dutton, 1996). Claire's loyalty to a cousin convicted of murder and sentenced to a Mexican jail prompted her to investigate, stirring up fear among the real killers. She risked her own well-being and Caron's for a solution that may leave readers less than satisfied.

Peter Rosen was out of town, giving Claire a taste of jealousy in *A Holly Jolly Murder* (Dutton, 1997) but that was only one of her problems. Caron's job at the mall was proving to be a liability—a $1,000,000 lawsuit. Claire, stung by inferences that she was stodgy, proved otherwise when she made connections with a druidical group, each member of which was a murder suspect.

Just when Claire and Peter were contemplating marriage, he revealed in *A Conventional Corpse* (St. Martin, 2000) that his former wife had requested that he become the father of her child. This added complication to their future was unacceptable to Claire. Their subsequent exchanges were supplications for understanding on his part and vicious rejections on hers. The narrative featured brittle dialogue as highly literate mystery authors converged on Farber College for a convention. Roxanne, editor at a major publishing company who had played a decisive role in the lives of five authors, was murdered. Overwhelmed by personal disarray and responsibilities at the conference, Claire still identified an unrepentant killer.

Joan Hess is one of an elite group of women writers (including Anne Perry, Margaret Maron, Elizabeth Peters, Carolyn Hart, Charlotte MacLeod, Agatha Christie, Marcia Muller, Susan Dunlap, and Lia Matera) who developed two or more mystery heroines, keeping them distinct and interesting.

Sheila Malory

Author: Hazel Holt

Sheila Malory was a tiny good-natured widow, whose charm belied her impressive credentials. Sheila credited Dorothy L. Sayers' *Gaudy Night* with encouraging her to attend Oxford. She worked as a literary critic without losing her taste for daytime soap operas and old Hollywood movies.

She lived in rural England with a Westie named "Tristan", a Siamese named "Foss", and a second less credentialed dog, Tess. Her husband Peter had been dead for several years. Her son Michael was initially studying law at Oxford. Although her father had been a clergyman, an inheritance from her mother left Sheila with no financial problems.

As *Mrs. Malory Investigates* a.k.a. *Gone Away* (St. Martin, 1989) began, old beau Charles Richardson returned from America with an attractive fiancée, Lee Montgomery. When Lee disappeared, Charles who had returned to the United States, asked Sheila to investigate. The discovery of Lee's corpse set Sheila on what seemed to be a fascinating game. Her enjoyment ended when she became personally involved with the suspects.

In *The Cruelest Month* (St. Martin, 1991), she returned to Oxford and the Bodleian Library for research. After library employee Tony Stirling found the body of a retired librarian under a pile of shelving, Sheila investigated. Her probe reunited Sheila with friends from her college days but disclosed humiliating revelations about the past.

Adrian Palfrey, the victim in *Mrs. Malory and the Festival Murders* (St. Martin, 1993) a.k.a. *Uncertain Death,* used his appointment as literary executor of the Lawrence Meredith reminiscences to embarrass and enrage fellow Taviscombe residents. Sheila, pleasantly inclined towards widower Will Maxwell, did not want him suspected of murder.

During *The Shortest Journey* (St. Martin, 1994), Sheila searched for an elderly woman who had disappeared from the local nursing home, leaving her potential heirs in confusion. Not even a marked grave ended the search.

In *Mrs. Malory: Detective in Residence* a.k.a. *Murder on Campus* (St. Martin, 1994), Sheila lectured at Wilmot College in Pennsylvania, where faculty infighting was a major sport. She accepted a formal resolution of a double murder investigation, even though she knew the real killer had not been identified.

Sheila ambled her way through another local crisis in *Mrs. Malory Wonders Why* (Dutton, 1995), when a visitor bearing gifts poisoned an elderly friend. Such a travesty of hospitality was not to be borne. Sheila had the assistance of her friend, Rosemary, and Rosemary's son-in-law Roger, now heading the Taviscombe police, in unraveling the schemes of an unscrupulous woman.

Sheila's son Michael chided her for being too tender-hearted in *Mrs. Malory: Death of a Dean* (Dutton, 1996) because she supervised a festival at the local cathedral even though she detested the arrogant dean. David, the dean's brother and a dear friend of Sheila's, became the primary suspect when the dean was poisoned while drinking his tea. Interesting supporting characters, as usual.

Everyone seemed to tolerate boring solicitor Graham Percy, as *Mrs. Malory and the Only Good Lawyer...* (Macmillan, London, 1997) began, but he had pushed someone too hard. As a friend of her husband's, Sheila had resigned herself to his annual visits. His murder while her guest led to a search of his possessions, which included blackmailing files. Sheila identified an unrepentant killer with whom she sympathized.

In *Mrs. Malory: Death Among Friends* (Signet, 1999), Freda Spencer had sewn the seeds of murder for decades by her domineering ways, her rejection of those she ought to love. When Freda was murdered, Sheila focused on one suspect after another: humiliated lover, rejected child, injured "friend", and hopeful beneficiary for the one who could no longer tolerate Freda's behavior.

Fatal Legacy (Macmillan, 1999) reunited Sheila with friends from her Oxford college days. Renowned author Beth Blackmore, recently dead from an overdose of medication, had named Sheila as her literary executor. An unpublished manuscript among Beth's papers disclosed a woman whom Sheila did not recognize, but whose search for fulfillment led to murder.

The return of youthful solicitor Thea Wyatt to Taviscombe in *Mrs. Malory and the Lilies That Fester* (Signet, 2001) seemed the answer to Sheila's prayers. Within months, the friendship between Thea and Michael (Sheila's thirty-year old son) led to an engagement. Their wedding plans were temporarily derailed when Thea was arrested for the murder of an unpleasant associate. Even when Thea had been personally exonerated, Sheila persisted until she identified the killer.

An opportunity to teach English at an exclusive girl's school might not have attracted Sheila in *Delay of Execution* (Macmillan, 2001), had it not been that Michael and Thea's marriage had left her lonely. She was to be a single term replacement for a dynamic teacher who had concentrated her efforts on a select group of students. Blakeney's School for Girls had a reputation for solid scholarship. Felicity Robinson, the new headmistress, planned to expand the science and mathematics department at a cost that some faculty considered excessive. Felicity's unexplained death put an end to the implementation but not to suspicions among students and staff.

The narratives were short, easy to read, and low-key. They provided villainous victims and highly motivated suspects but limited tension. Suspects rarely went to trial and physical evidence was not a major consideration.

Dawn Markey
Author: Caroline Burnes, pseudonym for Carolyn Haines

Along with Ann Tate and Veronica Sheffield, Dawn Markey was one of a trio of characters, each of whom played the dominant role in one of Caroline Burnes Harlequin novels, while having minor parts in others.

Phantom Filly (Harlequin, 1989) featured Dawn Markey who was responsible for Dancing Water Ranch while Ann Tate and Matt were on their honeymoon. A video made Dawn aware that Private Stock, a filly sired by Speed Dancer a horse that was stolen from the ranch four years before, was running races. If this phantom filly was currently a three-year old, then it might still be possible to find Speed Dancer. Dawn was not the only one who had received the tape. Luke O'Neil, a trainer with a dubious reputation, was also on the trail. Luke and Dawn joined forces against the "Boss," a man who wanted revenge against them and against Ann Tate, Veronica Sheffield and their spouses.

Although the love scenes were typical of pulp paperback romances, the series was interesting particularly when read in sequence—*A Deadly Breed* (Harlequin, 1988), *Measure of Deceit* (Harlequin, 1988) and *Phantom Filly* (Harlequin, 1989). Also see: Veronica Sheffield, page 266 and Ann Tate, page 279.

Helen Markham

Author: Eileen Dewhurst

Helen Markham was close to forty, frustrated as an actress, and mired in a second rate British repertory company. The end of her twelve-year marriage to John Markham was inevitable by the time they separated. John had been serially unfaithful. Her dear friend, Ken who had managed the production of the plays was too ill to continue. His replacement cast Helen in supporting roles, often playing elderly or disabled women.

An offer to play a strong role in a new television series provided an option for Helen in *Whoever I Am* (Doubleday, 1982), when she anticipated she would be fired. So she quit first, and then notified John that she was setting up her own home in a small coastal town. Rehearsals for the television series would not begin until fall but Helen's performance as an invalid in her most recent play brought her to the attention of British Intelligence. There had been two mysterious deaths in a nursing home utilized by the government for their agents in need of recuperation. Helen's assignment was to find the foreign agent responsible for the murders while posing as a developmentally disabled woman. Her agency contact Julian Jones filled other needs, although at one point she considered him a suspect.

Coincidences played a strong role in *Playing Safe* (Collins, 1985). Helen's resemblance to a distinguished physicist enabled her to portray the woman as a patient in another institutional setting. An unexpected pregnancy and danger to Julian forced her to play a more active role than in the previous book.

Daisy Marlow

Author: D. Miller Morgan

Daisy Marlow, a tough middle-aged investigator, was left with a San Diego detective agency when her husband Joe was killed on a stakeout. She was short, overweight and profane, addicted to hard liquor, designer lingerie, and jewelry. When not working, she lounged around the house in shapeless muumuus. Daisy carried a .357 Magnum, and drove a 1964 light blue Pontiac called "Edna Elizabeth."

At a time when her old beau, Las Vegas Police Captain Sam Milo was overwhelmed in *Money Leads to Murder* (Dodd, 1987), Daisy was hired to trace a missing club singer. She had to find out whether the young woman was missing or dead.

In *A Lovely Night to Kill* (Dodd, 1988), Daisy and Sam Milo investigated the arson of a house trailer, in which a man and two children were killed. The wife, Jeannie, escaped only to be abducted.

Clio Rees Marsh

Author: Jo Bannister

Clio Rees was in transition—an English medical doctor who became a mystery novelist; a "diminutive" single woman in her 40's who married a detective inspector.

In *Striving with Gods* (Doubleday, 1984) Clio would not accept the death of her friend Luke Shaw as part of a homosexual suicide pact. She moved into Luke's apartment, using her medical knowledge to pinpoint the killer. When the deduction ended, the action began.

By *Gilgamesh* (Doubleday, 1989), Clio had married Inspector Harry Marsh. In his absence, Clio visited David and Ellen Aston on an occasion when David was seriously injured and a John Frederick Herring horse painting stolen.

To recuperate, the Marshes sailed leisurely along the coast of Scotland in *The Going Down of the Sun* (Doubleday, 1989). While anchored in a secluded cove, they witnessed an explosion on the "Shara-Sun" and rescued the only survivor. He was subsequently accused of having killed his employer. This was a tense narrative, but Bannister held off her solution for a surprising finish.

This was an excellent series that used realistic medical clues and an attractive heroine. It went no further. In the Nineties Bannister introduced Inspector Liz Graham and her fellow professionals in a British police procedural.

Chris Martin

Author: Annette Roome

Auburn haired Chris Martin was in a mid-life crisis. Her children, Richard (20) and Julie (16), had no sympathy for their mother's belated ambition to become a newspaper reporter. Her unfaithful husband Keith preferred that she remain a housewife.

As *A Real Shot in the Arm* (Hodder, 1989; Crown, 1991) began, Chris found a job on the *Tipping Herald*. Her editor assigned her to cover a conference on Drug and Alcohol Abuse. During a recess in the proceedings, Chris discovered the body of high school teacher Michael Stoddard hanging from the fire escape. Chris began an affair with divorced fellow reporter Pete Schiavo. Even when she was taken hostage, Chris got no respect at home.

By *A Second Shot in the Dark* (Crown, 1992) Chris had moved to Pete's apartment. Daughter Julie joined her there, while Richard moved in with a friend. Pete's former wife's new husband was arrested for the murder of a married woman. The murder resembled others that had occurred in the area. Without encouragement, Chris investigated the wild parties held by the woman's employer. Dangerous, yes, but she had become a risk taker. It was too late to turn back.

A simple interview with former rock star, Rick Monday in *Bad Monday* (HarperCollins, 1998) expanded into a murder investigation. Add in a series of burglaries, and an exposé of environmental hazards in a housing development. Chris's investigation went far beyond the role assigned her by publisher Heslop, and even further beyond the limits set down by the local C. I. D. Although she kept her job under pressure, Chris's identification of Rick's killer had an unexpected outcome. She grew in her sense of independence from Heslop, from her lover, Pete, and from the demands of motherhood. Pete's suggestion that they marry was what Chris had thought she wanted. Now she was unsure.

Deceptive Relations (Collins, London, 1999) was disappointing. Chris muddled her way through a cluttered narrative that included two suicides, three murders, several threatening attacks and a trio of suspects. She found evidence of municipal misdeeds and obtained a confession from a killer, but only after exposing herself to considerable danger. Perhaps it was a time of uncertainty. Her former husband and his intended were expecting a child; her daughter would soon be leaving for college. These factors sensitized Chris to the fact that her own biological clock was running.

Interesting and unconventional.

Daphne Matthews

Author: Ridley Pearson

Daphne "Daffy" Matthews, a psychologist on the staff of the Seattle Police Department, lived alone on a houseboat. She and her associate Sgt. Lou Boldt shared a short-term physical relationship. However, he was married with a child.

Boldt was the primary character in *Undercurrents* (St. Martin, 1988), a police detective whose marriage was in deep trouble. A serial killer totally absorbed him at work. It also provided frequent contacts with Daphne whose skill in hypnosis and interrogation helped trap the killer.

Boldt had left the police force by *The Angel Maker* (Delacorte, 1993). He and Daphne had not seen one another for two years. While working as a volunteer at a local youth center, Daphne became aware of assaults, some ending in death, during which vital organs were removed from the victims. She suspected an organ harvesting crime, and needed Boldt's help. He had been spending his nights as a piano player and days acting as househusband while his wife supported the family. The criminals, their relationships, and motivations were significant elements of the narrative.

Boldt was working full time at the police department by *No Witnesses* (Hyperion, 1994). Daphne was seriously involved with wealthy food manu-facturer Owen Adler who was being threatened anonymously. He was to shut down his business and kill himself or his company would be bankrupted and he would be murdered. The culprit polluted Adler food products, trigger-ing police involvement. A wholesale slaughter was averted after Boldt and Matthews combined forces.

Daphne had not rid herself of her longing for Boldt, now the father of two children. During *Beyond Recognition* (Hyperion, 1997), she realized that there was no hope for a relationship, but that she did not love her fiancé Owen Adler enough to marry him. Meanwhile she lost her heart to a twelve-year-old who had been abused by his stepfather. She and Boldt trapped an arsonist who utilized high temperature accelerant to murder single mothers who resembled one another. Poor Daphne was left bereft of all the males in her life.

Boldt's wife Elizabeth, with whom he had reconciled, was ill with cancer as *The Pied Piper* (Hyperion, 1998) began. He spent most of his time at her hospital bed. The abduction of a four-month-old Seattle child had been connected to nine similar cases on the West Coast. These were serial crimes; not kidnapping for ransom; possibly connected to a moneymaking adoption racket. Boldt's supervisors wanted the case solved before the FBI took over. They came to realize that pressure had been placed on investigat-ing officers to leave the abductions unsolved.

By *The First Victim* (Hyperion, 1999), Liz's cancer was in remission, which she ascribed to prayer, a concept that Boldt could not accept. Daphne made minor appearances in support of the Boldt marriage and as occasional professional advisor to Lou. Melissa Chow, who was investigat-ing the illegal importation of young Asian women for sweatshops and brothels, disappeared. Boldt's efforts to break the smuggling ring and find Melissa were impeded by differing priorities between the Seattle Police Department and the Immigration Service.

The "blue wall" of solidarity among cops toppled in *Middle of Nowhere* (Hyperion, 2000) when members of the Guild (the bargaining unit for police officers and detectives below the rank of lieutenant) came down with "blue flu." A new police chief had ended overtime and second jobs to meet budget cuts. The men and women affected had budget problems of their own. Boldt, with Daphne's assistance, sought to separate the cases of burglary/attacks by professional criminals from those by rogue cops. In their probe they left themselves open to blackmail, but did not succumb to the pressure. Amidst mayhem and death, Daphne took personal risks unworthy of her training and experience.

These were tense action oriented narratives in which Daphne played a subordinate, but significant role.

Georgia Lee Maxwell

Author: Mickey (Michaele) Friedman

Divorcee Georgia Lee Maxwell decided that life as society editor for the *Florida Bay City Sun* no longer met her needs. She was tired of kowtowing to the local society leaders. Her short marriage to "good old boy" Lonnie Boyette had left her restless. She was too young to be a spinster, too smart to vegetate in Bay City. There was time to change her life.

In *Magic Mirror*, (Viking, 1988) Georgia assessed her skills. Although she had never attended journalism school, she could write and was conversant in French. For what *Good Look* magazine would pay, Georgia Lee was willing to go to Paris as a stringer. She witnessed an armed robbery/murder at the Musee Bellefroide while interviewing the dour art restorer. Georgia Lee had the excitement she had coveted. She was kidnapped, suspected by the police, and discovered the prosaic motive for the robbery.

Georgia was well enough established by *A Temporary Ghost* (Viking, 1989) to ghost write Vivien Howard's memoirs. Vivien intended not only to defend herself against the unproven charge that she had murdered her wealthy husband, but also to make money doing so. At Vivien's Provencal home, Georgia's fellow guests included the other suspects in Vivien's husband's murder. There was a disappointing climax to Georgia's efforts.

She was an interesting sleuth in a short series.

Dr. Tina May

Author: Sarah Kemp, pseudonym for Michael Butterworth

Pathologist Dr. Tina May served as consultant to Scotland Yard and appeared on a popular television program. She was a composed ash blonde who owned a three-floor building in which she occupied the two lower levels. Her alcoholic ex-husband Jock lived in the attic. This pleasant arrangement was damaged when Jock married Tina's secretary. Although successful, Tina was embittered by the sacrifices a woman was expected to make in a medical career. She had an intimate and loving relationship with her mentor, Dr. John Kettle. There were several other men during the series, but never one who was a serious long-term prospect.

No Escape (Doubleday, 1984) began with a green-eyed woman character, possibly amnesiac, who moved from job to job, leaving death and injury in her wake. Tina tied the deaths to a serial killer, presenting her speculations on television. Clues from the casebooks of a deceased doctor and her knowledge of the modus operandi took Tina beyond the obvious solution.

Tina became interested in the deaths of senior citizens who had withdrawn money from their banks shortly before being found drowned in their baths in *The Lure of Sweet Death* (Doubleday, 1986). The common thread, she discovered was the victims' desire for death.

What Dread Hand? (Doubleday, 1987) sent Tina on vacation to a colleague's cottage. She found no relief in the country. She was harassed, rejected by the locals, and upset by serial drownings and a coven of Satanists.

Quin St. James McCleary

Author: T. J. MacGregor, pseudonym for
Trish Janeschutz a.k.a. Alison Drake

See: Quin St. James, Page 256

Nina McFall

Author: Television actress Eileen Fulton

In the series subtitled *Take One for Murder*, Nina McFall was described as single, 5' 8", and redheaded with jade-green eyes. She was born and raised in Madison Wisconsin by a social activist mother and a physician father. After graduation from college, Nina taught high school while active in the local theatre. She found work in the Milwaukee Repertory Theatre and finally, tried her luck in New York City. The role of villainous career woman Melanie Prescott on *The Turning Seasons* made Nina famous. She was sexually active but discriminating, looking for the right man; perhaps, divorced Police Lt. Dino Rossi.

- In *Take One for Murder* (Ivy, 1988), Nina and Dino met when her producer was murdered. Rossi cultivated her initially to get inside information on possible suspects.

- By *Death of a Golden Girl* (Ivy, 1988), Nina and Dino were established lovers. Added characters in *The Turning Seasons* created stress that led to murder. The pattern that evolved was that Nina would ignore Dino's request to stay out of investigations. When she persisted, she would be threatened and/or attacked, but provide crucial clues.

- *Dying for Stardom* (Ivy, 1988), focused on the murder of a novice actress selected in a nationwide contest to play a role on *The Turning Seasons*.

- *Lights, Camera, Death* (Ivy, 1988) introduced several devoted viewers of the television series. One was so obsessed with Nina—or the character she portrayed—that Dino's life was endangered.

- In *A Setting for Murder* (Ivy, 1988), an antique broach, which Nina was to wear, triggered an absurd plot about insanity and remorse.

- *Fatal Flashback* (Ivy, 1989) moved the characters from New York City to a country home rented by Nina for the summer. The house had been the setting for murder ten years earlier. The convicted "killer" returned. Nina had Dino and cast members available as guests but the suspects were local.

The books developed Nina and Dino's affair and his son Peter's acceptance of Nina. The dialogue was at the level of a daytime serial.

Jenny McKay

Author: Dick Belsky a.k.a. Richard G. Belsky

Television station WTBK, which ranked 7th out of 7 local stations, sought to boost its ratings with *South Street Confidential*. The program featured Jenny at a difficult time in her personal life. She had turned forty after a failed marriage and an unsuccessful affair. For sympathy she depended on a miniature dachshund, Hobo and her mentor Joe Gergen.

In *South Street Confidential* (St. Martin, 1989) a.k.a. *Broadcast Clues* Jenny was less than enthusiastic about covering the wedding of Kathy Kerrigan and Bradley Jeffries. When Jenny arrived for an interview, she learned that the bride had disappeared. The wedding was postponed. Kathy was searching for her "deceased" father, whom she thought she had seen during television coverage of homeless men.

Jenny was demoted at WTBK for her use of foul language on the air as *Live from New York* (Jove, 1993) began. When an attractive hooker offered Jenny the inside story on a six million dollar bank theft, Jenny thought she had her ticket back to regular news. It was not that simple. The Mafia, an out-of-town assassin, and politicians had their own agendas.

Jerry Meredith, a lover whom Jenny had never quite forgotten, hit the big time in *The Mourning Show* (Berkley, 1994). He remembered Jenny when accused of his rich wife's murder. Pesin, Jenny's unscrupulous news director, temporarily bought her loyalty with promises of advancement. Shocked by the death of a young battered wife and the scorn of her friends and co-workers, Jenny reset her priorities.

Jenny was depressed as *Summertime News* (Berkley, 1995) began. The death of a young woman in a park would have been a routine story, except that she was living under an assumed name. Jenny, intrigued by the deception, and by the disappearance of a beloved family dog, tracked "Katie Thomas" in the past and the future.

Patience "Pay" McKenna
Author: Orania Papazoglou who also writes as Jane Haddam

Among the sleuths of the Eighties, romance writer Pay McKenna was notable for her dimensions (6 feet tall and 125 pounds) and her affluent New England heritage. In contrast, her best friend and former college roommate, Phoebe (Weiss) Damereaux, was 4' 11" short. A blonde with waist length hair, Pay grew up in Waverly, Connecticut, attended Emma Willard School and Greyson College for Women. Her parents, John and Louisa, enjoyed a 32-room Connecticut home. Pay occupied an unfurnished twelve-room New York City condo she had inherited from a friend.

Sweet Savage Death (Doubleday, 1984) took place during a convention of romance writers. The death of aging writer Myrra Agenworth was labeled a mugging until literary agent Julie Simms was found dead in Pay's locked apartment. Pay and Greek attorney Nick Carras sought the killer because Pay was the obvious suspect.

In *Wicked, Loving Murder* (Doubleday, 1985, also published in 2000 under the same title but as written by Jane Haddam), Pay reluctantly interviewed prominent romance writers for *Writing*, a second rate literary magazine. When she opened a closet in her new office, the corpse of the publisher's nephew fell out.

Pay offered fledgling writer Sarah English a place to stay and an introduction to "the girls" in *Death's Savage Passion* (Doubleday, 1986). When Pay was incapacitated for three days due to poison, no one would believe that Sarah had also been poisoned and died.

Pay adopted a child and seriously considered marriage to Carras. First she shared a book tour with a coterie of highly caricatured romance writers in *Rich, Radiant Slaughter* (Doubleday, 1988). She discovered a crusader against sexy romance novels dead under a table at "The Butler Did It," well known Baltimore mystery bookstore. Phoebe, unmarried and pregnant, was aware that she might be carrying a disabled child. Personal problems had to be ignored until Pay found the killer.

Wedding plans were underway in *Once and Always Murder* (Doubleday, 1991) when Pay returned to her extended family in Waverly. The planning was disrupted when a high school friend was found hanging in a greenhouse.

Marriage seemingly ended Pay's career.

Abby Novack McKenzie

Author: Al Guthrie

See: Abby Novack, Page 212

Francesca Wilson McLeish

Author: Janet Neel (Cohen)

See: Francesca Wilson, Page 307

Stoner McTavish (Lucy B. Stone)

Author: Sarah Dreher

Although Stoner McTavish was named Lucy B. Stone at birth in honor of the 19th century feminist, she chose her own version of the name – Stoner. Stoner McTavish's sexual orientation had been unacceptable to her parents. Rigid and insensitive, they killed her dog when she demanded independence. She had not grown into a happy woman. She was moody and suffered from nightmares, which she believed foretold her future. The sustaining person in Stoner's life had been her Aunt Hermione, a practitioner of spiritualism. Stoner divided her professional life between her Boston detective business and a travel agency that she operated with Marylou Kesselbaum.

Stoner's relationships had been tinged with violence. She and high school teacher Gwen accidentally killed Gwen's husband in *Stoner McTavish* (New Victoria, 1985). Gwen had been a battered wife, whose grandmother was a friend of Aunt Hermione. At the grandmother's request, Stoner had traveled to Wyoming to investigate the man whom Gwen, an heiress, had married so suddenly.

Aunt Hermione convinced Stoner to visit Maine in *Something Shady* (New Victoria, 1986) to investigate the disappearance of a nurse working at Shady Acres Mental Hospital. Gwen and Stoner encountered local hostility when they probed Shady Acres' non-medical activities.

In *Gray Magic* (New Victoria, 1987), Stoner and Gwen explained their relationship to Gwen's grandmother; then, went to Arizona to visit Stell, a friend of Stoner's. While there, they were drawn into a contest between the Hopi Indian spirits of good and evil.

During *A Captive in Time* (New Victoria, 1990), Stoner was transported into the Colorado Territory of the 1870's where she met a young woman whom she would never forget—according to review material.

In *Otherworld* (New Victoria, 1993) she visited Disney World, where her business partner Marylou was kidnapped—according to review material.

Gwen was still Stoner's "partner" in private life in *Bad Company* (New Victoria, 1995), when Stoner and Marylou relocated their travel agency in Shelbourne Falls, Massachusetts. The three were to share a house. While Marylou settled in, Stoner and Gwen visited Sherry Dodder, owner of an inn that catered to "wimmin" and produced feminist plays. The group was wracked with jealousy.

This series featured inventive plots but in *Shaman's Moon* (New Victoria, 1998) author Dreher moved deeper into a spiritual world, timeless and metaphysical where some readers may not care to travel. Was it a mystery at all? Perhaps, in a spiritual sense. What was the crime? Attempted theft of Aunt Hermione's soul. How could it be prevented? Only by Stoner's journey into that timeless, spaceless world to face the enemies (including herself).

Cathy McVeigh

Author: Eileen Dewhurst

See: Cathy McVeigh Carter, Page 56

Tish McWhinny

Author: B. (Barbara) Comfort.

Tish (Letitia) McWhinny, an artist who had trained in France, began her childless marriage when she was in her forties. After her husband's death, she resumed her career as a portrait painter, and was sustained by good friends like publisher Hilary Oats. She had multiple interests: cooking, her riding horse, and a brindle bulldog. She did not let widowhood end her life.

Tish was a very active sixty-five-year-old in *Phoebe's Knee* (Foul Play Press, 1986, reissued 1994). Her suspicions had been aroused by the arrival of a cult, the "Ring of Right", into quiet Lofton Village, Vermont. When reporter Lew Weber disappeared, Tish investigated the reclusive cultists and the death of their guru.

Tish was seventy-three in *Grave Consequences* (Foul Play, 1989, reissued 1994) but showed no sign of slowing down. She owned an Isuzu Trooper in which she chased thieves through the hills until someone sent her over a cliff. Tish absorbed Sophie, her niece's stepdaughter, into her household, and sought the kidnapper/killer of a museum volunteer.

In *The Cashmere Kid* (Foul Play, 1993), Sophie, now a goat farmer, temporarily left her assistant in charge. When he disappeared, so did her prize stud, "William the Conqueror". Tish and Hilary herded goats, chased toxic waste transporters, and found a regretful killer.

During *Elusive Quarry* (Countryman, 1995), Sophie divided her affections between two beaus. When Tish defended Sophie from charges of arson when her house was blown sky high, Hilary was on hand to help. He became a victim when his car was rigged to crash.

To please Hilary, Tish allowed herself to become involved in possible art fraud in *A Pair for the Queen* (Foul Play/Norton, 1998). After Hilary's beloved godson Bruce was murdered and a restored painting stolen, Tish had no choice but to investigate. Hilary was not only depressed—he was a suspect. The narrative was heavy on subplots (pornography, insurance fraud, kidnapping, former wives and former lovers) and marred by an abrupt ending. It was difficult to understand how Hilary and Tish could bypass the authorities for so long.

Alvira Meehan

Author: Mary Higgins Clark

Alvira Meehan had worked as a cleaning woman and her husband Willy as a plumber until they won the New York Lottery. Forty million dollars changed their lives, but not their natures. Both were in their fifties, enjoyed a secure marriage, but were childless. Alvira spent money on new clothes, dyed her hair brown, and enjoyed time at a fashionable California spa. Even though they purchased a condo that overlooked Central Park, they kept the small apartment in which they had lived before the windfall. The Meehans traveled and shared their largesse with others, but made conservative investments with at least half of their annual income.

The supporting characters of Alvira and husband Willy were so endearing in *Weep No More, My Lady* (Simon & Schuster, 1987) that Clark returned them in a book of their own. In *Weep No More...* Alvira had visited Baroness Min von Schreiber's spa to meet the elite, while improving her self-image. Her natural curiosity and guileless friendliness put her in the middle of a murder investigation that almost led to her death.

The Lottery Winner (Simon & Schuster, 1994) was a collection of short stories, many of which had been published previously, as follows:

- Alvira took an interest in a despondent young neighbor who had been convicted of a crime she did not commit;

- An elderly woman was accused of killing the husband who defrauded her of a lottery win;

- A corpse appeared in the Meehan's bedroom closet. Alvira helped the Baroness von Schreiber who ran the California spa, traced a kidnapped infant, and rescued Willy from kidnappers.

Alvira's investigative skills were supplemented by the use of a sunburst pin that contained a recording device. The pin had been given to Alvira by the New York Globe, which published her column.

All Through the Night (Simon & Schuster, 1999), was a Christmas treat with the entwined adventures of Alvira and Willy. The Meehans restored an abandoned child to her mother in time for the nativity pageant and confounded crooks who endangered Sister Cordelia's after-school care center. Short but sweet.

Clark joined with her daughter, Carol Higgins Clark, author of the Regan Reilly series, in *Deck the Halls* (Simon & Schuster, 2000). A pair of disgruntled bumblers had kidnapped Regan's father, Luke Reilly, and an employee of his funeral home. Hints dropped by Luke in a phone exchange and clues from friends brought about a rescue in time to save the victims from a cold, cold death. Regan and Alvira had met in the waiting room of a dental office. A light Christmas tale.

Susan Melville

Author: Evelyn E. Smith

Readers who believe courts no longer dispense justice and that criminals are coddled, will find an empathetic heroine in Susan Melville, avenger and hit woman. Susan not only believed in capital punishment, she dispensed it. Before her father Black Buck Melville had left for South America with the remains of the family fortune, Susan's life had been secure. She attended Vassar, planned to be an artist, but never expected to earn a living. She taught art in a private school until it went out of business but was soon reduced to crashing parties to get a meal.

Susan planned to commit suicide at a Charity Foundation dinner in *Miss Melville Regrets* (Fine, 1986). Buck had taught her to be an excellent shot so when she decided instead to shoot her landlord, she killed him. Her skill attracted Alex Tabor, currently seeking a socially acceptable assassin for his payroll. The murder launched Susan on a new career, which she eventually expanded to include persons who earned her disapproval; e.g. when the Melville Wing of the Museum of American Art was renamed. She no longer needed the payoffs. Her paintings were selling.

When artist Rafael Hoffman died at a gallery show in *Miss Melville Returns* (Fine, 1987), his wife said it was murder. Susan noticed a pattern connected to drug smuggling, and provided her own justice. She became a victim of the men who used her, including Tabor and Peter Franklin, the anthropologist/lover for whom she subsidized a foundation. They all had interests of their own, leaving Susan restless.

In *Miss Melville's Revenge* (Fine, 1989), she killed a diplomat who had abused his legal privileges. Her next target was already in America—Martillo, dictator of La Pradera, who had reputedly ordered the murder of Buck Melville. Fortunately she changed her mind.

Miss Melville Rides a Tiger (Fine, 1991) pit Susan against Berengaria Rundle, the false friend who became Buck Melville's lover, and drew Susan into schemes of charity fundraisers, Mafia overlords, and a Middle Eastern dynasty.

Heroes who robbed the rich and endowed the poor have always been a part of mythology. Susan, for all her wit and command of the social graces, was an arrogant killer who took upon herself the right to decide who should live or die.

Michelle Merrill

Authors: Carole Gift Page and Doris Elaine Fell

Rejected by her fiancé Scott, who ran off with one of the bridesmaids, Michelle Merrill moved out to California. She had attended a devoutly Christian college, Hopewell, where she perceived herself as a "rebel". Her rebellions amounted to little more than overproduction of popcorn and a chaste kiss with Scott on campus. She took her faith very seriously, expressing anger by saying "Oh, Shakespeare." Although her ultimate intention was to be a novelist, Michelle took a clerical position at Ballard Computer Design headed by handsome David Ballard.

An emergency made it necessary for Michelle, rather than Ballard's faithful secretary Eva Thornton, to accompany him on a trip during *Mist Over Morro Bay* (Harvest House, 1985). Bad weather and motor problems forced David, a former Navy pilot, to land far short of their destination. A casual contact to Jackie, Michelle's college roommate, made Michelle aware of the mysterious "death" of Jackie's husband, Steve Turman. Both Michelle and David made personal sacrifices to help Jackie, even when the investigation pitted them against a criminal conspiracy. In the process, Michelle's faith was restored. David, also a devout Christian, was attracted to that quality in Michelle.

David and Michelle's wedding plans were temporarily derailed in *Secret of the East Wind* (Harvest House, 1986), first by her father's insistence that they wait six months; then, by the return of Rob Thornton, believed dead in Vietnam, after a twelve year absence. As Michelle played a role in Rob's recovery, even planning a book on his experiences, David felt less important in her life. Until Rob was sure of his identity, Michelle could not put her needs first.

By *Storm Clouds Over Paradise* (Harvest House, 1986), David and Michelle were preparing for their wedding. At the last minute, Jackie had to cancel her participation. She and Steve were on the Syndicate's hit list and their location had been discovered. For a shrewd businessman, David showed little curiosity when he and Michelle were anonymously provided with a honeymoon on Solidad Island. Rather than peace and quiet, they encountered government manipulation, criminal activity, and a ghost from the past.

One of the four honorees on a Hopewell Alumni cruise to Alaska in *Beyond the Windswept Sea* (Harvest House, 1987) was targeted by a killer. David and Michelle, also an honoree, had other problems. He wanted to begin a family. She preferred to wait until her career was better established. They agreed to let the Lord make the decision, and He did. The identities of the potential killer and victim were obvious early in the narrative, diminishing the tension.

Although the books were comparatively simplistic, they had a certain charm. Not everyone orders steak tartare. Some readers will find the series a pleasant antidote to more salacious and violent narratives.

Debbie Miles

Author: Joseph R. Rosenberger

Debbie was a tall redhead with photographic recall, and a master's degree in parapsychology from the University of Southern California. She deserved better treatment from the author and from the misogynistic pseudo-patriots with whom she worked. She was devoutly committed to anti-Communism as a result of the death of her father, a U.S. military attaché in Rome who died at the hands of the Red Brigade. Her reaction had been to affiliate with COBRA (Counter-subversion Operations Bureau of Resistance and Action), a subversive arm of the National Security Agency. COBRA was expected to get results using any methods necessary, unhampered by laws and the United States Constitution. Readers who enjoy gratuitous violence, sleazy sex, foul language and dirty jokes need search no further.

In the first outing, *COBRA: The Heroin Connection* (Lorevan, 1986), the otherwise laudable goal of limiting the importation of drugs into the United States by a coalition of Russian agents and Mafia gangs was carried out via indiscriminate killing. Jon Skul, leader of the COBRA unit assigned to this task, was horrified that Debbie and the other female members of the group (the Doves) used sex to get information and blackmail foreign agents. He found himself attracted to her anyway. He and the males (the Eagles) used machine guns and bombs to wipe out the enemies of democracy.

The third in the series, *COBRA: The Red Dragon Operation* (Lorevan, 1987), moved the principal members of the unit to the West Coast to execute the leadership of Chinese triads. The new powers in the Chinese community were cooperating with Russian agents to blackmail Asian fisherman into spying on U.S. naval operations. Skul's heavy drinking worried Debbie as he and his cohort gleefully tortured, gassed and/or murdered not only Chinese gangsters but also innocent bystanders and San Francisco police officers. Her role was restricted to driving vehicles, while Brenda Fong, a Chinese COBRA dove, did the seduction.

COBRA: Nightmare in Panama (Lorevan, 1987) was more of the same although the setting was now Central America. Surprisingly the standard Russian villains had become temporary allies against Libyan terrorists determined to bomb the Panama Canal. Still, Debbie for all her education earned her paycheck and satisfied her patriotic impulses by exchanging sexual favors for information, driving get-away cars, and meeting Skul's personal needs. She did have an opportunity to kill someone (a patriotic Panamanian police officer trying to do his duty) during an escape.

Others: *Paris Kill-Ground, Project Andromeda: Belgrade Battleground*

Kinsey Millhone
Author: Sue Grafton

Kinsey Millhone and Sharon McCone accomplished for the female private investigator what Sam Spade and Lew Archer did for the male. They portrayed pragmatic professionals who persisted despite limited financial success and a diminished personal life.

Kinsey's parents had been killed when she was five years old in an accident that left her trapped in the car with her dead parents for several hours. A caring, but undemonstrative aunt raised her. Kinsey tried marriage twice, but revealed that she dumped her first husband, and the second left her. She described herself as having hazel eyes, dark hair, which she cut herself, a twice broken nose. She wore little or no makeup, jeans with cotton tops, boots or tennis shoes, a jacket or blazer when needed. She jogged regularly at three miles per day, six days a week, and worked out occasionally. Although she had few housekeeping skills, she knit and crocheted.

Kinsey had worked as a policewoman, then an insurance investigator, but craved independence. Professionally, she was thorough and resourceful, leaving intuition to her amateur sisters, utilizing index cards to record information and then assembling them in patterns. She followed her own standards: lying when convenient, killing when there was no alternative, and, on one occasion, when she was enraged. Although careful with money, she rarely had any to spare, living in cheap lodgings, drinking Chardonnay, and eating badly. Kinsey liked good food, and when she wanted to indulge herself emotionally went to Rosie's, where the proprietor attended to her personally.

Her office space was provided initially through a retainer agreement with California Fidelity (Cal Fid); later, by a similar arrangement with a small firm of attorneys. Her personal relationships were as sparse: her octogenarian landlord Henry Pitts, who was a regular confidante and supporter; Rosie; and off and on-again lovers e.g. police officers (Jonah Robb) or private investigators (Robert Dietz). The men tended to be married or rootless, unable to make a commitment, but she was too. Even when she discovered long lost relatives, she was hesitant about making a connection.

In *"A" Is for Alibi* (Holt, 1982), Nikki Fife left prison after serving eight years for the murder of her unfaithful husband, determined to prove her innocence. Kinsey researched the victim's wives, lovers, children, and business associates to find not one, but two killers. Beverly Danziger hired Kinsey in *"B" Is for Burglar* (Holt, 1985) to find her missing sister, but called off the search when Kinsey urged her to contact the police. Kinsey had another client willing to bankroll the case and believed there was a connection between the woman's disappearance and another death.

Bobby Callahan, who frequented the same gym as Kinsey, knew someone wanted him dead. An assault had left him too brain damaged to figure out why. During *"C" Is for Corpse* (Holt, 1986), he hired Kinsey to fill in the blanks. Three days later, Bobby was dead. John Daggett, who had destroyed families with his drunken driving, eased his conscience by siphoning stolen drug money to the survivors in *"D" Is for Deadbeat* (Holt, 1987). Someone preferred to have Daggett dead.

Kinsey was alarmed when $5,000 was deposited in her checking account in *"E" Is for Evidence* (Holt, 1988). She could not afford to have her credibility destroyed in the midst of an arson investigation for Cal Fid. As an added complexity Daniel Wade, Kinsey's drug addicted former husband, was involved. Her name cleared and her apartment in the process of repair, Kinsey was at loose ends in *"F" Is for Fugitive* (Holt, 1989). Dying Royce Fowler hired her to prove that his son Bailey had not killed a pregnant girlfriend. Kinsey moved temporarily to Floral Beach to get acquainted with their families but was made to feel unwelcome.

In *"G" Is for Gumshoe* (Holt, 1990), Kinsey searched for Irene Gersh's "wacky" mother, Agnes Grey, while evading a contract killer hired by a man she had sent to prison. Nevada detective Robert Dietz guarded Kinsey and helped when Agnes Grey was murdered. Her vulnerability was reflected in her fear of the assassin and her emotional dependence on Dietz.

Grafton left introspection behind for action in *"H" Is for Homicide* (Holt, 1991), beginning with the murder of a claims adjuster at Cal Fid. Kinsey investigated Bibianna Diaz, and her obsessive lover. Once Kinsey connected with this pair, she had tigers by the tail until rescued by an undercover police officer. There was no letdown in *"I" Is for Innocent* (Holt, 1992). Kinsey used the incomplete records of a deceased private investigator to re-examine a six-year-old murder where the primary suspect had been acquitted.

Grafton opened up Kinsey's past in *"J" Is for Judgment* (Holt, 1993), when Cal Fid hired her to locate Wendell Jaffe, a real estate developer. He had disappeared from his yacht five years before, leaving his business partner in financial ruin. After his widow had him officially declared dead, a man appearing to be Jaffe was sighted in Mexico. The investigation brought Kinsey into contact with her mother's wealthy family, estranged since Kinsey's mom married a lowly mail carrier. The eventual fate of the killer was left unsettled, as was Kinsey's intention to pursue closer ties with her family.

In *"K" Is for Killer* (Holt, 1994) a mother's determination to find the truth sent her to Kinsey with a pornographic tape in which her deceased daughter, Lorna, was depicted. Lorna had been a night person, hobnobbing with others whose schedules matched her own: teenage hookers, radio talk show hosts, and Mafia gangsters. When Kinsey found the killer, she went a step further and arranged for quick justice. *"L" Is for Lawless* ((Holt, 1995) seemed inconsistent with the Millhone character. Wasn't she was too shrewd to let a casual request by dear friend Henry Pitts send her on a cross country jaunt with a pseudo pregnant female and her bank robbing father, while pursued by a vicious killer? She ended up with a sore head, but reached out to her mother's family for the first time.

"M" Is for Malice (Holt, 1996) brought Dietz back into Kinsey's life after a two-year absence, but still unable to commit. Her cousin, Tasha, an attorney hired Kinsey to find a missing heir who had fled as a teenager in trouble. When Kinsey found Guy Malek, she was deeply affected. She sought to protect him from his past and his avaricious brothers, but failed. During *"N" Is for Noose*, (Holt, 1998), Kinsey was an unwelcome presence

in a small Eastern California town, investigating the death of a popular sheriff's deputy. His wife wanted to know what had disturbed Tom Newquist in the weeks before his heart attack. The premise that a woman would expend $1,500 for this information when she had limited resources weakened the narrative. Once accepted, the action was sustained, the characters as good as usual.

The husband whom Kinsey had "dumped" came back into her life in *"O" Is for Outlaw* (Holt, 1999). A chance phone call returned Kinsey to memories of her marriage to Mickey Magruder fourteen years before. She had been a police rookie and he, an experienced detective. An unopened letter made her aware that she had failed Mickey in a way that cost him the job he loved. Kinsey no longer loved Mickey. It was too late to make amends as he lay dying from his wounds, but not too late to find his killer. A depressing sub-text seemed to be that everyone cheated on his or her spouse or lover.

"P" Is for Peril (Puttnam's, 2001) left Kinsey's personal relationships on the back burner. As it began she had no man in her life, limited cash in her checking account, and a sense that it was time to seek new office space. She reluctantly took on Fiona, first wife of the missing Dr. Dowan Purcell, as a client, warning her that if the police department had failed to locate him in the weeks following his disappearance, she was unlikely to do so. Fiona was convinced that Crystal, Dow's second wife, was responsible. In short order, Kinsey discovered evidence of Medicare fraud in the nursing home managed by Dow, discrepancies in his bank accounts, and his body submerged near Fiona's home. Her latest beau turned out to have an unacceptable past and no future.

It was always important in reading the series to remember that the books are not set current to the date of publication, but take place in the 1980's. The series not only utilized successive letters of the alphabet in the title, but in many if not all of the books, the name of the primary character began with the same initial. (C = Callahan; D = Daggett; F = Fowler; etc)

Grafton used the alphabet to identify her books, but her plots were not formulaic. Along with several contemporaries, she opened the mystery genre to a new breed of heroine, independent, iconoclastic, and perceptive. Although not all books were of the same quality, their level was remarkable for such a long series. She has experimented with humor, pathos, and furious action, and succeeded with them all. An intensive examination of the Millhone series can be found in *"G" Is for Grafton* (Holt, 1997) by Natalie Hevener Kaufman and Carol McGinnis Kay.

Donna Miro

Author: Heather Graham (Pozzessere)

Donna Miro was one of six children (one sister, four brothers) in an Italian-American household that always had room for her friends. Lorna Doria, the lonely single child of older parents, spent her free time at the Miro home. They had been friends since childhood. Both had negative experiences in marriage. Donna's had ended in an annulment, leaving her free to marry again. Lorna's devoted husband, Jerry, died a natural death. Each had a career to sustain her. Donna was the bookkeeper for the Miro Olive Oil Company managed by her father. The family still felt the iron hand of Grandfather Miro and the less obvious guidance of his wife. Lorna, who had the security of inheritances from her parents and Jerry, ran an upscale antique store in Massachusetts.

Each of the two women took the lead role in one book.

Sensuous Angel (Dell, 1985) was characterized as a "Candlelight Ecstasy Romance" which should be a clue to serious mystery readers. There were crimes: murders, kidnapping, but the primary emphasis was on the growing attraction that Donna felt for an Episcopalian priest, Father Luke Trudeau. Donna visited New York in search of Lorna, unaware that she was in an NYPD witness protection program. In a surprising coincidence, Lorna's primary protector was Andrew, Luke's brother. Donna's reckless search for her friend put them all in danger.

The Roman Catholic Miro family survived Donna's wedding to Luke Trudeau. The focus shifted over to Lorna in *An Angel's Share* (Dell 1985). The master criminal who had initiated a series of murders to conceal his motive in killing his wealthy grandmother was out on bail. Lorna had witnessed his grandmother's murder. Donna had been kidnapped and interrogated by him. This time it was Lorna's difficulty in adjusting to Andrew's role as protector and sometime lover that engaged most of the narrative. A weak ending took care of the more mundane aspects of convicting a serial killer.

Kate Miskin

Author: P. D. James

Although she never approached the independent level of Cordelia Grey, Kate Miskin made a place for herself in later books featuring Inspector Adam Dagleish. Like Cordelia, Kate had an unconventional childhood. Her unwed mother died shortly after Kate's birth. She had never known her father's name and had ceased to wonder. She was raised by a grandmother who lived in a depressing housing development.

When Kate entered the Dagleish series, the police department offered her security. She was struggling to purchase an apartment of her own. Her upbringing in an overcrowded crime ridden building created in her a need for a quiet private place where she could enjoy her hobby—painting. Her grandmother's poor health and financial problems made it difficult for Kate to separate herself from her past. She was twenty-seven, involved with librarian Alan Scully when Dagleish added her to his special team. The unit had been created to deal with crimes, which "for political or other reasons, needed particularly sensitive handling."

The death of Sir Paul Berowne in *A Taste for Death* (Knopf, 1986) qualified for such treatment. Berowne had approached Dagleish earlier about anonymous letters accusing him of complicity in the deaths of several women, one his first wife. The manner of Berowne's death was bizarre, killed by his own razor in the vestry of a church in which he intended to spend the evening. A second man, a vagrant, lay there dead by the same weapon.

Kate, who had become a detective inspector by *Original Sin* (Faber & Faber, 1994), was no longer involved with Alan Scully. She and fellow D. I. Danny Aaron assisted Dagleish in the investigation of several deaths connected to a distinguished publishing house. Dagleish had dismissed earlier problems at Peverell Press as unworthy of his special squad, but revised that opinion. The primary victim, Chief Executive Officer Gerard Etienne, had multiple enemies, but the killer had acted out of a mistaken sense of revenge.

When Dagleish's special squad appeared again in *A Certain Justice* (Knopf, 1997), they explored the death of Venetia Aldridge, a hard-edged barrister. She had successfully defended Garry Ashe on a charge of killing his aunt. Venetia, who had an unhappy childhood, had managed to provide an equally unhappy one for her daughter Octavia. She was enraged when Ashe courted the young woman. Venetia had earned her enemies by rigidity and ambition, but pushed too far. Kate played a significant role in the investigation, accompanying Dagleish in his interviews, pursuing Octavia and Garry through the countryside. Dagleish and his new assistant Piers Tarrant sheltered Kate from the ultimate act of killing.

An anonymous letter to powerful Sir Alred Treeves in *Death in Holy Orders* (Knopf, 2001) cast doubt on the cause of his son Ronald's death at St. Anselm's theological college. Dagleish, who had tie s to the facility, agreed to investigate on his own time. Within days of his arrival, one dramatic murder and two more suspicious deaths changed the focus of his enquiries. Kate, Piers and other members of his team joined the investigation. Kate, in the throes of a professional crisis, found new resolve in her work. A report charging institutional racism within the Metropolitan Police, had deeply offended Kate, who was without racial prejudice. Dagleish not only identified a killer, but met a woman capable of giving him another chance at personal happiness.

Except for Cordelia Gray and Dagleish in the earlier books, James did not focus on her detectives. She explored the lives of victims and suspects, bringing them to life as ensemble players in her complex plots that frequently involved revenge for earlier wrongs.

Cassandra Mitchell

Author: L. (Laurali) R. Wright

Oh, the lot of the lonely librarian. *The Music Man* gave Miss Marian an opportunity to kick over the traces with a handsome rascal. In the mystery genre, librarians might be swept off their feet by male sleuths but, after the initial flurry of activity, they usually faded away.

Cassandra Mitchell, librarian in Sechelt, British Columbia, had an interesting debut in *The Suspect* (Viking, 1985), but met the fate of her fellow librarians in later books. At forty-one and unmarried, she was a tall graying dark haired woman with hazel eyes, searching for a long-term relationship. Cassandra had left an excellent professional position in Vancouver for Sechelt because her widowed mother had been placed in a nearby senior citizens residence. Her only brother lived in Edmonton. Through an impulsive letter to a lonely-hearts club, Cassandra met RCMP Sgt. Karl Alberg. When library patron George Wilcox became a suspect in the death of his former brother-in-law, she and Alberg dealt with a conflict of interest.

Cassandra was diverted in *Sleep While I Sing* (Viking, 1986) when she met handsome actor Roger Galbraith. Cassandra and Roger became lovers and her contacts with Alberg diminished until a corpse found in the nearby woods was connected to Roger.

A Chill Rain in January (Viking, 1990) focused on two other women: the isolated Zoe Strachan at the mercy of a blackmailing brother, and Ramona Orlitzke, an unhappy resident at the nursing home. Although Cassandra was with Karl when he found the body of a young man on an island beach in *Fall from Grace* (Viking, 1991) she took no part in the investigation of his death.

Alberg was 52, Cassandra almost 50 as *Prized Possessions* (Viking, 1993) began. Their affair had lasted eight years. At that time, Cassandra urged Alberg to become a private investigator and move to Vancouver. Although he proposed to Cassandra, they settled for living together. Meanwhile Alberg searched for a husband who had abandoned a "perfect" marriage. The case intertwined with that of a young developmentally disabled man whose innocent approaches to a woman led to several deaths.

Karl and Cassandra had been living together for eight months in *A Touch of Panic* (Scribners, 1994). She became the target of a seriously deranged fellow librarian seeking the "perfect woman." While Karl enjoyed a sailing vacation, Cassandra depended upon a chronic thief to rescue her from her determined suitor. Although Cassandra's role was expanded in this narrative, it was as victim, not as sleuth.

During *Mother Love* (Scribners, 1995), still emotionally affected by her kidnapping and abuse in the prior novel, Cassandra relied more and more on Karl's presence for her peace of mind. He had other responsibilities; i.e. a daughter who was getting married, and an intriguing murder case. Maria Buscombe had left her husband and daughter shortly after learning that she had been adopted. Why did she return now? Why did she have to be killed before she could reunite with her family?

In *Strangers Among Us* (Scribners, 1996), Karl and Cassandra set the wedding date (Valentine's Day). Karl was distracted by his concern for a runaway teenager who had hacked his parents to death and injured his young sister, but might be salvageable and by the presence of a former neighbor who blamed Karl for the savage attack that maimed his daughter.

Karl was concerned about a case that had gone unsolved while they were on their honeymoon in *Acts of Murder* (Scribners, 1997). He reviewed the records along with similar cases in Sechelt, at the urging of his new assistant, Edwina Henderson. Unfortunately the killer remained active until finally confronted by the police. Karl and Cassandra had decisions to make. She had inherited a considerable amount of money. He realized that he was burned out by his years as a police officer. Now he wanted to become a private investigator and move to Vancouver; now, she wasn't sure.

Although Cassandra was not the primary character, this was an excellent series with subtle undertones to the mystery plots.

Mom

Author: James Yaffe

Mom originally appeared in short stories printed in Ellery Queen Magazines during the 1950's and 60's. When female sleuths became topical, she moved easily into collections of short stories and novels. "Mom," who assisted her investigator/son Dave in solving crimes, changed along with the literary format. She left behind the opera, the Jewish deli, and the subways to go "West"; first, to visit her relocated son, then to establish a permanent residence. Now a widower, Dave was highly critical of the Colorado community where he worked as an investigator for the Public Defender's Office.

In *A Nice Murder for Mom* (St. Martin, 1988), Mom resumed the role she had played so well in the short stories; listening to Dave talk about his cases, identifying questions that would lead to a solution, but protecting his status as the investigator. She recognized a faked alibi before Dave did, but did not disclose the killer.

In *Mom Meets Her Maker* (St. Martin, 1990), she had a flashy red Toyota, a home, and a devoutly religious neighbor. Dave's intolerance for fundamentalists, small towns, and western attitudes contrasted with his mother's more generous acceptance of diversity. Dave, under Mom's direction, uncovered the mundane motive behind a murder with religious overtones.

In *Mom Doth Murder Sleep* (St. Martin, 1991), a local production of Macbeth ended with murder. In her assistance to Dave, Mom frequently omitted the rationale behind her questions. If she really wanted to advance his career, she might have pointed him in the correct direction and let him work out the solution on his own.

During *Mom Among the Liars* (St. Martin, 1992), Mom concealed her theory as to how brothel owner Edna Pulaski might have died by mistake. Mom did not share all of her discoveries. She distinguished between the weak and the vicious.

The format included a prologue and/or epilogue by Mom, often disclosing information she had withheld from Dave. Formulaic, but pleasant.

Yaffe's collection of short stories *My Mother, the Detective* (Crippen and Landru, 1997) (previously published in *Ellery Queen's Mystery Magazine*) was most interesting for his account of Mom's evolution. Her character was enlivened with wit and wisdom.

Rosie Monaghan

Author: Alan McDonald

The 1980's was a period of high unemployment in Great Britain, nowhere more so than in Liverpool. The Liverpudlians are a breed of their own, including many Irish immigrants. Roisin Theresa Monaghan, better known as Rosie, was the divorced mother of two children. Graham, her former husband, had remarried. Rosie maintained a low-level physical relationship with Jerry, whom she considered "too soft", but good in bed. Her son Bob (11) sought the company of his father, but Carol (9) saw him only under pressure. Rosie was good hearted, tough, with a sense of humor and intermittent optimism.

Rosie and the kids survived on Graham's tardy child support and the dole (British version of unemployment and/or welfare). She was not a lazy woman. She had put her typing and shorthand to use, worked as a store detective for six months, but was unemployed when *Unofficial Rosie* (Futura, 1988) began. Perennially short of money, Rosie decided her prior employment as a store detective could be the basis for a career as a private detective. Notices in the local storefronts did not produce the desired results. Even her new answering machine was a failure. Most calls were from an anonymous sex starved male. Her only serious client turned out to be a manipulative businessman who framed a city official with Rosie's unwitting help. Nevertheless before she was through, Rosie had proved to herself (if no one else) that she could solve a murder. Other: *Rosie Among Thorns*

Dittany Henbit Monk

Author: Alisa Craig, pseudonym for Charlotte MacLeod

See: Dittany Henbit, Page 126

Mona Moore

Author: Will Harriss

See: Mona Moore Dunbar, Page 78

Rain Morgan

Author: Lesley Grant-Adamson

Rain Morgan was an attractive blonde London newspaperwoman who did not always enter the narratives initially.

In *Death on Widow's Walk* (Scribners, 1985) a.k.a. *Patterns in the Dust,* she planned a solo vacation in a cottage offered by her lover's cousin. This proved to be a disastrous decision because she found a corpse deposited there. The locals, first very friendly, turned against Rain when she defended a juvenile delinquent accused of the killing. *The Face of Death* (Scribners, 1986) focused first on the unhappy marriage of Peter and Clara Dutton. Peter claimed that the amnesiac young woman injured in a traffic accident was his wife, Clara. The woman was less confident of her identity. Rain entered the story in its final stages to help "Clara" find herself.

Rain and her lover, Oliver, visited the French Riviera in *Guilty Knowledge* (St. Martin, 1988), intending to interview female artist Sabine Jourdain. The elusiveness of Sabine and the unusual techniques in recent work by painter Marius Durance alerted Rain and Oliver to murder and drug dealing.

By *Wild Justice* (St. Martin, 1988) Irish-American Hal MacQuillan had purchased the newspaper and was "ruining it". When MacQuillan was stabbed to death, editorial staff, anti-Irish protestors, and striking printers were suspected.

Curse the Darkness (St. Martin, 1990) ran to 500 pages. Casual acquaintance Alfred Wilson, once an outstanding playwright, invited Rain to his home where she found him hanging from the chandelier. Rain was intrigued by the twenty-year period during which Alfred could not write. A parallel plot concerned author John Gower, whose declining sales made him wonder if similar publicity would increase his popularity.

Ingenious plotting.

Theresa "Terri" Morrison

Author: Judi Miller

Terri Morrison was a New York City policewoman, fighting to make her way in a male dominated occupation. The daughter of a police officer, she married a co-worker. Bob wanted children while Terri's career came first so they separated. Terri, at 34, was tall with long dark hair and violet eyes. She had Sgt. Bernie Moskowitz, as her mentor, and Charlie Hawkins as her partner. Her promotion to detective third grade was mistakenly perceived by some as earned on her back.

A serial killer used singles ads to meet and murder women, leaving a flower behind. In *I'll be Wearing a White Gardenia* (Avon, 1985), Terri noticed that all victims were redheads. The task force made a quick arrest, and then disbanded, leaving Terri to clean up the paper work. Instead she canvassed florists and donned a red wig to attract the killer. Her obduracy caused trouble, but gave her time to rethink her marriage.

During *Phantom of the Soap Opera* (Dell, 1988), daytime television actress Kristi Marlowe was killed with a screwdriver. Although there was considerable interest in who would replace her in the series, competition diminished when two candidates were murdered. This could not have come at a worse time for the television series, celebrating its 25th anniversary by the "wedding" of two fictional characters. A special squad, including Terri, was assigned to investigate.

The two books had a lot in common: the psychopathic killer, women as victims, and serial murderers.

Mary Frances Mulrooney a.k.a. M. F.

Author: Jerry Ahern

Josh Culhane was the protagonist in *The Takers* (WorldWide Library, 1984), a hero similar to Indiana Jones. All such heroes need a supportive heroine, a role filled by Mary Frances Mulrooney—she preferred to be called M. F. Josh was the author of an adventure series. His twin brother Jeff, a Vietnam vet, who had worked for the Central Intelligence Agency, lived an adventurous life. Gradually Josh took over Jeff's lifestyle.

M. F.'s literary output was very different—non-fiction such as *Occult Murmurs, The Legend Beneath the Waves*. She made frequent appearances on television shows, as an expert on unexplained phenomena. She and Josh were occasional lovers. He alone was allowed to refer to her as "Fanny." She was characterized by her skills—she was a good shot, expert driver of her yellow Mustang, and by her eccentricities—she saved her frequent parking tickets and paid them in bunches, carried a huge purse, and smoked filtered cigarettes. She was also adamant about her independence.

The Takers could be more accurately described as a science fiction thriller than as a mystery. Josh and M. F. reconciled when the evil Sonia Steiglitz murdered his brother Jeff. For Sonia it had been an effort to please her controlling father Jeremiah. He was obsessed by a search for the starbase constructed under Antarctic ice thousands of years ago by creatures from another planet. Explosions, gunshots, mysterious gases joined with greed and treachery in a good yarn. Credibility was not part of the mixture.

There was a modicum more credibility and a better role for M. F. in *The Takers: River of Gold* (Worldwide, 1985) co-authored by S. A. Ahern, Jerry's wife. Corpses still littered the narrative's scenery from Istanbul to central Brazil. M. F. searched for the remnants of a tribe of Greek Amazonian women. Josh made his own trip into the interior, carrying what he believed to be $1,000,000 in gold to ransom Amelina Palmer. Scott, Amelina's wealthy husband, had saved Jeff Culhane's life in Vietnam, so Josh agreed to serve as the messenger. Toss in Russians seeking the Amazon women, Uruentes headhunters, cannibals seeking a main course, and enough plutonium to blow up an international conference.

J. D. Mulroy

Author: Richard Werry

J. D. Mulroy disliked her name, preferring to be known by her initials. She was a dark-haired graduate of the University of Michigan currently employed as a private investigator in Birmingham, Michigan. "Determinedly single," she had an ongoing relationship with Ed Rogers, a divorced attorney. At least two prior affairs had ended when the men realized she would never marry them. Her business associate Ahmad had been a professional football player and looked like it.

In *A Casket for a Lying Lady* (Dodd Mead, 1985), J. D. and Ahmad traveled to Florida on the trail of Cary McMurtie who had absconded with bearer bonds belonging to her brother and son. They headed for the home of Helga Lawrence whose disreputable husband Duncan had enticed Cary away. Deceived by the amiable Helga, J. D. might have been drowned at sea had she not hummed the Michigan fight song to alert Ahmad to her presence.

J. D. and Ahmad preferred to avoid domestic disturbances, but took a quick look at the dramatic change in broker Emmett Harney in *A Delicately Personal Matter* (Dodd Mead, 1986). Something was bothering Harney—something connected to the Colorado Beef House. Harry Jenkins, an associate of J. D.'s, was murdered while undercover at the restaurant. So there was no choice, they had to find his killer.

Fair to middling.

Kate Murphy

Author: Sr. Carol Anne O'Marie

See: Sister Mary Helen O'Connor, Page 213

Cassie Newton

Author: Joan G. Smith

Cassie Newton was a young woman who moved from her Bangor, Maine home to attend McGill University in Montreal in pursuit of a French degree. Her uncle, Victor Mazzini, a distinguished classical violinist, provided her with access to social events. His sophistication, free-spending habits, and luxurious lifestyle awed Cassie. Her own goal was a career in the diplomatic service.

In *Capriccio* (Jove, 1989), Uncle Victor disappeared just before a major concert appearance. Cassie initially thought that it might have been a publicity stunt. That possibility decreased when she learned that he had sold his car, his cottage, and stocks and had taken a large bank loan. A mysterious stranger, claiming to be a hardware dealer from the Midwest, seemed too eager to help Cassie find Victor. He was revealed to be John Weiss, a representative of a major insurance company. Weiss, who was based in London, continued to play a role in Cassie's life, but she remained in Montreal, sharing an apartment with a young friend.

Their innocent romance continued in *A Brush with Death* (Jove, 1990), when Weiss posed as a Texas tycoon to pursue art forgers and thieves. Cassie showed considerable courage, earning an engagement ring at the end.

These were light mysteries with a flighty heroine and a stalwart hero.

Ella Nidech

Author: Richard Hoyt

Espionage agent James Burlane worked with Ella Nidech in only two of his adventures, but she was a formidable ally. Ella, a "well stacked" brunette with green eyes, earned her position as head of the Hong Kong CIA office the hard way—proficiency in languages, a Ph.D. in International Affairs from Johns Hopkins, and rank in the top 2% of graduates of CIA training. Nevertheless, she was not unwilling to use sexual favors in her work.

As *The Dragon Portfolio* (TOR, 1986) began, the Hong Kong office had an opportunity to secure data about activities in China from an unknown source. Ella, who met the informant, might have been robbed of the documents had not Burlane intervened to kill an assailant. Confident that she could have handled the matter, she filed a sex discrimination suit against Burlane.

Burlane and Ella teamed again in *Siege* (TOR, 1987). Ella monitored a conspiracy between Russian agent Boris Suslov and Arab leader Muhammed Aziz under Burlane's supervision. It took them both to handle an attempt to turn Gibraltar over to enemy forces.

Espionage with elements of mystery, dominated by the male protagonist.

Pam Nilsen

Author: Barbara Wilson

Pam Nilsen and her twin sister, Penny, were natives of Seattle, Washington. After their parents died in a car crash, Penny married a man with whom Pam once had a heterosexual relationship. Pam took a female lover, Hadley. Pam worked as a printer in the family shop, now run by a group of activists. In her free time, she enjoyed gardening and mysteries.

During *Murder in the Collective* (Seal, 1984), the print shop considered a merger with a lesbian press, which Penny opposed. Vandalism at the plant and the murder of a young cameraman could be tied to the proposal or to jealousies among the group members. Even when Pam discovered the killer, she did not turn her in.

In *Sisters of the Road* (Seal, 1986) Pam identified a serial killer of young women in the Seattle area, but was raped by him. Men were frequently portrayed negatively in the series as pimps, sexually abusing fathers, or rapists. During *The Dog Collar Murders* (Seal, 1989), there was an internal struggle in the feminist/lesbian movement. Pam and Hadley explored adult entertainment stores and sexual videos to find the killer of a feminist who opposed pornography.

The series included explicit lesbian sex, but explored issues of general interest to women.

Rita Noonan

Author: Michael Hendricks

Rita Noonan was an experienced but erratic private investigator in the New York area. Her marriage to police officer Frank Noonan had ended in divorce.

In *Money to Burn* (Dutton, 1989), Bobby Wilcox hired Rita to find his missing stepsister, Lucy Randle. Wilcox could afford the fee, because, although he published a profitless poetry magazine, he and Lucy were independently wealthy. Rita had no scruples about sex with a client, depended upon information from her friend, police detective Max Wellman, and was quick on the trigger. The case turned out to be far more serious than Bobby had indicated.

Rita had become a partner in the agency by *Friends In High Places* (Scribners, 1990). "Wilsey" Weiss, a former cop in Frank Noonan's unit, came to Rita for help. He had been forced to resign because of alcohol abuse and a relationship with a call girl. The next day he was found dead in Rita's apartment. Not only Frank's reputation but also that of the department was at stake, because Weiss may have been writing an exposé.

Abby Novack

Author: Al Guthrie

Abby (Abigail) Novack and her husband Walter "Mac" McKenzie were among the new "couples" in mystery fiction during the Eighties. Abby, a tiny woman with brown hair and eyes, had recently returned to the Chicago suburbs from the West Coast. She had married young, but divorced her husband when she realized that he was a charming confidence man.

In *Private Murder* (Bantam, 1989), Abby came to Sarahville to visit her older sister Henrietta, just before she was murdered. Mac, a neighbor recently retired from the United States Air Force, was working as a "consultant" on a private investigator's license. Abby was the number one suspect in Henrietta's murder. Mac was number two so they joined forces to find the killer.

By *Grave Murder* (Zebra, 1990), Abby and Mac were married and living in a large Queen Anne house where Abby established her art and craft business. The couple enthusiastically joined in community activities; Mac, in the Merchant's Association; Abby, in the Historical Society. Their interests came into conflict when the two groups disagreed on a parking area. The death of an historical researcher investigating the property sent the McKenzies into World War II history. The risks taken by both Abby and Mac dampened their enthusiasm for criminal detection.

In *Murder by Tarot* (Zebra, 1992), Mac planned to let his investigator's license expire, but not until he found a ten-year-old girl's lost dog. Meanwhile Abby accepted a case on her own, investigating political corruption.

The McKenzies made an interesting start, but the series ended.

Sister Mary Helen O'Connor
Author: Sr. Carol Anne O'Marie

Sister Mary Helen O'Connor, a slightly overweight woman with gray hair and hazel eyes, had been an elementary teacher. Upon retirement, she resided at Mt. St. Francis College for Women in San Francisco, working part time in the alumnae office with leisure for solving mysteries. She accomplished this most frequently in tandem with Kate Murphy, a San Francisco police detective. During the series, Kate, the redheaded daughter of a police officer, rejoined the Catholic Church, married her policeman lover, Jack Basetti, and became a mother.

The two women met in *A Novena for Murder* (Scribners, 1984) when Prof. Phillip Villanueva of the college history department was murdered. Kate, and her avuncular partner, Dennis Gallagher, resented Mary Helen's intrusion in the investigation. Although Gallagher never did accept Mary Helen, she and Kate developed a working relationship in *Advent of Dying* (Delacorte, 1986). Suzanne Barnes, a shy secretary in the alumnae office, was killed. It was Mary Helen who discovered that Suzanne was a former nun who left the convent to marry a prisoner with whom she had been corresponding.

During *The Missing Madonna* (Delacorte, 1988), Mary Helen and fellow nun Sr. Eileen joined the OWLs (Older Women's League) gaining a new circle of friends, one of whom disappeared. Mary Helen's detection was based upon an obscure connection to a religious painting. As *Murder in Ordinary Time* (Delacorte, 1991) began, Mary Helen waited to be interviewed on a television program. Poisoned cookies and celebrity suspects kept her busy. A pregnancy did the same for Kate.

After winning a contest, Mary Helen and Eileen visited Spain in *Murder Makes a Pilgrimage* (Delacorte, 1993). Mary Helen compared her companions to characters from *Canterbury Tales* until the death of flirtatious Lisa Springer turned her thoughts to murder. Kate Murphy, restless as her maternity leave ended, provided evidence to identify the killer. This book rejuvenated a series that had showed signs of fatigue.

Not even a retreat, where spiritual values could be expected to dominate, kept Sr. Mary Helen from violence in *Death Goes on Retreat* (Delacorte, 1995). After a former seminarian was found dead on the retreat grounds, neither the priests nor the two nuns could leave. The official resolution of the investigation was unacceptable to Sr. Mary Helen, but she relied on the integrity of Sgt. Bob Little to see that justice was done.

Mary Helen and Eileen had become addicted to murder investigations by *Death of an Angel* (St. Martin, 1997). When Gemma Burke, alumna of Mount St. Francis and frequent donor to its causes, was murdered, the two nuns ignored the concerns of their religious superior and the warnings of Inspector Dennis Gallagher. Kate was not available, as Jack had been seriously injured in a related matter. As if murder were not enough to keep them busy, they prodded an obese library worker into changing her life, and then had to deal with the results.

Sisters Mary Helen and Eileen were reluctantly delivering St. Patrick's Day gifts to the benefactors of their convent during *Death Takes up a Collection* (St. Martin, 1998). They interrupted a tense encounter between Monsignor Joe Higgins and members of the St. Agatha parish council. His subsequent death by poisoning cast suspicion on the council members, several of whom had good reason to dislike the errant priest.

Sr. Eileen's departure for Ireland to care for a dying member of her family put a crimp in Mary Helen's deductions during *Requiem at the Refuge* (St. Martin, 2000). She was feeling her age and aware that the new Sister Superior preferred younger staff. Mary Helen made a preemptive strike, resigning from her post as head of the Development Office, and signing on to help Sr. Anne at the Refuge. The Refuge provided care for homeless and vulnerable women. When Melanie, a young prostitute, was murdered, her brutal pimp was the suspect of choice. However, Mary Helen, Kate Murphy, and a particularly ill-humored Inspector Dennis Gallagher could not ignore hints that a socially prominent couple might be worth a hard look.

Well written, low-keyed.

Rita Gardella O'Dea

Author: Andrew Coburn

Gardella was the operative word in Rita O'Dea's name. The daughter of a Mafia family, which had paternalistic attitudes towards females, she was under the spell of her brother Anthony, capo of the local criminal empire. Although she had married Tyrone O'Shea, a passive man whom she had convinced to have a vasectomy, it was Anthony whom she loved. Her father and mother now in their eighties were no longer active in the family businesses.

Anthony responded to her loyalty, if not her excessive affection, by protecting Rita financially, even making her the manager of a toxic disposal company. She was a dark-haired overweight woman in her forties who conveyed a sense of power. Rita appeared in three of Coburn's novels, but never as the primary character.

During *Sweetheart* (Macmillan, 1985), a murderous attack on the Gardella parents could not be ignored. Russell Thurston, an FBI agent determined to bring the Gardellas to justice, watched carefully. He believed that Tony would respond excessively, making the family vulnerable to an undercover agent. Their spouses betrayed both Rita and Tony. Tony paid the price at the hands of Mafia executioners. Rita was left unharmed. At the end, a new generation sought revenge on Thurston. Rita was not all bad. She had tried to convince Tony to let her run the toxic waste company honestly because she was concerned about cancer in children.

Rita was peripheral in *Love Nest* (Macmillan, 1987). She was concerned about the deaths of Melody, a young hooker, and Wally, an impotent youth, but she was neither the cause of the murders, nor did she solve them. Sonny Dawson, a middle-aged police officer in Andover, Massachusetts who had loved young Melody carried on the investigation. Rita, who had moved into the area, wanted to be accepted into local society. She had her own cause, revenge on a "friend," who had stood by when Tony was executed.

The title character in *Goldilocks* (Macmillan, 1989) was a conniving Vietnam veteran who preyed upon older women. His story was less memorable than the struggle of five teenagers, now in middle age, who had been raised in the projects of Lawrence, Massachusetts. Their loyalties and their betrayals consumed them: the Mafia godmother, the drink-drenched attorney and his hardworking wife, the crooked police captain, and the single upright man.

These were compelling stories in which Rita was a continuing character, less important in each book.

Lee Ofsted

Authors: Charlotte and Aaron Elkins

Lee Ofsted, a veteran of the U. S. Army, lacked many of the resources necessary for a professional career as a golfer. Her parents were low income. She had no major sponsor until *A Wicked Slice* (St. Martin, 1989) when the death of top golfer Kate O'Brian created an opening. Lee drew the attention of police detective Graham Sheldon because she found the body and bene-fited financially from Kate's death. He worked with Lee because of her insights into the other suspects and because he found her attractive.

Lee returned six years later in *Rotten Lies* (Mysterious Press, 1995) with no appreciable change in time. She had maintained a long distance relationship with Sheldon, limited by their careers. The death of Ted Guthrie, a contentious golf architect, during the High Desert Classic in New Mexico cost Lee her lead in the contest. A fill in appointment as color commentator on the American Sports Network enabled Lee to pay her bills, and pinpoint a killer while on the air.

The opportunity to vacation on an East Coast island while teaching business executives to play golf was irresistible in *Nasty Breaks* (Mysterious Press, 1997). Host Stuart Chappell had selected an inn on Block Island for a corporate seminar. The program was to include golf lessons, but, more importantly, the reorganization of company management. Five middle managers vied to become the executive vice president. Playtime was over when a kidnapping and a murder interfered. Lee and her friend Peg identi-fied the killer, but Graham Sheldon won the prize for a dramatic rescue.

Readers with the golf habit may find this series particularly interest-ing. Aaron Elkins was better known for his Dr. Gideon Oliver series, during which the forensic anthropologist involved his wife (see Julie Tendler Oliver) in some of his investigations.

Deirdre O'Hara

Author: Maurice Gagnon

Deirdre O'Hara, a tall, slim twenty-eight year old with blue/black hair and gray eyes, was a Montreal attorney. Her father, a wealthy Irish lawyer and his French Canadian wife had been killed in a plane crash. With a consider-able inheritance and a law degree, Deirdre had no financial problems. She joined her father's firm, specializing in marine insurance law. Deirdre was a risk-taker, scarred and physically abused during her investigations. She had lovers, but never married; smoked cigarettes in public but cigars and a pipe privately; handled guns and had killed. In her spare time she listened to classical music, golfed and rode a bicycle for exercise.

In *The Inner Ring* (Collins, 1985), Deirdre discovered the corpse of a badly abused young woman while cycling along the St. Lawrence Canal. To find the killer, she confronted rogue Royal Canadian Mounted Police, the KGB, and the Polish Secret Police. During *A Dark Night Offshore* (Collins, 1986), Deirdre probed the sinking of a Greek ship with a loss of 25 men.

Lloyds of London sent Deirdre and legal intern Jean Paul Clothier to sea to substantiate fraud.

In *Doubtful Motives* (Collins, 1987), Lloyds employed Deirdre when a Canadian industrialist and his crew were killed as they began a yearlong cruise. Although she had "more than normal observation powers," the investigation proved that she, too, could be blinded by her prejudices.

Deirdre's narratives have not been published in the United States. No other titles in the series are known. Gagnon used a diary technique for the books. His writing was methodical and wooden.

Elena Olivarez

Author: Marcia Muller

Elena Olivarez, a Mexican-American employed as the curator, and later director, of Santa Barbara's Museum of Mexican Arts, did not seek out criminal investigations. They occurred on her turf and within her circle of friends. Although her widowed mother worked as a domestic, Elena had graduated from the University of California at Santa Barbara and her sister was a college professor at the University of Minnesota.

In *The Tree of Death* (Walker, 1983), Frank De Palma, the obnoxious Museum director, was murdered soon after he fired Elena. To clear her name, Elena probed the tangled relationships of museum staff and volunteers discovering embezzlement and smuggling.

As *The Legend of the Slain Soldiers* (Walker, 1985) began, Elena's mother Gabriella contacted her. A friend, Ciro Sisneros, who had been writing a history of the Depression in Santa Barbara County, had been murdered. Painter Abuela Felicia described to Elena the injustices suffered by Mexican workers in the local harvests, even from their own countrymen.

Lt. Dave Kirk, who had cooperated with Elena in investigations, moved. She was left with a sense of rejection as *Beyond the Grave* (Walker, 1986 co-written by Muller and Bill Pronzini) began. Elena worked, across a century of time, with John Quincannon, Pronzini's nineteenth-century investigator. Quincannon's notes as to religious treasures were discovered in a marriage coffer purchased by Elena for the museum. Her quest for the treasures was interspersed with episodes relating to Quincannon's earlier search. Elena's understanding of the Catholic faith enabled her to find the relics and in doing so, she uncovered a murder. (See Selena Carpenter re Quincannon)

The Elena Olivarez stories were enriched by the ethnic and historical references. They lacked the wit and vigor of the McCone series, but had a charm of their own.

Julie Tendler Oliver

Author: Aaron Elkins

Julie Tendler was married at eighteen; then, divorced due to her husband's drug problems. After service in the military police, she earned a bachelor's degree in psychology, and a master's in ecology. By age thirty when she met Gideon Oliver, a forensic anthropologist, she had become a Chief Ranger in the National Park Service. Julie, an attractive brunette, could shoot and was adept at judo and karate.

In *The Dark Place* (Walker, 1983), Oliver came to Olympic National Park, because the disappearance of hikers in the area had been tied to rumors of a "Big Foot." Oliver was to examine bones from possible victims, but needed Julie's guidance. They searched the forest for remnants of a lost Indian tribe.

Murder in the Queen's Armes (Walker, 1985) took place on Julie and Gideon's honeymoon. Gideon was diverted into academic confrontations that led to multiple murders. Julie did not accompany Gideon to France for his adventures in *Old Bones* (Mysterious Press, 1987).

Oliver and his mentor, Abe Goldstein were the investigators in *Curses!* (Mysterious Press, 1989). Julie accompanied them to the Yucatan, where the reopening of an ill-fated archeological dig aroused greed, jealousy and murder among the excavators. The pattern continued in *Icy Clutches* (Mysterious Press, 1990), when Gideon accompanied Julie to a conference held in Alaska. Bored with his role as "spouse", Gideon researched a twenty-nine year old tragedy. Julie had the correct theory for the murderer's disappearance, but it was Oliver who identified him.

Alternately, Julie joined Gideon at a forensic anthropology conference at Whiteback Lodge in *Make No Bones* (Mysterious Press, 1991). A scientific exhibit containing bones of a deceased colleague was displayed but later disappeared. Questions were raised as to the death of Albert Jasper. Were those really his bones? Had his death been an accident? Julie added valuable observations and saved Gideon's life when he was attacked.

The opportunity for an expense paid trip to Egypt tempted Gideon in *Dead Men's Hearts* (Mysterious Press, 1994), but the project was rife with infighting. Julie experienced danger as a result of Gideon's investigation into the theft of ancient mummies and the discovery of a new corpse.

Twenty Blue Devils (Mysterious Press, 1997) offered Gideon the opportunity to probe the activities of the wealthy Druett clan of Papeete, the intricacies of the French oriented judicial system, and the U. S. witness protection program. He was asked to examine the skeleton of a young man killed on a hiking trip. Julie remained at home, limited to telephone contacts with her husband, during which, however, she perceptively analyzed the interactions of the Druett family. Julie had much to offer the series, but was underutilized.

Elkins wove a web of scientific jealousies and academic arguments that led to murder in *Skeleton Dance* (Morrow, 2000). Julie and Gideon were planning to spend his sabbatical in Europe, leisurely combining research with pleasure. Instead, Gideon was drawn into what became a triple homicide where the first step was to identify the victim. Julie, still a supervising park ranger at Olympic National Park, played helpmate again.

Peggy O'Neill

Author: M. D. Lake, pseudonym for Allen Simpson

Peggy O'Neill was a tall green-eyed redhead. She did not drink or allow smoking in her presence. She swam and bicycled regularly, and was sexually active but selective. She dropped one lover when his son came to live with him because she had no interest in marriage or children. Her father had been an abusive alcoholic who killed himself. Peggy, then a teenager, heard the shot and found the body. She described her mother as being whiny and pious. Peggy spent four years in the U. S. Navy before returning to her Minnesota alma mater as one of three campus policewomen.

In *Amends for Murder* (Avon, 1989), Peggy responded to a nuisance call only to find Professor Adam Warren dead. Dissatisfied by the lack of progress in the local police department, she began her own investigation. In *Cold Comfort* (Avon, 1990), Peggy connected the deaths of a pharmacy professor and a campus computer expert, exposing a scheme to provide American computer secrets to Communist countries.

During *Poisoned Joy* (Avon, 1992), Peggy withheld information about a personal friend suspected of murder from homicide detective Mansell "Buck" Hansen. She went off campus in *A Gift for Murder* (Avon, 1992), when she found the body of arrogant author Cameron Harris at the Towers building. Harris had planned a book, which might prove embarrassing to members of his writing group. In an extended narrative, Peggy ran an investigation parallel to that of the city police.

She learned that academic communities were not free of racial and religious prejudice in *Murder by Mail* (Avon, 1993). Her fellow police officers, African-American Paula Henderson and Caucasian Lawrence Fitzgerald set up housekeeping. Their probable tormentor was murdered. A bequest in his will set Peggy at odds with the University.

By *Once Upon a Time* (Avon, 1995), Lake's narrative skills had matured and Peggy had developed as a personality. Injured in her last adventure, she was on leave. She became interested in Pia Austin's obsession with Hans Christian Anderson while taking part in a university theater production of *The Emperor's Clothes*. Before she was through, Peggy had unmasked several suspects in the murder of Pia's father, but kept her insights from her mentor, Buck Hansen. She declined a promotion to detective, preferring to stay with her campus beat.

During *Grave Choices* (Avon, 1995), Peggy identified Daniel Sanchez as the fleeing suspect from the killing of an art professor. After he was charged with the crime, Peggy located the real killer.

Peggy had always preferred the night shift, but in *Flirting with Death* (Avon, 1996), she was stalked by a strange man who might have killed twice. She used her off-duty time to connect academic skullduggery with murder. During an evening work break in *Midsummer Malice* (Avon, 1997), Peggy chatted with Steadman George, a pianist fighting his alcoholism. Steadman recalled an adoption he had arranged twenty years before. His subsequent death was considered an accident, but Peggy wondered whether he had blackmailed the infant's adoptive parents or her putative father. Although Peggy did the detecting, it was the birth mother and her now grown daughter who confronted the killer.

Gary Mallory, who had been Peggy's lover for many years, wanted to buy a newspaper in Northern Michigan. Nevertheless in *Death Calls the Tune* (Avon, 1999), Gary revealed that he loved Peggy enough to continue living in the Twin Cities, if she would consider marriage and children. Peggy's troubled childhood had left her with no desire for either in her future. Her prior contact with rich and powerful Dulcie Turner led to a special assignment. She was to investigate the death of Dulcie's grandson. Music professor Evan Turner had been presumed to have fallen from a cliff at the University's Conference Center on Lake Superior. An examination of Evan's early life as a guitarist playing in clubs uncovered his love affair with a harpist who left him for a rival musician. This period of his life related to his death and the emergence of a "mystery woman" with whom Evan had been seen.

The narratives increased in complexity and readability over the years. One of the better series to remain in paperback.

Jocelyn O'Roarke

Author: Jane Dentinger

Like her author, Jocelyn "Josh" O'Roarke had been an actress, teacher and director. She was in her early thirties, of French-Irish descent with black curly hair and hazel eyes. From her brothers she had learned touch football and poker. Her father was dead but Frederick Revere, an older actor friend, had an avuncular role in her life. Josh was an agnostic and a dedicated liberal.

In *Murder on Cue* (Doubleday, 1983), Jocelyn's role in a play by college friend Austin Frost was minor, but she understudied the aging and unpopular lead, Harriet Weldon. When Weldon died after a blow from a stage sandbag, O'Roarke had to clear her name. Her relationship with Detective Phillip Gerrard helped. During *First Hit of the Season* (Doubleday, 1984), Josh played in an off-Broadway revival, panned by reviewer Jason Saylin. When someone laced Jason's cocaine with poison, Josh and Phillip found the real victim and the clumsy killer. Josh was too busy to consider Philip's proposal.

During *Death Mask* (Scribners, 1988), Josh was directing a play featuring Frederick Revere in an historic theatre soon to be demolished. The disastrous incidents that marred the production were connected to a major real estate deal. The relationship between Josh and Phillip was affected when she concealed vital facts during the investigation.

By *Dead Pan* (Viking, 1992) Phillip, tired of waiting, planned to marry someone else. Author Austin Frost offered Josh a role in a West Coast television movie. Josh was expected to offer emotional support to Ginger Jellicoe, an unstable former child star. Cinematographer Buddy Banks, who managed Ginger's trust fund died of chemical fumes. Josh showed a warm-hearted side to her nature in her commitment to help Ginger, and her six-year old daughter, Hilly.

The Queen Is Dead (Viking, 1994) returned Josh to New York City only long enough to agree to substitute in *The Winter's Tale* for murdered actress Tessa Grant. Phillip, who had broken his engagement, followed Josh to Corinth, New York, to reestablish their relationship. Josh knew many of the suspects personally, but learned more about them in a short time.

She was relieved to be back in New York City, as *Who Dropped Peter Pan?* (Viking, 1995) opened. While in between engagements, she took an interest in an off-off Broadway production of *Peter Pan*, which employed her friend P. J. Cullen. Having an aging male play the lead role appalled most of the cast, but artistic director Rich Rafelson had the clout to get the

222 Mystery Women: An Encyclopedia of Leading Women Characters in Mystery Fiction

part. He flopped in more ways than one when his harness tore, dropping him to his death. Although Josh investigated using Sgt. Thomas Zito as a resource, she solved the crime only with the help of Phillip Gerrard, who returned from an out of town assignment. Josh had to decide between Gerrard, and her West Coast lover, Jack Breedlove soon. Dentinger left the reader hanging too.

Initially abrasive, Jocelyn mellowed.

Karen Orr

Author: Frank Wyka

Twenty-nine year-old Karen Orr was a lesbian police detective in California. Her childhood provided only sad memories. Her deceased father had been an unhappy man, married to a woman who did not enjoy sex. Karen spent two years in uniform before becoming the only female on the Special Investigations Squad. She was concerned that the department might dismiss her if she disclosed her sexual orientation.

In *Wishful Thinking* (Carroll, 1988), Tom Baker asked his lover Ann to care for a kidnapped child. She did so under the impression that it was an effort to frighten the child's mother into being more responsible. When Tom's employer, the child's father, was murdered, Karen investigated. Fortunately Ann realized that the child was in danger.

During *Regression* (Carroll, 1989), Karen and her partner probed the death of psychologist David Epstein. Although most of his office files had been stolen, Karen traced current patients. She learned that Epstein used hypnotism on Teri Walker to recall the death of her parents while transporting drugs. Karen's homosexuality was a factor in her attraction to Teri.

Kieran O'Shaughnessy

Author: Susan Dunlap

Kieran O'Shaughnessy was a tiny woman with short black curly hair. She was single but shared her home with ex-jock Brad Tchernak, her houseman, and a huge mixed-breed dog. She was fiercely competitive, tough talking, and kept herself in excellent physical condition. Kieran had been fired after four years as a forensic pathologist because she made a serious error in an autopsy. After dismissal from the coroner's office, she traveled through Asia for several years; then returned to become a medical detective. A former Catholic, she had no tolerance for the church. She could not forget that her sister, who had been heavily involved in drugs and prostitution before her suicide, was denied a religious funeral.

Why then was she chosen by the Diocese of Phoenix, Arizona to solve the suicide/murder of a priest in *Pious Deception* (Villard, 1989)? Neither Father Vanderhooven's parents nor Kieran believed he had killed himself in autoeroticism. No one escaped tragedy in this narrative.

Kieran accepted Maureen Brant as a client in *Rogue Wave* (Villard, 1991) because she was interested in husband Garrett's paintings. Maureen suspected that Robin Matucci, operator of a fishing charter, had driven the car that left Garrett brain damaged. There were layers of deception: financial, political, and personal that had to be probed before an important initiative election.

Stuntman Greg Gaige had influenced Kieran when she considered a career as a gymnast. In *High Fall* (Delacorte, 1994), young Lark Sondervoil was killed, trying to duplicate Gaige's premiere stunt. Kieran refused to accept the death as an accident. Several of those present at the filming of Lark's stunt had been on scene when Gaige had been killed ten years before. Powerful film executives alternately helped and obstructed Kieran's investigation. She persisted, finding a new and old love in the process.

Kieran had known Dr. Jeff Tremaine from medical school when she considered him a stiff, rather dull man. She had met him again in Africa where they worked together for a short time in a clinic treating victims of Lassa fever. In *No Immunity* (Delacorte, 1998), Kieran agreed to confer with Jeff, then practicing in rural Nevada, on the death of an unidentified woman who might have died from a highly contagious hemorrhagic fever. She expected risk; she did not expect betrayal. She did not expect to be accused of breaking and entering, and possibly of murder. The narrative utilized frequent changes in viewpoint characters that may disrupt the flow of the plot for some readers. Kieran appeared in one story in Dunlap's collection, *Celestial Buffet*.

Bridget O'Toole

Author: Frank McConnell

Bridget O'Toole, a sixty-year-old nun, left the convent and the classroom to take over the O'Toole Investigative Agency when her father retired. Anyone expecting that the former Sister Juanita would be a Mother Teresa type was quickly disillusioned. Reminiscent of the Lam/Cool series, Harry Garnish, a foul-mouthed employee of the senior O'Toole, worked grudgingly with Bridget.

Harry handled the investigation in *Murder Among Friends* (Walker, 1983) when his friend Fred Healy was killed. He owed Healy that much; he had been sleeping with his wife. Bridget could lend a hand because the investigating officer had been her eighth grade pupil years before, but this was Harry's book.

In *Blood Lake* (Walker, 1987), Bridget assigned Harry to watch over Cheryl Howard at a Northern Wisconsin resort, but joined him later to solve the young woman's murder.

Kim Molloy, a former novice at Bridget's convent, contacted her for help in *The Frog King* (Walker, 1990). They called for Harry when Kim's stepdaughter disappeared. Bridget rode a Harley with "Cado" Molina, a Son of Satan, but Harry had most of the action.

Liar's Poker (Walker, 1993) had less of the McConnell humor. Harry was a darker character. Assigned to check out a religious cult to which a wealthy woman was making large donations, he bedded a nubile young woman after some serious drinking. Harry's contacts introduced him to college students who were harassed by professors and to a religious organization that was unknowingly supplying prostitutes. Bridget offered counseling, showing that she was less naive than Harry thought.

Bertha Cool had a few books of her own; Bridget never did.

Molly Palmer-Jones

Author: Ann Cleeves

Molly Palmer-Jones, a retired social worker, formed a professional partnership in a private enquiry agency with her husband, George. He had considerable involvement with the police force during his career in the British Home Office. He used his connections to obtain inside information, and worked easily with local officials when a crime occurred. Although she frequently felt ignored by George and the police with whom he worked, Molly had acquired excellent listening skills in her work, enabling her to gather information at a personal level. George, who suffered from depression, was happiest when bird watching, an addiction to which Molly was less seriously committed. Their cases arose from bird watching connections. She was a short plump woman in her sixties who gave little or no attention to her appearance. George saw her as the one person who would love and care for him in his moods. They had a happy marriage with children who had their own lives and never played roles in the series.

The couple had recently retired as *A Bird in the Hand* (Fawcett, 1986) opened with the discovery of an amateur ornithologist dead in a rural marsh. George and Molly knew the personal history of the victim before they were finished, but the solution was close to home. Members of the Gillibry Island Bird Trust met with bad news in *Come Death and High Water* (Fawcett, 1987). The land on which the observatory stood was to be sold. When the owner was murdered, George called for Molly.

During *Murder in Paradise* (Fawcett, 1989) a young bride trying to adjust to the insular community to which her husband returned, found herself involved in murder.

George had never forgotten aristocratic Eleanor Masefield, whose charm had bewitched him as a youth. So, in *A Prey to Murder* (Fawcett, 1989) he answered her call for help. She wanted protection for falcon eggs in an aerie located by her deceased husband. All Molly wanted, after Eleanor was killed, was to open George's eyes to the woman Eleanor had become. Her insights explained the killer's motives.

By *Sea Fever* (Fawcett, 1991), George and Molly had established a formal investigation agency. A client sent them to find his son, then with ornithologists observing an extraordinary gathering of sea birds. Shortly after they met the young man, he was murdered.

Molly's unconventional Aunt Ursula was dead when they arrived for an unplanned visit in *Another Man's Poison* (Fawcett, 1993). There was a connection between her death and the serial poisoning of birds and small animals in the area. It was Molly who picked up on the nuances of family controversy in the manor house.

James Morrissey, a prominent naturalist, was dead at the opening of *The Mill on the Shore* (Fawcett, 1994). The local police considered his death, after serious disability, to be suicide. His widow hired George to investigate. He insisted that Molly be there to help. George and Molly discovered how Morrissey's death was tied to industrial pollution and its continuing impact on local waters.

The setting moved to Texas in *High Island Blues* (Fawcett, 1996), when an investigation into a charitable scam enabled George to monitor a major migration of birds. A trio of men, originally from England, and a young female hitchhiker they had absorbed into their group, reunited at the migration, along with ornithology enthusiasts from abroad. Someone with a long memory found a reason to kill. Molly had no active role, but was the first to sense the motivation for the crime.

Not everyone will enjoy the ornithological details, although a great deal can be learned in a pleasant manner from the narratives. Most readers will be fascinated by the finely drawn characters of those obsessed with birds and the impact on those who love them.

Melita Pargeter

Author: Simon Brett

For those who like a touch of spice and larceny in their sleuths, Melita Pargeter can be a treat. A childless widow in her sixties, she was plump, her golden hair now white, but she was not a sweet old lady. Sweet young ladies become sweet old ladies. Melita was generous, non-judgmental, and pragmatic. The deceased Mr. Pargeter shielded her from the details as to how he earned his fortune, but prepared her for widowhood. He left her very comfortable financially; but also provided her with burglar tools and a directory of nefarious associates that was even more valuable. Melita enjoyed good food and wine, fur coats and brightly colored silks, limousines and theatre. She was a reader who frequented libraries wherever she lived, and a shrewd judge of character.

In *A Nice Class of Corpse* (Scribners, 1987), Melita resided at the Devereux Hotel for retirees even though the manager doubted that she was the "right kind." Combining her skills of listening and watching with burglary, Melita identified a thief and murderer.

The Devereux was unsuitable for Melita so she moved to a six-unit housing development in *Mrs., Presumed Dead* (Scribners, 1989). Even before her arrival a murder had occurred in Unit #6. Melita used Mr. Pargeter's notebook to enlist a housebreaker, a private detective, and a police informer in her investigation.

In *Mrs. Pargeter's Package* (Scribners, 1991), Joyce Dover, a recent widow, had asked Melita to accompany her on a trip to Corfu. A woman of Melita's experience should have been suspicious when Joyce asked her to carry a bottle of ouzo through customs. She was not prepared to find Joyce's dead body the first morning after their arrival.

Mrs. Pargeter's Pound of Flesh (Scribners, 1993) sent Melita off to a "fat farm," not that Melita intended to participate in the regimen. She merely accompanied her friend Kim Thurrock, who was anxiously awaiting her husband's release from prison. Melita was suspicious of the facility's close ties to the diet products of popular author Sue Fisher. Had they contributed to the deaths of staff members? No informer, Melita worked this out without involving the police.

Before his death, Mr. Pargeter had purchased a secluded plot of land on which to build a comfortable home. As *Mrs. Pargeter's Plot* (Macmillan, 1996) began, Melita's efforts to carry out his wish were stymied. Concrete Jacket, her contractor, was accused of murdering a potential blackmailer whose corpse had been deposited on the plot. Summoning allies from the past, Melita set out to prove Concrete's innocence, even though he refused to cooperate in his own defense. A recently released convict with badly orchestrated attempts at restitution enlivened the proceedings.

Mr. Pargeter's address book had bequeathed Melita with a list of "providers of future assistance." In *Mrs. Pargeter's Point of Honor* (Macmillan, 1998), she used those resources to assist Veronica Chastaigne, widow of a prosperous thief. Veronica's poor health made her anxious to return stolen works of art to their rightful owners. Unfortunately, Veronica's son opposed this decision. Thanks to kindly but inept Detective Inspector Craig Wilkinson, who admired Melita, the mission was accomplished.

A reader comfortable with dramatic license in the plotting will enjoy Melita's acquaintance.

Claire Parker

Author: Laurence Gough

Divorced homicide detective, Jack Willows teamed with Claire Parker in a Canadian police procedural based in Vancouver, British Columbia. Claire was initially twenty-eight years old, 5' 7" tall, slim, with black hair and dark brown eyes. She had strong feelings about drug pushers because her brother had been an addict. Claire had been at the top of her class at the Police Academy but was initially deployed undercover as a narcotics agent.

When Jack's partner Norm Burroughs was dying of cancer, Claire substituted. Resented by Jack at first, she saved his reputation, which established rapport. They began a relationship when his wife, Sheila took the children and left. Both Claire and Jack had killed in the line of duty, but suffered trauma as a result. Generally Claire appeared to be competent but lacking in warmth in the early books.

During *The Goldfish Bowl* (St. Martin, 1988), when Willows' long time partner was dying of cancer, Claire took his place. There was a sniper out there, somehow connected with a singles club. Claire's deductive thinking found the pattern that led to the killer but not before there was an excess of violence.

A contract killer and his Los Angeles employer were spotlighted in *Silent Knives* a.k.a. *Death on a No. 8 Hook* (St. Martin, 1988). Mannie Katz had been hired to kill several teenage prostitutes. Claire and Jack each discovered one of the corpses; then, tied their cases together through tattoos. Although Jack and Claire became intimate, he was lonely for his children and hoped to reconcile with his wife.

Serious Crimes (Viking, 1990) took place soon after Jack's wife left. He was feeling sorry for himself, and Claire was unable to divert his attention. It took the murder of Chinese newspaper publisher Kenny Lee, and a series of senseless juvenile delinquencies to focus him on his job. As always, Gough explored the motives behind the criminal acts; two young men, each thinking that he is duping the other, both destined for trouble.

In *Hot Shots* (Viking, 1990), distressed businessman Alan Paterson discovered a jettisoned drug shipment. Meanwhile Claire and Jack investigated the murder of the drug runner responsible for the mistake.

Inept killers left corpses all over *Accidental Deaths* (Viking, 1991). Junior, a.k.a. "Newt" Newton who had a score to settle with Claire, sent first one, then another hired gun after her. True love diverted the first potential killer. Clumsiness felled the second. Unaware of her danger, Jack and Claire solved crimes involving the Asian community.

Greg, a talented make-up artist used his skills to carry out a series of bank robberies in *Fall Down Easy* (Gollancz, c. 1992). He knew he had stayed too long in the Vancouver area, but wanted that last big score. A victim of his raid on the Bank of Montreal had surrendered a briefcase containing records of major drug laundering. Greg considered the information to be his chance for wealth. Jack and Claire, working well together professionally although their personal relationship was on hold, eventually discovered Greg's pattern and set a trap.

Sheila dropped Sean and Annie, their two children, off with Jack for an indeterminate period of time in *Killers* (McClelland & Stewart, 1993). This was a distraction for both him and Claire, who had been trying to build a life together. They needed to focus on the murder of a libidinous researcher at the local aquarium whose infidelities caught up with him in a shark tank. Realizing that Jack was depressed, Claire drew him back into her life, prodding him to accept that his marriage had ended.

The criminals had more trouble with one another and a vengeful police officer than they did with Parker and Willows during *Heartbreaker* (McClelland & Stewart, 1995). When Shelley, a small time thief, picked up an attractive female hitchhiker he did not realize how much baggage she carried from her past. Claire and Jack never solved the case.

Jack decided to file for divorce in *Memory Lane* (McClelland & Stewart, 1997), but soon became preoccupied with the death of a police officer. The focus of the narrative moved back and forth from the investigation to the troubles of Ross Larson. Larson was a parolee who had carried on a pen-pal relationship with Shannon, the girlfriend of his deceased cellmate, Garret Mosby. Mosby had shared his innermost secrets with Ross. What everyone wanted to know was did that information include where he had hidden the loot from his last robbery.

Karaoke Rap (McClelland & Stewart, 1997) was populated by inept, aging, sex-ridden criminals. Two bungling kidnapers took a sleazy financier and his mistress hostage, expecting his wife to pay ransom. They were unaware that the financier was a delinquent debtor of aging mob boss, Jake Cappalletti. Claire and Jack were diverted when the kidnapers shot Sean, Jack's son, but managed to connect the incidents and foil the villains.

During *Shutterbug* (McClelland & Stewart, 1998), Wayne, Cappalletti's competition, sent him a warning by killing off drug dealers. April, Wayne's wife, had an assignment of her own, preparing a small time crook to bear the responsibility for Wayne's crimes. Parker and Willow, working their way through the details of buying his wife's share of the house, had the case. By this time, Willow's two children lived contentedly with him and Claire, having little contact with their mother.

Like other businesses, criminal enterprises were subject to glitches caused by incompetent lower staff. In *Funny Money* (McClelland & Stewart, 2000), Hector and Carlos, couriers for ten million dollars in counterfeit U.S. currency, were instructed to delay delivery to mob boss Jake Cappalletti until he recovered from a stroke. Hector's misplaced generosity in giving $960 worth of "funny money" to Chantal, a young hooker placed the couriers and Chantal in danger. Claire and Jack were assigned to investigate the murder of Chantal's pimp, which delayed Claire's recognition that she was pregnant and wanted the baby. They had not married as yet and she was uncertain as to how Jack would handle the news that he would be a father again at age forty-six.

Gough's narratives were tough and realistic, but humorous, focusing more on the criminals than the investigation, providing excellent characterizations.

Amelia Trowbridge Patton

Author: Roger Ormerod

Many of the traditional British detectives (Lord Peter Wimsey, Roderick Alleyn) met their future wives when the women were suspects in murder cases. Amelia Trowbridge was a woman of spirit and ingenuity, but was distinguished from Harriet Vane and Troy Alleyn in that she was a murderess.

Patton was a widower in *The Hanging Doll Murder* a.k.a. *Face Value* (Scribners, 1984), when Amelia reported her husband missing. He was within days of retirement and in no mood for challenges. Amelia had been a prison visitor and advocate for Clive Kendall, a paroled child molester. A disfigured corpse in an empty cottage might be Kendall, but Amelia identified it as her husband. In a startling denouement, Patton disclosed Amelia's motivation for helping Kendall to get parole.

During *Still Life with Pistol* (Scribners, 1986), Patton accompanied Amelia to a summer course in painting promoted by an old friend. The vacation involved a murder that he investigated but Amelia, then not his wife, played no role. In *An Alibi Too Soon* (Scribners, 1988) Patton learned that his mentor, Llewellyn Hughes had been desperately trying to reach him. When Patton and Amelia arrived, the Hughes home was on fire and Hughes was dead. Patton's suspicion that Hughes' memoirs would expose police corruption kept him on the case even though he had no official status. Amelia's participation in this book was limited to jealousy of another woman and personal danger when Patton came close to the truth.

Amelia's Uncle Walter, who feared his own children, made Amelia the residual legatee to his substantial estate in *An Open Window* (Constable, 1988). Although it was Walter who was murdered, Amelia may have been the intended victim of a trailer explosion.

Amelia, possessed of a substantial income, was enjoying marital bliss with Patton in *Death of an Innocent* (St. Martin, 1989). A novelist friend and her husband asked Patton to investigate a break-in at their home. Amelia and Patton worked together to discover the killer of a young woman seeking her birth mother.

Richard returned to the location where he had served as a police official in *Guilt on the Lily* (St. Martin, 1989). He had responded to a plea from actress Linda Court, but she was dead when he arrived. Patton's replacement resented his involvement, threatening to re-open the Kendall murder case, which might implicate Amelia. After the death of a young policewoman, Amelia insisted that Patton solve the murders, while she diverted his successor.

Because he had been a police officer so long, Richard recognized in *No Sign of Life* (Constable, 1990) that although his 1977 Stag had been stolen, it was not the vehicle that the Felixstone police discovered near the docks. This mattered because that car had been involved in vehicular homicide. Richard knew the probable owner of the car, Hugh Lambert and his family whom he'd met ten years before while a detective sergeant. He knew where the answers were to be found in Sweden so that is where he and Amelia traveled in the damaged vehicle knowing that they would attract the notice of the police. Richard's intimate knowledge of the Lambert family made itr possible for him to identify two killers, but because he was no longer a police officer, he didn't have to tell…or did he? Amelia was held hostage for a while by the family of a victim, but without any harm coming to her.

Although Richard expressed his need to have Amelia with him when he worked because she "noticed all the little details," she generally played a passive role. The death of Eric Prost had been Richard's first case as a detective inspector. He had arrested Julian Caine on the basis of the evidence presented to him. In *When the Old Man Died* (Constable, 1991), a new development released Caine, forcing Richard to reconsider. Once he decided that Caine had not been the killer, it was incumbent on him to discover the culprit before another murder was committed.

The past intruded again in *Shame the Devil* (Constable, 1993), when a legacy of cameras and photographic equipment turned Richard's attention to a kidnapping case he'd worked fifteen years before. The kidnappers had been identified and imprisoned but the child and the young woman who had cared for him (and the ransom money) had never been found. The kidnappers approached Richard for help in finding the money. He was more interested in finding the truth, even though it brought shame and death to those involved. Amelia had discouraged this project, but went along to support his efforts.

Richard could not stop for an overnight away from home without encountering murder. In *A Mask of Innocence* (Constable, 1994), he and Amelia escorted Mary Pinson to the home of Sir Rowland Searle where she had once been a servant. Mary had cared for Amelia's Uncle Walter for many years and had a life interest in living in the home he bequeathed to Amelia. One glance at the youngest child of the recently deceased master of the house made it plain to Richard and Amelia that Mary had provided more than domestic service to Sir Rowland. Besides a legacy of £10,000, Mary was reunited with a daughter she had never known. The will contained other provisions—the family genealogy and other surprises which led to murder.

Although Amelia was resourceful and supportive, she had a sharp tongue, which she did not hesitate to use. What had been intended as an overnight visit to celebrate the birthday and engagement of Amelia's god-daughter, Mellie, became an extended stay in *Stone Cold Dead* (Constable, 1995). Richard's discovery of the corpse of a young policewoman cast suspicion on members of the household.

Worthwhile low key series, although the sleuthing was Richard's prerogative.

Amanda Pepper

Author: Gillian Roberts, pseudonym for Judith Greber

Although Amanda Pepper was a single high school teacher who solved mysteries with the assistance of a police officer, she was no clone of Hildegarde Withers. Thirty-year-old teachers were no longer categorized as spinsters. Moreover, the relationship between Amanda and C. K. Mackenzie went well beyond the platonic level. Amanda, described as "good-sized" with red-brown hair, taught at an exclusive private school.

In *Caught Dead in Philadelphia* (Scribners, 1987), Amanda found drama teacher Liza Nichols dead. She had excellent reasons for her own investigation: police detective Mackenzie suspected her; she had ignored Liza when the young woman sought her out; and whoever killed Liza might believe she had confided in Amanda.

Amanda wanted to provide her students with a dose of reality, so in *Philly Stakes* (Scribners, 1989) she developed a project to "help the homeless." Her conservative principal diverted the plan into a holiday party at a student's home, but wished he had not when the host was subsequently murdered.

Amanda returned in *I'd Rather Be in Philadelphia* (Ballantine, 1992), plagued by restless students and competition for Mackenzie's attention. Volunteer work at a used book sale set her on the trail of a battered wife. In *With Friends Like These* (Ballantine, 1993), familial loyalty sent Amanda to the posh birthday party of television producer Lyle Zacharias. When the guest of honor collapsed and died, the Pepper family had a motive, but so did other guests and service personnel.

How I Spent My Summer Vacation (Ballantine, 1994) found Amanda in Atlantic City. She took advantage of freebies offered by her friend Sasha Berg, a photographer on assignment, but paid a high price. While Amanda spent an all-nighter with the visiting C. K., Sasha was set up as prime suspect for the murder of an unscrupulous investment advisor. Unable to leave Sasha in jail, Amanda spent the rest of her vacation risking mayhem to prove that her friend was no killer.

During *In the Dead of Summer* (Ballantine, 1995), Philadelphia was hot. Classrooms at Philly Hill were not air-conditioned. Teaching *Romeo and Juliet* to ethnically diverse students was an invitation to murder. Mackenzie, recovering from a leg injury, warned Amanda to stay out of it, but did not expect her to do so. Her best student disappeared in the midst of gang fighting. Fellow teachers were harassed. A young man in love was crucified in the school gym. Enough was enough.

Amanda's good spirits revived for *The Mummers' Curse* (Ballantine, 1996) centering on the traditional parade that kept local clubs busy all year round in their preparations. When a participant was murdered, a fellow teacher used Amanda as an alibi, not realizing that she had attended with Mackenzie. The only way Amanda could help both her friend and Mackenzie was to investigate. The only way she could explain a murder weapon in her purse was to discover who put it there. Teachers will relate to Amanda's problems with an under-motivated but vindictive student. Philly Prep was competing for wealthy, upper class students in the area, which affected the principal's decisions.

In *The Bluest Blood* (Ballantine, 1998), Principal Havermeyer dodged unfavorable publicity brought about when a generous donation was used to purchase art and literary material offensive to Moral Ecology, a fundamentalist religious group. The lifestyle and personalities of the donors, Neddy and Tee Roederer had awed Amanda who considered Havermeyer unprincipled. The leader of Moral Ecology was murdered and Neddy died mysteriously. Amanda's concern centered on two students connected to the victims, whose lives were in disarray.

The impact of the Columbine High School tragedy on teachers was explored in *Adam and Evil* (Ballantine, 1999). Amanda worried about the stability of Adam, a senior in her English class. His parents were in denial about his bizarre behaviors. Havermeyer had no intention of offending generous donors. That all changed when Adam was accused of murder. Amanda risked more than life and limb in working her way out of academic burnout.

Author Roberts, who is a member of a book group, placed Amanda in such a setting in *Helen Hath No Fury* (Ballantine, 2000). Helen Coulter, a participant in the group had inveighed against a character's death by suicide as cowardly. When Helen "fell" from the roof garden of her home, why was almost everyone but Amanda so sure that it must be suicide? C. K. not only shared his first name with Amanda, but agreed to share his life with her.

Amanda was an attractively complex character in narratives with relevant social themes. The comic relief was based primarily on the efforts of her happily married sister, Beth, and her Florida based mother to find Amanda a conventional marriage—something appropriate for Philadelphia.

Andrea Perkins

Author: Carolyn Coker, pseudonym for Alison Cole

Artists and art historians possess acute visual perception that can be an asset to an investigator. American Andrea Perkins, who had copper colored hair and olive green eyes, spent much of her professional life in Italy. She had hoped for a career as an artist, but finding her skills inadequate, became an accomplished art restorer.

Formerly an art history instructor at Harvard, she was "on loan" as an assistant curator at the Galleria dell'Accademia in Florence as *The Other David* (Dodd, 1984) began. When an elderly priest brought a painting to Andrea at the Galleria, she suspected that it might be a Michelangelo, a portrait of his statue of David. Before the painting could be examined it was stolen. The investigation by Police Captain Aldo Balzani began a long-term relationship. Andrea visited Ferrara to restore paintings belonging to the Gonzaga family during *The Vines of Ferrara* (Dodd, 1986). Pressures within the household built as first one member, then another died from poisoned wine.

The identity of the criminals was made clear early in *The Hand of the Lion* (Dodd, 1987). Georges Tropard planned to kidnap Connie Gilbert's granddaughter, seeking an ancient death mask as the ransom. Not only did Andrea's attention to detail provide information for Balzani, but she saved the child's life. During *The Balmoral Nude* (St. Martin, 1990), Andrea worked at the Victoria and Albert Museum in London. Her interest in art, and old beau Clayton Foley's interest in Andrea drew her into a mystery. The murder was solved when the killer betrayed himself; then, was killed by a jealous lover. Interesting questions were: Who painted the nude? and Who were the models?

Appearance of Evil (St. Martin, 1993) retained Andrea as the titular sleuth and utilized her knowledge of English painting and genetic defects, but focused on African-American California policewoman Tina Roberson, and her womanizing partner, Eduardo Lopez. The police were investigating a nude corpse found adjacent to the Huntington Museum where Andrea was refurbishing Gainsborough's "Blue Boy."

These were entertaining narratives with a bonus in the glimpses of restoration and verification of art works.

Darina Lisle Pigram

Author: Janet Laurence

See: Darina Lisle, page 169

Marvia Plum

Author: Richard A. Lupoff

Marvia Plum transformed Hobart (Bart) Lindsey's life. A humdrum employee of International Surety, he had devoted his life to caring for his chronically mentally ill mother. She had never recovered from the death of her sailor husband during the Korean War. Then he met Marvia. She was an African-American policewoman in Berkeley, California, who challenged his perceptions of life, and warmed his heart and his bed.

Her own life had been difficult. While serving overseas in an Army military police unit, she had an affair with a commissioned officer. Her pregnancy created a problem for him, and could have meant a dishonorable discharge for her. Their solution was a quick marriage, a quick divorce, and Marvia's resignation from the service. She returned to California where her parents and brother Tyrone lived. With her skills, she found employment in the police force. Unable to care for her son, Jamie (10) as the series began, Marvia placed him with her parents. This made her vulnerable when her former husband, James Wilkerson, showed an interest in custody.

During *The Comic Book Killer* (Bantam, 1988), Bart challenged a dealer's insurance claim for 35 missing comic books, considering the amount excessive. His father had been a cartoon artist before he went into the service, but Bart had to be educated about comic book values. The mystery of these particular books went far beyond their intrinsic value and deep into Bart's past. While working with Marvia, he also received an education into the indignities suffered by African-Americans.

Attention was given to Bart's success in handling big claims. He was assigned to investigate the theft of a 1928 SJ Duesenberg Phantom convertible worth $425,000 in *The Classic Car Killer* (Bantam, 1992). He was no longer seeing Marvia and had settled back into his restricted existence. She lent a hand and the expertise of her brother Tyrone. Together, they discovered what made the Dusie irreplaceable. Realizing that his life would be incomplete without Marvia, Bart proposed but was rejected.

Bart was drafted into SPUDS (Special Projects Unit) of International Surety, where he was assigned only to the most difficult cases. Marvia had valuable insights for him in *The Bessie Blue Killer* (St. Martin, 1994). A movie based on the exploits of an African-American flying squadron during World War II was interrupted by murder on the set. International Surety was liable under an umbrella policy that covered costs incurred if production were halted. Marvia took Bart into the African-American South, and the history of discrimination against African-American servicemen during the War. James Wilkerson helped save young Jamie from a man who never put the past behind him. In the process of Bart's awakening, his mother found new strength, became independent, remarried and set him free.

There seemed no reason why early African-American films should be targeted for arson, but they were in *The Sepia Siren Killer* (St. Martin, 1994), International Surety had absorbed the original insurer of Pacific Film Archives, so Bart was the investigator. Mrs. Wilbur, Bart's former secretary, befriended an elderly client whose room had been burned. Bart and Marvia were together a great deal now on a personal level and discussed this case. They learned that producers for a time made parallel movies: one with a Caucasian cast, the other with an African American cast. Someone wanted those films destroyed.

The Cover Girl Killer (St. Martin, 1995) began with the death of an elderly man who had willed his fortune to "the girl on the cover" of the book, "Death in the Dark", published by an obscure Chicago firm. Bart and Marvia confronted an old foe while probing the history of Americans who had fought against the Fascists in Spain. They were lovers and had talked marriage. Bart was stunned when Marvia announced plans to marry Willie Fergus, an older police officer, whom she had known while in the service. Her son was to stay with his grandmother at least temporarily.

Bart moved to Denver to work out of the main SPUDS office, trying to put Marvia out of his mind during *The Silver Chariot Killer* (St. Martin, 1996). Subsequently, he was assigned to investigate the death and possible betrayal of a friend and fellow agent.

The marriage to Willie Fergus had been a disaster, sending Marvia back to California within months, as *The Radio Red Killer* (St. Martin, 1997) began. She was immediately assigned to the death of blind, left wing radio broadcaster "Radio Red" Bob Bjorner, during which she frequently wished she had Bart to help. She relied on MOM (motive, opportunity and method) to identify the murderer, but had to kill to save her son's life.

Before...12:01...And After (Fedogan & Bremer, 1996) included one Lupoff story about Marvia, during which she investigated serial killings of the more annoying residents of a business district.

Carrie Porter

Author: Elizabeth Travis

Ben and Carrie Porter left jobs at Foote & Marshall to start their own publishing company. Leaving behind their adult children Terry and Brooke, they moved to central Connecticut. Carrie, a tall blonde, managed the financial and sales aspects of the business, while Ben edited, cooked, and painted.

All was not quiet in Connecticut in *Under the Influence* (St. Martin, 1989). Philandering artist Greg Dillon was murdered with Ben's knife. For all of her business efficiency, Carrie assumed the passive role of the 1950's spouse, as Ben proved his innocence by trapping the killer.

In *Finders, Keepers* (St. Martin, 1990), the Porters combined their European vacation with detection. Author Charles Melton's will left the copyright to his book to whichever heir could locate the entire manuscript within one year. Carrie's journal became part of the story, detailing the alliances, jealousies, deception, theft, and inevitably murder among the competitors.

Eugenia Potter

Authors: Virginia Rich and Nancy Pickard

Eugenia Potter, a blonde with graying hair, had been born in a small town in northeastern Iowa. She and her husband, Lew, spent most of their married life either on their Arizona ranch or in Northcutt's Harbor, Maine. Although the couple had three grown children, Eugenia was very independent after Lew's death.

In *The Cooking School Murders* (Dutton, 1982), Eugenia, while revisiting Iowa, promoted an haute cuisine class taught by culinary expert James Redmond. Within a short time, three members of class died mysteriously. Although Eugenia cast her suspects in various scenarios, only when the killer confronted her, did she understand the years of resentment that underlay the murders.

The Baked Bean Supper Murders (Dutton, 1983) took place in Northcutt's Harbor where Eugenia planned to make her home. Her curiosity about the death of friend and neighbor Harvard Northcutt, and the explosion that killed two other residents, led to serious trouble.

Over the years "Genia" and seven other vacationing wives, whose husbands commuted from Nantucket Island to their work, had banded into "Les Girls." *The Nantucket Diet Murders* (Delacorte, 1985) found them renewing their acquaintanceship. A lover of good food, Genia was appalled by her friends' absorption into the diet regimens of Count Tony Ferencz. When Oscar deBevereaux, a local attorney, and his faithful secretary died mysteriously, Eugenia made it her business to see that the wrong person was not arrested for the crime.

After Virginia Rich's death, Nancy Pickard used Rich's characters and a tentative story outline to publish *The 27*Ingredient Chili Con Carne Murders* (Dutton, 1993). Eugenia returned to her Arizona ranch in response to a plea from foreman Ricardo Ortega. Ortega had arranged a neighborhood meeting that Eugenia was to attend, but was missing when she arrived. After Ricardo's body was discovered, his granddaughter Linda disappeared. Uncertain as to whom her allies might be, Eugenia located the young woman before a killer did. An unexpected bonus was the appearance of former suitor Jed White, eager to resume their relationship.

Pickard continued the series at a high level in *The Blue Corn Murders* (Delacorte, 1998). Restless and interested in archeology since she discovered a pottery shard on her ranch, Eugenia attended a special week for women at the Medicine Wheel Archeological Camp in Colorado. The "Hike Into History" week was troubled by staff dissension; i.e. conflict between those who wanted the site restricted to professional archeologists and those who recognized the financial advantages of having tuition paying amateurs involved. Add in an unfaithful husband who had to decide between two women. Eugenia found allies among the staff and participants to solve the mysteries.

It took a family crisis to lure Genia away from her beloved ranch in *The Secret Ingredient Murders* (Delacorte, 2001). She not only visited Devon, Rhode Island in response to a plea from Lew's niece, Donna Eden, but stayed on to cooperate with old friend Stanley Parker on a cookbook of Rhode Island recipes. After Stanley was murdered, Genia came to realize how controlling he had been. His generosity had been marred by manipulation. Genia's beloved grandnephew Jason was a vulnerable suspect in the murder. The clue to the real killer had been in Genia's kitchen all along.

These were pleasant books to read, to keep and read again, as one would a favorite cookbook. They were filled with a joy of food and the companionship that accompanies sharing a meal. Pickard's plotting was at least equal to Rich's, and she retained the flavor of the original series.

Georgina Powers

Author: Denise Danks

Englishwoman Georgina Powers was in emotional distress as *User Deadly* a.k.a. *The Pizza House Crash* (Futura, 1989; St. Martin's, 1992) began, coping with her husband's infidelity and the pending divorce. Her position as a scientific reporter for Technology Press required concentration. Georgina's cousin, Julian Kirren was to be posted to the United States for employment with a major corporation. He died in what appeared to be a sex related suicide. It became apparent that Julian, Georgina's former husband Eddie, and an ambitious female executive were influencing stock purchasers with subliminal messages.

Better Off Dead (Macdonald, 1991) found Georgina drinking too much, unable to find full-time employment, and lonely. She had no desire for the homosexual liaison offered by Carla Blue, an old friend who had become a rock star. Nevertheless, when Carla died suspiciously, Georgina had to know whether she had been murdered and by whom. Even when successful, she could not return to work, but visited the United States instead.

Frame Grabber (St. Martin, 1993) tied computers, pornography, sex, and detection together in a narrative that may leave some readers baffled. While in New York City, Georgina fell under the influence of Dr. David Jones, a developer of virtual reality in computer systems. Even the knowledge that David's wife cooperated in her seduction did not satisfy Georgina.

In *Wink a Hopeful Eye* (Macmillan, 1993), Georgina was joined by pal Charlie East, her former husband Eddie, and rough lover/computer executive, Shinichro Saito. They entwined Georgina in the world of high stakes poker with computer chips at risk, and South American drug lords as players. The pregnant Georgina lost her unborn child through mistreatment, but persevered to write a news story on the investigation.

Even loyal fans may find *Phreak* (Gollancz, 1998) more depressing than they can handle. Georgina had cut back on alcohol, but continued to enjoy pot and casual sex. Her cozy sharing of an apartment with Richard, a colleague at Technology Week, ended when his purportedly pregnant girlfriend moved in. Georgina was engrossed in a telephone scam when, one by one, her contacts were brutally murdered. If Tony Levi, a former lover had not protected her, she could have been next in line.

This was a difficult series to read. It was complicated by British jargon and computer talk, replete with sex and violence.

Celia Prentisse

Author: Andrew Taylor

Celia Prentisse, a scrupulously conscientious Englishwoman, had one weakness: William Dougal, the wild young man whom she had never forgotten. He was the son of Major Ted Dougal, a retired British Intelligence officer who was Celia's godfather and neighbor. Criminal behavior and a lack of responsibility had characterized William's ten years in America. (See *Caroline Miniscule* (Dodd Mead 1983) and *Waiting for the End of the World* (Dodd, 1984)

William returned to England and a patina of respectability just as Celia's father was being buried in *Our Fathers' Lies* (Dodd, 1985). Neither Celia nor William believed that Richard Prentisse had committed suicide. They had no idea that the roots of his death went back into a World War I cover-up that led to further injustices. There was an intervening Dougal adventure, *An Old School Tie* (Dodd, 1986).

Celia had made a new life for herself by *Freelance Death* (Dodd, 1988) working for a public relations firm. William engaged in historical writing, theft, and corpse disposal. He and Celia resumed their relationship. When he disclosed his activities, she shut him out of her life, aware that she was carrying his child. Fatherhood was a revelation to William.

In *Blood Relation* (Gollancz, 1990), Celia, now in a successful public relations partnership, allowed William conditional access to their daughter, Eleanor. The claims of family did not keep William from being drawn into the schemes of his old criminal mentor, Hanbury. Celia's motherhood had made her more tolerant. Even though she was aware of William's criminal activities she accepted him back into the household.

This arrangement lasted several years, but in *Odd Man Out* (Gollancz, 1993) William killed Miles, a friend of Celia's on whom she was depending for new capital for her business. The murder placed him in Hanbury's debt for disposing of the corpse. The possibility of reconciliation with Celia continued after William freed himself from Hanbury's power.

Lady Margaret Priam

Author: Joyce Christmas

When the series began Lady Margaret Priam was a tall fair-haired divorcee in her thirties whose only child had died in infancy. A member of a distinguished family, she had access to exclusive social circles in England and the United States. Lady Margaret earned extra income working for an oriental antique shop run by her friend, Bedros Kasparian. She had attended school in Switzerland and "dabbled in art studies at the Courtauld." Her two most frequent companions were: young Prince Paul Castrocani, son of an Italian nobleman and an American heiress, and her lover, Sam De Vere, a divorced police inspector.

In *Suddenly in Her Sorbet* (Fawcett, 1988), Margaret attended a charitable benefit sponsored by socialite Helene Harpennis. When Helene was poisoned, De Vere sought out Margaret both because he was attracted to her and because she had relevant information about the suspects. In *Simply to Die For* (Fawcett, 1989), Margaret was intrigued by the mysterious death of Ann Stafford, mother of a reluctant debutante whom Margaret sponsored in society. The connection drew Margaret into the personal affairs of the very private Stafford family who could not ignore a second murder at the debutante's coming out party.

By *A Fete Worse Than Death* (Fawcett, 1990) Margaret was astute enough to call the police immediately when her friend Emma, "Lady Ross", was found dead in her bath. Her decision to stay out of the investigation wavered when a young African-American deliveryman was accused of the murder. In *A Stunning Way to Die* (Fawcett, 1991) Margaret accompanied the corpse of Sylvia Code to Los Angeles. Because her employer, Bedros Kasparian, was suspected in Sylvia's murder, Margaret joined the California social whirl to find a killer, falling prey to all of the worst features of the Had I But Known (HIBK) heroine.

Margaret was more credible in *Friend or Faux* (Fawcett, 1991) when she returned to England. Her brother David, the Earl of Brayfield, needed help in dislodging a guest, Ramsamai Singh, the former Maharajah of Tharpur. The reclusive Maharani's murder during a country weekend was more than Margaret could handle, so De Vere provided support.

During *It's Her Funeral* (Fawcett, 1992), Margaret, at the request of Texas heiress Carolyn Sue Hoopes, represented the landlord's viewpoint in a neighborhood dispute about urban renewal. Public relations expert Rebecca Wellington and her attorney/husband opposed low-income activist Frances Rassell. When Rassell's corpse was discovered at a nearby construction site, Carolyn Sue hired Margaret to find the killer and protect the viability of her project.

Prince Paul dominated the first half of *A Perfect Day for Dying* (Fawcett, 1994) when, having been terminated at the bank, he accepted a position as major domo of the Caribbean estate of a wealthy English businessman. As he became enmeshed with the personal and criminal aspects of the Farfaine family and their jet set friends, he needed Margaret's help.

Gloria Anton, good friend of columnist Poppy Dill, sought Margaret's prestige in *Mourning Gloria* (Fawcett, 1996). Margaret was indebted to Poppy so she agreed to help with a fund raising project to be held in the house where Gloria's brother had died mysteriously. Not only Gloria, but also Margaret, became a target for killers who wanted the past forgotten. Margaret and Sam De Vere finally made a commitment—but see later books.

Dianne Stark, a friend of Margaret's, was disturbed when her younger sister "temporarily" joined her household. Karen had been trouble for Dianne in her first marriage and she did not want it to happen again. During *Going Out in Style* (Fawcett, 1998), Karen was murdered in front of the Stark home. Was she the intended victim, or was Dianne? There was guilt enough to go around, but Margaret decided not to share everything she knew with the police department.

Friendship was again the cause of Margaret's involvement in a murder investigation, but *Dying Well* (Ballantine, 2000) might well have been subtitled *All About Lucy*. Margaret agreed to help Texas heiress Lucy Rose Grant to find employment, a place to live and suitable friends to please Carolyn Sue. Sophisticate that she was, Margaret seemed slow to realize how the manipulative young woman would use her employment as social secretary to Roberta Reeves. She drove a wedge between Roberta (and her husband, Dale) and their children. She became part of the Reeves household with the goal of becoming the second Mrs. Reeves.

A Better Class of Murder (Fawcett, 2000) combined the talents of Margaret with those of Christmas's other sleuth, Betty Trenka (See Volume 3). Margaret was asked to make Betty's stay in New York City a pleasant experience to accommodate Carolyn Sue. Burned previously by the Texas hellcat, Lucy, Margaret was relieved to find Betty a pleasant and interesting guest. Although she intended to see the sights, Betty was serving as a representative of software expert, Ted Kelso. Gerald Toth, who had once shared a short-term affair with Margaret, had solicited Kelso to test a new product. From Betty, Margaret learned of the death of Xaviera, the beauty after whom Toth had named his corporation, but who had betrayed him. Margaret contributed to Betty's success in identifying Xaviera's killer.

The quality of writing was above average for paperback originals, providing interesting reading at an affordable price.

Kori Price

Author: Mary Margaret Pulver

See: Kori Price Brichter, Page 42

Molly Rafferty

Author: Sophie Belfort

The descendant of working class Irish immigrants, Molly Rafferty rose to academic status (History of Renaissance and Reformation professor) and linguistic competence (Italian and Latin). Little of her Irish heritage was evident.

In *The Lace Curtain Murders* (Atheneum, 1986), Molly, then a professor at Boston's Scattergood College, worked with police detective Nick Hannibal to solve the murder of a right wing female Congressional candidate. Molly was single, unsure of her relationship with Italian-American Nick, because her prior lover had rejected her to marry a woman of his own Jewish faith.

In *The Marvell College Murders* (Fine, 1991), Molly was on staff at Marvell College, and living with Nick. High school teacher Margaret Donahue, a friend of Molly, had been awarded a mid-career fellowship to the Marvell Center for Participating Politics. Virginal Margaret was exposed to her own sexuality, to high-powered academic politics, and to murder. Molly and Nick assisted her, but played subordinate roles.

In *Eyewitness to Murder* (Fine, 1992), Molly confronted World War II Nazis and Middle European conspiracies. Molly's mentor Caleb Tuttle had served in Army Intelligence. His murder, assigned to Nick, occurred before Molly left to take part in a Krakow, Poland conference. Cornelius Healey, a bigoted right-wing columnist whom Molly detested, was a fellow traveler. While in Europe, Molly and "good" German Wulfgang Ritter pursued a renegade priest and a misguided youth who was in search of his family's lost wealth.

Belfort's talents were evident in her sensitive treatment of personal relationships, such as Margaret Donahue's romantic interlude with union organizer Jack Larson.

Deb Ralston

Author: Lee Martin, a.k.a. Martha Webb,
pseudonyms of Anne Wingate

Deb Ralston differed on a personal level from the hard-edged professional investigators. She was a police officer who shared her life with a husband and children. A Nancy Drew/Hardy Boys reader as a child, she aspired to become a Texas Ranger but had been rejected. As the series opened, Deb had been a Fort Worth police officer for over fifteen years. Deb and Harry, a helicopter test pilot, did not have a token child but a houseful. Their first three multi-ethnic children (Vicky, Becky, and Hal) had been adopted. The Ralstons related to their community differently than most fictional professionals. They attended church services, played bingo at the Elks, and were involved in their children's activities.

Older daughter Vicky was married and expecting a child; Becky (19) and Hal (15) lived at home as *Too Sane a Murder* (St. Martin, 1984) began. When Deb entered the scene of a multiple murder, she accepted that former mental patient Olead Baker was the killer. After getting to know Olead, Deb not only became convinced of his innocence but involved her family in supporting him.

Deb was jogging when she discovered the corpse of a pregnant woman in *A Conspiracy of Strangers* (St. Martin, 1986). An ankle bracelet identified the young woman. Deb uncovered a racket that supplied infants to adoptive parents. She learned that she was pregnant for the first time at age 42.

In *Murder at the Blue Owl* (St. Martin, 1988), Deb attended a party for multi-married Margali Bowman. Later, she researched the deaths of Margali's former husbands to learn why she had been poisoned. *Death Warmed Over* (St. Martin, 1988) explored the impact of dead children, grieving parents, and the corpse of an elderly man on police officers. Deb used her resources: Dr. Susan Braun, Aline Brinkley of the Dallas Police Department and husband Harry to pull this one out.

Late in her surprise pregnancy, with Harry in the hospital, Deb coped with a runaway teenage son in *Hal's Own Murder Case* (St. Martin, 1989). Sixteen-year-old Hal and his girlfriend had decamped on a hitchhiking vacation. Before Deb could locate them, Hal had been jailed on suspicion of killing a young woman in New Mexico. Hal was cleared before infant Cameron Martin joined the family.

Her maternity leave over, Deb returned to work in *Deficit Ending* (St. Martin, 1990). Harry's injury had ended his professional flying, so he was job hunting. When a young woman was taken hostage in Deb's presence, she identified the culprits. Forgetting to follow the manual, she failed to provide for backup. *The Mensa Murders* (St. Martin, 1990) suffered from loose ends and an obvious murderer. Deb and policewoman Sarah Collins trailed a killer who overestimated his own intelligence.

As *Hacker* (St. Martin, 1992) began, Deb experienced "burn out." She was so overwhelmed by her family and personal problems that she had become unresponsive to tragedies on the job. One case, in which a young drifter was the most likely suspect in an ax murder, was reminiscent of *Too Sane a Murder*. Hal's girlfriend Lori was in a coma at the hospital after a car accident. Deb checked a virus on a computer network, and the tendency of powerless women to use axes to kill. The coincidence that tied the two story lines together was convenient.

During *The Day that Dusty Died* (St. Martin, 1994), Deb reluctantly accepted a short-term transfer into the sex crimes unit. Her personal experience with incest had sensitized her. She challenged her fellow officers to come to the aid of children who showed signs of sexual abuse. The narrative incorporated subplots that highlighted abuse as well as the danger that innocent persons can encounter when their acts are misinterpreted.

Inherited Murder (St. Martin, 1994) took Deb off the job as the Ralston family journeyed to Salt Lake City. Son Hal was about to embark on his mission year for the Mormon (Latter Day Saints) Church. It was to be a farewell celebration. Motels were out of the question for the Ralstons. They settled for a "Bed and Breakfast" operated by Georgina Grafton. Georgina's mentally ill sister was brutally murdered during the stay. Deb's unofficial investigation delved into Multiple Personality Disorders and Utah history.

The circus world has fascinated people for generations, and Deb was no exception. In *Bird in a Cage* (St. Martin, 1995), she and Harry were present when a young pregnant aerialist fell during a nightclub performance. Only by immersing herself in the history of the special families who compose most of the world's aerial acts could Deb unravel the rivalries and hatreds that lasted over the generations.

Deb enjoyed the multiple ancestries of her birth and adopted children. In *Genealogy of Murder* (St. Martin, 1996), she encountered a killer to whom an historical heritage was more important than life, or at least than other people's lives.

The Thursday Club (Bookcraft, 1997), which included two murders and two unplanned deaths, was dependent upon coincidence and human errors, amateur psychological evaluations, and unforced confessions. Deb had been jogging with Jeanne Minot when her paraplegic husband Curtis was killed. Deb then became a one-woman task force as the corpses piled up and suspects poured their hearts out to her.

A reader who enjoys both Erma Bombeck and mystery stories should try the series particularly the earlier books.

Dolly Rawlins

Author: Lynda La Plante

Dolly Rawlins thought she would never recover from the shock when she learned that her husband, Harry, and three confederates had been burned to death trying to rob an armored car. Harry had provided Dolly with a good life, but kept his business affairs to himself.

In *The Widows* (Sphere, 1983; Warner, US, 1994), Dolly was provided with access to Harry's "ledgers" which contained plans for another major robbery. Gathering the widows of the three other burn victims, Dolly put Harry's plans into action, just as he would have wanted. The women added a few surprises of their own. Dolly made one big mistake, which eventually put her behind bars.

She earned a reputation as a leader among the women prisoners. When *She's Out* (Pan, 1995) opened, Dolly was due for release. The police were watching to see where she hid the loot from the last caper. Far more dangerous was a group of former convicts who pretended to support Dolly's plan to build a home for the children of women in prison.

La Plante has spread herself generously across television screens and book pages. This was not one of her better efforts.

Annabel Reed

Author: Margaret Truman

See: Annabel Reed Smith, Page 268

Clio Rees

Author: Jo Bannister

See: Clio Rees Marsh, Page 183

Caitlin Reese

Author: Lauren Wright Douglas

Thirty-nine-year old Caitlin Reese was a lesbian private investigator working in Victoria, British Columbia. She had spent seven years in France while her father served overseas. He was a stern short-tempered man, who caused Caitlin to leave home at sixteen. A scholarship enabled her to attend the University of Toronto. After graduation from law school, she worked for seven years in the Crown Prosecutor's Office. Burned out, she neither went into private practice as an attorney, nor maintained an office as an investigator, but accepted clients by referral only. Caitlin was 5' 8" with red brown hair and gray-green eyes. She had several cats, triggering her interest in animal rights.

In *The Always Anonymous Beast* (Naiad, 1987), Caitlin was hired by Val Frazier, a married television anchorwoman who was being threatened. A blackmailer possessed letters exchanged between Val and her lover, Professor Tonia Konig. Caitlin recommended that Val and Tonia come out of the closet but agreed to retrieve the letters. In *Ninth Life* (Naiad, 1990), Caitlin was to take delivery of a package for a new client. At the pickup site, a young woman was seen speeding away pursued by two men in a car. The "package" was a badly injured cat, which was later connected to animal abuse by corporate interests testing chemical reactions.

The Daughters of Artemis (Naiad, 1991) explored the reaction of a militant segment of the lesbian community to rape. Caitlin learned that a rapist she had sent to prison while a crown prosecutor had been released. The man was vengeful and dangerous so Caitlin went to Saanich where his prior victim still lived. While there she came into contact with a para-military female group that devised their own punishments for rapists.

A Tiger's Heart (Naiad, 1992) harkened back to a time when Caitlin had cared deeply for Jonna Rowan, a part Native American high school classmate. Jonna had chosen a heterosexual marriage. Over twenty years later, a frightened Jonna sent her ten-year-old daughter to Caitlin for protection just before she was murdered. In *Goblin Market* (Naiad, 1993) schoolteacher Laura Neal had been receiving pictures through the mail. A friend who intercepted them hired Caitlin to locate the sender. Blind criminologist Eliane St. Cyr had developed a system for identifying prospectively violent persons. She connected the letters to a potential killer.

The repercussions from a child molestation case, which Caitlin had plea-bargained while a crown prosecutor, had not ended as *A Rage of Maidens* (Naiad, 1994) began. The molester had served his time and was employed at a recreation center. Alicia, the victim, had moved away with her mother, leaving behind her father and Andrea, the sister who had reported the incident. Caitlin, whose past included molestation by a non-family member, sought to trap the offender who was active again. Then she protected the woman who killed him.

The narratives contained considerable violence and explicit sex. Plots focused on issues of general interest; rape and animal abuse within a lesbian context, but had an anti-male subtext.

Janet Wadman Rhys
Author: Alisa Craig, pseudonym of Charlotte MacLeod

Janet Wadman was a farmer's daughter from Pitcherville, New Brunswick. An attractive woman with bronze hair and dark gray eyes, she had been raised by an older brother and his wife after the death of her parents. Upon graduation she worked as a secretary in St. John, New Brunswick but returned to Pitcherville to recover from surgery. She was devout, virginal, and rather prim.

In *A Pint of Murder* (Doubleday, 1980), Janet was convinced that eighty-seven-year-old Agatha Treadway did not die a natural death. A home canner, Agatha would never risk food poisoning. Janet was the only one questioning the death until the Royal Canadian Mounted Police, in the person of Madoc Rhys, came on the scene.

Janet continued to see Madoc, even being introduced to his distinguished parents in *Murder Goes Mumming* (Doubleday, 1981). Janet's employer invited the young couple to a Christmas weekend. The dysfunctional host family did not realize they had a policeman guest.

Janet led off again in *A Dismal Thing to Do* (Doubleday, 1986), when her car was stolen, her purse disappeared, and she was in danger of rape or death. Once rescued, Janet was vulnerable because she could identify the attackers. *Trouble in the Brasses* (Avon, 1989) ignored Janet except to confirm her marriage to Madoc and her pregnancy. Madoc intervened when members of his father's symphonic orchestra were killed.

The Wrong Rite (Morrow, 1992) was subtitled *A Madoc and Janet Rhys Mystery*, but her role was supplementary. The Canadian Rhys family en masse visited Wales for the 89th birthday celebration of Madoc's great uncle. Cousin Mary, a genealogist and gem cutter, exploded during the festivities because gunpowder had been placed in her pockets. Janet's primary contribution was an observation that cleared Daffyd, Madoc's brother, of suspicion.

Amanda Roberts

Author: Sherryl Woods

Amanda Roberts was a liberal urban reporter, who abandoned her career to move to rural Georgia where her husband had found work. The narrative played on the culture clash between an ex-student rebel from an educated family and the more conservative setting. Her husband's affair with a college student ended the marriage. Stunned, Amanda, a journalist with a law degree, stayed on to work at the local weekly paper.

By *Reckless* (Popular Library, 1989), Amanda was eager to return to work on a major newspaper. While covering a local food demonstration, she witnessed the death of Chef Maurice. Amanda solved the murder, began a romance, and was offered a job on a nearby Atlanta newsmagazine.

During *Body and Soul* (Popular Library, 1989), an assignment to cover a local health club turned into a murder investigation. Retired police detective Joe Donelli and secretary Jennie Lee were there to help Amanda when she needed it.

In *Ties That Bind* (Warner, 1991), Amanda was left waiting at the altar by Donelli. His car had been bombed. He had disappeared. Bucking the local police and FBI and diverted by a juvenile delinquent, Amanda came to understand Joe's other responsibilities. Nevertheless she postponed any consideration of marriage. *Stolen Moments* (Warner, 1995, reprint of Severn House 1991) brought Mark, Amanda's former husband, back into her life. He and elderly socialite Martha Wellington were active in the historical preservation movement. The theft of an antique gun triggered an expose of a group undermining preservation. Amanda paid a price for her scoop.

As *Bank on It* (Warner, 1993), began, Joe and Amanda were still estranged. Knowing that Amanda was bored with her job, her editor sent her to meet an unknown informant in a graveyard. After the informant was murdered, Amanda's interference endangered a government investigation. Jogging was a chore for Amanda in *Hide and Seek* (Warner, 1993). She met interesting people, one of whom was murdered a short time later, the sixth serial killing of a professional woman.

Life had stabilized for Amanda by *Wages of Sin* (Warner, 1994). She and Joe were married. They were planning the adoption of Pete, the thirteen-year-old they had taken into their home. Domesticity did not keep Amanda from investigating the presumed suicide of a talented female political figure, who had everything to live for. Armand Le Conte, the mysterious power broker who had assisted Amanda in the past, spirited away her chief suspect.

In Deadly Obsession (Warner, 1995), she and Joe learned more about Pete's unhappy family life. Why would blue-blooded Hamilton Kenilworth accept the responsibility for the death of his runaway wife, Margaret? Amanda found out, but suppressed the story.

With a happy marriage and an adopted teenager, Amanda took the next step towards domestication in *White Lightning* (Warner, 1995). She became pregnant. She learned that her elderly friend Martha Wellington was dying. Martha could not rest in peace until Amanda unraveled a fifty-year-old mystery. She had loved a married bootlegger convicted of killing a revenue agent. She never believed him guilty. Now his grandson, Willie, was in jail for a similar murder. Overcoming early nausea and problems at work, Amanda, Joe and Jenny Lee solved both crimes.

Countess Aline Griffith Romanones

Author: Aline, Countess Romanones

Readers who shook their heads in disbelief at Helen MacInnes or Ann Bridges' upper class secret agents should read the non-fiction adventures of Aline Griffith Romanones. Griffith, a native of Pearl River, New York, and a graduate of a Catholic college for women, sought active participation in the Second World War.

While working as a Hattie Carnegie model, she told a blind date about her ambition, not realizing that he would pass the information on to the War Department. Aline, who spoke both French and Spanish, trained with the OSS (Office of Strategic Services). By the time she finished training, Aline could pick a lock, send coded messages, and kill an enemy.

During *The Spy Wore Red* (Random, 1987), Aline was in neutral Spain where she mingled in elite social circles, investigating ties between prominent Spaniards and the fascist governments of Italy and Germany. The OSS was aware that there was a mole in their Intelligence System, but only at the Normandy landing did Aline realize it was a friend from her recruit class. In 1947 Aline left the service to marry Luis, the Count of Quintanilla (name later designated as Romanones).

The Spy Went Dancing (Putnam, 1990) covered her postwar services. She had settled into a routine as hostess, wife, and mother to three sons, but agreed to help uncover a spy at NATO. During *The Spy Wore Silk* (Putnam, 1991), Aline accompanied Luis on a business trip to Morocco where there were rumors of a plot to kill King Hassan, an American ally. Bill Casey, later head of the CIA, worked with Aline to foil the coup.

Romanones, the author, left reality behind in *The Well-Mannered Assassin* (Putnam, 1994) in which she mixed fact and fiction. Aline's connections with Carlos the Jackal, an acknowledged assassin, were explored at great length. He supposedly was so impressed by her kindness and nobility that he risked his liberty to warn Aline of danger. Aline deceived her adoring husband by working for the CIA against his wishes, tracing smugglers and rescuing a battered wife.

Eleanor Roosevelt

Author: Elliott Roosevelt, her son was listed as the author,
but at least some of the books are reputed to have been ghost written

Like Hillary Clinton, Eleanor Roosevelt was ridiculed and praised, vilified and sanctified. A remote cousin of her husband, she was a shy, intelligent young woman, devoted to the scapegrace father who died early in her life. She spent much of her youth in boarding schools, led a sequestered life in early adulthood moving from the tyranny of her grandmother to the domination of her mother-in-law. Franklin was a handsome man. They made an unusual couple—the Ugly Duckling married to Prince Charming. Eleanor never grew to be a beautiful woman, but became a poised, articulate champion for equal opportunity and civil rights. FDR, when president, valued her insights, but must at times have wished she had a sense of humor. Was this the Eleanor portrayed in Elliott's series?

Eleanor would have been loyal to staff as she was to her young English secretary in *Murder and the First Lady* (St. Martin, 1984) even when she was accused of gem theft and the murder of her former lover. FDR might have encouraged Eleanor to play cupid and solve a murder that had ramifications for international finance as he did in *The Hyde Park Murder* (St. Martin, 1985).

The name-dropping was excessive in *Murder at Hobcaw Barony* (St. Martin, 1986), when financier Bernard Baruch included Eleanor as a guest at his South Carolina estate, along with Joan Crawford, Tallulah Bankhead, Humphrey Bogart, and an obnoxious producer destined to be murdered. In *The White House Pantry Murder* (St. Martin, 1987) Winston Churchill visited. The discovery of a dead man in the walk-in refrigerator sparked Eleanor's support of a young staff secretary. An investigation exposed the presence of a Nazi agent on the White House staff.

Eleanor was in London for *Murder at the Palace* (St. Martin, 1988) when old friend Sir Alan Burton, was accused of murder. Then, back to

Washington for *Murder in the Oval Office* (St. Martin, 1989), where there was the familiar pattern of Eleanor befriending a suspect and then using her influence in the investigation.

The series' plots reflected the 1980's headlines in *Murder in the Rose Garden* (St. Martin, 1989). When the daughter of a deceased Mississippi Senator was found dead on the White House premises, Eleanor worked with Missy Le Hand, FDR's secretary to find the killer. The books had become repetitious by *Murder in the Blue Room* (St. Martin, 1990) when Elliott died. Another body in the White House, a sprinkling of famous names, and Eleanor methodically listing and eliminating suspects. The series did not end with Elliott's death, but continued with *Murder in the Red Room* (St. Martin, 1992), the corpse being a professional killer; *Murder in the West Wing* (St. Martin, 1992); tied to Huey Long's Louisiana politicking; *Murder in the East Room* (St. Martin, 1993) where Eleanor's rapport with the servants provided a clue.

During *A Royal Murder* (St. Martin, 1994), Eleanor and an entourage that included U.S. intelligence agents traveled to the Bahamas to visit the Duke and Duchess of Windsor. The murder of a Swedish industrialist who had supplied war goods to Hitler's troops brought Eleanor and a cooperative African-American police commissioner into an investigation of pro-Nazi businessmen who took advantage of the Windsors' self-centered naivete.

Then came *Murder in the Executive Mansion* (St. Martin, 1995) during which the King and Queen of England visited the White House. The staff was so pre-occupied that they failed to notice a body in the linen closet.

Murder in the Chateau (St. Martin, 1996) stretched credulity, presenting Mrs. Roosevelt as her husband's representative at a secret meeting between Free French generals and prominent German officers, seeking a negotiated peace early in the Second World War. Mrs. Roosevelt assisted in covering up murders in order to keep the conference going, but was determined to identify the killers before she left Vichy, France. Touches of romance between Eleanor and a raffish Irish mercenary were unconvincing.

Murder at Midnight (St. Martin, 1997) returned to the early days of the Roosevelt administration. Franklin had assembled his Brain Trust (professors and economists who assisted in the development of government policy), a few of whom lived at the White House for short periods of time. When Judge Horace Blackwell, a former prosecutor in New York City, was discovered dead in his bedroom, the African-American maid who initially found him was jailed. Eleanor, concerned that the woman would be "railroaded", directed the police towards other suspects.

The diminutive but powerful Madame Chiang Kai-Shek was a guest in the White House during *Murder in the Map Room* (St. Martin, 1998).

The murder of a Chinese shoe salesman in the room adjacent to the Oval office brought Eleanor into a case that involved drug smuggling and international espionage. The White House had not run out of rooms, but Eleanor ventured out again in *Murder in Georgetown* (St. Martin, 1999). At the request of Louis Howe, Eleanor had recommended young Jessica Dee for a position on Senator Huey Long's staff. When an official of the Federal Reserve Board was murdered, Jessica who had been his lover, was suspected. The narrative targeted the Kennedys, the Boston Irish, and General Douglas MacArthur.

FDR and Churchill met with top military officers at the White House to discuss opening a second front in *Murder in the Lincoln Bedroom* (St. Martin, 2000). Meanwhile Eleanor assisted the Secret Service and District Police in their investigation of the death of a disloyal presidential assistant. They learned that the victim had planned to kill FDR, but had become a burden to his fellow plotters. How were guns and assassins entering the heavily guarded White House?

Eleanor had help from several officials during the series: Sir Alan Burton of British Intelligence, Secret Service Agent Stan Szczygiel, and Lt. Edward Kennelly of the D. C. police, who had great affection for her. A hit list of public figures now deceased were criticized, even vilified, during the mysteries including Nelson Rockefeller, Henry Ford II, Huey Long, Lyndon Johnson, Sam Rayburn, the Windsors, and Alfred Sloan.

Rune

Author: Jeffrey Wilds Deaver a.k.a. William Jeffries

Rune was a free spirit, who lived first as a squatter in an abandoned New York City building, then moved to a houseboat tied to a city wharf. She had tried a variety of jobs (and names) since she left home. They ranged from the conventional (waitress, shoe clerk) to the marginal (street sales, clerking in a porno video store, gopher for a pair of Australian filmmakers) to the successful, assistant cameraman for Network News. Her objective was to write, direct, and produce her own documentary.

Physically, she was tiny and slight with auburn hair that she dyed, cut and styled in assorted punk fashions. Her clothing was eclectic, mixing colors, patterns, fabrics, and styles. Rune had limited formal education, but followed her enthusiasms; i.e. taking college courses in mythology and collecting children's fairy tales. She lived in a physically dangerous neighborhood, unaware of her vulnerability, a mixture of bravado (carelessly inviting men to her apartment), insecurity (she seemed unsure of her own sexuality), and naivete. She was wary of commitment, easily bored, and impulsive. Rune acknowledged that she lived in a dream world, visualizing the grimy dangerous metropolis as a magic land. She preferred her version to reality.

In *Manhattan Is My Beat*, (Bantam, 1989), Rune was drawn into murder when she called on a customer of her video store employer, only to find the police department investigating his death. She believed that the victim was on the trail of a million-dollar ransom and decided to find both the money and the killer. Rune's chance appearance outside a porno theatre just before it was bombed in *Death of a Blue Movie Star* (Bantam, 1990) enabled her to produce a documentary on the life of a porno queen. It also connected her with Detective Sam Healy, a divorced older man, who provided stability in her life. The finished film bore the name, Irene Dodd Simons, as producer, possibly Rune's name.

She parlayed her temporary job as a cameraman into an opportunity to produce a major story in *Hard News* (Doubleday, 1991). Rune believed that Randy Boggs was innocent of the murder of a former network executive, even though he had been convicted of the crime. Interesting. Earlier works in this series have been reprinted, possibly as a result of Deaver's other series featuring Lincoln Rhynes.

Maggie Ryan

Author: P. M. (Patricia) Carlson

As the series began, Maggie Ryan was a tall, slim brunette undergraduate majoring in English and mathematics at Hargate University in upper New York State. She spoke French, had been a gymnast, swam and bicycled for pleasure; played the flute in a student orchestra and was involved in the university theatre.

In *Audition for Murder* (Avon, 1985), set in the 1960's, Maggie worked the lights in a college production of *Hamlet*, which employed professional actors. Nick O'Connor and his drug and alcohol addicted wife Lisette played major roles. Although the play succeeded, Lisette was a casualty. Maggie had become a graduate student in statistics when *Murder Is Academic* (Avon, 1985 but set in 1968) began. Nick O'Connor and Maggie dated casually, and then became serious. The narrative explored not only Maggie's concerns but also the reactions of other women on campus to a rapist and a murderer.

Nick had a major role in *Murder Is Pathological* (Avon, 1986). Vandalism, the slaughter of test animals, and the death of a custodian disrupted Maggie's work in a biology lab. Nick, temporarily at leisure, hired on as a substitute custodian. He needed Maggie's gymnastic skills and his own escape tactics to avert a multiple murder. Nick was a sturdy balding older man but Maggie recognized that he had the capacity for love that would make him a wonderful husband.

In *Murder Unrenovated* (Bantam, 1988), set in 1972, the couple moved to Brooklyn. Maggie was pregnant, working as a statistician. Their new residence had an obstreperous elderly tenant in the basement and the corpse of a young man on the premises.

By *Rehearsal for Murder* (Bantam, 1988) Maggie had her Ph.D. in theoretical statistics while new father Nick worried about finances. He was rehearsing a play with potential for a long run if the star part were well cast. When the female lead was first injured and then died, Maggie and Nick found a questionable solution.

Murder in the Dog Days (Bantam, 1991) involved the again pregnant Maggie in the problems of her brother and his wife, Olivia. A co-worker of Olivia died under suspicious circumstances while Maggie was visiting. An interesting aspect was the exchanges among Donna, the abused wife of the victim, Holly, an ex-Vietnam war nurse now a police detective, and Maggie, who had opposed the war.

Maggie took her children on a short-term assignment in *Murder Misread* (Doubleday, 1990). Over a three-day period, she was embroiled in academic controversy, child molestation, and murder. *Bad Blood* (Doubleday, 1991) was a moving book in which murder and detection were secondary to the trauma felt when fifteen-year-old Ginny Marshall left her adoptive parents to find her birth mother. Maggie, who bore Ginny as an unwed teenager, was caring, mature, and resourceful in helping the girl and her adoptive parents and in solving a murder.

The development of Maggie's character from the college student of the 1960's to the wife and mother of the 1970's was paralleled by the increase in Carlson's literary skills. The early books foreshadowed the sensitivity and warmth that ripened in the later books.

Rachel Sabin

Author: Wayne Warga

Rachel Sabin, who had long black hair and dark blue eyes, was described as "well-built." Her physical charms were balanced with a Master's degree in Fine Arts and a part-time teaching job at Cal State-Long Beach. A moderate feminist, she enjoyed cooking at home, and in her spare time was an art dealer. What more could Jeffrey Dean, a former foreign correspondent who became a rare book dealer in Los Angeles, require as a romantic interest?

The couple met in *Hardcover* (Arbor House, 1985) at a book fair to which Rachel had accompanied her Aunt Lena, a rare book dealer. Dean had learned that forged books were being sold at the fair; one, a book he had previously handled. Their romance progressed as they uncovered an international plot.

Rachel received additional exposure in *Fatal Impressions* (Morrow, 1988). Her Frank Stella print was on loan to curator Henry Thurmon, when he was killed. The substitution of art fakes was tied into foreign intrigue.

During *Singapore Transfer* (Viking, 1991), Dean decided their personal relationship was too confining. He set off on an adventure of his own, an assignment in the East, which included diversion by a lovely Chinese-American customs agent. Rachel joined him later in Hawaii, but was "tied-up" for the real action.

Quin St. James

Author: T. J. MacGregor, pseudonym for
Trish Janeschutz a.k.a. Alison Drake

Quin was tall and thin with dark brown hair and a constant appetite for junk food. Before working as a private investigator, she had been a teacher. Mike McCleary, then a Miami police officer, came into her life in *Dark Fields* (Ballantine, 1987), when he investigated the death of her lover. Their initial relationship was adversarial, but they became intimate. When Quin and Mike co-operated to solve the crime, their affinity was a problem for Robin, Mike's female police partner.

By *Kill Flash* (Ballantine, 1987), Quin and Mike were married and partners in a detective agency. They monitored a television series produced by Gill Kranick, a boyhood friend of Mike's. After a major star was killed and Gill threatened with death, Quin went undercover as an actress while Mike openly investigated the murder.

During *Death Sweet* (Ballantine, 1988), a client who wanted an investigation of his half-sister's death hired Mike and Quin. Mike had an affair with a former lover, causing a rift in the marriage.

In *On Ice* (Ballantine, 1989), Mike awakened, sharing a bed with a dead woman, not only unaware of how he came to be there, but also with amnesia so serious that he could not remember Quin. As *Kin Dread* (Ballantine, 1990) began, Mike and Quin, although estranged, ventured into the Everglade swamps, where they encountered members of an inbred clan. This was more an adventure, than a mystery. Quin's pregnancy ended the separation.

Spree (Ballantine, 1992) was an orgy of blood, madness and brutality. "Cat", McCleary's actress sister, who had been living on an isolated farm connected to witches, was a victim. Quin refused to be left behind even though she had an infant to care for. It took Mother Nature to get Quin out of this one. Quin speculated on how motherhood and marriage cramped her style as a partner in the detective agency. In *Storm Surge* (Hyperion, 1993), Quin and Mike investigated the death of a former CIA employee. They challenged renegade government officials with the help of a hurricane.

The twilight zone of the series was intensified in *Blue Pearl* (Hyperion, 1994), during which an uneducated Peruvian mystic was accused of the death of his socialite wife. As in other narratives, the unidentified killer's thoughts and feelings were expressed periodically in italics. At the request of Fitz Eastman, a Palm Beach detective, Mike had been secretly investigating the heiress's murder. Only when Mike was gunned down while jogging, did Quin learn of his involvement, clear Alejandro Domingo, and rescue his daughter from scientific experimenters. Mike left the hospital to unmask an ambitious politician. Mike and Quin competed with one another while trying to save their marriage.

In *Mistress of the Bones* (Hyperion, 1995), Quin, managing a pre-school child along with hot flashes to remind her of her age, accompanied Mike to Tango Key. Mike and Quin had been named as joint executors of the will of bail bondsman Lou Hernando. The couple moved into Lou's house, reputedly haunted by a dead woman with whom he had fallen in love. The police had settled on a seventeen-year-old delinquent as Lou's murderer. Mike and Quin risked their future together to prove otherwise. There was a surprising conclusion.

MacGregor offered intricate plots with complex characters, occasionally wandering off into ruminations by the killers, astrology, I-Ching, dream and nightmare sequences.

Fiona Kimber-Hutchinson Samson

Author: Len Deighton

Bernard Samson was the hero of what became a triple trilogy:

- *Berlin Game*, (1983); *Mexico Set* (1985); *London Match*, (1986); all by Knopf;

- *Spy Hook* (Knopf, 1988); *Spy Line* (Knopf, 1989) and *Spy Sinker* (Harper, 1990). Fiona, his wife and mother of their two children, was woven into the first five books and had a compelling role in *Spy Sinker*.

- *Faith* (Harper, 1994); *Hope* (Harper, 1995) and *Charity* (Harper Collins, 1996).

Fiona was a fascinating character. Like Bernard, she was employed by MI5, the British Intelligence Agency. The daughter of a financier, she had attended Oxford where she flirted with Communism. She worked for a travel agency until she entered the Intelligence service. Once hired, she rose rapidly as a brilliant scholar and a fine linguist.

Fiona had an aristocratic appearance, beautiful with long dark hair. She had one sister, Tessa, who played a role in several books. Although Fiona had independent wealth, Bernard refused to allow it to be used for family expenses. Theirs was a strange match. Bernard had humble origins, did not attend college, and was never really accepted by Fiona's family. He narrated all books except *Spy Sinker*, so Fiona was portrayed through his viewpoint—the elusive woman who rose to the top levels at MI5 only to defect, who schemed to have their children abducted and brought to East Germany, and whom he could never forget even though he took a mistress, Gloria. Only in *Spy Sinker* did a different Fiona emerge. The books should be read in order. Once begun, the reader will find it difficult to stop. PBS televised a fascinating series based on the second trilogy.

After several other unconnected books, Deighton returned to the Samsons in *Faith* (Harper, 1994). Bernard remained the focus, torn between his love for Gloria and his long-term adoration of Fiona. She was presented less sympathetically on her return from Russia: a difficult, ambitious wife; a neglectful mother; and a doting daughter. Bernard returned to the field-work that he preferred and was assigned to bring in a major defector, Verdi, whom he did not trust. Bernard knew that his detractors in the London office were working to damage him, and that Fiona had attached her career to his nemesis, the ambitious Dickie Cruyer.

As *Hope* (Harper, 1995) began, Fiona's brother-in-law, George Kosinski, a member of a prominent Polish family but a British citizen, still would not accept the death of his wife, Tessa. Deluded into the belief that she was alive and pregnant with their first child, he defected, and only Bernard could bring him back. Bernard's obsession with the cause of Tessa's death dominated Charity (HarperCollins, 1996), pitting him against forces within British Intelligence who wanted a cover-up. Only when he laid that to rest, could he rebuild a life with Fiona and the children. Her role was to wait.

The final trilogy lacked the emotional tension of the earlier narratives.

Abigail "Sandy" Sanderson

Author: E.X. Giroux, pseudonym for
Canadian Doris Shannon to whom some of the books are credited

Although a supporting character, Sandy Sanderson played roles ranging from nursemaid and substitute mother for introspective barrister Robert Forsythe to independent investigator. She was a parson's daughter who initially worked for Robert's father. At that time she took on a semi-maternal status because Robert's mother had died. She understood loneliness, having been sent to a childless aunt in London when her parents could no longer support their large family.

Later, as a tall single gray-haired woman in her fifties, she acted as secretary to Robert, offering an exceptional visual and aural memory, quick wit, and dedication. She had few private interests and even fewer vices (smoked and enjoyed a double malt whiskey).

Robert and Sandy were introduced in *A Death for Adonis* (St. Martin, 1984), when she joined his self-imposed professional exile. He had been accused, but not found guilty, of misconduct. Robert was jolted out of his seclusion by a request that he reopen a twenty-five-year-old criminal case.

It was Sandy who brought Forsythe to the Norfolk estate where a film company was remaking *Wuthering Heights* in *A Death for a Darling* (St. Martin, 1985). Although the obnoxious male lead Mickey Dowling was a candidate for murder, it was actress Marcia Mather and hostess Honey Farquson who were poisoned.

Robert and Sandy's services were sought when a light-fingered hitchhiker was interned in the Dancer family crypt in *A Death for a Dancer* (St. Martin, 1985). Sandy's sprained ankle kept her prone for most of the action. In *A Death for a Doctor* (St. Martin, 1986), Sandy went undercover to probe the murder of four members of Dr. Paul Foster's family, but let Robert handle the deductive process.

An elderly rake, looking up his illegitimate children, should expect to meet with hostility. In *A Death for a Dilettante* (St. Martin, 1987), Winslow Penndragon was murdered. Although Sandy was on the premises, Robert solved the case. In *A Death for a Dietitian* (St. Martin, 1988), she was the "detective" at a mystery party on a secluded island when two of the guests were killed. Although Forsythe returned in *A Death for a Dreamer* (St. Martin, 1989), Sandy had a large role in the investigation of deaths at a nursing home.

In *A Death for a Double* (St. Martin, 1990), Buffy, Sandy's nephew, felt indebted to Anthony Funicelli, a rich Italian-American. Funicelli had brought his young wife to England for the birth of their child. It was look-alike cousin, Fredo who was murdered.

Robert and Sandy journeyed to British Columbia in *Death for a Dancing Doll* (St. Martin, 1991). Rebecca Holly had never accepted the determination that her granddaughter Thalia committed suicide. Robert sent Sandy to Hollystown, a rural community dominated by the family. He withdrew from the case when convinced that his client withheld valuable information, but resumed the investigation when Rebecca was murdered. Sandy had no impact in *Death for a Dodo* (St. Martin, 1993) in which Robert solved a seventeen year-old crime while recuperating from surgery.

Sandy's adulation of Robert was just bearable in a series with excellent plotting. She saw herself as an assistant gathering information but lacking Forsythe's ability to fashion a solution from the data.

Vonna Saucier

Author: J. Madison Davis

Vonna Saucier, an African-American private investigator, became professionally and personally intimate with Dub Greenert, when he joined the Devraix private investigative agency in New Orleans. She was a warm loving woman, who had served in the U. S. Army prior to employment as an investigator.

Greenert, a white divorced detective, was a graduate of the Citadel, scion of a military family, and a Vietnam veteran. He worked out of the Pittsburgh area, but came to New Orleans in *White Rook* (Walker, 1989) to investigate the death of a restaurateur that had been labeled a suicide. The case evolved into an undercover operation for Greenert into the activities of a white supremacist organization, which recruited mercenaries. Vonna and Dub became lovers. Her role as an investigator was subsidiary to his, but expanded in the fast acting conclusion.

The interracial romance was under stress, partly because she and Dub were dieting, as *Red Knight* (Walker, 1992) opened. Mrs. O'Dell, the widow of the victim in the earlier book, hired Dub to protect a white attorney. He was being harassed by both African-Americans and whites as a result of a book detailing activities in the civil rights movement of the Sixties. When the attorney was kidnapped and his alcoholic, promiscuous wife was murdered, Dub and Vonna worked together to uncover unsuspected motives for the crimes.

Catherine Sayler
Author: Linda Grant, pseudonym for Linda V. Williams

Catherine Sayler conveyed efficiency and professionalism as a private investigator. In her personal life, she had a pet snake, a mouse, and two cats—one at home, one at the office. She played the classical guitar; read Dylan Thomas; drank foreign beers and studied Aikido. No wonder she occasionally had migraines. The daughter and ex-wife of police officers, Catherine realized that her decision to become a private investigator was partly responsible for the breakup of her marriage to Dan Walker. She specialized in commercial crime. Her lover, Peter Harmon, also a private investigator, preferred defense investigations and divorce work. Catherine was described as a 5' 7" tinted blonde in her late thirties.

Random Access Murder (Avon, 1988) intertwined Catherine's personal and professional life. Marilyn Wyte, a woman Peter had been investigating, was found dead with a piece of Peter's shirt in her hand. *Blind Trust* (Scribners, 1990) began when bank executive Daniel Martin hired Catherine, and eventually Peter, to investigate a flaw in the bank's security system that must be corrected within fourteen days. Their progress threatened someone because Peter was shot, leaving Catherine to carry on.

She convinced embezzler Owen Merrick to sign a confession with a promise of non-prosecution that was betrayed in *Love Nor Money* (Scribners, 1991). When Merrick committed suicide, Catherine was determined to help his family even if she had to resort to blackmail. Her runaway niece Molly moved in with Catherine and Pete. An old friend was accused of murdering a judge who had molested children. The three story lines were well blended.

A Woman's Place (Scribners, 1994) was set in an established computer corporation that had recently absorbed an innovative but misogynistic upstart company. The corporate president hired Catherine's firm to discover who was playing crude pranks on the female staff. By the time she and Jesse, her African-American assistant, went undercover, the pranks had escalated into vicious threats and murder. In personal danger, Catherine relied on force to protect herself.

Jesse had become a partner by *Lethal Genes* (Scribners, 1996). The relationship between Catherine and Peter was tenuous, a matter he dealt with by an extended visit to Guatemala. In his absence the agency immersed itself in DNA's, corn genetics, and murder. The University of California-Berkeley plant genetics laboratory staff expected a major breakthrough with commercial applications. Greed and ambition among staff members sabotaged the project.

Catherine, Jesse, Peter, and young Molly worked together in *Vampire Bytes* (Scribners, 1998). The narrative mixed live action role-playing, the death of a computer wizard who had absconded with vital source codes, and the disappearance of a young girl who had lost touch with reality. Catherine challenged the Palo Alto police department that suspected her of involvement in a satanic cult.

Grant's narratives are well above average for female private investigators, but will primarily appeal to those with an interest in computer mysteries.

Rebecca Schwartz

Author: Julie Smith

Rebecca Schwartz had followed in the footsteps of her attorney father Isaac, although her mother had hoped that she would become a concert pianist. She regularly consulted a psychiatrist, smoked pot, and maintained a one hundred gallon aquarium. Rebecca had studied drama and enjoyed theatre. In the law office that she shared with Chris Nicholson, another woman attorney, Rebecca cultivated an eclectic clientele.

For a lark she played piano in a bordello in *Death Turns a Trick* (Walker, 1982). Unfortunately her escort recognized his sister Kandi as one of the "girls." After Kandi was murdered in Rebecca's apartment, she fought off a rapist, went to jail, and ran her Volvo into another car to solve the case. In *The Sourdough Wars* (Walker, 1984), a theatre benefit raised money by auctioning off the cryogenically frozen sourdough starter of the famous Martinelli bakery. After pal Peter Martinelli was murdered and the starter stolen, Rebecca endured a repeat trip to the jail, and was almost murdered. Rebecca's family was uncomfortable with her boyfriend, Rob Burns, a newspaperman. He was only half-Jewish.

During *Tourist Trap* (Mysterious Press, 1986), she and Rob discovered the crucified body of a Phoenix tourist when they attended a sunrise Easter service. Warnings were sent to Rob indicating that the "Tourist Trapper" intended to kill again. His coverage of the incidents caused a rift with Rebecca who considered it inflammatory. The promised "accidents" continued: an uncontrolled cable car, an elevator crash, and a traffic pile-up on the Golden Gate bridge. When Rebecca and Rob worked together to uncover the perpetrators, they resumed their affair.

Dead in the Water (Ivy, 1991) began when Marty Whitehead, a fellow tropical fish enthusiast, was accused of killing her boss at the Monterey Bay Aquarium. Rebecca was not only present when the body was discovered, but acted as Marty's attorney and baby-sitter for her two children. Rebecca met the next significant man in her life, Julio, a marine biologist with a nine-year-old daughter, Esperanza.

Although Rebecca realized that Julio offered better long-term prospects (if she wanted them), she spent *Other People's Skeletons* (Ivy, 1993) with former beau Rob Burns. Rob and Rebecca were drawn together when her law partner was accused of the hit and run death of Jason McKendrick, the Chronicle's entertainment critic. Rebecca's agnosticism was challenged by awareness that many of those most important in her life (Chris, Julio, and her father) held beliefs she had never suspected. The lump in her breast made her conscious of her own mortality. The narrative included about thirty pages of gross-me-out details as to how the killer intended to dispose of his victims.

Although an attorney, Rebecca rarely used her legal skills.

Aline Scott

Author: Alison Drake, pseudonym for
Trish Janeschutz a.k.a. T.J. MacGregor

The grittiest female sleuths may have lived in Chicago and New York and the most liberated and casual on the West Coast. Florida has at least a claim to the most sensual. Aline Scott was described as tall, slender, thirty-four years old, with wavy cinnamon hair worn in a ponytail and "vibrant" blue eyes. While employed by the Tango Key Police Department, she owned a part-interest in two bookstores on the mainland managed by a partner. Her house pet was a skunk (Wolfe) rather than a cat or dog.

Steve Murphy was Aline's lover as *Tango Key* (Ballantine, 1988) began. Their relationship became troubled when he showed an interest in

Eve, a married woman who resembled his murdered wife. When Eve's husband was killed, Ryan Kincaid, local private investigator, was hired to discover the murderer.

Fevered (Ballantine, 1988) found Aline and Kincaid in an established relationship, marred by his long foreign vacations that Aline could not share. After the vicious murders of Judge Henry Michael and his family, Kincaid and Aline ran parallel investigations complicated by their prior lovers.

Aline and Kincaid had separated by *Black Moon* (Ballantine, 1989). She was spending her leisure time with Simon Martell, the county prosecutor. Kincaid and Aline could not ignore one another when they both became involved in the death of a mysterious dancer.

Margaret Wickerd had escaped from a mental institution, leaving two corpses behind in *High Strangeness* (Ballantine, 1992). Aline realized that Margaret was merely a pawn in a conspiracy among government officials, military leaders, and scientists. The premise bordered on science fiction, and might disappoint a traditional mystery reader.

Hana Shaner

Author: Roma Greth

Hana Shaner, a Pennsylvania manufacturer, was not only interesting in her own right but numbered among her friends and acquaintances members of the little understood Amish community. Although a Unitarian Universalist, Hana appreciated the "plain people." She had become self-sufficient at any early age. After her mother deserted the family, Hana's father included Hana in his home-furnishing business. Upon assuming control at his death, she opened up a line of women's clothing. At forty, green-eyed Hana's blonde hair had turned white, but she remained trim. She shared her family estate with a collection of dogs and cats. The establishment was presided over by housekeeper Sal Nunemacher and major domo Mr. Fred.

Hana was disturbed in *...Now You Don't* (Pageant, 1988), when her assistant Grace Urich disappeared. She moved into Grace's home, checking the neighborhood for clues as to what might have happened. Her insistence that a recently dug trench be uncovered, and that the body revealed there was not Grace, left the local police unsure as to whether Hana was a bumbling amateur, a suspect, or deranged.

During *Plain Murder* (Pageant, 1989), Hana's housekeeper Sal asked Hana for help when police sergeant Will Kochen investigated the death of a young Amish man in the family barn. She was far more likely to get information from the closed Amish society than an outlander like Kochen. When a second youth was murdered, Hana and Will combined to find the killer. The narrative provided a realistic and sympathetic look at a subculture, seeking to protect its youth from outside influences.

Lucy Shannon

Author: Dick Belsky a.k.a. Richard G. Belsky

Lucy Shannon, a tough-talking reporter on the New York Blade, had earned her reputation in Vietnam. She was confrontational with the police, the administration of the Blade, and her co-workers. A short blonde in her thirties, she was single initially, but sexually active, eschewing monogamy even in her affairs. Once assigned to a story, she was tenacious, stealing papers and pictures from those she interviewed, and concealing information from the police.

During *One for the Money* (Academy, Chicago 1985), Lucy covered the murder of an ambitious young actress, whose battered corpse had been found in her parents' upscale apartment. Nancy Kimberly had worked at a record shop where a customer had left behind a mysterious briefcase. Whatever the case contained, it was important enough to trigger several additional murders, and danger to Lucy.

Lucy did not reappear for twelve years, when *Loverboy* (Avon, 1997) by Richard Belsky was published. They had been tough years for Lucy: three failed marriages, a battle with alcoholism, and a decline in her professional status. (However, she was still in her thirties.) In her prime, Lucy had covered "Loverboy", a serial killer who attacked young couples trysting in parks. A film company, making a movie on the case, invited Lucy to play herself in the motion picture. The disappearance of a young woman led to the discovery of corpses in a manner reminiscent of Loverboy. Lucy had made mistakes during the original investigation: falling in love with detective Jack Reagan, and concealing Reagan's murder of a suspect. They came back with a vengeance as she followed the case to its bitter end.

Emma Shaw

Author: Hazel Wynn Jones

Emma Shaw, who worked as a script supervisor in the English movie business during the 1950's, hoped to write and direct her own productions. When she and assistant director Hal Halliwell came together in *Death and the Trumpets of Tuscany* (Doubleday, 1989), she was in love with him, but he was married. Because she had lived in Rome for years, Emma was chosen as the guide for actors and staff in Italy during the filming of *Trumpets of Tuscany*. When several deaths occurred on the set, Emma knew who stood to gain. She and Hal eventually married but separated when his ambitions left no room for hers. While she achieved a modest success in documentary films, Halliwell became a prominent producer.

They met again quite by accident in *Shot on Location* (Doubleday, 1991) when she observed the film company. Hal needed a temporary script supervisor, so she signed on. The sexual peccadilloes of the cast and crew fueled death and accidents on the set. Emma's eye for detail led to a solution in which the killer decided his own fate.

Technical details were well integrated by Jones, a veteran of the film industry, but the narratives were plodding.

Veronica Sheffield

Author: Caroline Burnes, pseudonym for Carolyn Haines

Along with Ann Tate and Dawn Markey, Veronica Sheffield was one of a trio of characters, who each played the dominant role in one of Caroline Burnes Harlequin novels, while having minor parts in others.

Reporter Veronica Sheffield balanced her growing attraction to State Senator Jeff Stuart against her suspicion that he was corrupt in *A Deadly Breed* (1988). The opponents of a Mississippi racetrack were determined to keep even honest gambling (an oxymoron?) out of the state. Local horse breeder Ann Tate provided shelter for Veronica when her life was threatened.

Although the love scenes were typical of pulp paperback romances, the series was interesting particularly when read in sequence—*A Deadly Breed* (Harlequin, 1988), *Measure of Deceit* (Harlequin, 1988) and *Phantom Filly* (Harlequin, 1989). Also see: Dawn Markey, page 181 and Ann Tate, page 279.

Ellie Simon

Author: Dorothy Cannell

See: Ellie Simon Haskell, Page 120

Evangeline Sinclair

Author: Marian Babson

See: Trixie Dolan, Page 77

Veronica Slate

Author: Lary Crews

A glance at the paperback covers featuring Veronica Slate would provide readers with a preview. She was a tall green-eyed divorcee, who survived a youthful marriage to an abusive U. S. Navy pilot. The divorce occurred in Texas, but Veronica moved to Florida. She graduated from college, and found work, first as a secretary, and then on a late night talk show for WAQT, Tampa Bay. Her father Archie had been both a sheriff and a FBI investigator, but retired when his wife was killed by a car bomb. Veronica lived with two cats (Rum Tum Tugger and Jennyanydots) and later added David Parrish, a homicide investigator to the household.

In *Kill Cue* (Lynx, 1988), disk jockey Danny Keaton romanced Veronica until he fell in love with homosexual actor, Glenn Gregory. When Danny was murdered during his radio show, Veronica's investigation led to her meeting with Parrish.

Extreme Close-Up (Lynx, 1989) concerned the relationships of the two most important men in Veronica's life. Her Dad had acquired a lady friend. David's ex-wife Angela was in town making a movie. Angela's murder was designed to implicate David, the beneficiary on her life insurance. In *Option To Die* (Lynx, 1989), the serial murderer was obvious early in the book, during which Veronica left David and the cats behind to visit her Dad and his lady-friend, Barbara. Veronica developed clues to prove that the deaths were not random, but purposeful revenge.

Crews often described characters by reference to celebrities. Veronica looked like Connie Sellecca; David, her lover, was likened to "Joe," Rhoda's television husband. The books had colorful settings, and convoluted plots.

Annabel Reed Smith

Author: Margaret Truman

Annabel had many of the stereotypical qualifications to become a fictional sleuth: red hair and green eyes; young attorney, tired of the large firm setting; interest in the arts, and a background in the political scene. Her initial goal had been success as a lawyer. Burned out, she turned her interest in Pre-Columbian art into a career as the owner of an art gallery.

In *Murder at the Kennedy Center* (Random House, 1989), Annabel was the minor partner in a trio of amateur sleuths, subordinated not only to Mac Smith, a law professor whose wife and child had been killed in a car accident, but to his associate, private investigator Tony Buffalino. *By Murder at the National Cathedral* (Random, 1990), the couple had married. Subsequently, the officiating clergyman was murdered. On their English honeymoon, Annabel's escape from an arranged accident and the discovery of a second corpse did not deter the couple from continuing their investigation of the priest's death.

Annabel's attitude towards Mac's participation in criminal work was a reluctant acceptance, coupled with willing assistance once he took on a case. She had a broader role in *Murder on the Potomac* (Random, 1994), primarily through her position on the Board of Directors of the National Building Museum. Wendell Tierney, a Washington power in industry and the arts, used Mac's friendship to entice him into probing the death of his devoted administrative assistant. Neither Mac nor Annabel had significant roles in *Murder at the Pentagon* (Random, 1992).

Annabel's art expertise gave her an advantage over Mac in *Murder at the National Gallery* (Random, 1995), but the narrative revolved around staff members at the Gallery. Luther Mason, senior curator with a long-term obsession for Caravaggio, betrayed a lifetime of dedication. He conspired to substitute two copies of "Grottesca", and keep the original for himself. The greed and subsequent murders of Mason's conspirators eventually brought his downfall.

When Congressman Paul Latham reluctantly agreed to be nominated as Secretary of State, he asked Mac Smith to serve as his counsel before the Senate hearings during *Murder in the House* (Random, 1997). Latham anticipated difficult questions about his connection with international businessman Warren Brazier. He did not anticipate his own murder in a secluded park. Mac's probe into the death involved the Russian Mafia, but had no role for Annabel.

Annabel and Mac moved to the prestigious Watergate Complex, which included both co-op apartments and more temporary living facilities. They were long-time friends of Vice President Joe Aprile and his wife Carole, Annabel's college roommate. During *Murder at the Watergate* (Random, 1998), Joe was a candidate to replace the current president. He had problems disassociating himself from current policies of which he did not approve; e.g. U. S. tolerance of weak drug control efforts by the Mexican government. Mac, while acting as an administration representative investigated the deaths of several others who opposed the current policy.

Annabel was at the center of *Murder at the Library of Congress* (Random, 1999) while Mac limped around, postponing needed knee surgery. Her stint at the Library was preparation for an article she was writing on Christopher Columbus. The project took a lower priority when a distinguished researcher was murdered. He had been selling Library information to a private citizen. Although there was more than enough greed involved, sexual rejection had led to the killing.

Jill Smith

Author: Susan Dunlap

Jill Smith, a college dropout from New Jersey, ended up as a Berkeley police officer. She had left college for the police force to subsidize husband Nat's education, but came to enjoy her work. Once he graduated, Nat wanted a conventional housewife. She was tall and trim with gray-green eyes and brown hair; dressed casually in L. L. Bean, Eddie Bauer, and Land's End. After the divorce, she lived in a finished porch tacked on the back of her landlord's house, spending her nights in a sleeping bag on the floor. She preferred junk food to her own cooking. At work she was a thorough professional except for chronic tardiness at staff meetings. Jill had an unenviable assignment as a police officer in that highly anti-establishment community, Berkeley, California. The Berkeley police were not like other urban departments.

In *Karma* (Raven, 1981), Jill attended a Buddhist blessing ceremony out of curiosity, but remained as "officer on the scene" when the Bhutanese lama was murdered. Personal relationships dominated *As a Favor* (St. Martin, 1984). Nat was concerned about the disappearance of a co-worker. Police officer Seth Howard, Jill's best friend, needed help because someone was trashing his car.

By *Not Exactly a Brahmin* (St. Martin, 1985), Jill had been assigned to Homicide. Ralph Palmerston, a wealthy philanthropist with failing eyesight, should not have been driving a car, particularly not when someone had perforated his brake lines. Jill's investigation into the death of Liz Goldenstern, a paraplegic activist for the rights of the handicapped in *Too Close to the Edge* (St. Martin, 1987), left her enjoying a new closeness with Seth Howard.

After an injury in a helicopter crash, Jill took sick leave, returning with misgivings in *A Dinner to Die For* (St. Martin, 1987). Her first assignment was to investigate the death of Mitch Biekma, a restaurateur who had been poisoned in his own establishment. Dunlap often had a semi-humorous subplot in her books, Seth's Halloween costume, thefts of running shoes, or trashed police cars. *Diamond in the Buff* (St. Martin, 1990) gave free rein to her lighter side. Jill was directed to mediate a neighborhood feud. Instead she found herself investigating a murder arising out of an ill-fated mountaineering expedition. Relaxing somewhat, she moved in with Seth Howard. Very soon, Jill realized she was incapable of sharing Howard's pleasure in being a leaseholder, and she was unsure whether their relationship could work.

Death and Taxes (Delacorte, 1992) put Jill on the trail of a clever murderer who killed an Internal Revenue agent with a pressure-induced injection of poison. Jill and Howard had reached a level of tolerance by *Time Expired* (Delacorte, 1993), but the police department was beset with pranks that escalated into serious problems. During her investigation, she renewed acquaintanceship with Madeleine Riordan, a dying activist who had opposed Jill in the courtroom. Madeleine's death in a community based group home raised questions, which Jill answered in time to save a life. The narrative combined insights and tension into a neat package.

When Jill returned in *Sudden Exposure* (Delacorte, 1996), she had been forced back into uniform patrol by the return of a detective with more tenure. Her lessened authority in homicide cases did not stop her. She investigated the murder of an itinerant secretary, caught in a controversy between an obsessive former Olympic athlete and an aging radical. Jill successfully balanced her loyalty to the Berkeley police department with her need to find a killer. The usual humorous subplot was an exchange between Jill and Howard whereby he suspended his obsessive home repairs while she abstained from junk food.

Seedy private investigator Herman Ott detested the police and the feeling was mutual. His special rapport with Jill threw her life into shambles during *Cop Out* (Delacorte, 1997). Her belief that Ott was incapable of murder was tied to her feeling for Berkeley as a place where she could function under her own standards as a policewoman and an individual. She risked the loss of comradeship with fellow police officers, her job, and most importantly the trust she shared with her lover, Seth Howard. Jill also appeared in five short stories in Dunlap's collection, *Celestial Buffet*.

Dunlap created above average narratives that combined humor, character insights, and action.

Xenia Smith

Author: Annette Meyers

See: Leslie Wetzon, Page 303

Joan Spencer

Author: Sara Hoskinson Frommer

In her forties, Joan Spencer faced an accelerated empty nest. Her husband Ken, a minister, died of a heart attack. Her son Andrew was in high school. Her older daughter Rebecca had left home. Joan's parents' home in Oliver, Indiana had been left vacant after their deaths. She moved there, and became active in cultural affairs. Joan had left Oliver to attend Oberlin College where she met Ken and traveled with him as he ministered to churches. On her return, she joined the local symphony orchestra, playing the viola. A friend found her a part-time job at the senior citizen center.

As *Murder in C Major* (St. Martin, 1986) began, there were sour notes among the musicians. Oboist George Petris had been included because of his technical ability, not his social skills. He became ill during rehearsal, and was dead on arrival at the hospital. The symphony manager, Yoichi Nakamura, identified the symptoms as similar to fugu poisoning. The possibilities of ingesting fluid by a reed player were obvious. Joan had other suggestions to offer Lt. Fred Lundquist, the assigned investigator when a second symphony player was murdered.

Joan's daughter, Rebecca, returned to her mother's home after a two-year estrangement in *Buried in Quilts* (St. Martin, 1994). Part of the attraction was the Alcorn County Quilt Show managed by domineering Mary Sue Ellett. Mary Sue was found buried under her own mother's collection of quilts by Joan and another member of the orchestra. The investigation became a family affair, and reunited Joan with her recalcitrant admirer, Lt. Lundquist.

When a tornado struck Oliver, Indiana during *Murder & Sullivan* (St. Martin, 1997), Joan became acquainted with Judge David Putnam and his wife, Ellen. Life went on in the small community after the wreckage was cleared. Projects included a performance of little known, *Ruddigore*, an operetta by Gilbert & Sullivan. Because she played in the orchestra, Joan was present when David was murdered during the performance. Although her early suspicions were misplaced, Joan's curiosity brought her to the attention of the killer.

Joan and Lt. Fred Lundquist edged cautiously towards a romantic relationship. In a narrative that vibrated with Frommer's appreciation of music, Joan befriended the young man who might become her son-in-law. As *The Vanishing Violinist* (St. Martin, 1999) began, she and Fred planned to marry in the near future. The kidnapping of a performer in an international violin competition and the hit-and-run death of a local policeman diverted them.

Pleasant and informational.

Sara Spooner

Author: Judith Kelman

Sara Spooner seemed an unlikely investigator and prosecutor for the New York City District Attorney's office, particularly as head of the newly established sex crimes unit. While raising her family she had commuted from her home in Stanford, Connecticut. The bulk of her fourteen years with the District Attorney's office had been spent as junior head of Homicide. Her husband Ben's infidelity led to a divorce, causing her to move from Stanford to be closer to her job. Initially she moved in with her sister Honey who had a Manhattan apartment.

Where Shadows Fall (Berkley, 1987) was not a legal thriller. Three years after her son, Nicky, had committed suicide, Sara was still consumed with grief and a need to understand. Her over-protective behavior towards her daughter Allison drove them apart. An investigation into multiple suicides on a college campus absorbed her time to the exclusion of her regular responsibilities at work. She risked her life in the apprehension of a crazed killer, but resolved at the end to try to mend her marriage.

Obviously the reconciliation attempt failed, because Sara and Ben were divorced in *Hush, Little Darlings* (Berkley, 1989). To enjoy this narrative it would be necessary to believe that a forty plus assistant district attorney would be doing her own investigations. Assigned a case in which four young girls had been sexually assaulted, then left with no recollection of the physical event, Sara became over-involved. She moved on to the judiciary at the end; this was not necessarily an improvement for the legal system. Sara was not a credible character.

Joanna Stark

Author: Marcia Muller

Joanna Stark had a troubled adolescence. She never had a close relationship with her father. Her alcoholic mother committed suicide on learning that her husband had been unfaithful while she was institutionalized. Joanna left home, spending two years at Wellesley, then traveling Europe and Asia on her own. On her return she married David Stark, who had been her father's college roommate. Joanna had a stepson, E. J., who was aware that Joanna and his father had been intimate before his mother died. At the time of David's death from bone cancer, Joanna was 42, E. J. was 22, and they had reached an accommodation. She also reconnected with Nick Alexander, her former partner in Security Systems, International, and became active in the business.

In *The Cavalier in White* (St. Martin, 1986), the firm was hired to recover Franz Hals' *The White Cavalier,* stolen from the de Young Museum in San Francisco. E. J. discovered that he had been adopted and reconciled with the birth mother he had never recognized.

There Hangs the Knife (St. Martin, 1988) highlighted Joanna's ongoing feud with art thief Antony Parducci, the father of her son. She was determined to connect Parducci to major art thefts in Europe, but failed to trap him. During *Dark Star* (St. Martin, 1989), Joanna could not let go of her past, even though E. J. had begun a life of his own in a small winery. Parducci resurfaced, drawing Joanna into a search that eventually exposed an old art insurance scam.

Gertrude Stein

Author: Samuel M. Steward

Perhaps Gertrude Stein and her companion, Alice B. Toklas, were too unconventional (and too dead) to be disturbed by sleazy mysteries that capitalized on their careers. Expatriate Stein, whose poetic variations were longer remembered than her influence on the artistic and literary Parisian community in the Twenties, deserved better treatment.

Murder Is Murder Is Murder (Alyson, 1985) chronicled the two women, then vacationing in Southern France, as they searched for the missing father of their gardener. In *The Caravaggio Shawl* (Alyson, 1989), Toklas' knowledge of art history detected the imperfections in a forged Caravaggio in the Louvre. When Alice discovered the corpse of a Louvre guard, she and Gertrude set out to find the killer. For their heroics in the investigation, Gertrude and Alice received the Legion of Honor. Steward's narrative was heavily concerned with the amorous intrigues of gay narrator Johnny McAndrews, a Chicago student who had insinuated himself into the Stein/Toklas household.

Joan Stock

Author: Leonard Tourney

A mystery heroine might be unrealistic in Elizabethan times except as the wife of a male sleuth; however, Joan Stock's participation increased over the series. Her husband, Matthew, was a stolid conscientious man, aware that his wife had skills that he could not duplicate. Joan was described as a small dark woman in her 40's who carried major household and business responsibilities, overseeing the servants and apprentices.

The Players' Boy Is Dead (Harper, 1980) established the middle aged couple in Chelmsford. Matthew was busy with his substantial drapery and clothing business and his position as village constable. No murder had occurred within his jurisdiction until he was called upon by Sir Harry Saltmarsh, the local squire. Saltmarsh had no expectation that Matthew would solve the crime, even less that he would suspect a member of the gentry.

In *Low Treason* (Dutton, 1982), Matthew worried over the disappearance of Thomas, a young jeweler's apprentice. Joan, who had remained at home while Matthew sought the boy in London, experienced a "glimmering," an extra sensory experience, telling her that both Thomas and her husband were in danger. When she warned Matthew that the jeweler was involved in a Papist plot, she and Matthew were thrown into Newgate prison. An attempt to murder Matthew failed when Joan killed the assailant.

During *Familiar Spirits* (St. Martin, 1985), a fifteen-year-old girl was hung as a witch on the testimony of an older couple. At Joan's instigation, Matthew proved that evil in the community was based on human greed, blackmail, and deception, not witchcraft. When the Stocks attended the Fair to show their wares in *The Bartholomew Fair Murders* (St. Martin, 1986), Matthew was concerned about the death of an itinerant puppeteer in his own district. Further deaths were heightened by the presence of

Queen Elizabeth. Matthew solved the murders, but it was Joan who saved Queen Elizabeth from an assassin.

By *Old Saxon Blood* (St. Martin, 1988), Elizabeth was sufficiently impressed with the Stocks to send them to the estate of a distinguished soldier who had recently been murdered. They served as the replacement steward and housekeeper, but were allowed only one month to find the killer. It was Joan's attention to physical characteristics that solved the mystery and explained the mitigating circumstances.

In *Knaves Templar* (St. Martin, 1991), the preface introduced an angry woman whose husband had been executed causing her child to be born dead. When, five years later, Matthew was sent to investigate student murders in Middle Temple, London, Joan accompanied him. Her entry into the Temple was barred by the male-only rules. Joan ventured into dangerous sections of the city, from which she was rescued by Nan, a friendly prostitute. Before the criminals were apprehended, Joan's affection for Nan almost caused her death.

During *Witness of Bones* (St. Martin, 1992), politicians jailed Matthew as the murderer of a London cleric, hoping to implicate his mentor, Lord Cecil. Queen Elizabeth was dying. The struggle for control of the government was fierce. Even when "shanghaied" on a ship to Europe, Joan won over an adversary, and returned to save Matthew and Cecil.

Tourney returned Joan and Matthew to earlier times in *Frobisher's Savage* (St. Martin, 1994). Matthew, although accepted as part of the local business economy, had no official role as the narrative began. When Adam Nemo, a native of Greenland brought to England by explorer Martin Frobisher, discovered a family massacre, he was a convenient suspect. At the request of the parson, Matthew served as constable, but was challenged by those who wanted the killer to be an outlander. While Matthew actively protected Adam from mob violence, Joan asked the questions which led to the killer.

Dee Street

Authors: Hannah Wakefield, pseudonym for
Sarah Burton and Judith Holland

Dee Street was not one of the Sixties protestors who ended up as a corporate executive or candidate for public office. She walked away from a law practice in the United States, unable to live in a system in which violence had become commonplace. England, with its gun control and structured society, met her personal needs. A law firm, composed of female attorneys, suited her professional standards. A short, plump woman with dark curly hair, Dee had been raised in an unconventional home in Los Angeles. Her attorney father never married her mother, his secretary.

In *The Price You Pay* (Women's Press, 1987; St. Martin's, 1990) Dee was coming off two years of celibacy when she met Dr. David Blake again. She was attracted to the handsome psychiatrist whom she had not seen in six years, until she learned he was married to renowned journalist Amanda Finch. She and Blake kept in contact. She drew his will, but declined to draft Amanda's because of the conflict of interest. Her efforts to avoid Blake ended when Amanda and a young Chilean schizophrenic were discovered dead.

As *A Woman's Own Mystery* (St. Martin, 1991) began, Dee's relationship with David had ended, but she feared she might be pregnant. She was drugged, tied up and placed in a car; then, transported to a secluded location. Flashbacks connected the abduction with her investigation in a custody suit, followed by the murder of a kindly Irish nurse. Dee's rosy view of the British government did not survive her treatment at their hands.

After a five-year lay-off in which the Aspinwall Street firm expanded, Dee re-appeared in *Cruel April* (The Women's Press, 1996). Growth had not meant prosperity. The failure of the Weaverstown Housing Association, a major client, to pay its legal fees forced the firm to consider cutting staff or entering into a merger. The refusal of Aspinwall Street to continue to provide legal services widened the breach between Dee and her long time friend, Janey Riordan, a WHA official. When Janey was murdered, Dee became a suspect, but was uncertain as to whether clues had been planted against her by the real killer or by a police inspector whom she had humiliated in court. This was a lengthy narrative that blended personal crises with international crime and pollution.

These were hard-edged feminist novels that emphasized a political viewpoint.

Dixie Flannigan Struthers

Author: L. V. Sims

Dixie Flannigan Struthers was a police sergeant with six years experience. She was only five feet tall, and had auburn hair and green eyes with gold flecks. After her divorce from Donald, she shared her Santa Cruz, California mountain home with her retired policeman/grandfather, Patrick Flannigan; the African-American housekeeper, Reversa; and Poke, a wolfhound. Dixie's deceased father had also been a policeman. Her mother Rose's second husband, Franklin Marks, did not approve of her choice of career. Unfortunately neither did some of her fellow police officers or her supervisor, Lt. Di Franco. She boasted an IQ of 168 and a degree from Stanford; drove a BMW, flew her own plane, and was independently wealthy. Maybe that was part of the problem.

In *Murder Is Only Skin Deep* (Charter, 1987), beautician Charles Bouchard was murdered by pesticides mixed into his hair dye. Although Dixie and her partner Herb Woodall were assigned to the case, Di Franco undercut her authority. Dixie bypassed official channels, operating as a lone wolf, but was rescued by a fellow officer who owed her a favor.

Her rescuer, Pete Willis had a favorite niece, Gretchen, who, in *Death Is a Family Affair* (Charter, 1987), was found badly mutilated in a closet at the local Mystery House. Pete, who perceived the girl as neglected by her divorced mother, interfered in the official investigation. Dixie and Herb learned that Gretchen spent her time with a group of delinquent teenagers.

In *To Sleep, Perchance to Kill* (Charter, 1988), Victor Peters, an aging computer industry executive who was unwilling to retire, became the victim of high tech murder. Although the killer used the latest technology, the motive for murder went back to World War II.

Sabina Swift

Author: Dorothy Sucher

When a man and woman are teamed as sleuths, the usual formula has been older man/younger woman—example—C. B. Greenfield/Maggie Rome; exception—Bertha Cool and Donald Lam. Narrator Victor Newman portrayed Sabina Swift, his middle-aged employer, as a vivacious older woman, happily married to physicist Bruno Herschel, busy with her detective agency but making time for painting. She was compulsively neat and interested in details. Her art product for a month might be one flower or one tree. Although not a college graduate, she was well read and had traveled extensively. Sabina had been a widow with a daughter, now grown, when she met Bruno. He was still married when they began their affair, but divorced in order to marry her. Her one idiosyncracy was the constant wearing of high heels.

In *Dead Men Don't Give Seminars* (St. Martin, 1988), sparks were expected to fly at the Lake Champlain Physics Institute when Nobel prizewinners Herve Moore-Gann and Saul Sachs met after years of feuding. Moore-Gann, aware of Sachs' poor health, sought reconciliation. When Moore-Gann died after drinking a cocktail, Sabina retained the glass for testing. Newman investigated other conference guests, because Sabina advised him that the poisoned cocktail might have been intended for a different victim. Her literary knowledge provided a clue when insights from Ford Madox Ford's *The Good Soldier* disclosed the motivation of the killer. This was the pattern that Vic and Sabina followed (à la Wolfe/Goodman). He gathered information, which she synthesized into a solution.

In *Dead Men Don't Marry* (St. Martin, 1989), Fran, an older friend of Vic's, was killed in a railroad accident shortly after her marriage. He was troubled when he followed up on the death of Ruthann, killed under similar circumstances. Her widower had left shortly after the accident. After Vic and Sabina profiled the serial killer of lonely women, she assumed the role of prospective victim, making good use of her high heels when it came to life or death.

Hilary Tamar

Author: Sarah Caudwell, pseudonym for Sarah Cockburn

See: Julia Larmore, Page 159

Tina Tamiko

Author: Paul Bishop

Calico Jack Walker, an experienced police officer ready for retirement, drew professional and personal support from Tina Tamiko. Her father, a prosperous Japanese-American businessman with three sons, had remarried after the death of his first wife. Tina's mother, an Englishwoman, died of cancer just before Tina's eighteenth birthday. Tina's decision to enter the police academy horrified her father and half-brothers who held to more traditional values. They were even less supportive of her relationship with Walker.

Calico Jack had put in thirty years on the force and Tina had just finished probation when they were paired in *Citadel Run* (TOR/Tom Doherty, 1988). Their first assignment, the apprehension of a youthful arsonist, was only moderately successful. Their further escapades were tied to Calico Jack's problems with his former wife, her lover who outranked him on the police force, a convict determined to have him killed, and a wild bet. Tina was loyal to her partner to her own detriment. Her status as a racial minority female made her too valuable to dismiss from the force.

By *Sand Against the Tide* (TOR, 1990), Calico Jack and son Ron were in partnership in the charter fishing business. Tina, promoted to detective and Jack, retired from the police, had an established relationship. They worked together against an ambitious police official who had been driven to crime by his wife, drug smugglers, and an attempt to besmirch Calico's erratic friend, Detective Wild John Elliot.

Ann Tate

Author: Caroline Burnes, pseudonym for Carolyn Haines

Along with Veronica Sheffield, and Dawn Markey, Ann Tate was one of a trio of characters, who each played the dominant role in one of Caroline Burnes Harlequin novels, while having minor parts in others.

Ann was the central figure in *Measure of Deceit* (Harlequin, 1988) in which Dawn Markey, a horse trainer, and Veronica Sheffield, now married to Jeff Stuart made brief appearances. Ann's efforts to save the family horse-breeding farm had met with continuing disasters—the disappearance of her husband Robert, along with a valuable stallion, and the death of her father. Stockbroker Matt Roper appeared with a mare to be bred at a time when accidents in the stables damaged the operations reputations. Ann wrestled with doubts about Matt, the man with whom she was falling in love.

Although the love scenes were typical of pulp paperback romances, the series was interesting particularly when read in sequence—*A Deadly Breed* (Harlequin, 1988), *Measure of Deceit* (Harlequin, 1988) and *Phantom Filly* (Harlequin, 1989). Also See: Dawn Markey, page 181 and Veronica Sheffield, page 266.

Kate Byrd Teague

Author: Wendy Hornsby

Although Kate Teague was a divorced California academic, the underlying theme in *No Harm* (Dodd, 1987) was reminiscent of English cozies that featured the inheritance of property within an extended family. Kate attended the funeral of her murdered mother Margaret who had been neither a loving wife nor mother, but did not deserve to be battered to death. Kate's father was one of three sons of grandfather Archie Byrd. He or one of his brothers could have sired the illegitimate grandchild who might inherit from the Byrd estate. Lt. Roger Tejeda rescued Kate when her life was

3333

threatened, a favor which she returned in a violent conclusion. Tejeda had long-term medical problems as a result of his injuries.

In *Half a Mind* (North American Library, 1990), Tejada battled blackouts and memory loss to keep his job. While on medical leave, he and Kate marshaled evidence against a serial killer and his family.

Murky, but above average in interest.

Julie Tendler

Author: Aaron Elkins

See: Julie Tendler Oliver, Page 218

Sally Tepper

Author: Frank King, a.k.a. Lydia Adamson

Sally Tepper was a dog person, pure and simple. She collected urban strays that she found eating out of garbage cans, shivering as they tried to keep warm. She was a bit of a stray herself, a tall, large boned redhead dressed in sweaters and overalls. Although working more frequently in a restaurant than a theater, she considered herself an actress.

As *Sleeping Dogs Die* (Dutton, 1988) began, Sally had five dogs in her Hell's Kitchen apartment. The murder of blind Albert Fuchs and his seeing-eye dog appalled Sally who loved them both. Albert remembered his friends. He left Sally a joint bank account of $191,000 and a mystery to solve, together with street cop, Tommy Hughes. Sally had no real use for money, so she donated it to the families of murdered police officers, and adopted another dog.

In *Take the D Train* (Dutton, 1990), Charlie Seven, one of a group of street people who "hung" together, was found hanging in a subway station. Charlie's death might be one of a series, and his friends could be in danger. Fortunately, Sally had a skeptical side to her nature that discarded the easy theories.

Author King must also like cats, horses and birds because, under the name Lydia Adamson, he authored three other series in which animals played significant roles. See Volume 3 for Lucy Wayles, Dr. Deirdre Nightingale, and the very popular Alice Nestleton series.

Jennifer Terry

Author: B. J. (Brenda Jane) Hoff

See: Jennifer Terry Kaine, Page 152

Lisa Thomas

Authors: Catherine Lewis and Judith Guerin

Lisa Thomas was a lecturer in the Department of Psychological and Socio-logical Enquiry at Justice Barry College of Technology in Melbourne, Australia. The narratives featured biting descriptions of student/faculty/staff interaction in a third rate academic setting.

The death of Richard Johnston, an unpopular professor at the college in *Unable By Reason of Death* (Penguin, 1989) sent his fellow academics into confusion. So many disliked him with good reason that there was considerable speculation as to who had made the move. A second murder and a suicide did nothing to dispel the uncertainty. Further disclosures of embezzlements, sex for good grades, and drug sales had everyone working on their resumes. Lisa helped a young teacher who had been initially arrested for the murder. When she discovered the real killer, she proved to be no better than her co-workers. She traded her silence for a job recommendation.

That sense of contentment at the conclusion of a mystery story that a crime has been solved and justice has prevailed was unavailable in *Not in Single Spies* (Penguin, 1992). Lisa and her ambitious friend Jacinta had taken over Johnston's project, the development of a gas which could be used to make large groups docile. In their opinion, CX-221 was ready for human testing. That explained why Lisa was climbing to the roof of the administration building to spray the office of the college president. Their work was interrupted by a police investigation when Joanna Shoemaker, a mole implanted in their project by its American grantor, was murdered. The gas proved to have serious side effects when withdrawn, a rebound that made the victims hostile.

The series was irreverent and clever.

Lizzie Thomas

Author: Anthony Oliver

The pairing of retired Detective Inspector John Webber and domestic servant Lizzie Thomas was unusual because of her occupation and appearance. Lizzie was short and dumpy with dark permed hair and black eyes, a shrewd Welsh woman, and the widow of a coal miner. She had little formal education, although she spoke and read French which she had learned during World War II. Lizzie had moved to Suffolk near her daughter Doreen, but there was a prickly relationship between the women. After Doreen's first husband, Rupert, died in a suspicious accident, she married "Betsey" Townsend, an effeminate but kindly antique dealer.

Doreen might not have intended Rupert's death in *The Pew Group* (Doubleday, 1981) but she had tripped him at the head of the stairs. Someone else was responsible for the disappearance of the Pew Group, a valuable piece of Staffordshire pottery, last seen at Rupert's wake. Detective Inspector John Webber had left his job and his wife, and returned to his native area. He and Lizzie worked together surrounded by colorful suspects.

During *The Property of a Lady* (Doubleday, 1983), Lizzie accompanied Doreen and Betsey to the Dunwold Fair from which young Mark Carter had disappeared. Mark's erratic character, and the complexities of his family and friends enlivened the narrative. *The Elberg Collection* (Doubleday, 1985) enabled Lizzie to use the French she had learned from refugees. She and Webber investigated the death by fire of a couple walking a French beach. The daughter of the victims did not accept the local police designation of accidental death which was supported by both French and British intelligence services.

Art dealer Joseph Greenwood was carrying a large sum of money on his buying trip near Flaxfield in *Cover-Up* (Doubleday, 1987) but it disappeared when he died of a heart attack. Prodded by Lizzie, Webber and a young police constable found unexpected traces of murder and theft.

Sex and violence were treated irreverently in the Flaxfield setting, akin to Colin Watson's portrayal of Flaxborough. (See Lucilla Edith Cavell Teatime, Volume 1)

Alice B. Toklas

Author: Samuel Steward

See: Gertrude Stein, Page 273

Sheila Travis

Author: Patricia Houck Sprinkle

Sheila Travis was a widow nearing forty when she returned to the United States from Japan. Her faithless husband Tyler had served in the diplomatic service. A tall (5' 9") dark-haired American, she had been born in Shikoku, Japan but sent to Atlanta for high school. After Tyler's death, Sheila's experience qualified her for work at the Markham Institute, a foreign affairs post-graduate facility located in Chicago.

She had just discovered an aging corpse in the cellar in *Murder at Markham* (St. Martin, 1988) when joined by Aunt Mary Beaufort. Mary, a diminutive but dominating personality, was responsible for the deductive reasoning that led Sheila to the murderer. While visiting South Carolina in *Murder in the Charleston Manner* (St. Martin, 1990), Sheila helped family friends, who had been plagued by accidents. She researched their family history where motives for two murders were hidden.

During *Murder on Peachtree Street* (St. Martin, 1991), Sheila was employed by a Japanese corporation with American headquarters in Atlanta. When the head of the film division of a Hosokawa subsidiary was murdered, Sheila kept her employers informed. Aunt Mary would not settle for anything less than full participation in the investigation. Sheila, temporarily homeless in *Somebody's Dead in Snellville* (St. Martin, 1992), was invited by neighbor Sara Sims Tait to dinner with the Sims/Shaw family. Sara's mother, who opposed the sale of the family farms, was shot. A retarded family member, under suspicion, was found hanging in the barn. Sheila, at Aunt Mary's urging, continued her contacts with the family long enough to discover the killers, but allowed them to carry out their own sentence.

Death of a Dunwoody Matron (Doubleday, 1993) took Sheila, and cousin Amory Travis into the upper levels of Atlanta society, reuniting them with high school friends. When a former beau was the prime suspect in his wife's death, Sheila not only assisted in his defense but offered Aunt Mary's home to his small son.

Aunt Mary and her contemporaries played significant roles in *A Mystery Bred in Buckhead* (Bantam, 1994). Now aging, the elite senior citizens were pressured to reveal the tragic circumstances of a 1944 party. The event had been recounted fictionally in a narrative draft by a famous Atlanta author. Only by unraveling the past misadventures could Sheila discover who was willing to kill to protect a reputation. Sheila did not work with Aunt Mary this time. She considered her a possible suspect.

The two women developed a pattern. Sheila was reluctant to become involved, but skillful in her assessment of relationships. Aunt Mary, with time on her hands, arrogantly interfered in investigations. Aunt Mary took a back seat in *Deadly Secrets on the St. Johns* (Bantam, 1995), when Sheila accompanied her lover Crispin on a visit to Jacksonville, Florida. When Daphne, the wife of an announced candidate for Congress, was poisoned at a celebration, Sheila barely knew the suspects. They were all close friends of Crispin. Their relationship was not only threatened by her investigation, but by her jealousy. She had to prove herself to a ten-year-old rival for Crispin's affection before she solved the murder.

A comfortable series.

Ms. Michael Tree

Authors: Max Allan Collins and artist Terry Beatty

Unlike Modesty Blaise, Michael Tree never made the transition from comic strips to novels, although her adventures appeared in bound volumes. She was depicted as tall, hard-faced, and full figured with padded shoulders, brown eyes and red-brown hair. She wore dark colors, frequently including gloves. Her dresses and shirts had high collars.

The Files of Ms. Tree (Renegade, 1984) included two comic strip narratives. As *An Eye for an Eye* began, Ms. Tree explained how she (then Michael Friday, daughter of a cop, Joe, probably) and Mike Tree met. As a meter maid, she had ticketed his car. She and Mike had both tried law school but quit when their money ran out. While he fought in Vietnam, she protested the war. After they became lovers, he convinced her to work for his detective agency. Ms. Friday, after a start as a secretary, was promised a full partnership. When the firm expanded, she earned her license and a proposal. Within hours of the wedding, Mike was gunned down. His widow wanted revenge. In the second story, *Death Do Us Part* she went to a resort looking for a rest, but found adventure and mystery.

In *The Cold Dish* (Renegade, 1985) Volume Two of *The Files of Ms. Tree*, Michael learned that her husband had an ex-wife, Anne and a son, Michael, Jr.. Michael connected Anne's death in a hit-and-run accident to mobster Dennis Muerta, the man responsible for her husband's murder. Her response was violent private vengeance.

The Mike Mist Case Book (Gary Kato also credited as artist, Renegade, 1988), Volume Three of *The Files of Ms. Tree*, collected short episodes featuring Mike Mist, and three longer stories with Mist and Ms. Tree working as a team. The three volumes were presented in a magazine size paperback.

Collins and Beatty also put together a paperback size book of comic strips, *Ms. Tree* (Paperjacks, 1968). It contained three more adventures, during which stepson Mike, Jr. ran away from home, Muerta was killed before he could be convicted, and Ms. Tree's new partner was suspected of the murder. Ms. Tree, notorious for her quick trigger, took a stand on abortion.

There are at least 43 issues of the Ms. Tree Comics, some available through used comic book dealers.

Jane Tregar

Author: Ellen Godfrey

Jane Tregar was a petite blonde in her mid-thirties, divorced from Bernie. A wealthy Swiss businessman, he had been much older than Jane when they married. He had written her off when she failed to fill his job description as hostess, wife and mother. After the divorce, their two sons remained in his custody. She had only limited access to the children. Jane (like her author) was a native of the United States who had moved to Canada. Her Jewish mother was from Montreal. Her American father, an atheistic scientist, had been blacklisted during the McCarthy era. She had a degree in psychology with considerable computer expertise. Not surprisingly she was able to utilize it in a top-level position in an executive search firm located in Toronto.

In *Murder Behind Locked Doors* (Penguin, Canada 1988), Brian Taylor, corporate president, planned to expand by a merger or joint marketing agreement with a major U.S. data processing firm. The death of chief financial officer Gary Levin created a problem that Jane was expected to solve by finding a suitable replacement. The matter became more serious when Gary's death was determined to be murder and the corporate executives were the primary suspects. Emboldened by her successful role in identifying the killer and by the presence of a new man in her life, Jane resolved to fight for custody of her children.

Georgia Disappeared (Penguin, 1992) centered upon charismatic Georgia Arnott, manager of a development team at a computer software corporation. She had not been seen for two weeks when Jane, a personal friend, learned of the situation. Jane was urged by Georgia's husband to find his wife. She became Georgia's replacement managing the volatile staff members on the Crystal Project. When Georgia's body was found, Jane added finding a killer to her agenda.

Godfrey had two other series:

- The first featured septuagenarian Rebecca Rosenthal, the fourth generation of a Jewish family living in Canada. See Volume 1.
- The second was a mystery series featuring Janet Barkin designed for readers who had become literate as adults. See Volume 3.

Diana Tregarde

Author: Mercedes Lackey

Lackey, an acknowledged science fiction/fantasy writer, did not stray far from the genre in this three book series featuring sorcerer Diana Tregarde. Diana had inherited her powers from a great-grandmother who trained her in the magical arts without making Diana's solidly Episcopalian mother aware of the fact. She attended college where she built up a coterie of fellow "sensitives." Most of the others had put their mystical experiences behind them when they entered careers and marriages. Physically Diana was a tiny brown-haired woman in her twenties. She supported herself as a romance writer because it would have been unethical for her to be paid for her services as a sorceress. Ranking as a "guardian", she was expected to make herself available to those who asked for help. She had a black belt in karate, but it was her powers as a sorceress that both protected her from danger and made it possible for her to overcome evil forces.

An earthquake in Mexico City unleashed the power of an ancient Aztec god in *Burning Water* (TOR/Tom Doherty, 1989). Months later five of his disciples began a series of ritual killings in Dallas, Texas. Detective Mark Valdez, overwhelmed by the increasing frequency and escalating violence of the incidents, called upon his college friend, Diana Tregarde. Diana used police records and the computer to identify the cult pattern. With the help of Native American mystics, a Hispanic bruja, and a college professor, she tied the killings to Aztec mythology in time to save the young woman with whom Mark was in love.

As *Children of the Night* (TOR 1990) began, Diana was clerking in an occult supply store to help a pregnant friend. The curious, the vulnerable, and the evil approached her. Andre, the vampire with whom she fell in love, needed help to rescue gypsy children from a covey of "hunters." Diana, who was dedicated to protecting the innocent, rallied other allies to release the children and overcome the evil forces.

Two other friends from Diana's college days, Larry and Miri Kestrel needed help in *Jinx High* (TOR, 1991). The Kestrels, who had sensitive powers of their own, lived in an exclusive suburb of Tulsa, Oklahoma. While Miri was in Japan, Larry became aware that their son, Deke, was in danger from an insidious force. The boy had left behind his loyal friends and attached himself to the followers of Fay Harper, a reckless teenager without parental guidance. Perhaps Fay didn't want parental guidance. She was at least 300 years old, presently occupying a youthful body. Larry sought Diana's help. Diana involved Mark Valdez. They focused on weakening the power that energized Fay so that Diana could overcome her.

Kate Trevorne

Author: Paula Gosling

Lt. Jack Stryker, a moody work-obsessed homicide investigator, was the primary sleuth in the series. Kate Trevorne first encountered him during the Sixties when she was a Michigan campus rebel and he was a uniformed cop. He remembered her "ass".

They met again in *Monkey Puzzle* (Doubleday, 1985), during which mutilations based on "See No Evil, Hear No Evil, Speak No Evil" occurred in a series of murders. The first victim, a loathsome pornographer and blackmailer was a faculty colleague of Kate's. Kate and Jack's initial hostility became a love affair, but only after they took opposite sides in the guilt of Richard Wayland, formerly close to Kate.

Four years later in *Backlash* (Doubleday, 1989) Stryker was in rare form, investigating a cop killer and fending off an attractive female FBI agent. Kate, still his lover, had been shelved temporarily while she attended a conference in London, where she was also tempted.

Kate re-emerged in *The Body in Blackwater Bay* (Mysterious Press, 1992) when she and Jack shared her traditional family summer vacation home on Paradise Island. Her cottage was part of a tightly controlled enclave whose inhabitants had formed close friendships over the years. Those ties were fraying as the original owners died or sold out. Jack was supposed to be taking it easy, but, when artist Doria Grey was accused of murdering her abusive husband, he was drawn into the investigation. The local police wanted his expertise. Kate wanted him to prove her friend, Doria, innocent.

Amelia Trowbridge

Author: Roger Ormerod

See: Amelia Trowbridge Patton, Page 229

Amy Tupper

Author: Josephine Bell, pseudonym for Doris Bell Ball

Amy Tupper, a former actress, was a hospital patient in *Wolf! Wolf!* (Walker, 1980) when Eurasian nurse Tan Sunee was murdered. Amy had seen a serial murderer, who had recently been released from prison, on the premises. She was determined to connect him to the killing, even if it put her back in the hospital.

In *A Question of Inheritance* (Walker, 1981), Amy encountered actress Maisie Atkins who, twenty years earlier, had substituted an adopted child for her deceased son in order to control an inheritance. She contacted Amy to help the living child obtain the heritage he deserved.

Anna Tyree

Author: Dave Pedneau

The potential conflict of interest between lovers or spouses in mystery series arises frequently when one of the pair is a journalist and the other is a police officer or detective needing to withhold information to carry out an investigation.

Early on in her career as a crime reporter, Anna Tyree had been renamed as Annie Tyson-Tyree. Her editor had considered it a better byline on a story. She had been ambitious when younger. At age 31, living in Milbrook, a small West Virginia town, she had mellowed. She was described as auburn haired and "well-endowed."

A.P.B.: All Points Bulletin (Ballantine 1987) described the meeting between Anna (the name she preferred) and Whit Pynchon, investigator for the district attorney's office. She had heard that he was rude, difficult to get along with, and contentious. Their first encounter did nothing to convince her otherwise. They had frequent contacts when a serial killer targeted police officers' wives. Tressa, Whit's teenage daughter, played Cupid with surprising results. Anna made a significant contribution to the case. She suggested a hypnotechnician to enable an injured suspect to recall the scene of the crime. The information came in time to save Tressa from becoming a victim.

Anna's relative tranquillity in the countryside disappeared in *D.O.A.: Dead on Arrival* (Ballantine, 1988), when she reported on the death of seven-year-old Jenny during an attempt to kill her mother, Mary Hairston. The administrative decision at the newspaper to limit coverage of the incident made no sense to Anna, particularly since Mary, a pregnant widow, had worked at the Journal. Her continued work on the matter was sparked by two teenagers, one of whom was Tressa, Whit's daughter. By this time, Whit had become Anna's lover. Generally of a moody temperament, Whit's spirits picked up when he had an interesting case to work but he managed to irritate city and county police officials along the way. Pedneau introduced an interesting moral issue—artificial life support for a pregnant woman until her child could be delivered.

It must have been difficult to recruit law enforcement officers in Raven County. The attrition among state troopers, county and local police officers in *B.O.L.O.: Be on the Lookout* (Ballantine, 1989) was heavy as they tangled with rural families who had turned from bootlegging to drug smuggling. Anna, now the editor at the Journal, ran an undercover operation to discover the suppliers of the drugs which ended badly.

The series' female characters took a lot of physical abuse in *A.K.A.: Also Known As* (Ballantine, 1990). Anna spent almost two-thirds of the narrative chained and otherwise humiliated by a sadistic killer. Julia, Whit's former wife, was brutally murdered. Kathy Binder, publisher of the Journal and a close friend of Anna's, was seriously injured when a car in which she was riding was forced off the road. Finally, Tressa was betrayed by someone she thought she could trust. Whit frustrated by the vendetta against him and the women in his life, turned in his badge, but needed official help to identify the source.

Anna played a minor role in *B. & E.: Breaking and Entering* (Ballantine 1991), during which Whit, the District Attorney, and the Sheriff's department combated right-wing terrorists. They had been informed by the F.B.I. that a gun stolen in a local robbery was used to kill a witness who was bringing evidence to officials. Local delinquents in Raven County were recruited to steal weapons for the Aryan Front by members who infiltrated the community. As usual Whit was rude and uncooperative. As too common by now, Anna was taken hostage. As always, the fatalities mounted. It's a wonder there was anyone left in Milbrook.

Whit and Anna negotiated during *N.F.O.: No Fair Deal* (Ballantine, 1992). After two years in a monogamous relationship, she wanted a commitment. Whit would agree but he had an agenda of his own—he wanted to spend the rest of his life on the South Carolina coast. Anna's current position as editor of the Journal could not be easily duplicated in a new setting. The abduction of a small girl from a day care center did not evoke the usual hostility between the newspaper and law enforcement agencies. Both emphasized the child's safety. Even the identification of the killer did not resolve what happened to little Marcia.

Harriet Unwin

Author: Evelyn Hervey, pseudonym for H. R. F. Keating

Harriet Unwin, a "foundling", in Victorian England, had been taught to read by a kindly mistress. She had become a governess and an attractive young woman by *The Governess* (Doubleday, 1983). Her discovery of a petty thief in the household brought her no credit. Instead she became a suspect when the head of the family was murdered, forcing her to escape from jail to prove her innocence.

In *The Man of Gold* (Doubleday, 1985), Harriet's compassion for children motivated her to accept a low paying position in the Partington home. Richard, a widower with two children, was dependent on the generosity—or penuriousness—of his domineering father. When the old miser was poisoned, Richard was accused of the crime, and Harriet named as his accomplice. She cleared Richard, but rejected his proposal.

In *Into the Valley of Death* (Doubleday, 1986), housemaid Mary Vilkins, who grew up in the orphanage with Harriet, sent a call for help. Jack Steadman, landlord of the local inn, was accused of murder. Harriet enlisted retired Superintendent Heavitree and took a local job to become part of the community.

Harriet used her limited education to advantage in her investigations checking records, posing as a lady private detective and a magazine reporter. Domestic service was never a popular line of work for mystery heroines, even when written by a skilled practitioner like H. R. F. Keating. Elma Craggs, another of Keating's hardworking lower class sleuths was profiled in Volume 1.

Claudia Valentine

Author: Marele Day

Tall redheaded Claudia Valentine was an Australian private investigator who saw her two children only during scheduled visitation. They lived with her ex-husband Gary and his second wife. Claudia was herself the product of a broken home, not by divorce, but desertion. She had sought her alcoholic father among the vagrants on city streets without success. Her mother Mina, a former actress, did well by Claudia, sending her to Sydney Girls High School and the University where she graduated with honors. Restless, Claudia backpacked through Europe, eventually marrying Gary at a London registry office, but they were incompatible. Claudia built a life of her own, but smoked too often, drank too much, and drove her 1958 Daimler too fast.

In *The Life and Crimes of Harry Lavender* (Allen, 1988), former classmate Marilyn Edwards hired Claudia to prove that her brother Mark had been murdered. Claudia contacted Mark's surfing companions but her best source of information was viciously murdered. The trail led to high-powered smugglers, one of whom had a secret to protect.

In *The Case of the Chinese Boxes* (Allen, 1989), the proceeds from a bank robbery included valuable lacquer boxes stored by members of the powerful Chinese community. Restaurateur Victoria Chen was unwilling to disclose the contents of her boxes, but hired Claudia to retrieve them. The hunt for the elusive boxes entrapped Claudia in a "tong" war, dependent only on mysterious investigator James Ho.

Claudia's mother Mina revived her career as an ostrich dancer in *The Last Tango of Dolores Delgado* (Allen, 1992). At her urging, Dolores, the dancing star of the nightclub show, hired Claudia as a companion. She was at loose ends, personally and professionally, so accepted the job. This seemed a simple assignment until Dolores died in her dancing partner's arms. Claudia's exploration of the secret life of Dolores brought unexpected disclosures, prompting her to masquerade as the dancer.

Mina's marriage to an old friend in *The Disappearance of Madalena Grimaldi* (Walker, 1996) reawakened Claudia's need to learn what had happened to her father. Mina said he had died. There was someone buried under the name, Guy Valentine. During her search for an Italian teenager, she learned why "Guy Valentine" had to die, and where he still lived.

Dee Vaughn

Author: Jennifer Jordan

Dee and Barry Vaughn were throwbacks to the Nick and Nora Charles era, so intertwined that they shared the narration. Dee (for Diana) was a tiny redhead. Although a magazine journalist with an English literature degree, she worked as a temporary secretary when the periodical folded. Barry combined his career as a British college lecturer with writing "humorous mysteries."

In *A Good Weekend for Murder* (St. Martin, 1987), the couple was invited to a party hosted by malicious author Charles Wild, during which he introduced his prospective third wife to her predecessors. Few of the guests had any positive feelings for Wild, so his death, as a result of a severed brake line in his car, came as no surprise. The setting changed to a holiday guesthouse, but the use of the cozy circle of suspects continued in *Murder Under the Mistletoe* (St. Martin, 1989). Barry and Dee spent Christmas at the Sussex holiday inn run by Robin and Betty Brewer. Among their fellow guests was Miranda Travers, a man-eating model whom the Vaughns had met in Italy. Travers' behavior was so atrocious that when she died, the Vaughns pressed to have her death investigated by their friend Scotland Yard Inspector Kenneth Graves.

Book Early for Murder (St. Martin, 1993) focused on a "two-centre" mystery holiday, in which the participants spent one weekend playing the mystery game and a second one at a different location, relaxing. Professional actors mixed with the guests at both settings. A series of accidents at the second location ended when a blackmailer was murdered in the pool.

The narratives were choppy, partly due to the switching of narrators.

Gillian Verdean

Author: Tony Gibbs, pseudonym for Wolcott Gibbs, Jr.

Thanks to an inheritance from a great-uncle, Gillian left her job as office manager at Constable Sails to cruise the seas. Her bequest was a lovely old sailboat suitable for deep sea chartering in the Caribbean. Because her education at a small Connecticut college had not prepared her to handle the ship, she hired Jeremy Barr as master of the Glory, and Patrick O'Mara as mate. Barr was a distant unhappy man, still dealing with the accidental death of his unfaithful wife.

Gillian knew that her great-uncle Dennis was dying as *Dead Run* opened (Random House, 1988). She did not expect to find him beaten to death in his cabin, while Barr lay drunk in his berth. She also knew that Dennis had not always operated within the law, but was confused by threats from two sinister groups who declared that Dennis had property that belonged to them. O'Mara, under pressure from soldiers of fortune with whom he had served, picked up Gillian and insinuated himself into the crew. Unsuspecting, Gillian worked with the repentant Barr and the conscience stricken O'Mara to save herself and an undesirable treasure from Dennis's assailants.

In *Running Fix* (Random, 1990), Sol Barber begged Gillian and her crew to find his daughter Sarah, Gillian's college roommate. Gillian knew that Sarah was unstable, but she could not resist his plea. In alternating chapters Gillian, Barr, and O'Mara described their search for the yacht, "Sea Horse." It was not only the vicious Roger Huddleston, editor of a failing liberal publication, that the trio had to overcome. Treachery was closer to home.

By *Landfall* (Morrow, 1992), Gillian and Jeremy had become lovers, and O'Mara accepted their relationship. Jeremy, under pressure to carry out another CIA assignment, withheld information from Gillian. A sinister clergyman had taken control of a small Caribbean island. Jake Adler, an Army colonel tied to an ultra conservative military group, had his own plan to investigate the possible coup. O'Mara found solace with Isabel Machado, Adler's companion, whose loyalty was questionable. Gillian killed to protect herself.

Rosie Vicente

Author: Shelly (Rochelle) Singer

Lesbian carpenter Rosie Vicente worked as a part-time assistant to detective Jake Samson. Jake, an ex-police officer, was never licensed as a private detective, but carried out investigations in the Oakland/San Francisco area. Rosie, who rented a small cottage on his property, was available when needed, earning a 15% share of Jake's fees. Although Rosie's sexual orientation was mentioned, there were no intimate scenes. Her behavior was more circumspect than that of Jake, who slept around without any emotional involvement.

In *Samson's Deal* (St. Martin, 1983), Jake probed the death of Margaret Harley, wife of an alleged Communist professor. Rosie came to Jake's assistance with a two-by-four when he was attacked, and went undercover in a conservative organization that had picketed the professor. In *Free Draw* (St. Martin, 1984), they worked together on the murder of the vice president of a correspondence school.

Full House (St. Martin, 1986) tapped a lighter vein. Jake, with Rosie's help, searched for Tom "Noah" Gebhart who was building two arks in expectation of a flood. A lot of money disappeared with Noah and so did a woman, who was later found dead. It was human sperm, not spit, that was thrown in the ocean in *Spit in the Ocean* (St. Martin, 1987), when the North Coast Sperm Bank was robbed. Rosie and Jake worked systematically checking lists and schedules while posing as reporters.

Rosie encouraged Jake to check out VIVOS, an environmental political party in *Suicide King* (St. Martin, 1988) but Jake did the detecting when Joe Richmond, VIVOS candidate for governor was murdered.

Rosie's return over ten years later in literary time was disappointing. *Royal Flush* (Perseverance Press, 1999) was subtitled "a Jake Samson and Rosie Vicente mystery", but it didn't play out that way. Their relationship had changed. Rosie had left the cottage, drawn away by her attraction for a woman whom Jake did not like. She was growing older and found work as a carpenter no longer met her needs. When her relationship ended, Rosie worked for a detective agency long enough to qualify for her own license. Now she reached out to Jake, who was ready for a change. He agreed to move to Marin County where he could work under her license. Less surprisingly he took on a major case of which Rosie disapproved, going underground with a group of right-wing bigots. Although Rosie made occasional appearances among the Aryan Command members, she played no significant role. Forget the subtitles; give Rosie some action.

Emma Victor

Author: Mary Wings

Emma Victor was consistent—a lesbian, a feminist, a leftist, and a war protestor. She had formerly worked as a doctor's assistant. As *She Came Too Late* (Crossing, 1987) opened, Emma was employed by the Women's Hotline in Boston. In violation of Hotline rules, she met with an anonymous caller who needed help, but found her dead. She contacted the police, but stonewalled their investigation, preferring to handle the matter herself.

Emma had moved to California by *She Came in a Flash* (New American Library, 1988), where she worked as a public relations specialist. After a blackout, she returned to consciousness in a confined area. Flashbacks described Emma's effort to convince Lana Flax to leave the Vishni Divine Inspiration Commune, and her discovery of Lana's body.

When the personal papers of a deceased gay politician, for whom Emma had been press secretary, came into her possession in *She Came by the Book* (Berkley, 1996), Emma was placed in danger. A woman wearing clothing similar to hers was poisoned. A lesbian mystery writer was suspected of the crime. Emma was hired to find the real killer from among multiple suspects.

The Castro Theatre's Lesbian and Gay Film Festival in San Francisco, an event that Emma had eagerly awaited, was the background for *She Came to the Castro* (Berkley, 1997). She had recently ended a relationship, and was caught up in the drive to legalize marriage between same sex couples. A candidate for mayor, sympathetic to homosexual marriages, was being blackmailed. Emma agreed to be courier for the payment, even to trying to identify the blackmailer. She had not expected to find dead bodies or to lose a relationship that had become important to her.

Emma found new romance but in a disastrous setting in *She Came in Drag* (Berkley, 1999), when she guarded medical researcher, Rita Huelga. Rita had outed a prominent African-American singer with whom she had a relationship that started in high school. Dr. Huelga was at risk not only from this revelation on a national television program, but from the sponsors of her anti-cancer research who suspected that she was concealing her results.

Alicia Von Helsing

Author: Joseph Mathewson

Alicia Von Helsing, the descendant of distinguished American families, had an enduring marriage with heart specialist Eric Von Helsing. With both children grown and out of their Greenwich Village home, Alicia used her Vassar education as a newspaper columnist. She was a risk-taker who carried a gun, a weapon she had learned to shoot at exclusive Foxcroft Academy.

In *Alicia's Trump* (Avon, 1980), she visited her godson, gay painter Ronnie Griswold, only to find him murdered. She used tarot card paintings and a tape Ronnie left behind to find the motive for his death. Alicia's investigation was sidetracked when she came upon another young man who had been killed with her gun. The police were more interested in Alicia's alibi than in her theories.

Although she had agreed at her husband's request to avoid such controversies, Alicia found her promise impossible to keep in *Death Turns Right* (Avon, 1982). Her childhood friend Jenny was married to Saul Rosen, publisher of a conservative magazine. Saul, who had shifted his allegiance from Zionism to reactionary politics, had alienated old friends and co-workers. Still, Alicia and Eric were stunned when Saul was shot and killed by a "black" man. Alicia saw a lot of frantic action.

Evelyn Wade

Author: Remar Sutton

Evelyn Wade was an Atlanta widow in her seventies, who had taken part-time employment as a telephone surveyor. In *Long Lines* (Weidenfelt, 1988), while interviewing a young man, the conversation was interrupted by sounds of violence. Initially she could not recall the telephone number to refer it to the authorities. By the time Evelyn had established the origin of the call, a killer was en route to silence her.

With a change of setting, Evelyn appeared in *Boiling Rock* (British-American, 1991). On a church activity, she visited the Grand Bahamas to teach English to Haitians. Area dolphins began beaching themselves on shore. Several young tourists died while swimming off Boiling Rock. The examining pathologist was killed in a traffic accident. Evelyn worked with a voodoo woman to tie it all together.

Nyla Wade

Author: Vicki P. McConnell

Nyla Wade, a young divorcee with a journalism degree, was working for a paint company. She first appeared in *Mrs. Porter's Letter* (Naiad, 1982), one of the early lesbian mysteries acknowledged by reviews in professional library journals. Nyla had purchased a used desk in which she discovered love letters, which affected her so deeply that she researched the two women involved. The investigation paralleled Nyla's awareness of her own sexual orientation and the existence of a lesbian community.

By *The Burnton Widows* (Naiad, 1984), Nyla had moved from Denver to Burnton, Oregon. The narrative detailed the lives of successive owners (all women) of a dwelling variously referred to as "the Castle" or "the widow's house." The building was to be torn down to make room for a tourist project until Nyla organized opposition.

In *Double Daughter* (Naiad, 1988), Nyla's lesbian relationship was troubled so she returned to Denver Community College, where she connected with the gay/lesbian community. Lesbian Pat Stevens was seriously injured in a hit and run, followed by organized incidents aimed at homosexuals. Nyla located the driver, but had to be rescued herself.

This series may be uncomfortable for some readers because of its anti-male bias.

Janet Wadman

Author: Alisa Craig, pseudonym of Charlotte MacLeod

See: Janet Wadman Rhys, Page 248

Penny Wanawake

Author: Susan Moody

Penny was the daughter of Dr. Benjamin Wanawake, United Nations representative from Senangaland, and Lady Helen Hurley, member of the British nobility. She had been educated at a Swiss finishing school and then attended the Sorbonne and Stanford. A commercial photographer, she had published a photo book, *The Women of Washington*.

A more lucrative enterprise was her share in the RH Domestic Agency. RH was run by Miss Antonia Ivory, a tenant in Penny's London building, and was used by Barnaby Midas, Penny's lover, to locate homes to rob. Given her wealthy family, Penny did not need to work so she donated her ill-gotten gains to African relief programs. She owned homes in New York City, California, and London, but also spent time with her mother in Sussex. Single, she had an ongoing, but not exclusive, relationship with Barnaby, an Eton/Oxford graduate and jewel thief. Penny's appearance was distinctive. At six foot tall, she wore high heels and did her hair in cornrows.

In *Penny Black* (Fawcett, 1986), model Marfa Lund, the daughter of a white supremacist U. S. Senator, but a friend and classmate of Penny, was murdered in a Los Angeles airport restroom. Penny visited Washington, D.C., where she made an adventure out of the investigation, but had to be rescued by Barnaby. Author/teacher Max Maunciple included thinly disguised characters in his crime novels revealing intimate information in *Penny Dreadful* (Fawcett, 1986). While many of those he defamed were attending a performance at Max's school, he drank poisoned gin.

While Miss Ivory and Barnaby were planning a jewel robbery in *Penny Post* (Fawcett, 1986), Penny investigated threats to Kendal Sartain, husband of old friend Emerald Blake. The Sartain family had not welcomed Emerald, who was of mixed parentage. When Kendal was killed, Penny protected Emerald and her unborn child. Barnaby wanted Penny to marry him in *Penny Royal* (Fawcett, 1987) but she was not ready for monogamy. She visited an Italian archeological dig, where a distinguished scientist had disappeared with two gold statuettes.

In *Penny Wise* (Fawcett, 1989), she cruised aboard Costas Kyriakouis's yacht. When a fellow passenger did not survive the journey, Penny was hired to investigate. Moody overendowed the narrative with characters, only to hurry through the conclusion. Penny's father, Dr. Benjamin Wanawake, was kidnapped in *Penny Pinching* (Fawcett, 1989). Penny's search was complicated by the murder of a woman who closely resembled her.

R.H. Domestic Agency had problems finding suitable nannies in *Penny Saving* (Joseph, 1990), so Penny substituted for the unavailable Miss Ivory. The prior nanny in a placement had disappeared and the police were treating the incident as number four in a series of "nanny killings."

This has been an interesting series. Watch for Moody's later series featuring bridge expert Cassandra Swann. (See Volume 3).

V. I. (Victoria Iphigenia) Warshawski

Author: Sara Paretsky

Chicago might be "Second City" to some but its female sleuth, V. I. Warshawski may have been the #1 mystery heroine of the 1980's. Not because V. I. was warm and endearing. On the contrary, she was tough, without tolerance for those who disagreed with her convictions, but, at least, she had convictions. V. I. was perpetually angry about something, challenging not only individuals, but also institutions—city government, unions, business corporations, the Catholic Church, and the medical profession.

Victoria Iphigenia Warshawski was the only child of Tony, a Polish police sergeant, and Gabriella, a Jewish/Italian singer. Her father's death—he was killed in action—remained an unsolved murder. Her mother died painfully of cancer. V. I. played high school basketball well enough to go to the state tournament with her team and earn a basketball scholarship to the University of Chicago. While attending law school, V. I. met and married Richard Yarborough. Their marriage lasted about fourteen months, during which time they realized how little they had in common. She was socially conscious; he was socially ambitious. His life style bored her; hers, appalled him. V. I. began her legal work as a public defender, but abandoned law to become a private investigator.

V. I. had a personal life. She sang lieder, played the piano, and not only enjoyed good food, but also could cook. She was disinterested in her appearance or in housekeeping but treasured Venetian glass left by her mother, and expensive Italian shoes. She was 5' 8", trim, liked to run and work out, swam at the Y, followed the Cubs, and had firm friendships. Dr. Lotty Henschel, who operated a health clinic, loved V. I. as a daughter. Landlord Sal Contreras fussed over her. Newspaperman Murray Ryerson had been a lover and remained a friend, particularly when there was the potential of a good story.

Indemnity Only (Dial, 1982) brought the seamier aspects of Chicago to life. While V. I. preferred financial investigations, she could not afford to refuse other assignments. Andrew McGraw hired her to find his daughter, a murder suspect. The pattern was established. V. I. either began with an innocuous case or helped a friend or family member, but the investigation eventually included murder.

It was cousin Boom-Boom, an ex-hockey player working on the loading docks, who sought her help in *Deadlock* (Dial, 1984). When Boom-Boom was killed. V. I. refused to let his murderer escape.

Only a deathbed promise to her mother would motivate V. I., an atheist, to assist pious Great Aunt Rosa in *Killing Orders* (Morrow, 1985). Securities for which Aunt Rosa was responsible had been counterfeited. V. I. challenged not only a reactionary lay organization but also the Catholic hierarchy. Warshawski set double-barreled aim on the medical profession and the pro-life movement in *Bitter Medicine* (Morrow, 1987). Consuelo Alvarado, a pregnant sixteen-year-old, was riding in V. I.'s car when she began premature labor. Not only did Consuelo and the baby die, but so did her African-American obstetrician. V. I. had to know why.

When she returned to her old neighborhood for a basketball team reunion, she agreed to help Caroline Djiak find her father in *Blood Shot* (Delacorte, 1988). Her probe evolved into a conflict with a major chemical industry that risked the lives of its employees. The skeleton in the Warshawski closet, Aunt Elena, appeared in *Burn Marks* (Delacorte, 1990). She was an alcoholic whose single-room-only apartment building was burned out. Elena introduced V. I. to the world of the homeless, the unwed mothers, and to those who manipulated them.

Peppy, a dog co-owned by V. I. and her landlord, acquainted her with Hattie Frizell, a recluse under the control of a grasping neighborhood couple in *Guardian Angel* (Delacorte, 1992). The death of a unionworker, who suspected misuse of the pension fund, worried V. I. at a time when she was introspective about her present life. She began a new relationship with an African-American police detective assigned to the case.

Tunnel Vision (Delacorte, 1994) evidenced an awareness by V. I. that her impulsiveness and tunnel vision involved her friends in difficult situations. She enticed a juvenile delinquent, whom she had pledged to help, into burglary. She risked the well being of Lotty's significant other, Max. She took old friend Sal Contreras into a rat-infested tunnel. When on one of her crusades, V. I. was reckless. She was determined to rescue a battered woman fleeing with her children. She investigated irregularities among banks, agricultural corporations, and charitable groups. Finally, she cleared a young girl accused of murdering her mother.

Windy City Blues (Delacorte, 1995) collected short stories written over the prior thirteen years. They added interesting notes to V. I.'s background—her affection for Chicago and its neighborhoods; the reason behind her middle name Iphegenia, an opera in which her mother sang the lead role; the impact of sports in her life; her willingness to use mob connections to get information; and her unwavering loyalty to Lotty and her high school friends and coaches.

Hard Time (Delacorte, 1999) portrayed a more vulnerable V. I., still driven, but more aware of the impact of her actions on those around her. She confronted corrupt politicians, a media mogul, and a bent cop. When a stint in prison left her emotionally and physically wounded, V. I.'s old friends and some surprising new ones (a priest and a sensitive boy) rallied around.

Lotty Herschel had been more than a friend to V. I. She was a mother substitute who had nurtured her since her college days. *Total Recall* (Delacorte, 2001) tested their relationship. A bill to deny the right to do business in Illinois to insurance companies that had failed to honor claims from Holocaust victims was at risk. African-Americans wanted a similar restriction on businesses that had insured slave owners and dealers. Insurance companies wanted it killed. V. I. entered the conflict on behalf of an African-American family whose policy claim was rejected by Ajax Insurance Company. Her case intersected with the plea of Paul, a young man who was seeking family having just learned that he was a Jew. Lotty reacted angrily when Paul claimed that Lotty and Max Loewenthal might be "family." V. I. could not understand her vehemence, her fears, or her rejection of those who loved her.

The consistently high quality of Paretsky's writing kept the series enjoyable, although at times her sleuth came across as single minded. Paretsky is a skilled writer with swift paced plots, crisp and colorful dialogue.

Delilah West

Author: Maxine O'Callaghan

Delilah West was the widow of Jack West, her former partner in West and West Detective Agency in Orange County, California. Delilah's mother had died when she was five; her police officer father, when she was a college freshman. Delilah joined the police force, then switched to Jack's agency, after which they married. She was described as thin with cinnamon hair and brown eyes.

In *Death Is Forever* (Raven, 1980), Delilah suffered from depression. She had been present when Jack was murdered but blanked out on the killer's face. Her current missing person case was similar to the one on which Jack had been working at the time of his death. Delilah was implicated as a murder suspect when she was knocked unconscious and left in a cheap hotel room with the corpse of Jack's killer.

Friend Rita Braddock, who ran an answering service, worried about the disappearance of the young woman who had been engaged to her son Michael in *Run from Nightmare* (Raven, 1981). Delilah's investigation brought about a near death experience that left her ready to begin life without Jack.

As *Hit and Run* (St. Martin, 1989) began, Delilah was broke, living in her office, working as a waitress and store detective on the side. While jogging, she was jarred by a passing car, heard a thump and discovered a corpse in the road. Her information enabled the police to locate and arrest Michael Morales for vehicular homicide, but Delilah believed that the victim was already dead when Morales hit him.

Set-Up (St. Martin, 1991) found Delilah doing better financially, still involved in an "off again, on again" relationship with public defender Matt Scott. She continued to get referrals from businessman, Eric Lundstrom, a former lover. Two cases, the identification of Sandy Renkowski as an embezzler and the investigation of threats against Councilwoman "Bobbi" Calder, merged when Bobbi was accused of Sandy's murder.

Delilah began *Trade-Off* (St. Martin, 1996) with a newly decorated office and a Beretta .22 mini automatic, which she hoped she would never use. She could not leave the home of Benjamin Wylie, who had hired her to find his missing stepdaughter, without checking on the unusual odor emanating from the neighboring yard. She discovered the corpse of Kate Sannerman, once a prosperous real estate broker, more recently addicted to drugs. Wylie would not accept Delilah's theory that the disappearance and the murder were connected. Fired by Wylie, Delilah found a new client, loving assistance from Eric Lundstrom, and saved her own life with the Beretta.

Delilah, never comfortable that she belonged in Eric's circle of friends, was even less so in *Down for the Count* (St. Martin, 1997). She met Nicki, his eighteen-year-old daughter while vacationing in Vermont. She had left behind a larcenous corpse and a frightened boy. Delilah returned home to a kidnapping for which she blamed herself.

Delilah was a tough lady with few personal ties except Rita and an interest in renewing the relationship with Lundstrom. When it suited her purpose, she lied, misrepresented, moved corpses, and withheld information.

Helen West

Author: Frances Fyfield (Hegarty)

Helen West, a tiny slim divorcee, was employed as a Crown Prosecutor in the British legal system, but did not always work comfortably within the bureaucracy. Although professional, she fostered a lingering empathy for the underdog, had no patience with bunglers, and was a perfectionist about her own work. On a personal level she was artistic, liked rich colors, and had a high tolerance for disorder within her life and home.

Helen met Detective Chief Superintendent Geoffrey Bailey in *A Question of Guilt* (Pocket, 1989), when both were involved in the trial of hired killer Stan Jaskowski. Fyfield did an excellent job of juxtaposing the attitudes of police officer and prosecuting attorney, of methodical Bailey and mercurial West as the trial proceeded. Helen's personal inquiry endangered her life and left her with a facial scar.

Both Helen and Geoffrey had left London by *Not That Kind of Place* (Pocket, 1990). He requested a transfer because of burnout. She earned one by her uncooperative attitude. They lived together in Branston village, but did not marry. Helen's new and unsympathetic supervisor assigned her to trivial cases. An important murder case was considered inappropriate because of a conflict of interest. Although Helen and Geoffrey protected innocent suspects, neither could convict the guilty. The charm of the rural area wore thin so both arranged transfers back to London.

In *Deep Sleep* (Pocket, 1991), Helen was irritated by an incomplete police report on the death of Margaret Carlton. In response Bailey complained that Helen interfered with police business. Still, Helen's careful planning and Bailey's prompt action saved a young mother and her son from murder. During *Shadow Play* (Pantheon, 1994), Geoffrey's absence on business was a relief to Helen because their relationship had been strained. She was stressed by office problems and her inability to convict a child molester. Helen entered into an alliance with Rose Darvey, a bitter young woman whose terror of the dark matched her own. Even after Rose worked out her problems, Helen remained adrift, wanting something more than her current arrangement with Geoffrey.

In *A Clear Conscience* (Pantheon, 1995), Geoffrey's investigation into the death of a boxer killed in the parking area of a pub involved the victim's sister. Cath was a battered wife in whom Helen had taken an interest. After Cath left her husband Joe, she lost her job because of a false accusation of theft, and had to endure further oppression from Joe. Although both Geoffrey and Helen knew the extreme measures taken by women who cannot escape their abusers, they declined to take action. The relationship between Geoff and Helen was tested by their interplay in the case, leading to a compromise. They would marry, but continue to live apart.

Even that concession was jeopardized during *Without Consent* (Viking, 1997), when Geoff refused to accept that his protege and friend Sgt. Ryan was capable of rape and murder. Ryan's sexual indiscretions were well known, but they had not involved violence. Helen through her legal assistant became aware of a serial attacker who brought sexual humiliation to women, but whom his victims refused to identify.

Fyfield, a solicitor, used her insights into police procedure, legal bureaucracy and the role of females in the system. Her characters—on both sides of the law—were complex; her plots laden with sensuality. No tidy endings should be expected.

Leslie Wetzon

Author: Annette Meyers

Xenia Smith and Leslie Wetzon were a double-barreled threat as executive placement experts operating within the Wall Street financial community. Their primary functions were to recruit stock market professionals or to relocate those who were no longer content with their current employment. Playing both sides of the transaction, they operated on tips, gossip, and inside information garnered during long luncheons, quick cocktails, and endless phone calls.

Leslie was more appealing, a small, slim, ash blonde who had been a professional dancer. If Leslie seemed a trifle innocuous for a "headhunter," Xenia compensated. A tall angular woman with short dark hair and green eyes, she was a single parent. Ruthless and competitive, Xenia had earned a Ph.D. from Columbia in psychology, and had worked at the Menninger Clinic in Kansas City for five years.

In *The Big Killing* (Bantam, 1989), stockbroker Barry Stark left Leslie at a table at the Four Seasons to make a phone call, but was murdered before he could return. This incident brought Leslie into contact with Detective Silvestri, who dated Xenia first but prudently switched to Leslie.

Retired social worker Hazel Osborne had acted as a surrogate mother for Leslie whose parents died when a drunken driver hit their car. In *Tender Death* (Bantam, 1990), Hazel asked Leslie to investigate the "suicide" of a friend. Against Silvestri's advice, Leslie persisted in learning more about the connection between health care workers who assisted wealthy senior citizens and stockbrokers. The man behind the scheme was too close for comfort.

As *The Deadliest Option* (Bantam, 1991) began, Leslie was a guest at "Goldie" Barnes retirement party. He was poisoned. Two factions competing for control of the company hired Smith & Wetzon (pun to be ignored) to find the Barnes' killer.

During *Blood on the Street* (Doubleday, 1992), Silvestri was attending a nine-month training session, leaving Leslie vulnerable for a new romance. Patient widower Alton Pinkus was willing to fill the role. When the corpse of agency client Brian Middleton was discovered in a city park, he was identified through Wetzon's business card. An investor who had suffered losses when Brian handled her money was concerned because her daughter was missing and the two incidents might be connected.

In *Murder: The Musical* (Doubleday, 1993), Leslie was drawn back into the world of the theatre. Her friend Carlos Prince choreographed *Hotshot: The Musical*. When she and Carlos visited the theater, they found the stage manager with her head bashed in. Leslie discovered who was skimming the profits. She also lost a fiancé and a friend, gained a dog, and conquered her nightmares.

Silvestri and Leslie were together again in *These Bones Were Made for Dancing* (Doubleday, 1995). The great joy in her life was participation in a concert performance of *Combinations*, the musical in which she and Carlos had danced seventeen years before. Terri Matthews, one of the original performers could not be found—unless, the bones that Silvestri was trying to identify were hers.

Leslie and Xenia were not getting along well. Leslie felt her life was out of control in *The Groaning Board* (Doubleday, 1997). Smith was making unilateral decisions about their agency. Silvestri moved out of her apartment. Her response was to begin a new romance and to befriend Micklynn Devora, the creative partner in a restaurant/catering business. Micklynn became first a suspect in a murder case, and then a victim.

The books provided inside information about the financial world and were enlivened by the theatre settings. Many of the supporting characters were unpleasant but then Wall Street and Broadway do not attract the shy and humble.

Johanna "Jo" Wilder a.k.a. Johannah*

Author: Agnes Bushell

Her name was spelled Johanna in the first book and Johannah in copies of the second.

Johanna "Jo" Wilder, a tall, dark, angular woman in her thirties, had been a ballet dancer under the name Jana Wilde. She dropped out of prominence, changing her name several times. Her parents and only brother were killed in a car accident, ostensibly by communists.

By her first appearance in *Shadowdance* (The Crossing Press, 1989) set in 1980, Jo had established herself as a private investigator. She and her partner, Ruth Wilson, a former police officer, operated a small agency in Portland, Maine. Jo, a lesbian, agreed to help the Portland Feminist Alliance who were dedicated to a "world without men", because they were regularly vandalized. Having apprehended the probable culprits, Jo gave herself a vacation in New York City, enjoying the ballet until a principal dancer died on stage. Jo used her family's Russian connections, her friends in the world of ballet, and Wilson's police connections to find a killer. Jo's affair with a feminist Russian poet was doomed.

The murder of several homosexuals over a six-month period in *Death by Crystal* (Astarte Shell Press, 1993) concerned Jo and her friends. When Peter Lawrence, a gay Native American artist was arrested for a murder that took place in his apartment, his attorneys hired Wilder and Wilson. Their search for information about the victim, possibly involved in drug traffic, brought them into personal danger.

Grace Willis

Author: A. J. Orde pseudonym for
Sheri S. Tepper a.k.a. B. J. Oliphant

This series pulled a switch on the gambit of having a heroine gain inside information about an investigation from the police officer with whom she was having an affair. Here the amateur male sleuth, Denver interior decorator Jason Lynx, obtained his help from female detective Grace Willis. Grace listened to his theories, then tapped into the department computers or records to bolster them.

Lynx was a widower, struggling with the memory of an accident during which his wife Agatha disappeared, leaving their infant son in a coma from which he never recovered. During *A Little Neighborhood Murder* (Doubleday, 1989), when Jason visited neighbor George Whitney, he noticed a suspicious package, a bomb according to the police department. Although George did not explain why anyone wanted him dead, someone did. The next day both he and his wife were brutally murdered. Grace, assigned to the case, worked with Jason.

Grace barely managed financially because she supported Ron, her homosexual brother. She flew to San Francisco whenever he needed her, and provided whatever funds were necessary. She shared her older home with "Critter," a 28-pound Maine Coon bullcat. The running gag in her appearances was her hearty appetite, coupled with her trim figure.

In *Death and the Dogwalker* (Doubleday, 1990) Jason, an orphan, adopted and raised by kindly antique dealer Jacob Buchnam, ignored letters indicating that he could find his birth family for a price. Jason found another corpse, acquaintance Frederick Foret, propped against a tree in a nearby park. Even when Jason solved the case, he was unsure of how to handle the new information. Grace supported his decision, but they were both troubled.

By *Death for Old Time's Sake* (Doubleday, 1992), both Jason's son and his dear friend Jacob Buchnam had died. Jason, as Jacob's executor, delivered a bequest to Planned Parenthood, so was present at the death of protester Simonetta Fixe. He solved her murder and learned about his parents, but was unsure whether or not to contact his family. Grace helped him decide by rejecting his proposal.

Bruce Norman knew he could depend on Jason in *Looking for the Aardvark* (Doubleday, 1993), when his half brother Ernie Quevada was murdered. Jason diverted himself by concentrating on Ernie's young widow, but then needed Grace's help to sort out his feelings. At the conclusion, they thought seriously about moving on to marriage and a family.

Their plans were deflected in *A Long Time Dead* (Fawcett Crest, 1995), when brother Ron returned to Grace's home to die of AIDS. He was fatally injured when he, Grace, and Jason inspected property on which Jason was to design and furnish a Center for Environmental Research. It was unclear whether Ron was the intended victim for the set trap. Jason, not Grace, investigated the family history of the property owners. Their relationship jelled to the point where a wedding date was set.

After Grace and Jason were married in *A Death of Innocents* (Fawcett, 1997), they purchased a rundown mansion that would meet both their professional and personal needs including a nursery. The discovery of a corpse by workmen deeply disturbed Grace who felt she could only live in the house if a thorough investigation were made. This would extend to the personal lives of the family that had formerly owned the property. Grace's professional ethics had to be balanced against her wellbeing and that of their unborn child.

Francesca Wilson

Author: Janet Neel (Cohen)

When Francesca Wilson was twelve, her invalid father died. Her fragile but resolute mother supported five children by working as a probation officer. As a result, Francesca assumed the role of "little mother" to four musically talented brothers. Their relationship worked at the time, but created problems in their adult lives. Francesca became a tall slim woman with dark hair and blue eyes. She maintained her figure in spite of her appetite by jogging in the evening.

Francesca, who earned a Cambridge law degree, was very bright, but easily bored. She had a short-term photographic memory but spread herself too thin. She was a terrific dancer, played the piano, and sang alto. After an unhappy marriage, Francesca entered the Civil Service, helped by her godfather, a senior officer at the Department of Trade and Industry (DTI). She was stationed in the United States until an affair with a married U.S. Senator caused her recall to England. It was hard to keep track of Francesca's four brothers: Charlie, the eldest; Peregrine "Perry" who abandoned classical music to become a pop star; and the twins, Jeremy and Tristram. Her eventual husband, Inspector John McLeish considered them a surfeit of siblings.

Francesca evaluated Britex, a British fabric manufacturer, for possible government subsidies in *Death's Bright Angel* (St. Martin, 1989). When the firm's purchasing manager was murdered in London, McLeish believed that the victim knew his attacker. Francesca's glance at internal documents at Alutex, another subsidy prospect, placed her in jeopardy, but provided the motive for murder. Francesca and McLeish became intimate. He wanted, at least monogamy, and preferably marriage.

While on vacation in *Death on Site* (St. Martin, 1989), Francesca and McLeish witnessed a climbing "accident" from which they rescued mountaineer Alan Fraser. Later, McLeish became convinced that Alan's fall had not been an accident. Francesca had a subordinate role in the investigation. In *Death of a Partner* (St. Martin, 1993) Francesca left England to "rescue" Tristram, charged by U. S. Customs with drug possession. McLeish, resenting her absence, was vulnerable to Catherine, an attractive and ambitious female police sergeant working with him on the murder of lobbyist Angela Morgan. Francesca had input when she returned because she knew Angela personally. Realizing that Catherine and McLeish were intimate, she nurtured her own attraction to a married American. Confronted with mutual infidelity, Francesca and McLeish made a commitment to marry.

Their son William complicated Francesca's professional life so that in *Death Among the Dons* (St. Martin, 1994), she postponed her return to DTI. The death of the warden of Gladstone College created a professional opportunity for Francesca as a part time bursar. McLeish had no official role as Francesca and the new warden straightened out the college's problems and identified the prior warden's killer.

Francesca's commitment to monogamy was tested in *A Timely Death* (Constable, 1996), when she met Matt, an idealistic young solicitor, while volunteering at a battered woman's shelter. McLeish had a similar temptation when his probe of the death of a conniving developer crossed paths with a fraud investigation by Catherine Crane, his former lover. The interests of Matt and Francesca, McLeish and Catherine were interwoven in a tense narrative.

Francesca was preoccupied with a toddler, a second pregnancy, her brother Tristram's operatic career, and the part-time job as bursar at Gladstone College as *To Die For* (Constable, 1998; St. Martin, 1999) opened. She made time to help Gladstone alumna Judith Delves deal with the financial chaos at the restaurant that she and her recently murdered partner owned. When a series of tragedies followed the murder, it was John McLeish who sorted things out.

With a two-year-old and the new baby expected within months, Francesca tried to cut back on her outside activities, but it wasn't easy. Dame Sarah located a replacement for her as Bursar at Gladstone College, but other responsibilities were not to be denied. As godmother for her cousin Wendy's teenaged son, Jamie, Francesca supplied not only musical training but also a place of refuge when his father Steve declined into one of his schizophrenic periods. During *O Gentle Death* (Constable, 2000) both Francesca and John McLeish were drawn into the lives of four teenagers, students at the Faraday Foundation School, which specialized in nurturing artistic talents. One of the four, Catriona, an unstable young woman had frequently attempted suicide, but her death was proven to be murder. Among the suspects were groups of parents, stepparents, fellow students, and faculty members. Although Francesca bore a second healthy son and almost became a victim, the investigative roles in the narrative fell to John and his gay assistant, D. I. Kevin Camberton.

An offbeat police procedural/amateur female sleuth duo who juggled roles as parents and spouses with their professional lives.

Miriam Winchester

Author: Nina Romberg

Miriam Winchester was an elderly Native American woman, a blend of Caddo, Comanche, and Irish, all cultures with mystical traditions. A lithe woman with silver hair and green eyes, she had never married, living alone in a rural area in East Texas. The granddaughter of a shaman, she could recognize the evil spirits, then call upon good spirits to combat them.

Sunny Hansen, a painter who fled an abusive husband, became Miriam's neighbor in *The Spirit Stalker* (Pinnacle, 1989). Sunny's reticence to call attention to herself caused her to lie to the police when she observed a serial killer at work. The love of a former athlete and Miriam's spirits helped Sunny when she confronted evil, which had been released by man's abuse of the environment and taken human form.

When Miriam glanced into her backyard in *Shadow Walkers* (Pinnacle, 1993), she saw Sadie, a bedraggled runaway, scavenging from food put out for the birds and squirrels. She quietly set out bread, cheese and tomatoes for the child. Eleven-year-old Sadie, who had left an abusive foster home, thought she had found a safe haven in abandoned buildings inhabited by other runaways. The fragile bonds within the group were destroyed when a locked room was opened, disclosing memorabilia of the Nazi movement. The evil released could only be overcome by Miriam's spiritual powers.

Jane Winfield

Author: Audrey Peterson

Jane Winfield and her co-protagonist, Andrew Quentin, were neither spouses nor lovers. He was a widower, whose wife had been killed by a drunken driver. She married British solicitor James Hall who represented her when she was accused of murder. Jane was the daughter of a widowed history professor. Her mother, who died when Jane was twelve, had left her a small annuity. Jane moved to England on a two-year fellowship to study the music of Marius Hart, while working towards a Ph.D. in Music History.

In *The Nocturne Murder* (Arbor, 1987), Jane was arrested when her lover, music critic Maxwell Fordham, was found dead in her room. Quentin, her American supervising professor, came to her assistance. Jane's participation in the investigation was passive. Her sojourn into the countryside in *Death in Wessex* (Pocket, 1989) coincided with Quentin's visit to friends in the area. This put them both on scene when fifteen-year-old Carla Braden was kidnapped. Jane's musical knowledge enabled her to rescue the girl.

By *Murder in Burgundy* (Pocket, 1989), James Hall and Jane were married but he remained in London while Jane and Andrew joined the extended O'Connor family on a boat tour through rural France. "Poppa" O'Connor was under pressure to will his fortune to his stepchildren, but he wanted to find his "own" son. Someone killed him first.

Jane had her Ph.D. and was working as a publicist for the Southmere Opera Festival in *Deadly Rehearsal* (Pocket, 1990). When James visited, he discovered the body of Julian Kingsley at the base of a stone tower. Unfortunately James and Kingsley's wife Margaret had been lovers.

A daughter Laura had joined the Hall family as *Elegy in a Country Graveyard* (Pocket, 1990) began. Jane was shocked when she and a distant cousin inherited money from her great-aunt, killed in a hit and run accident. Aunt Carlotta had taught pianist Silvio Antonelli. Her journals would be valuable in a biography that Jane was writing. Although Jane had the major role in other books, Quentin was the primary figure in *Lament for Christabel* (Pocket, 1991). He was in love for the first time since his wife died, but with a woman accused of killing her husband.

Although the series never rose above average, Peterson was a competent writer. When hardcovers are so expensive, good paperback originals like the Winfield/Quentin series are a bargain.

Caledonia Wingate

Author: Corinne Holt Sawyer

See: Angela Benbow, Page 37

Alexandra "Alex" Winter

Author: Susan Steiner

Alexandra "Alex" Winter, a tall redheaded divorcee, was an apprentice detective in the Abramowitz & Bailey Agency in *Murder on Her Mind* (Fawcett, 1985) when handsome Jay Southwood sought help. Unsure of her skills, but encouraged by Jay, she investigated a potential blackmailer. The more Alex learned about her client, the more she wondered if she were on the right side.

Library: No Murder Aloud (Fawcett, 1993) contained interesting "touches"—a library in a castle, irises planted by a distinguished horticulturist, and a picture purportedly painted by Judy Garland. Alex was hired by wealthy Barron Dysart III to prove that his sister's suitor was a "gigolo." Instead, she became enmeshed in the murder of a real estate broker determined to sell out the library.

Lettie Winterbottom

Author: Leela Cutter

Lettie Winterbottom was cast in the mold of the eccentric spinsters who populated so many English cozy mysteries. She was a mystery writer in her sixties, feeling her age, known to doze off while speaking, suffering periods of mental confusion. This presentation will not endear the series to the mature female mystery readers who do not consider senility either humorous or a common characteristic of sixty-year-old females.

Murder After Tea Time (St. Martin, 1981) was funny once the reader adapted to Cutter's camp style. Her niece, Julia Carlisle, realized that Lettie had wandered off. She traced her aunt by means of excerpts from her last book that contained a "thinly veiled" description of a dysfunctional family. There had probably been a murder, but where was the corpse?

Who Stole Stonehenge? (St. Martin, 1983) featured an unusual crime: the removal of the ponderous structures during a snowstorm. Lettie believed she could explain the method used. She, Julia, and Australian journalist J. D. Hilsebeck set out to win the reward. Lettie was physically active: skiing, boating down the river, and flying to Ireland to find the relocated monuments.

Glenna Hardcastle, a colorful romance novelist invited Julia and Lettie to a party promoting a Museum of Historical Romance in *Death of the Party* (St. Martin, 1985). Lettie, who declined, missed the murder of Freddie, Glenna's nephew, but investigated it anyway. She went behind convent walls and into the compound of a beauty salon to gather information.

Lettie and Julia's incredible adventures were witty and amusing.

Matilda Worthing

Author: John Keith Drummond

Matilda Worthing, a retired court reporter, had auburn hair turning gray and thick glasses covering dark blue eyes. She shared her home in Jolliston, California, with Martha Shaw, a former co-worker. Matilda used reference materials and her courtroom experience in her criminal investigations.

Lady "Lally" Fairgrief, Matilda's ninety-five year old aunt visited opera tenor Rudolph Besserman during *Thy Sting, O Death* (St. Martin, 1985). Besserman's family was in an uproar when he died of complications from bee stings. Lally was convinced that a murderer was loose so she introduced Matilda and Martha as household help. *'Tis the Season to Be Dying* (St. Martin, 1988) described Matilda (short and slender, over seventy) and Martha (taller, older, heavier, white hair, with colorful clothes). At their annual Christmas open house, Matilda's nephew Larry Worthing brought a friend who drew them into another murderous, mercenary family.

In *Mass Murder* (St. Martin, 1991), Matilda and Martha investigated the murders of clergymen, including one at their own church, who had been poisoned by communion wine. The police, reluctant to become involved, preferred to let the amateurs work it out. Matilda did, but allowed the murderer to find his own punishment.

For a person who worked within the criminal justice system, Matilda was surprising reluctant to share the results of her investigations with the police.

Elizabeth Lamb Worthington

Author: B. J. Morison

Most children in adult mystery fiction have been singularly unappealing. Elizabeth Lamb Worthington was an exception. Elizabeth, raised in Europe by her mother, knew nothing of her father's family.

In *Champagne and a Gardener* (Thorndike, 1983) Elizabeth's mother, Jane Lamb, accepted a position as secretary to society dowager Mrs. Elizabeth Elbridge Worthington. The Worthington summer homes were located on Mount Desert Island at some distance from Bar Harbor, Maine. Mrs. Worthington had three adult children: Sarah Worthington Halstead, married to an attorney; Peter, the black sheep son in Peru managing a mine; and Isabella von Litchtenfeld, a divorcee who delighted in scandalizing the community. Lettice Parker, an annoying neighbor, was found beaten to death, triggering an investigation by Elizabeth and her young cousin, Persis. The re-introduction of Jane to Peter Worthington completed Elizabeth's family.

In *Port and a Star Boarder* (Thorndike, 1984), Elizabeth's new friend, a fifteen-year-old amateur inventor, was found badly beaten. Then a local lobsterman was killed in an explosion. Elizabeth had promised to stay out of trouble, but she noticed everything that went on around her. As Elizabeth and Persis wandered on the beach in *Beer and Skittles* (Thorndike, 1985) they found the corpse of a young man. Elizabeth was mature enough to understand such complexities as blackmail and illegitimacy, but needed help when the action moved to drug dealing, arson, and murder.

In *The Voyage of the Chianti* (North Country, 1987), neighbor Vittorio Vincentia invited Elizabeth and Persis to accompany Viola, his mildly retarded granddaughter, on a yachting trip. This was not a happy ship and after a series of incidents, Viola was smothered to death.

By *The Martini Effect* (North Country, 1992), Elizabeth was ready for high school. She settled for St. Augustine's on the Island, rather than an exclusive mainland boarding school. The parents of a male student drowned in a scuba diving accident demanded a police investigation that reunited Elizabeth with Lt. Buzzie Higgins.

The series was most effective in the earlier books.

Author /Character Index

Although some characters appear in all volumes of a shared series, only those in which a significant role is played will be listed. Only those books in which her actions affect the plot are listed below. Books listed in Hubin or another reliable authority as including the identified sleuth but not available for a personal review are listed with an asterisk. All titles, publishers and dates of publication were taken from my personal book reviews but were rechecked for accuracy with recognized authorities such as Hubin, Heising, *Twentieth Century Crime* and *Mystery Writers*. Any errors are my own. *Indicates a book unavailable for personal review.*

Bannister, Jo
Clio Rees Marsh 183
    Gilgamesh   *The Going Down of the Sun*
    Striving with Gods

Barnes, Linda
Carlotta Carlyle 51
    Cold Case   *Coyote*
    Flashpoint   *Hardware*
    The Snake Tattoo   *Snapshot*
    Steel Guitar   *A Trouble of Fools*

Barnes, Trevor
Blanche Hampton 116
    A Midsummer Killing   *Taped*
    A Pound of Flesh a.k.a. Dead Meat

Beck, K.K. a.k.a. Katherine Marris
Iris Cooper 63
    Death in a Deck Chair   *Murder in a Mummy Case*
    Peril Under the Palms

Belfort, Sophie
Molly Rafferty 243
    Eyewitness to Murder   *The Lace Curtain Murders*
    The Marvell College Murders

Bell, Josephine—pseudonym for Doris Bell Ball
Amy Tupper 288
    A Question of Inheritance   *Wolf! Wolf!*

Belsky, Dick a.k.a. Richard G. Belsky
Jenny McKay 188
    Live from New York   *The Mourning Show*
    Summertime News
    South Street Confidential a.k.a. Broadcast Clues
Lucy Shannon 265
    Loverboy   *One for the Money*

Bennett, Liza
Peg Goodenough 107
    Madison Avenue Murder   *Seventh Avenue Murder*

Berne, Karin—pseudonym for Sue Bernell and Michaela Karni
Ellie Gordon 107
    Bare Acquaintances   *False Impressions*
    Shock Value

Berry, Carole
Bonnie Indermill 137
    The Death of a Dancing Fool   *The Death of a Difficult Woman*
    Death of a Dimpled Darling   *Death of a Downsizer*
    Good Night, Sweet Prince   *Island Girl*
    The Letter of the Law   *The Year of the Monkey*

Cannell, Dorothy
    Ellie Simon Haskell 120
        Bridesmaids Revisited   *Femmes Fatale*
        How to Murder the Man of Your Dreams
        How to Murder Your Mother-in-Law
        Mum's the Word
        The Spring Cleaning Murders   *The Thin Woman*
        The Trouble with Harriet   *The Widow's Club*

Carlson, P. M. (Patricia)
    Maggie Ryan 254
        Audition for Murder   *Bad Blood*
        Murder in the Dog Days   *Murder Is Academic*
        Murder Is Pathological   *Murder Misread*
        Murder Unrenovated   *Rehearsal for Murder*

Castle, Jayne—pseudonym for Jayne Krentz
    Gwen Jones 148
        Desperate Games   *The Chilling Deception*
        The Fatal Fortune   *The Sinister Touch*

Caudwell, Sarah—pseudonym for Sarah Cockburn
    Julia Larmore, Selena Jardine and Hilary Tamar 159, 145, 278
        The Shortest Way to Hades   *The Sibyl in Her Grave*
        The Sirens Sang of Murder   *Thus Was Adonis Murdered*

Chase, Elaine Raco
    Nikki Holden 135
        Dangerous Places   *Dark Corners*

Christmas, Joyce
    Lady Margaret Priam 240
        Dying Well   *A Fete Worse Than Death*
        Friend or Faux   *Going Out in Style*
        It's Her Funeral   *Mourning Gloria*
        A Perfect Day for Dying   *Simply to Die For*
        A Stunning Way to Die   *Suddenly in Her Sorbet*
        A Better Class of Murder

Churchill, Jill—pseudonym for Janice Young Brooks
    Jane Jeffrey 147
        A Farewell to Yarns   *Fear of Frying*
        From Here to Paternity   *The Class Menagerie*
        Grime and Punishment   *A Groom with a View*
        A Knife to Remember   *The Merchants of Menace*
        Mulch Ado About Nothing   *A Quiche before Dying*
        Silence of the Hams   *War and Peas*

Clark, Mary Higgins
    Alvira Meehan 193
        All Through the Night   *The Lottery Winner (ss)*
        Weep No More, My Lady

Godfrey, Ellen
   Jane Tregar 285
      Georgia Disappeared   *Murder Behind Locked Doors*

Gordon, Alison
   Kate Henry 128
      The Dead Pull Hitter   *Night Game*
      Prairie Hardball   *Safe at Home*
      Striking Out

Gosling, Paula
   Kate Trevorne 287
      Backlash   *The Body in Blackwater Bay*
      Monkey Puzzle

Gough, Laurence
   Claire Parker 227
      Accidental Deaths   *Fall Down Easy*
      Funny Money   *The Goldfish Bowl*
      Heartbreaker   *Hot Shots*
      Karaoke Rap   *Killers*
      Memory Lane   *Serious Crimes*
      Shutterbug   *Silent Knives a.k.a.*
                                         Death on a No.8 Hook

Grafton, Sue
   Kinsey Millhone 197
      "A" Is for Alibi   *"B" Is for Burglar*
      "C" Is for Corpse   *"D" Is for Deadbeat*
      "E" Is for Evidence   *"F" Is for Fugitive*
      "G" Is for Gumshoe   *"H" Is for Homicide*
      "I" Is for Innocent   *"J" Is for Judgment*
      "K" Is for Killer   *"L" Is for Lawless*
      "M" Is for Malice   *"N" Is for Noose*
      "O" Is for Outlaw   *"P" Is for Peril*

Graham, Heather (Pozzessere)
   Donna Miro & Lorna Doria 201
      An Angel's Share   *Sensuous Angel*

Granger, Bill a.k.a. Joe Gash
   Karen Kovacs 156
      The El Murders   *Public Murders*

Grant, Linda—pseudonym for Linda V. Williams
   Catherine Sayler 261
      Blind Trust   *Lethal Genes*
      Love Nor Money   *Random Access Murder*
      Vampire Bytes   *A Woman's Place*

Grant-Adamson, Lesley
   Rain Morgan 207
      Guilty Knowledge   *Curse the Darkness*
      The Face of Death   *Wild Justice*
      Death on Widow's Walk a.k.a. Patterns in the Dust

Hart, Ellen—pseudonym for Patricia Boehnhardt

Jane Lawless 162

Faint Praise	*Hallowed Murder*
Hunting the Witch	*A Killing Cure*
The Merchant of Venus	*Robber's Wine*
A Small Sacrifice	*Stage Fright*
Vital Lies	*Wicked Games*

Hartland, Michael

Sarah Cable 46

Frontier of Fear	*Seven Steps to Treason*
The Year of the Scorpion	

Hendricks, Michael

Rita Noonan 212

Friends in High Places	*Money to Burn*

Hervey, Evelyn—pseudonym for H. R. F. Keating

Harriet Unwin 290

The Governess	*The Man of Gold*
Into the Valley of Death	

Hess, Joan a.k.a. Joan Hadley

Arly Hanks 117

Madness in Maggody	*Maggody and the Moonbeams*
Maggody in Manhattan	*Maggody Loves Misery*
The Maggody Militia	*Malice in Maggody*
Martians in Maggody	*Miracles in Maggody*
Mischief in Maggody	*Mortal Remains in Maggody*
Much Ado in Maggody	*Murder@Maggody.com*
O Little Town of Maggody	

Claire Malloy 177

Strangled Prose	*Dear Miss Demeanor*
A Really Cute Corpse	*A Diet to Die For*
Roll Over and Play Dead	*Death by the Light of the Moon*
Poisoned Pins	*Tickled to Death*
Busy Bodies	*Closely Akin to Murder*
A Holly Jolly Murder	*A Conventrional Corpse*
Murder at the Murder at the Mimosa Club	

Hoff, B. J. (Brenda Jane)

Jennifer Terry Kaine 152

Dark River Legacy	*Storm at Daybreak*
The Tangled Web	*Vow of Silence*
The Captive Voice a.k.a. The Domino Image	

Holland, Isabelle

Claire Aldington 28

A Death at St. Anselm's	*A Fatal Advent*
Flight of the Archangel	*The Long Search*
A Lover Scorned	

Kellerman, Faye
>   *The Forgotten*   *Grievous Sin*
>   *Jupiter's Bones:*   *Prayers for the Dead*
>   *The Ritual Bath*   *Sanctuary*
>   *Serpent's Tooth*   *Stalker*

Kelly, Nora
>   *Bad Chemistry*   *In the Shadow of Kings*
>   *My Sister's Keeper*   *Old Wounds*

Kelly, Susan
>   *The Summertime Soldiers*   *And Soon I'll Come to Kill You*
>   *The Gemini Man*   *Out of the Darkness*
>   *Trail of the Dragon*   *Until Proven Innocent*

Kelman, Judith
>   *Hush, Little Darlings*   *Where Shadows Fall*

Kemp, Sarah—pseudonym for Michael Butterworth
>   *The Lure of Sweet Death*   *No Escape*
>   *What Dread Hand?*

Kenney, Susan
>   *Garden of Malice*   *Graves in Academe*
>   *One Fell Sloop*

Kijewski, Karen
>   *Alley Kat Blues*   *Copy Kat*
>   *Honky Tonk Kat*   *Kat Scratch Fever*
>   *Kat's Cradle*   *Katapult*
>   *Katwalk*   *Stray Kat Waltz*
>   *Wild Kat*

King, Frank—a.k.a. Lydia Adamson
>   *Sleeping Dogs Die*   *Take the D Train*

Kittredge, Mary
>   *Dead and Gone*   *Murder in Mendocino*
>   *Poison Pen*

Knight, Kathryn Lasky
>   *Dark Swan*   *Mortal Words*
>   *Mumbo Jumbo*   *Trace Elements*

Lackey, Mercedes
  Diana Tregarde. 286
    Burning Water   *Children of the Night*
    Jinx High

Lake. M. D.—pseudonym for Allen Simpson
  Peggy O'Neill 219
    Death Calls the Tune   *Amends for Murder*
    Cold Comfort   *Flirting with Death*
    A Gift for Murder   *Grave Choices*
    Midsummer Malice   *Murder by Mail*
    Once Upon a Time   *Poisoned Joy*

LaPierre, Janet
  Meg Halloran 114
    Baby Mine   *Children's Games*
    The Cruel Mother   *Grandmother's House*
    Old Enemies   *Unquiet Grave*

LaPlante, Lynda
  Dolly Rawlins 246
    She's Out   *The Widows*

Laurence, Janet
  Darina Lisle 169
    Appetite for Death   *Death a la Provencale*
    Death and the Epicure   *A Deepe Coffyn*
    Diet for Death   *Hotel Morgue*
    Mermaid's Feast   *Recipe for Death*
    A Tasty Way to Die   *Death at the Table*

Lewin, Michael Z.
  Sgt. Carollee Fleetwood 91
    And Baby Will Fall   *Hard Line*
    Late Payments

Lewis, Catherine and Judith Guerin
  Lisa Thomas 281
    Not in Single Spies   *Unable By Reason of Death*

Livingston, Nancy
  Mavis Bignell 39
    Death in a Distant Land   *Death in Close-Up*
    Fatality at Bath & Wells   *Incident at Parga*
    Quiet Murder   *Unwillingly to Vegas*

Lochte, Dick
  Serendipity "Sarah" Dahlquist 65
    Laughing Dog   *Sleeping Dog*
    Lucky Dog and Other Tales of Murder

Longley, W. B.—pseudonym for Robert J. Randisi
  Liz Archer a.k.a. Angel Eyes 29
    Avenging Angel   *Bullets & Bad Times**
    Chinatown Justice   *Death's Angel**
    Logan's Army   *The Miracle of Revenge**
    *Six Gun Angel**   *Wolf Pass**

Character Index: Volumes I & II

I refers to Volume I and II refers to Volume II of the series

I refers to Volume I and II refers to Volume II of the series

I refers to Volume I and II refers to Volume II of the series

LuEllen *II*-173
Lyons, Pauline I-236

M
MacDonald, Lynn I-56
Macintosh, Isabel *II*-175
Mack, Madelyn I-13
MacPherson, Elizabeth. *II*-176
MacVeigh, Sue I-57
MacWilliams, Eve. I-132
Maddox, Kate *II*-176
Maddox, Sue Carstairs I-236
Madeiras, Zee *II*-177
Maigret, Madame. I-132
Malloy, Claire *II*-177
Malory, Sheila *II*-179
Markey, Dawn *II*-181
Markham, Helen. *II*-182
Marlow, Daisy *II*-182
Marple, Jane I-58
Marsden, Kit I-133
Marsh, Clio Rees. *II*-183
Marsh, Emma I-60
Marsh, Helen I-237
Marsh, Kate I-61
Marshall, Megan I-238
Marshall, Suzanne "Suzy" Willett . I-133
Martin, Chris *II*-183
Martin, Octavia "Tavy". I-238
Marvin, Dr. Joan. I-62
Matthews, Daphne. *II*-184
Matthews, Freya I-238
Maughan, Leslie I-63
Maxwell, Georgia Lee *II*-186
May, Dr. Tina *II*-187
McCleary, Quin St. James *II*-187
McCone, Sharon I-239
McFall, Nina. *II*-187
McGurk, Gail I-63
McIntosh, Ann I-134
McKay, Jenny *II*-188
McKenna, Patience "Pay" *II*-189
McKenzie, Abby Novack. *II*-190
McKinnon, Georgine Wyeth . . . I-135
McLean, Anne "Davvie" Davenport I-64
McLeish, Francesca Wilson . . . *II*-190
McLeod, Kitty I-135
McNeill, Anne Holt I-64

McTavish, Stoner *II*-191
McVeigh, Cathy *II*-192
McWhinny, Tish. *II*-192
Mead, Selena I-242
Meehan, Alvira. *II*-193
Melville, Susan. *II*-194
Mercer, Penny I-66
Merrill, Michelle. *II*-195
Merton, Sally I-135
Mettie, Caroline "Cad" I-6
Miles, Debbie *II*-196
Millhone, Kinsey. *II*-197
Miro, Donna. *II*-201
Miskin, Kate. *II*-201
Mitchell, Cassandra *II*-203
Mitchell, Gail Rogers I-243
Mom. *II*-205
Monaghan, Rosie *II*-206
Monk, Dittany Henbit. *II*-206
Moore, Mona *II*-206
Morgan, Mary I-243
Morgan, Rain *II*-207
Morganthau, Molly I-14
Morrison, Theresa "Terri" *II*-207
Morrison-Burke, Hon. Constance I-243
Mott, Daisy Jane I-67
Mott, Lucy. I-67
Ms. Squad I-244
Mulcahaney, Norah. I-245
Mulrooney, Mary Frances
a.k.a. M. F. *II*-208
Mulroy, J. D.. . . . . *II*-209
Murdoch, Emily I-136
Murdoch, Rachel and Jennifer . . . I-68
Murphy, Kate *II*-210
Myrl, Dora. I-14

N
Nevkorina, Natasha. I-136
Newberry, Millicent I-15
Newton, Cassie *II*-210
Nidech, Ella *II*-210
Nightingale, Amanda I-247
Nilsen, Pam *II*-211
Noonan, Rita *II*-212
Norrington, Jennifer I-248
Norris, Mrs. Annie I-136
North, Norah. I-249

I refers to Volume I and II refers to Volume II of the series

I refers to Volume I and II refers to Volume II of the series

S

I refers to Volume I and II refers to Volume II of the series

Book Titles Index

All titles were taken from my personal book reviews or from advance notices of books and were rechecked for accuracy with recognized authorities such as Hubin, Heising, Twentieth Century Crime and Mystery Writers, and with newsletters by mystery book stores. Any errors are my own. Those titles marked with an asterisk (*) are believed to be in existence or to be published soon but were not currently available.

Title of Book	Author	Character
#		
The 27* Ingredient Chili Con Carne Murders	Nancy Pickard	Eugenia Potter
A		
"A" Is for Alibi	Sue Grafton	Kinsey Millhone
A.K.A.: Also Known As	Dave Pedneau	Anna Tyree
A.P.B.: All Points Bulletin	Dave Pedneau	Anna Tyree
Accidental Deaths	Laurence Gough	Claire Parker
Act of Faith	Michael Bowen	Sandrine Casette Curry
Act of Revenge	Robert K. Tanenbaum	Marlene Ciampi
Acts of Murder	L. (Laurali) R. Wright	Cassandra Mitchell
Adam and Evil	Gillian Roberts	Amanda Pepper
Advent of Dying	Carol Anne O'Marie	Sr. Mary Helen O'Connor
Albatross	Evelyn Anthony	Davina Graham
An Alibi Too Soon	Roger Ormerod	Amelia Trowbridge Patton
Alicia's Trump	Joseph Mathewson	Alicia Von Helsing
All Dressed Up to Die	Robert Nordan	Mavis Lashley
All Hallows' Evil	Valerie Wolzien	Susan Henshaw
All that Glitters	Elizabeth Powers	Viera Kolarova
All Through the Night	Mary Higgins Clark	Alvira Meehan
Alley Kat Blues	Karen Kijewski	Kat Colorado
Alternate Sides	Marissa Piesman	Nina Fischman
The Always Anonymous Beast	Lauren Wright Douglas	Caitlin Reese
Amateur City	Katherine Forrest	Kate Delafield
Amends for Murder	M. D. Lake	Peggy O'Neill
American Quartet	Warren Adler	Fiona Fitzgerald
American Sextet	Warren Adler	Fiona Fitzgerald
And Baby Will Fall	Michael Z. Lewin	Sgt. Carollee Fleetwood
And Soon I'll Come to Kill You	Susan Kelly	Liz Connors
And Then There Was Nun	Monica Quill	Sr. Mary Theresa "Emtee" Dempsey

Angel and the French Widow	Anthea Cohen	Agnes Carmichael
Angel Dust	Anthea Cohen	Agnes Carmichael
Angel in Action	Anthea Cohen	Agnes Carmichael
Angel in Autumn*	Anthea Cohen	Agnes Carmichael
Angel in Love	Anthea Cohen	Agnes Carmichael
The Angel Maker	Ridley Pearson	Daphne Matthews
Angel of Death	Anthea Cohen	Agnes Carmichael
Angel of Retribution	Anthea Cohen	Agnes Carmichael
Angel of Vengeance	Anthea Cohen	Agnes Carmichael
Angel Without Mercy	Anthea Cohen	Agnes Carmichael
An Angel's Share	Heather Graham	Donna Miro & Lorna Doria
Another Man's Poison	Ann Cleeves	Molly Palmer-Jones
Antipodes	Maria-Antonia Oliver	Lonia Guiu
The Apostrophe Thief	Barbara Paul	Marian Larch
Apparition Alley	Katherine Forrest	Kate Delafield
Appearance of Evil	Carolyn Coker	Andrea Perkins
Appetite for Death	Janet Laurence	Darina Lisle
The Art of Survival	A. E. Maxwell	Fiora Flynn
As a Favor	Susan Dunlap	Jill Smith
Ashes to Ashes	Mary Monica Pulver	Kori Price Brichter
At the Edge of the Sun	Anne Stuart	Maggie Bennett
Audition for Murder	P. M. Carlson	Maggie Ryan
Avenging Angel	W. B. Longley	Liz Archer a.k.a. Angel Eyes
The Avenue of the Dead	Evelyn Anthony	Davina Graham

B

"B" Is for Burglar	Sue Grafton	Kinsey Millhone
B. & E.: Breaking and Entering	Dave Pedneau	Anna Tyree
B.O.L.O.: Be On the Lookout	Dave Pedneau	Anna Tyree
Baby Doll Games	Margaret Maron	Lt. Sigrid Harald
Baby Mine	Janet LaPierre	Meg Halloran
Baby, Would I Lie?	Donald E. Westlake	Sara Joslyn
Backhand	Liza Cody	Anna Lee
Backlash	Paula Gosling	Kate Trevorne
Bad Blood	P. M. Carlson	Maggie Ryan
Bad Chemistry	Nora Kelly	Gillian Adams
Bad Company	Liza Cody	Anna Lee
Bad Company	Sarah Dreher	Stoner McTavish
Bad Monday	Annette Roome	Chris Martin
Badger Game	Michael Bowen	Sandrine Casette Curry
The Baked Bean Supper Murders	Virginia Rich	Eugenia Potter
The Balmoral Nude	Carolyn Coker	Andrea Perkins
The Bandersnatch	Mollie Hardwick	Doran Fairweather
Bank on It	Sheryl Woods	Amanda Roberts
Bare Acquaintances	Karin Berne	Ellie Gordon
The Bartholomew Fair Murders	Leonard Tourney	Joan Stock
The Bay Psalm Book Murder	Will Harriss	Mona Moore Dunbar
A Beautiful Place to Die	Philip R. Craig	Zee Madeiras Jackson
Beauty Dies	Melodie Johnson Howe	Maggie Hill, Claire Conrad
Beer and Skittles	B. J. Morison	Elizabeth Lamb Worthington
Berlin Game	Len Deighton	Fiona Kimber-Hutchinson Samson
The Bessie Blue Killer	Richard A. Lupoff	Marvia Plum
A Better Class of Murder	Joyce Christmas	Lady Margaret Priam
Better Off Dead	Denise Danks	Georgina Powers
The Beverly Malibu	Katherine Forrest	Kate Delafield

C

Cajun Nights	D. J. Donaldson	Kit Franklyn
Calling Juliet Bravo	Mollie Hardwick	Juliet Bravo a.k.a. Jean Darblay
The Calling	Jerry Jenkins	Jennifer Grey
Canary	Nathan Aldyne	Clarissa Lovelace
Capriccio	Joan G. Smith	Cassie Newton
*A Captive in Time**	Sarah Dreher	Stoner McTavish
The Captive Voice a.k.a. *The Domino Image*	B. J. Hoff	Jennifer Terry Kaine
The Caravaggio Shawl	Samuel Steward	Gertrude Stein & Alice B. Toklas
Carpenter and Quincannon	Bill Pronzini	Sabina Carpenter
The Case of the Anxious Aunt	Anna Clarke	Paula Glenning
The Case of the Chinese Boxes	Marele Day	Claudia Valentine
The Case of the Hook-Billed Kites	J. S. Borthwick	Sarah Deane
The Case of the Ludicrous Letters	Anna Clarke	Paula Glenning
The Case of the Paranoid Patient	Anna Clarke	Paula Glenning
A Case of Vineyard Poison	Philip R. Craig	Zee Madeiras Jackson
Casebook of Constance and *Charlie, Volume I*	Kate Wilhelm	Constance Leidl
Casebook of Constance and *Charlie, Volume II*	Kate Wilhelm	Constance Leidl
The Cashmere Kid	B. (Barbara) Comfort	Tish McWhinny
A Casket for a Lying Lady	Richard Werry	J. D. Mulroy
Casting for Murder	Mikel Dunham	Rhea Buerklin
Catnap	Gillian Slovo	Kate Baeier
Caught Dead in Philadelphia	Gillian Roberts	Amanda Pepper
The Cavalier in White	Marcia Muller	Joanna Stark
Celestial Buffet (ss)*	Susan Dunlap	Kieran O'Shaughnessy, Jill Smith
A Certain Justice	P. D. James	Kate Miskin
Chain Letter	Claire McNab	Inspector Carol Ashton
Champagne and a Gardener	B. J. Morison	Elizabeth Lamb Worthington
Charity	Len Deighton	Fiona Kimber-Hutchinson Samson
The Charles Dickens Murders	Edith Skom	Beth Austin
Chase the Storm	Alison Tyler	Jennifer Heath
*Chase the Sun**	Alison Tyler	Jennifer Heath
Chase the Wind	Alison Tyler	Jennifer Heath
Children of the Night	Mercedes Lackey	Diana Tregarde
Children's Games	Janet LaPierre	Meg Halloran
A Chill Rain in January	L. (Laurali) R. Wright	Cassandra Mitchell
The Chilling Deception	Jayne Castle	Gwen Jones
Chinatown Justice	W. B. Longley	Liz Archer a.k.a. Angel Eyes
A Chorus of Detectives	Barbara Paul	Geraldine Farrar
The Christie Caper	Carolyn G. Hart	Annie Laurence Darling
Citadel Run	Paul Bishop	Tina Tamiko
A Civil Death	Joyce & John Corrington	Denise Lemoyne
The Glass Menagerie	Jill Churchill	Jane Jeffry
The Classic Car Killer	Richard A. Lupoff	Marvia Plum
A Clear Conscience	Frances Fyfield	Helen West
Cliff Hanger	Philip R. Craig	Zee Madeiras Jackson
Close Call	Gillian Slovo	Kate Baeier
Close Quarters	Marissa Piesman	Nina Fischman
Closely Akin to Murder	Joan Hess	Claire Malloy
Cobalt	Nathan Aldyne	Clarissa Lovelace
*Cobra: Belgrade Battleground**	Joseph Rosenberger	Debbie Miles
Cobra: Nightmare in Panama	Joseph Rosenberger	Debbie Miles

D

Dark Swan	Kathryn Lasky Knight	Calista Jacobs
Darkness Before the Dawn	Anne Stuart	Maggie Bennett
The Daughters of Artemis	Lauren Wright Douglas	Caitlin Reese
The Day That Dusty Died	Lee Martin	Deb Ralston
Dead and Gone	Mary Kittredge	Charlotte Kent
Dead Certain	Claire McNab	Inspector Carol Ashton
Dead Crazy	Nancy Pickard	Jenny Cain
Dead in the Water	Julie Smith	Rebecca Schwartz
Dead Man Running a.k.a.	Jean Warmbold	Sarah Calloway
June Mail		
Dead Man's Thoughts	Carolyn Wheat	Cass Jameson
Dead Meat a.k.a. A Pound of Flesh	Trevor Barnes	Blanche Hampton
Dead Men Don't Give Seminars	Dorothy Sucher	Sabina Swift
Dead Men Don't Marry	Dorothy Sucher	Sabina Swift
Dead Men's Hearts	Aaron Elkins	Julie Tendler Oliver
Dead Pan	Jane Dentinger	Jocelyn O'Roarke
The Dead Pull Hitter	Alison Gordon	Kate Henry
Dead Run	Tony Gibbs	Gillian Verdean
The Deadliest Option	Annette Meyers	Leslie Wetzon & Xenia Smith
Deadlock	Sara Paretsky	V. I. Warshawski
Deadly Aims	Ron Gerard	Jane Britland
Deadly Breed	Caroline Burnes	Ann Tate, Veronica Sheffield
Deadly Deceit	Erica Quest	Kate Maddox
Deadly Devotion	Patricia Wallace	Sydney Bryant
Deadly Grounds	Patricia Wallace	Sydney Bryant
A Deadly Judgment	Jessica Fletcher & Donald Bain	Jessica Fletcher
Deadly Obsession	Sherryl Woods	Amanda Roberts
Deadly Rehearsal	Audrey Peterson	Jane Winfield
Deadly Secrets on the St. Johns	Patricia Houck Sprinkle	Sheila Travis
Deadly Sights	Ron Gerard	Jane Britland
Deadly Valentine	Carolyn G. Hart	Annie Laurence Darling
A Deadly Vineyard Holiday	Philip R. Craig	Zee Madeiras Jackson
Dear Miss Demeanor	Joan Hess	Claire Malloy
Death a la Provencale	Janet Laurence	Darina Lisle
Death Among the Dons	Janet Neel	Francesca Wilson
Death and Letters	Elizabeth Daly	Clara Gamadge
Death and Taxes	Susan Dunlap	Jill Smith
Death and the Dogwalker	A. J. Orde	Grace Willis
Death and the Epicure	Janet Laurence	Darina Lisle
Death and the Trumpets of Tuscany	Hazel Wynn Jones	Emma Shaw
Death at a Discount	Valerie Wolzien	Susan Henshaw
A Death at St. Anselm's	Isabelle Holland	Claire Aldington
Death at the Table	Janet Laurence	Darina Lisle
Death at Victoria Dock	Kerry Greenwood	Phryne Fisher
Death Beneath the Christmas Tree	Robert Nordan	Mavis Lashley
Death Benefits	Michael A. Kahn	Rachel Gold
Death Beyond the Nile	Jessica Mann	Tamara Hoyland
Death by Analysis	Gillian Slovo	Kate Baeier
Death by Crystal	Agnes Bushell	Johannah "Jo" Wilder
Death by Misadventure a.k.a.	Kerry Greenwood	Phryne Fisher
Cocaine Blues		
Death by the Light of the Moon	Joan Hess	Claire Malloy
Death Calls the Tune	M. D. Lake	Peggy O'Neill
Death Club	Claire McNab	Inspector Carol Ashton
Death Comes Staccato	Gillian Slovo	Kate Baeier
Death Down Under	Claire McNab	Inspector Carol Ashton

Deception on His Mind	Elizabeth George	Barbara Havers
Deceptive Relations	Annette Roome	Chris Martin
Deck the Halls	Mary & Carol Higgins Clark	Alvira Meehan
Dedicated Angel	Anthea Cohen	Agnes Carmichael
Deep Sleep	Frances Fyfield	Helen West
A Deepe Coffyn	Janet Laurence	Darina Lisle
The Defector	Evelyn Anthony	Davina Graham
Deficit Ending	Lee Martin	Deb Ralston
Delay of Execution	Hazel Holt	Sheila Malory
A Delicately Personal Matter	Richard Werry	J. D. Mulroy
Depraved Indifference	Robert K. Tanenbaum	Marlene Ciampi
Design for Murder	Carolyn G. Hart	Annie Laurence Darling
Designer Crimes	Lia Matera	Laura Di Palma
Desperate Games	Jayne Castle	Gwen Jones
Destroying Angel	Anthea Cohen	Agnes Carmichael
The Devil's Code	John Sandford	LuEllen
Diamond in the Buff	Susan Dunlap	Jill Smith
Diet for Death	Janet Laurence	Darina Lisle
A Diet to Die For	Joan Hess	Claire Malloy
Digging Up Momma	Sarah Shankman	Samantha Adams
A Dinner to Die For	Susan Dunlap	Jill Smith
The Disappearance of Madalena Grimaldi	Marele Day	Claudia Valentine
The Disenchanted Diva	Rosemarie Santini	Rosie Caesare
A Dismal Thing to Do	Alisa Craig	Janet Wadman Rhys
Ditch Rider	Judith Van Gieson	Neil Hamel
The Dog Collar Murders	Barbara Wilson	Pam Nilsen
Dolly Is Dead	J. S. Borthwick	Sarah Deane
The Domino Image a.k.a. The Captive Voice	B. J. Hoff	Jennifer Terry Kaine
Don't Leave Me This Way	Joan Smith	Loretta Lawson
Double Bluff	Claire McNab	Inspector Carol Ashton
Double Daughter	Vicki McConnell	Nyla Wade
The Double Minded Men	Philip R. Craig	Zee Madeiras Jackson
Doubtful Motives	Maurice Gagnon	Deirdre O'Hara
The Down East Murders	J. S. Borthwick	Sarah Deane
Down for the Count	Maxine O'Callaghan	Delilah West
The Dragon Portfolio	Richard Hoyt	Ella Nidech
The Dreaming Damozel	Mollie Hardwick	Doran Fairweather
Dude on Arrival	J. S. Borthwick	Sarah Deane
Due Diligence	Michael A. Kahn	Rachel Gold
Dupe	Liza Cody	Anna Lee
Dying for Stardom	Eileen Fulton	Nina McFall
A Dying Light in Corduba	Lindsey Davis	Helena Justina
Dying Well	Joyce Christmas	Lady Margaret Priam

E

"E" Is for Evidence	Sue Grafton	Kinsey Millhone
The El Murders	Bill Granger	Karen Kovacs
The Elberg Collection	Anthony Oliver	Lizzie Thomas
Elected to Death	Valerie Wolzien	Susan Henshaw
Elegy in a Country Graveyard	Audrey Peterson	Jane Winfield
Elusive Quarry	B. (Barbara) Comfort	Tish McWhinny
Emma Chizzit and the Mother Lode Marauder	Mary Bowen Hall	Emma Chizzit

Firm Ambitions	Michael A. Kahn	Rachel Gold
First Hit of the Season	Jane Dentinger	Jocelyn O'Roarke
First Kill All the Lawyers	Alice Storey	Samantha Adams
The First Victim	Ridley Pearson	Daphne Matthews
Flashpoint	Linda Barnes	Carlotta Carlyle
Flight of the Archangel	Isabelle Holland	Claire Aldington
Flirting with Death	M. D. Lake	Peggy O'Neill
Flowers of Evil	John Sherwood	Celia Grant
A Flush of Shadows (ss)	Kate Wilhelm	Constance Leidl
Flying Too High	Kerry Greenwood	Phryne Fisher
The Fool's Run	John Sandford	LuEllen
For the Sake of Elena	Elizabeth George	Barbara Havers
The Forgotten	Faye Kellerman	Rina Lazarus
The Fortieth Birthday Party	Valerie Wolzien	Susan Henshaw
Frame Grabber	Denise Danks	Georgina Powers
Free Draw	Shelley Singer	Rosie Vicente
Freelance Death	Andrew Taylor	Celia Prentisse
Fresh Kills	Carolyn Wheat	Cass Jameson
Friend or Faux	Joyce Christmas	Lady Margaret Priam
Friends in High Places	Michael Hendricks	Rita Noonan
Frobisher's Savage	Leonard Tourney	Joan Stock
The Frog King	Frank McConnell	Bridget O'Toole
From Here to Paternity	Jill Churchill	Jane Jeffry
Frontier of Fear	Michael Hartland	Sarah Cable
Fugitive Colors	Margaret Maron	Lt. Sigrid Harald
Full Cry	Teona Tone	Kyra Keaton
Full Frontal Murder	Barbara Paul	Marian Larch
Full House	Shelley Singer	Rosie Vicente
Full Stop	Joan Smith	Loretta Lawson
Funeral Sites	Jessica Mann	Tamara Hoyland
Funny Money	Laurence Gough	Claire Parker

G

"G" Is for Gumshoe	Sue Grafton	Kinsey Millhone
Gallow's Bird	Margaret Duffy	Ingrid Langley Gilliard
Garden of Malice	Susan Kenney	Roz Howard
The Garden Plot	J. S. Borthwick	Sarah Deane
Gateway	Jerry Jenkins	Jennifer Grey
The Gathering Place	Jon Breen	Rachel Hennings
Gatsby's Vineyard	A. E. Maxwell	Fiora Flynn
The Geezer Factory Murder	Corinne Holt Sawyer	Angela Benbow, Caledonia Wingate
The Gemini Man	Susan Kelly	Liz Connors
Genealogy of Murder	Lee Martin	Deb Ralston
Generous Death	Nancy Pickard	Jenny Cain
The George Eliot Murders	Edith Skom	Beth Austin
Georgia Disappeared	Ellen Godfrey	Jane Tregar
Getting Mine	Jean Femling	Martha "Moz" Brant
A Gift for Murder	M. D. Lake	eggy O'Neill
Gilgamesh	Jo Bannister	Clio Rees Marsh
Gin and Daggers	Jessica Fletcher & Donald Bain	Jessica Fletcher
Goblin Market	Lauren Wright Douglas	Caitlin Reese
The Going Down of the Sun	Jo Bannister	Clio Rees Marsh
Going Out in Style	Joyce Christmas	Lady Margaret Priam
The Gold Curse	Herbert Resnicow	Norma Gold
The Gold Deadline	Herbert Resnicow	Norma Gold

The Hanging Garden	John Sherwood	Celia Grant
A Hard Bargain	Lia Matera	Laura Di Palma
Hard Line	Michael Z. Lewin	Sgt. Carollee Fleetwood
Hard News	Jeffrey Wilds Deaver	Rune
Hard Time	Sara Paretsky	V. I. Warshawski
Hardcover	Wayne Warga	Rachel Sabin
Hardware	Linda Barnes	Carlotta Carlyle
Havana Twist	Lia Matera	Willa Jansson
A Hazard of Losers	Lloyd Biggle, Jr	Raina Lambert
He Huffed and He Puffed	Barbara Paul	Marian Larch
He Was Her Man	Sarah Shankman	Samantha Adams
Head Case	Liza Cody	Anna Lee
Heading Uptown	Marissa Piesman	Nina Fischman
Heartbeat	Jerry Jenkins	Jennifer Grey
Heartbreaker	Laurence Gough	Claire Parker
Helen Hath No Fury	Gillian Roberts	Amanda Pepper
Hell Bent for Heaven	Shannon OCork	T. T. Baldwin
Hell's Angel	Anthea Cohen	Agnes Carmichael
Hidden Agenda	Anna Porter	Judith Hayes
Hidden Agenda	Lia Matera	Willa Jansson
Hide and Seek	Sherryl Woods	Amanda Roberts
High Fall	Susan Dunlap	Kieran O'Shaughnessy
High Island Blues	Ann Cleeves	Molly Palmer-Jones
High Strangeness	Alison Drake	Aline Scott
The Highland Fling Murders	Jessica Fletcher & Donald Bain	Jessica Fletcher
Highland Laddie Gone	Sharon McCrumb	Elizabeth MacPherson Dawson
Hit and Run	Maxine O'Callaghan	Delilah West
Ho-Ho Homicide	Corinne Holt Sawyer	Angela Benbow, Caledonia Wingate
A Holly, Jolly Murder	Joan Hess	Claire Malloy
Honeymoon with Murder	Carolyn G. Hart	Annie Laurence Darling
Honky Tonk Kat	Karen Kijewski	Kat Colorado
Hooray for Homicide	James Anderson	Jessica Fletcher
Hope	Len Deighton	Fiona Kimber-Hutchinson Samson
Hot Shots	Laurence Gough	Claire Parker
Hotel Morgue	Janet Laurence	Darina Lisle
Hotshots	Judith Van Gieson	Neil Hamel
How I Spent My Summer Vacation	Gillian Roberts	Amanda Pepper
How to Murder the Man of Your Dreams	Dorothy Cannell	Ellie Simon Haskell
How to Murder Your Mother-in-Law	Dorothy Cannell	Ellie Simon Haskell
Hunting the Witch	Ellen Hart	Jane Lawless
Hush, Little Darlings	Judith Kelman	Sara Spooner
Hush, Money	Jean Femling	Martha "Moz" Brant
The Hyde Park Murder	Elliott Roosevelt	Eleanor Roosevelt

I

"I" Is for Innocent	Sue Grafton	Kinsey Millhone
I.O.U.	Nancy Pickard	Jenny Cain
I'd Rather Be in Philadelphia	Gillian Roberts	Amanda Pepper
I'll Be Wearing a White Gardenia	Judi Miller	Theresa "Terri" Morrison
Icy Clutches	Aaron Elkins	Julie Tendler Oliver
If I'd Killed Him When I Met Him...	Sharon McCrumb	Elizabeth MacPherson Dawson
Immaculate Deception	Warren Adler	Fiona Fitzgerald

Knight Fall a.k.a. Murder at the War	Mary Monica Pulver	Kori Price Brichter
Knight Must Fall	Theodora Wender	Glad Gold
Knock 'Em Dead	Jessica Fletcher & Donald Bain	Jessica Fletcher

L

"L" Is for Lawless	Sue Grafton	Kinsey Millhone
The Lace Curtain Murders	Sophie Belfort	Molly Rafferty
Ladies' Night	Elizabeth Bowers	Meg Lacey
Lady on the Line	Teona Tone	Kyra Keaton
Lament for Christabel	Audrey Peterson	Jane Winfield
Landfall	Tony Gibbs	Gillian Verdean
Last Act in Palmyra	Lindsey Davis	Helena Justina
The Last Annual Slugfest	Susan Dunlap	Vejay Haskell
Last Chants	Lia Matera	Willa Jansson
Last Judgement	Anna Clarke	Paula Glenning
Last Seen in London	Anna Clarke	Paula Glenning
The Last Tango of Dolores Delgado	Marele Day	Claudia Valentine
Late Payments	Michael Z. Lewin	Sgt. Carollee Fleetwood
Laughing Dog	Dick Lochte	Serendipity "Sarah" Dahlquist
The Legend of the Slain Soldiers	Marcia Muller	Elena Olivarez
Lessons in Murder	Claire McNab	Inspector Carol Ashton
Let Us Prey	Monica Quill	Sr. Mary Theresa "Emtee" Dempsey
Lethal Genes	Linda Grant	Catherine Sayler
The Letter of the Law	Carole Berry	Bonnie Indermill
Liar's Poker	Frank McConnell	Bridget O'Toole
Liberty Square	Katherine Forrest	Kate Delafield
Library: No Murder Aloud	Susan Steiner	Alexandra "Alex" Winter
The Lies That Bind	Judith Van Gieson	Neil Hamel
The Life and Crimes of Harry Lavender	Marele Day	Claudia Valentine
Lights, Camera, Death	Eileen Fulton	Nina McFall
A Little Class on Murder	Carolyn G. Hart	Annie Laurence Darling
A Little Neighborhood Murder	A. J. Orde	Grace Willis
A Little Yuletide Murder	Jessica Fletcher & Donald Bain	Jessica Fletcher
Live from New York	Dick Belsky	Jenny McKay
Logan's Army	W. B. Longley	Liz Archer a.k.a. Angel Eyes
London Match	Len Deighton	Fiona Kimber-Hutchinson Samson
Long Lines	Remar Sutton	Evelyn Wade
The Long Search	Isabelle Holland	Claire Aldington
A Long Time Dead	A. J. Orde	Grace Willis
Looking for the Aardvark	A. J. Orde	Grace Willis
The Lottery Winner (ss)	Mary Higgins Clark	Alvira Meehan
Louisiana Fever	D. J. Donaldson	Kit Franklyn
Love Nest	Andrew Coburn	Rita Gardella O'Dea
Love Nor Money	Linda Grant	Catherine Sayler
Lovely in Her Bones	Sharon McCrumb	Elizabeth MacPherson Dawson
A Lovely Night to Kill	D. Miller Morgan	Daisy Marlow
A Lover Scorned	Isabelle Holland	Claire Aldington
Loverboy	Richard G. Belsky	Lucy Shannon
Lovers and Other Killers	James Anderson	Jessica Fletcher
Low Treason	Leonard Tourney	Joan Stock
Lucky Dog and Other Tales of Murder	Dick Lochte	Serendipity "Sarah" Dahlquist
The Lure of Sweet Death	Sarah Kemp	Dr. Tina May

M

"M" Is for Malice	Sue Grafton	Kinsey Millhone
MacPherson's Lament	Sharon McCrumb	Elizabeth MacPherson Dawson
Madison Avenue Murder	Liza Bennett	Peg Goodenough
Madness in Maggody	Joan Hess	Arly Hanks
Maggody and the Moonbeams	Joan Hess	Arly Hanks
Maggody in Manhattan	Joan Hess	Arly Hanks
Maggody Loves Misery	Joan Hess	Arly Hanks
The Maggody Militia	Joan Hess	Arly Hanks
Magic Mirror	Mickey Friedman	Georgia Lee Maxwell
Make No Bones	Aaron Elkins	Julie Tendler Oliver
Malice Domestic	Mollie Hardwick	Doran Fairweather
Malice in Maggody	Joan Hess	Arly Hanks
The Man of Gold	Evelyn Hervey	Harriet Unwin
The Man Who Killed His Brother	Reed Stephens	Ginny Fistoulari
The Man Who Risked His Partner	Reed Stephens	Ginny Fistoulari
The Man Who Tried To Get Away	Reed Stephens	Ginny Fistoulari
Manhattan Is My Beat	Jeffrey Wilds Deaver	Rune
Manhattans & Murder	Jessica Fletcher & Donald Bain	Jessica Fletcher
The Mantrap Garden	John Sherwood	Celia Grant
The Mark Twain Murders	Edith Skom	Beth Austin
Marriage Is Murder	Nancy Pickard	Jenny Cain
Martians in Maggody	Joan Hess	Arly Hanks
The Martini Effect	B. J. Morison	Elizabeth Lamb Worthington
Martinis & Mayhem	Jessica Fletcher & Donald Bain	Jessica Fletcher
The Marvell College Murders	Sophie Belfort	Molly Rafferty
A Masculine Ending	Joan Smith	Loretta Lawson
A Mask of Innocence	Roger Ormerod	Amelia Trowbridge Patton
Mass Murder	John Keith Drummond	Matilda Worthing
Material Witness	Robert K. Tanenbaum	Marlene Ciampi
Mean Streak	Carolyn Wheat	Cass Jameson
Measure of Deceit	Caroline Burnes	Ann Tate, Veronica Sheffield, Dawn Markey
Memory Lane	Laurence Gough	Claire Parker
Menacing Groves	John Sherwood	Celia Grant
The Mensa Murders	Lee Martin	Deb Ralston
The Merchant of Venus	Ellen Hart	Jane Lawless
The Merchants of Menace	Jill Churchill	Jane Jeffry
Mermaid's Feast	Janet Laurence	Darina Lisle
Mexico Set:	Len Deighton	Fiona Kimber-Hutchinson Samson
Middle of Nowhere	Ridley Pearson	Daphne Matthews
A Midsummer Killing	Trevor Barnes	Blanche Hampton
Midsummer Malice	M. D. Lake	Peggy O'Neill
The Mike Mist Case Book (Volume III of The Files of Ms. Tree)	Max Allan Collins	Ms. Michael Tree
The Mill on the Shore	Ann Cleeves	Molly Palmer-Jones
Ministering Angel	Anthea Cohen	Agnes Carmichael
Mint Julep Murder	Carolyn G. Hart	Annie Laurence Darling
*The Miracle of Revenge**	W. B. Longley	Liz Archer a.k.a. Angel Eyes
Miracles in Maggody	Joan Hess	Arly Hanks
Mischief in Maggody	Joan Hess	Arly Hanks
Miss Melville Regrets	Evelyn E. Smith	Susan Melville
Miss Melville Returns	Evelyn E. Smith	Susan Melville
Miss Melville Rides a Tiger	Evelyn E. Smith	Susan Melville
Miss Melville's Revenge	Evelyn E. Smith	Susan Melville

Missing Joseph	Elizabeth George	Barbara Havers
The Missing Madonna	Carol Anne O'Marie	Sr. Mary Helen O'Connor
Missing Susan	Sharon McCrumb	Elizabeth MacPherson Dawson
Mist Over Morro Bay	Carole Gift Page & Doris Elaine Fell	Michelle Merrill
Mistress of the Bones	T. J. MacGregor	Quin St. James
Model Murder	Erica Quest	Kate Maddox
Mom Among the Liars	James Yaffe	Mom
Mom Doth Murder Sleep	James Yaffe	Mom
Mom Meets Her Maker	James Yaffe	Mom
Money Burns	A. E. Maxwell	Fiora Flynn
Money Leads to Murder	D. Miller Morgan	Daisy Marlow
Money to Burn	Michael Hendricks	Rita Noonan
Monkey Puzzle	Paula Gosling	Kate Trevorne
Morbid Symptoms	Gillian Slovo	Kate Baeier
Mortal Remains in Maggody	Joan Hess	Arly Hanks
Mortal Sins	Anna Porter	Judith Hayes
Mortal Words	Kathryn Lasky Knight	Calista Jacobs
Mother Love	L. (Laurali) R. Wright	Cassandra Mitchell
The Mother Shadow	Melodie Johnson Howe	Maggie Hill, Claire Conrad
Mourning Gloria	Joyce Christmas	Lady Margaret Priam
The Mourning Show	Dick Belsky	Jenny McKay
Mrs. Malory and the Festival Murders a.k.a. Uncertain Death	Hazel Holt	Sheila Malory
Mrs. Malory and the Lilies That Fester	Hazel Holt	Sheila Malory
Mrs. Malory and the Only Good Lawyer...	Hazel Holt	Sheila Malory
Mrs. Malory Investigates a.k.a. Gone Away	Hazel Holt	Sheila Malory
Mrs. Malory Wonders Why	Hazel Holt	Sheila Malory
Mrs. Malory: Death Among Friends	Hazel Holt	Sheila Malory
Mrs. Malory: Death of a Dean	Hazel Holt	Sheila Malory
Mrs. Malory: Detective in Residence a.k.a. Murder on Campus	Hazel Holt	Sheila Malory
Mrs. Pargeter's Package	Simon Brett	Melita Pargeter
Mrs. Pargeter's Plot	Simon Brett	Melita Pargeter
Mrs. Pargeter's Point of Honor	Simon Brett	Melita Pargeter
Mrs. Pargeter's Pound of Flesh	Simon Brett	Melita Pargeter
Mrs. Porter's Letter	Vicki McConnell	Nyla Wade
Mrs., Presumed Dead	Simon Brett	Melita Pargeter
Ms. Tree	Max Allan Collins	Ms. Michael Tree
Much Ado in Maggody	Joan Hess	Arly Hanks
Mulch Ado About Nothing	Jill Churchill	Jane Jeffry
Mum's the Word	Dorothy Cannell	Ellie Simon Haskell
Mumbo Jumbo	Kathryn Lasky Knight	Calista Jacobs
The Mummers' Curse	Gillian Roberts	Amanda Pepper
Murder & Sullivan	Sara Frommer	Joan Spencer
Murder Across and Down	Herbert Resnicow	Isabel Macintosh
Murder After Tea Time	Leela Cutter	Lettie Winterbottom
Murder Among Friends	Frank McConnell	Bridget O'Toole
Murder and the First Lady	Elliott Roosevelt	Eleanor Roosevelt
Murder at Hobcaw Barony	Elliott Roosevelt	Eleanor Roosevelt
Murder at Markham	Patricia Houck Sprinkle	Sheila Travis
Murder at Midnight	Elliott Roosevelt	Eleanor Roosevelt
Murder at the Blue Owl	Lee Martin	Deb Ralston
Murder at the Friendship Hotel	Charlotte Epstein	Dr. Janet Eldine
Murder at the Kennedy Center	Margaret Truman	Annabel Reed Smith

Murder in the Red Room	Elliott Roosevelt	Eleanor Roosevelt
Murder in the Rose Garden	Elliott Roosevelt	Eleanor Roosevelt
Murder in the West Wing	Elliott Roosevelt	Eleanor Roosevelt
Murder in Two Acts	David Deutsch	Jessica Fletcher
Murder in Writing	Anna Clarke	Paula Glenning
Murder Is Academic	P. M. Carlson	Maggie Ryan
Murder Is Murder Is Murder	Samuel Steward	Gertrude Stein & Alice B. Toklas
Murder Is Only Skin Deep	L. V. Sims	Dixie Flannigan Struthers
Murder Is Pathological	P. M. Carlson	Maggie Ryan
Murder Keeps a Secret	Haughton Murphy	Cynthia Frost
Murder Machree	Eleanor Boylan	Clara Gamadge
Murder Makes a Pilgrimage	Carol Anne O'Marie	Sr. Mary Helen O'Connor
Murder Misread	P. M. Carlson	Maggie Ryan
Murder Observed	Eleanor Boylan	Clara Gamadge
A Murder of Crows	Margaret Duffy	Ingrid Langley Gilliard
The Murder of Sherlock Holmes	James Anderson	Jessica Fletcher
Murder Ole!	Corinne Holt Sawyer	Angela Benbow, Caledonia Wingate
Murder on Campus a.k.a. Mrs. Malory: Detective in Residence	Hazel Holt	Sheila Malory
Murder on Cue	Jane Dentinger	Jocelyn O'Roarke
Murder on Her Mind	Susan Steiner	Alexandra "Alex" Winter
Murder on Martha's Vineyard	David Osborn	Margaret Barlow
Murder on Peachtree Street	Patricia Houck Sprinkle	Sheila Travis
Murder on the Ballart Train	Kerry Greenwood	Phryne Fisher
Murder on the Chesapeake	David Osborn	Margaret Barlow
Murder on the Potomac	Margaret Truman	Annabel Reed Smith
Murder on the QE2	Jessica Fletcher & Donald Bain	Jessica Fletcher
Murder Saves Face	Haughton Murphy	Cynthia Frost
Murder Takes a Partner	Haughton Murphy	Cynthia Frost
Murder Times Two	Haughton Murphy	Cynthia Frost
Murder Under the Mistletoe	Jennifer Jordan	Dee Vaughn
Murder Unrenovated	P. M. Carlson	Maggie Ryan
Murder: The Musical	Annette Meyers	Leslie Wetzon & Xenia Smith
Murder@Maggody.com	Joan Hess	Arly Hanks
Murder…Now and Then	Jill McGown	Inspector Judy Hill
Murders and Acquisitions	Haughton Murphy	Cynthia Frost
Murders in Volume 2	Elizabeth Daly	Clara Gamadge
The Murders of Mrs. Austin and Mrs. Beale	Jill McGown	Inspector Judy Hill
My Body Lies Over the Ocean	J. S. Borthwick	Sarah Deane
My Mother, the Detective (ss)	James Yaffe	Mom
My Sister's Keeper	Nora Kelly	Gillian Adams
A Mystery Bred in Buckhead	Patricia Houck Sprinkle	Sheila Travis
The Mystery Lady	Anna Clarke	Paula Glenning

N

"N" Is for Noose	Sue Grafton	Kinsey Millhone
N.F.O.: No Fair Deal	Dave Pedneau	Anna Tyree
The Nantucket Diet Murders	Virginia Rich	Eugenia Potter
Nasty Breaks	Charlotte and Aaron Elkins	Lee Ofsted
Neon Dancer	Matthew and Bonnie Taylor	A. J. Egan
Neon Flamingo	Matthew and Bonnie Taylor	A. J. Egan
Nevsky's Demon	Dmitri Gat	Charity Day
Nevsky's Return	Dmitri Gat	Charity Day
New Orleans Requiem	D. J. Donaldson	Kit Franklyn

Original Sin	Mary Monica Pulver	Kori Price Brichter
Original Sin	P. D. James	Kate Miskin
The Other David	Carolyn Coker	Andrea Perkins
Other People's Skeletons	Julie Smith	Rebecca Schwartz
The Other Side of Death	Judith Van Gieson	Neil Hamel
The Other Woman	Jill McGown	Inspector Judy Hill
Otherworld*	Sarah Dreher	Stoner McTavish
Our Fathers' Lies	Andrew Taylor	Celia Prentisse
Out of the Darkness	Susan Kelly	Liz Connors
Outbreak	Robin Cook	Dr. Marissa Blumenthal

P

"P" Is for Peril	Sue Grafton	Kinsey Millhone
A Pair for the Queen	B. (Barbara) Comfort	Tish McWhinny
A Palette for Murder	Jessica Fletcher & Donald Bain	Jessica Fletcher
Parrot Blues	Judith Van Gieson	Neil Hamel
Parson's Pleasure	Mollie Hardwick	Doran Fairweather
Past Due	Claire McNab	Inspector Carol Ashton
Past Imperfect	Margaret Maron	Lt. Sigrid Harald
Patterns in the Dust a.k.a. Death on Widow's Walk	Lesley Grant-Adamson	Rain Morgan
Paying the Piper	Sharon McCrumb	Elizabeth MacPherson Dawson
Payment in Blood	Elizabeth George	Barbara Havers
The Peanut Butter Murders	Corinne Holt Sawyer	Angela Benbow, Caledonia Wingate
Penny Black	Susan Moody	Penny Wanawake
Penny Dreadful	Susan Moody	Penny Wanawake
Penny Pinching	Susan Moody	Penny Wanawake
Penny Post	Susan Moody	Penny Wanawake
Penny Royal	Susan Moody	Penny Wanawake
Penny Saving	Susan Moody	Penny Wanawake
Penny Wise	Susan Moody	Penny Wanawake
A Perfect Day for Dying	Joyce Christmas	Lady Margaret Priam
A Perfect Match	Jill McGown	Inspector Judy Hill
Perfectly Pure and Good	Frances Fyfield	Sarah Fortune
Peril Under the Palms	K. K. Beck	Iris Cooper
Perish in July	Mollie Hardwick	Doran Fairweather
Personal Effects	Marissa Piesman	Nina Fischman
The Pew Group	Anthony Oliver	Lizzie Thomas
Phantom Filly	Caroline Burnes	Ann Tate, Dawn Markey
Phantom of the Soap Opera	Judi Miller	Theresa "Terri" Morrison
Philly Stakes	Gillian Roberts	Amanda Pepper
Phoebe's Knee	B. (Barbara) Comfort	Tish McWhinny
Phreak	Denise Danks	Georgina Powers
Picture of Innocence	Jill McGown	Inspector Judy Hill
The Pied Piper	Ridley Pearson	Daphne Matthews
A Pint of Murder	Alisa Craig	Janet Wadman Rhys
Pious Deception	Susan Dunlap	Kieran O'Shaughnessy
Plain Murder	Roma Greth	Hana Shaner
The Players' Boy Is Dead	Leonard Tourney	Joan Stock
Playing for the Ashes	Elizabeth George	Barbara Havers
Playing Safe	Eileen Dewhurst	Helen Markham
Plots and Errors	Jill McGown	Inspector Judy Hill
The PMS Outlaws	Sharon McCrumb	Elizabeth MacPherson Dawson
Poison Pen	Mary Kittredge	Charlotte Kent
Poisoned Joy	M. D. Lake	Peggy O'Neill

The Ritual Bath	Faye Kellerman	Rina Lazarus
River of Gold	Jerry Ahern	Mary Frances Mulrooney a.k.a. M. F.
Robber's Wine	Ellen Hart	Jane Lawless
Rogue Wave	Susan Dunlap	Kieran O'Shaughnessy
Roll Over and Play Dead	Joan Hess	Claire Malloy
Rook Shoot	Margaret Duffy	Ingrid Langley Gilliard
Rosie Among Thorns*	Alan McDonald	Rosie Monaghan
Rotten Lies	Charlotte and Aaron Elkins	Lee Ofsted
Royal Flush	Shelley Singer	Rosie Vicente
A Royal Murder	Elliott Roosevelt	Eleanor Roosevelt
Ruddy Gore	Kerry Greenwood	Phryne Fisher
Rum & Razors	Jessica Fletcher & Donald Bain	Jessica Fletcher
Run from Nightmare	Maxine O'Callaghan	Delilah West
Running Fix	Tony Gibbs	Gillian Verdean

S

Safe at Home	Alison Gordon	Kate Henry
Samson's Deal	Shelley Singer	Rosie Vicente
Sanctuary	Faye Kellerman	Rina Lazarus
Sand Against the Tide	Paul Bishop	Tina Tamiko
Say No to Murder	Nancy Pickard	Jenny Cain
Scavengers	Yvonne Montgomery	Finny Aletter
Scene of Crime	Jill McGown	Inspector Judy Hill
Sea Fever	Ann Cleeves	Molly Palmer-Jones
A Second Shot in the Dark	Annette Roome	Chris Martin
The Secret Ingredient Murders	Nancy Pickard	Eugenia Potter
Secret of the East Wind	Carole Gift Page & Doris Elaine Fell	Michelle Merrill
Senator Love	Warren Adler	Fiona Fitzgerald
Sensuous Angel	Heather Graham	Donna Miro & Lorna Doria
The Sepia Siren Killer	Richard A. Lupoff	Marvia Plum
Serious Crimes	Laurence Gough	Claire Parker
Serpent's Tooth	Faye Kellerman	Rina Lazarus
Set Up	Claire McNab	Inspector Carol Ashton
A Setting for Murder	Eileen Fulton	Nina McFall
Set-Up	Maxine O'Callaghan	Delilah West
Seven Kinds of Death	Kate Wilhelm	Constance Leidl
Seven Steps to Treason	Michael Hartland	Sarah Cable
Seventh Avenue Murder	Liza Bennett	Peg Goodenough
The Seventh Crossword	Herbert Resnicow	Isabel Macintosh
Shadow Play	Frances Fyfield	Helen West
Shadow Walkers	Nina Romberg	Miriam Winchester
Shadowdance	Agnes Bushell	Johanna "Jo" Wilder
Shadows in Bronze	Lindsey Davis	Helena Justina
Shadows in Their Blood	Marian Babson	Trixie Dolan, Evangeline Sinclair
Shadows on the Mirror	Frances Fyfield	Sarah Fortune
Shaman's Moon	Sarah Dreher	Stoner McTavish
Shame the Devil	Roger Ormerod	Amelia Trowbridge Patton
Shattered Moon	Kate Green	Theresa Fortunato
She Came by the Book	Mary Wings	Emma Victor
She Came in a Flash	Mary Wings	Emma Victor
She Came in Drag	Mary Wings	Emma Victor
She Came to the Castro	Mary Wings	Emma Victor
She Came Too Late	Mary Wings	Emma Victor
She Walks in Beauty	Sarah Shankman	Samantha Adams
She's Out	Lynda LaPlante	Dolly Rawlins

The Spirit Stalker	Nina Romberg	Miriam Winchester
Spit in the Ocean	Shelley Singer	Rosie Vicente
Sports Freak	Shannon OCork	T. T. Baldwin
Spree	T. J. MacGregor	Quin St. James
The Spring Cleaning Murders	Dorothy Cannell	Ellie Simon Haskell
Spy Hook	Len Deighton	Fiona Kimber-Hutchinson Samson
Spy Line	Len Deighton	Fiona Kimber-Hutchinson Samson
Spy Sinker	Len Deighton	Fiona Kimber-Hutchinson Samson
The Spy Went Dancing	Aline, Countess Romanones	Countess Aline Griffith Romanones
The Spy Wore Red	Aline, Countess Romanones	Countess Aline Griffith Romanones
The Spy Wore Silk	Aline, Countess Romanones	Countess Aline Griffith Romanones
Squeezeplay	David Nighbert	Sgt. Molly Flanagan
Stage Fright	Ellen Hart	Jane Lawless
Stalker	Faye Kellerman	Rina Lazarus
Stalker	Liza Cody	Anna Lee
Star Witness	Lia Matera	Willa Jansson
Staring at the Light	Frances Fyfield	Sarah Fortune
A Star-Spangled Murder	Valerie Wolzien	Susan Henshaw
Statutory Murder	Dicey Thomas	Bertha Barstow
Steel Guitar	Linda Barnes	Carlotta Carlyle
Still Life with Pistol	Roger Ormerod	Amelia Trowbridge Patton
Stilled Life	Mikel Dunham	Rhea Buerklin
Stolen Moments	Sheryl Woods	Amanda Roberts
Stone Cold Dead	Roger Ormerod	Amelia Trowbridge Patton
Stoner McTavish	Sarah Dreher	Stoner McTavish
Storm at Daybreak	B. J. Hoff	Jennifer Terry Kaine
Storm Clouds Over Paradise	Carole Gift Page & Doris Elaine Fell	Michelle Merrill
Storm Surge	T. J. MacGregor	Quin St. James
Strangers Among Us	L. (Laurali) R. Wright	Cassandra Mitchell
Strangled Prose	Joan Hess	Claire Malloy
Stray Kat Waltz	Karen Kijewski	Kat Colorado
Strikezone	David Nighbert	Sgt. Molly Flanagan
Striking Out	Alison Gordon	Kate Henry
Striving with Gods	Jo Bannister	Clio Rees Marsh
The Student Body	J. S. Borthwick	Sarah Deane
The Student Body	Valerie Wolzien	Susan Henshaw
Study in Lilac	Maria-Antonia Olvier	Lonia Guiu
A Stunning Way to Die	Joyce Christmas	Lady Margaret Priam
Sudden Exposure	Susan Dunlap	Jill Smith
Suddenly in Her Sorbet	Joyce Christmas	Lady Margaret Priam
Sugar Plum Dead	Carolyn G. Hart	Annie Laurence Darling
Suicide King	Shelley Singer	Rosie Vicente
A Suitable Vengeance	Elizabeth George	Barbara Havers
Summertime News	Dick Belsky	Jenny McKay
The Summertime Soldiers	Susan Kelly	Liz Connors
The Sunflower Plot	John Sherwood	Celia Grant
Survival Instincts	Marissa Piesman	Nina Fischman
The Suspect	L. (Laurali) R. Wright	Cassandra Mitchell
Sweet, Savage Death	Orania Papazoglou	Patience "Pay" McKenna
Sweet, Sweet Poison	Kate Wilhelm	Constance Leidl

Trick or Treachery	Jessica Fletcher & Donald Bain	Jessica Fletcher
Trio in Three Flats	Eileen Dewhurst	Cathy McVeigh Carter
Trouble in the Brasses	Alisa Craig	Janet Wadman Rhys
A Trouble of Fools	Linda Barnes	Carlotta Carlyle
The Trouble with Harriet	Dorothy Cannell	Ellie Simon Haskell
Troubled Waters	Carolyn Wheat	Cass Jameson
True Justice	Robert K. Tanenbaum	Marlene Ciampi
Trust Me on This	Donald E. Westlake	Sara Joslyn
Tunnel Vision	Sara Paretsky	V. I. Warshawski
Twenty Blue Devils	Aaron Elkins	Julie Tendler Oliver
Twilight	Nancy Pickard	Jenny Cain
Two for the Lions	Lindsey Davis	Helena Justina

U

Unable By Reason of Death	Catherine Lewis & Judith Guerin	Lisa Thomas
Uncertain Death a.k.a. Mrs. Malory and the Festival Murders	Hazel Holt	Sheila Malory
Under Contract	Liza Cody	Anna Lee
Under Suspicion	Claire McNab	Inspector Carol Ashton
Under the Influence	Elizabeth Travis	Carrie Porter
Undercurrents	Ridley Pearson	Daphne Matthews
Uneaseful Death	Mollie Hardwick	Doran Fairweather
The Unforgiving Minutes	Mary Monica Pulver	Kori Price Brichter
Union Jack a.k.a. Conferences Are Murder	Val McDermid	Lindsay Gordon
Unofficial Rosie	Alan McDonald	Rosie Monaghan
Unorthodox Methods	Deborah Valentine	Katharine Craig
Unorthodox Practices	Marissa Piesman	Nina Fischman
Unquiet Grave	Janet LaPierre	Meg Halloran
Until Proven Innocent	Susan Kelly	Liz Connors
Unwillingly to Vegas	Nancy Livingston	Mavis Bignell
Urn Burial	Kerry Greenwood	Phryne Fisher
User Deadly a.k.a. The Pizza House Crash	Denise Danks	Georgina Powers

V

Vampire Bytes	Linda Grant	Catherine Sayler
The Vanishing Violinist	Sara Frommer	Joan Spencer
The Veil of Ignorance	Monica Quill	Sr. Mary Theresa "Emtee" Dempsey
Veiled Threat	Jerry Jenkins	Jennifer Grey
Venus in Copper	Lindsey Davis	Helena Justina
Verdict Unsafe	Jill McGown	Inspector Judy Hill
Vermilion*	Nathan Aldyne	Clarissa Lovelace
A Very Venetian Murder	Haughton Murphy	Cynthia Frost
The Vines of Ferrara	Carolyn Coker	Andrea Perkins
Vineyard Blues	Philip R. Craig	Zee Madeiras Jackson
Vineyard Shadows	Philip R. Craig	Zee Madeiras Jackson
Vital Lies	Ellen Hart	Jane Lawless
Vital Signs	Robin Cook	Dr. Marissa Blumenthal
Vow of Silence	B. J. Hoff	Jennifer Terry Kaine
The Voyage of the Chianti	B. J. Morison	Elizabeth Lamb Worthington

Y

Yankee Doodle Dead	Carolyn G. Hart	Annie Laurence Darling
The Year of the Monkey	Carole Berry	Bonnie Indermill
The Year of the Scorpion	Michael Hartland	Sarah Cable
You Have the Right to Remain Silent	Barbara Paul	Marian Larch

Mystery Women—Chronology

Year in which female character made first published appearance in a novel or collection of short stories. The chronological listing of female sleuths refers to first significant appearance. An asterisk (*) indicates that the character made at least three appearances. © Indicates copyright date, used when publication date was unavailable.

Volume I

1861:	Mrs. Paschal
1864:	Mrs. G.
1875:	Valeria Woodville
1884:	Madeline Payne
1894:	Loveday Brooke
1895:	Caroline "Cad" Mettie
1897:	Amelia Butterworth*; Dorcas Dene
1898:	Hagar Stanley
1899:	Lois Cayley; Madame Koluchy
1900:	Dora Myrl*; Hilda Wade
1903:	Madame Sara
1905:	Polly Burton; Henrietta Van Raffles
1906:	Frances Baird
1910:	Lady Molly Robertson-Kirk
1911:	Letitia "Tish" Carberry
1912:	Judith Lee

1913:   Constance Dunlap ©; Ruth Fielding* (Juvenile)

1914:   Madelyn Mack; Mercedes Quero*

1915:   Molly Morganthau*; Violet Strange

1917:   Millicent Newberry*; Evelyn Temple; Olga von Kopf

1922:   Prudence "Tuppence" Beresford*

1923:   Rosie Bright; Sylvia Shale

1924:   Fidelity Dove

1925:   Eileen "Bundle" Brent; Sophie Lang; Blue Jean Billy Race; Madame Rosika Storey*

1926:   Juliet Jackson*

1927:   Meg Garret *; Leslie Maughan in U.S.; Jane Ollerby

1928:   Angela Bredon; Lynn MacDonald*

1929:   Dame Adela Beatrice Bradley*; Four Square Jane; Sarah Keate*; Maud Silver* in U.S.

1930:   Nancy Drew* (Juvenile); Ellen Gilchrist; Gwynn Leith; Gail McGurk*; Jane Marple*; Kate Marsh*; Polack Annie; Harriet Vane*; Louisa Woolfe*; Daphne Wrayne*

1931:   Fah Lo Suee*; Solange Fontaine; Prudence Whitby; Hildegarde Withers*

1932:   Hilda Adams*; Avis Bryden*; Angeline Tredennick; Mrs. Caywood "Julia" Weston

1933:   Amanda Fitton Campion; Lizzie Collins*; Olga Knaresbrook; Della Street; Mrs. Elizabeth Warrender*

1934:   Nora Charles; Clarice Claremont; Susan Dare; Peggy Fairfield; Anne Layton; Ariadne Oliver*; Alice Penny; Matilda Townsend*

1935:   Jane Amanda Edwards*; Emma Marsh*; Penny Mercer*; Matilda Perks; Palmyra Pym*

1936:   Iris Pattison Duluth*; Baroness Clara Linz in U.S.; Anne Holt McNeill*; Dr. Joan Marvin; Georgia Cavendish Strangeways; Ethel Thomas*

1937:   Adelaide Adams; Carey Brent*; Theolinda "Dol" Bonner; Patricia "Pat" Preston Cordry*; Grace Latham*; Anne "Davvie" Davenport McLean*; Daisy Jane Mott; Lucy Mott in U.S.; Tamara Valeshoff

1938:   Agatha Troy Alleyn; Mary Carner*; Kay Cornish*; Valerie Dundas; Coco Hastings; Carole Trevor; Lace White*

1939:   Hilea Bailey*; Janet "Janie" Allen Barron*; Bertha Cool*; Helene Brand Justus*; Sue MacVeigh*; Emma Marsh*; Rachel and Jennifer Murdoch*; Anne Seymour Webb; Susan Yates*

1940:   Ethel Abbott; Amanda and Lucy Beagle; Margot Blair*; Jane Carberry*; Elsie Mae Hunt*; Pamela "Pam" North*; Miss Mabie Otis*; Katherine "Peter" Piper*; Sister Ursula; Haila Rogers Troy*; Agatha Welch

1941:   Jean Abbott*; Eleanora Burke; Gypsy Rose Lee; Sarah DeLong O'Brien; Andrea Reid Ramsay; Hannah Van Doren*; Kitty McLeod Whitney*

1942:   Arabella "Arab" Blake*; Louise "Liz" Boykin Parrott*; Grace Pomeroy

1943:   Christine Andersen; Georgine Wyeth McKinnon; Doris "Dodo" Trent; Nell Witter*

1944:   Kit Marsden Acton*; Judy Ashbane; Maria Black*; Lorna Donahue; Vicky Gaines; Lady Lapin Hastings*; Abbie Harris*; Bessie Petty and Beulah Pond*

1945:   Nora Hughes Blaine; Amy Brewster*; Dr. Mary Finney*; Jenny Gillette Lewis*

1946:   Elizabeth; Eve MacWilliams; Maggie Slone; Tessie Venable

1947:   Hortense Clinton*; Gale Gallagher; Suzanne "Suzy" Willett Marshall; Terry Terence*; Julia Tyler*; Lucy Pym

1948:   Jane Hamish Brown*; Eve Gill*

1949:   Miriam Birdseye*; Emily Murdoch Bryce*; Janice Cameron and Lily Wu*; Marka de Lancey*

1950:   Sumuru*; Ma Tellford*; Hilda Trenton

1951:   Petunia Best; Liane "Lee" Craufurd*; Shirley Leighton Harper*; Laura Scudamore, The Sinister Widow*; Ginger Tintagel; Sarah Vanessa*

1952:   Ann McIntosh*

1953:   Nell Bartlett; Norma "Nicky" Lee*

1954:   Sally Dean; Sally Strang*

1955:   Miss Flora Hogg*; Mavis Seidlitz*; English translations of Souer Angele*

1956:   Eileen Burke*; Sally Merton Heldar*; Marion Kerrison; Julia Probyn*; Daye Smith*

1957:   Mrs. Annie Norris*; Honey West*

1958:   Mother Paul*

1959:   Arabella Frant; Madame Maigret (in U.S. in her only major role); Kate Starte; Marla Trent

1960:   Forsythia Brown*; Kate Harris; Emmy Tibbett* in U.S.

1962:   Myra Savage in U.S.

1963:   Hilary Brand*; June Beattie

1964:   Telzey Amberdon*; Maxene Dangerfield*; Charmian Daniels* in U.S.; Kate Fansler*; Mary Morgan Kelly*; Sue Carstairs Maddox; Selena Mead

1965:   Modesty Blaise*; Jane Boardman; Amanda Curzon*; Emma Greaves*; Anna Zordan*

1966:   Sibyl Sue Blue; Mrs Elma Craggs in U.S.; Lee Crosley*; April Dancer*; Mrs. Emily Pollifax*; Effie Schlupe*

1967:   Madame Dominique Aubry in U.S.; Felicia Dawlish; Eve Drum*; Julia Homberg*; Freya Matthews; Emma Peel*; Sylvia Plotkin*; Regina; Charity Ross; Paola Smith; Lucilla Edith Cavell Teatime*

1968:   Julie Barnes of Mod Squad*; Angel Brown*; Dominique Frayne; Tracy Larrimore*; Amanda Nightingale*; Stevie O'Dowda; Christie Opara*; Miss Emily Seeton*; Dr. Grace Severance*; Katy Touchfeather

1969: Lisa Clark*; Gail Rogers Mitchell; Jennifer Norrington* in U.K.; Claudine St. Cyr*; Kate Theobald*

1970: Tessa Crichton* in U.K.; Kiss Darling*; Millicent Hetherege; Hon. Constance Morrison-Burke*; Deirdre O'Connor; Sheila Roath; Charity Tucker*

1971: Cherry Delight*; Donna Bella*; Cynthia Godwin; Lucy Ramsdale*; Helga Rolfe* in U.K.; Kitty Telefair*

1972: Lucy Beck*; Arlette Van Der Valk Davidson as a primary*; Laurie Grant*; Cordelia Gray in U.K.; Jacqueline Kirby*; Octavia "Tavy" Martin in U.S.; Norah Mulcahaney*; Hilary Quayle*

1973: Vicky Bliss*; Thea Crawford; Helen Blye Horowitz*; Cleopatra Jones; Baroness Penelope St. John-Orsini*; Miss Melinda Pink*

1974: Shauna Bishop*; Vera Castang; Catherine Alexander Douglas*; Rosa Epton* in U.S.; Ann Fielding Hales; Susan Silverman*; Kate Weatherly*

1975: Pepper Anderson*; Claire Reynolds Atwell*; Helen Bullock*; Constance Cobble; Amelia Peabody Emerson*; Angela Harpe*; Ms. Squad; Dr. Nora North*; Molly Owens*; Minnie Santangelo; Bea Wentworth*

1976: Jannine Austin*; Edwina Charles* in U.K.; Julie Hayes*; Dr. Hannah Land; Natasha O'Brien; Lexey Jane Pelazoni; Anna Peters*; Rebecca Rosenthal; Jaime Sommers; Morgan Studevant

1977: Mici Anhalt*; Jana Blake; Charlie's Angels*; Betty Crighton Jones*; Sharon McCone*; Jemima Shore*; Persis Willum*

1978: Marilyn Ambers*; Kay Barth*; Tory Baxter*; Margaret Binton*; Dulcie Bligh; Darby Castle; Virginia Freer*; Helen Keremos*; Hildy Pace*; Maxine Reynolds*; Delia Riordan*; Sarah Saber; Helen Marsh Shandy; Terry Spring*

1979: Adrienne Bishop; Janna Brill*; Cody in England*; Maggie Courtney*; Charlotte Eliot; Margo Franklin*; Carol Gates*; Alison B. Gordon*; Kate Graham; Anna Jugedinski*; Sarah Kelling*; Valerie Lambert*; Ann Lang; Pauline Lyons*; Megan Marshall; Charlotte Ellison Pitt*; Maggie Rome*; Penelope Spring*; Julia Sullivan; Nell Willard

Volume II

1980:   T. T. Baldwin*; Juliet Bravo* a.k.a. Jean Darblay; Ginny
            Fistoulari*; Karen Kovacs*; Clarissa Lovelace*; Joan Stock*;
            Amy Tupper; Alicia Von Helsing; Janet Wadman (Rhys)*;
            Delilah West*

1981:   Cathy McVeigh Carter*; Sr. Mary Theresa "Emtee" Dempsey*;
            Fiona Fitzgerald*; Davina Graham* in U.S.; Lt. Sigrid Harald*;
            Dittany Henbit*; Viera Kolarova; Julia Larmore, Selena
            Jardine, and perhaps Hilary Tamar*; Anna Lee* in U.S.; Jill
            Smith*; Lizzie Thomas* in the U.S.; Lettie Winterbottom*

1982:   Charity Day; Sarah Deane*; Maggie Elliott*; Sgt. Carollee
            Fleetwood; Tamara Hoyland* in U.S.; Helen Markham;
            Kinsey Millhone*; Eugenia Potter*; Rebecca Schwartz*;
            Katherine Forrester Vigneras; Nila Wade*; V. I. Warshawski*

1983:   Mona Moore Dunbar; Norma Gold*; Jennifer Grey*;
            Inspector Judy Hill*; Roz Howard*; Cass Jameson*; Kyra
            Keaton; Elena Olivarez*; Julie Tendler Oliver; Jocelyn
            O'Roarke*; Bridget O'Toole*; Dolly Rawlins in U.K.; Fiona
            Kimber-Hutchinson Samson in U.S.; Harriet Unwin*; Rosie
            Vicente*; Elizabeth Lamb Worthington*

1984:   Gillian Adams*; Lauren Adler; Rev. Claire Aldington*; Sarah
            Cable*; Jenny Cain*; Agnes Carmichael* in U.S.; Iris Cooper*;
            Kate Delafield*; Vejay Haskell*; Rachel Hennings; Sgt.
            Hilary Lloyd in U.S.; Elizabeth MacPherson*; Dr. Tina May*;
            Patience "Pay" McKenna*; Mary Frances Mulrooney; Pam
            Nilsen*; Sr. Mary Helen O'Connor*; Amelia Trowbridge
            Patton in U.S.; Andrea Perkins*; Deb Ralston*; Clio Rees
            (Marsh)*; Eleanor Roosevelt*; Abigail "Sandy" Sanderson*;
            Ellie Simon (Haskell)*; Ms. Michael Tree*

1985:   Liz Archer a.k.a. Angel Eyes*; Kate Baeier* in U.S.; Susan
            Bright*; Liz Connors*; Serendipity "Sarah" Dahlquist; Donna
            Miro and Lorna Doria; Geraldine Farrar; Jessica Fletcher*; Fiora
            Flynn*; Paula Glenning*; Glad Gold; Ellie Gordon*; Celia
            Grant* in U.S.; Marian Larch*; Isabel Macintosh*; Stoner
            McTavish*; Michelle Merrill (Ballard)*; Cassandra Mitchell*;
            Rain Morgan*; Theresa "Terri" Morrison; J. D. Mulroy; Rita
            Gardella O'Dea; Deirdre O'Hara* in Canada; Celia Prentisse;

Maggie Ryan*; Rachel Sabin; Lucy Shannon; Gertrude Stein; Kate Trevorne; Alexandra "Alex" Winter; Matilda Worthing*

1986: Jane Britland; Rosie Caesare; Sarah Calloway*; Doran Fairweather*; Theresa Fortunato; Cynthia Frost; Judith Hayes in U.S.; Calista Jacobs*; Gwen Jones*; Rina Lazarus (Decker); Denise Lemoyne; Claire Malloy*; Tish McWhinny*; Susan Melville*; Debbie Miles*; Kate Miskin; Ella Nidech; Molly Palmer-Jones*; Molly Rafferty*; Catherine Sayler*; Joan Spencer*; Joanna Stark*; Penny Wanawake* in U.S.

1987: Finny Aletter; Jane Bailey*; Maggie Bennett*; Mavis Bignell* in U.S.; Dr. Marissa Blumenthal; Carlotta Carlyle*; Marlene Ciampi (Karp)*; Lisa Davis; A. J. Egan; Lindsay Gordon*; Lonia Guiu in U.S.; Meg Halloran*; Arly Hanks*; Jennifer Heath*; Nikki Holden; Bonnie Indermill*; Willa Jansson*; Charlotte Kent*; Raina Lambert*; Annie Laurance (Darling)*; Constance Leidl*; Daisy Marlow; Alvira Meehan*; Melita Pargeter* in U.S.; Amanda Pepper*; Caitlin Reese*; Countess Aline Griffith Romanones*; Quin St. James*; Sara Spooner; Dee Street* in U.K.; Dixie Flannigan Struthers*; Kate Byrd Teague; Anna Tyree*; Dee Vaughn*; Emma Victor*; Jane Winfield (Hall)*

1988: Samantha Adams*; Inspector Carol Ashton*; Angela Benbow and Caledonia Wingate*; Kori Price Brichter*; Sydney Bryant*; Angel Cantini; Laura Di Palma*; Trixie Dolan and Evangeline Sinclair* in U.S.; Lydia Fairchild*; Kit Franklyn*; Ingrid Langley Gilliard* in U.S.; Rachel Gold*; Neil Hamel*; Barbara Havers*; Susan Henshaw*; Sara Joslyn; Meg Lacey; Loretta Lawson* in U.S.; Kate Maddox*; Daphne Matthews*; Georgia Lee Maxwell; Nina McFall*; Mom*; Karen Orr; Claire Parker* in U.S.; Marvia Plum*; Lady Margaret Priam*; Catherine Sayler*; Aline Scott*; Hana Shaner; Veronica Slate*; Sabina Swift; Tina Tamiko; Ann Tate, Dawn Markey and Veronica Sheffield; Sally Tepper; Sheila Travis*; Jane Tregar; Claudia Valentine* in Australia; Gillian Verdean*; Evelyn Wade

1989: Beth Austin*; Margaret Barlow*; Bertha Barstow; Martha "Moz" Brant*; Rhea Buerklin; Emma Chizzit*; Kat Colorado*; Katharine Craig; Sandrine Casette Curry*; Dr. Janet Eldine in U.S.; Nina Fischman*; Phryne Fisher* in Australia; Anne Fitzhugh; Sgt. Molly Flanagan; Sarah Fortune*; Clara Dawson Gamadge*; Peg Goodenough; Blanche Hampton*; Kate Henry in U.S.*; Lady Jane Hildreth* in U.S.; Maggie Hill and Claire Conrad; Harriet Jeffries*; Jane Jeffry*; Helena Justina; Jennifer Terry Kaine*; Mavis Lashley*; Jane Lawless*; Darina Lisle* in U.K.; LuEllen*; Sheila Malory*; Chris Martin* in U.K.; Jennie McKay*; Rosie Monaghan in Australia; Cassie Newton; Rita Noonan; Abby Novack (McKenzie)*; Lee Ofsted*; Peggy O'Neill*; Kieran O'Shaughnessy*; Carrie Porter; Georgina Powers* in U.K.; Anabel Reed Smith*; Amanda Roberts*; Rune*; Emma Shaw in U.S.; Diane Tregarde*; Lisa Thomas in Australia; Leslie Wetzon and Xenia Smith*; Johanna Wilder; Grace Willis; Francesca Wilson* in U.S.; Miriam Winchester

Volume III

The following is a preliminary expectation of sleuths to be covered in the final volume of the series. Whether or not a character has made three or more appearances is based upon information through November 2001. Additional sleuths will undoubtedly be added to this list before Volume 3 is published. A third book may have been published subsequent to November 2001. New series are added regularly as work on Volume 3 continues.

1990: Irene Adler*; Gabrielle Amato; Connie Bartholomew; Goldy Bear (Schultz)*; Mildred Bennett*; Helen Black*; Nora Bonesteel*; Claire Breslinsky*; Paris Chandler; Edwina Crusoe*; Lark Dailey*; Abigail Danforth*; Poppy Dilworth*; Flavia Di Stefano*; Brigid Donovan*; Faith Fairchild*; Charlotte Graham*; Mary "Harry" Haristeen*; Alison Hope*; Jeri Howard*; Dewey James*; Jessica James*; Jazz Jasper*; Sister Joan*; Joanne Kilbourn*; Willow King*; Michelle "Mickey" Knight*; Skip Langdon*; Hester Latterly*; Lavinia London; Annie MacPherson*; Shirley McClintock*; Madison McGuire*; Cat Marsala*; Jayne Meadows; Alice Nestleton*; Chicago Nordejoong*; Patricia Pratt*; Gwen Ramadge*; Lucia Ramos; Cassandra Reilly*; Vonna Saucier; Kay Scarpetta*; Anna Southwood*; Aurora Teagarden*; Nicky Titus*; Nikki Trakos; Holly Winter*

1991:   Jessie Arnold*; "Petey" Biggers*; Verity Birdwood*; Rev.
         Theodora Braithwaite*; Nell Bray*; Hollis Carpenter; Midge
         Cohen; Melissa Craig*; Lauren Crowder; Molly DeWitt*;
         Phrynne Fisher*; Jan Gallagher*; Simona Griffo*; Dr. Bernie
         Hebert; Barbara Holloway*; Lil Hubbert*; Kate Jasper*;
         Virginia Kelly*; Libby Kincaid*; Amanda Knight; Lauren
         Laurano*; Whitney Logan; Devon MacDonald*; Wanda
         Mallory*; Judith McMonigle (Flynn)*; Kathy NcNeely; Robin
         Miller*; Meredith Mitchell*; Lane Montana; Dr. Jean
         Montrose*; Kate Mulcay (one earlier book in 1958 as Kate
         Kincaid)*; Kit Powell; Claire Sharples*; Delta Stevens*; Blaine
         Stewart*; Lucy Stone*; Jane Tennison* in U.K.; Rev. Ziza Todd;
         Ginny Trask; Ronnie Ventana*; Liz Wareham; Fanny Zindel

1992:   Kristin Ashe; Temple Barr*; China Bayles*; Molly Bearpaw*;
         Becky Belski; Christine Bennett*; Ellie Bernstein; Constable
         Judy Best*; Elizabeth Blair*; Julie Blake*; Joanna Blalock*;
         Victoria Bowering*; Smokey Brandon*; Harriet Bushrow*;
         Rosalie Cairns*; Claire Camden*; Dr. Jessica Coran*; Karen
         Crist; Victoria Cross; Jane Da Silva*; Molly De Witt*; Catherine
         Edison; Elizabeth Elliot*; Casey Farrel*; Sister Frevisse*; Leslie
         Frost; Nell Fury*; Callahan Garrity*; Liz Graham*; Charlie
         Greene*; Blanche Hampton*; Leah Hunter*; Laura Ireland;
         Lucy Kingsley*; Kate Kinsella in U.S.*; Deborah Knott*; Emma
         Lord*; Marti MacAlister*; Maggie MacGowan*; Caroline Masters*;
         Christine McCall*; Annie McGrogan; Laura Michaels*; Kate
         Millholland*; Britt Montero*; Freddie O'Neal*; Maddy Phillips*;
         E.J. Pugh*; Agatha Raisin*; Regan Reilly*; Lil Ritchie; Maxene
         St. Clair*; Charlotte Sams; Kate Shugak*; Diana Speed; Lee
         Squires*; Elena Timafeyeva; Glynis Tryon*; Samantha Turner*;
         Amanda Valentine*; Jackie Walsh*; Aunt Dimity Westwood
         and Lori Shepherd*; Blanche White*; Hannah Wolfe*; Susan
         Donavan Wren*

1993:   Laura Ackroyd*; Angelina Amalfi*; Tory Bauer*; Angela
         Biwaban*; Joanna Brady*; Barbara "Bo" Bradley*; Kate
         Brannigan*; Sr. Cecile Buddenbrooke*; Caley Burke*; Maxey
         Burnell*; Cat Caliban*; Nora Callum; Cliveley Sisters; Nancy
         Clue and Cherry Aimless*; Henrie O'Dwyer Collins*; Nancy
         Cook; Mary Di Nunzio; Jessica Drake*; Kay Engels; Laura
         Fleming*; Caz Flood* in U.K.; Insp. Liz Graham*; Amanda

Hazard*; Marty Hopkins*; Jo Hughes*; Kate Ivory*; Gemma James*; Hepzipah Jeffries*; Claire Jenner (Claiborne)*; Tyler Jones*; Alison Kaine*; Irene Kelly*; Kimmey Kruse; Barrett Lake*; Catherine Le Vendeur*; Wyn Lewis*; Kathryn Mackay*; Kate MacLean; Royce Madison; Casey/Kate Martinelli*; Dr. Lauren Maxwell*; Kathleen O'Shaunessey*; Jane Perry*; Anna Pigeon*; Dr. Amy Prescott*; Gin Prettifield; Imogen Quy; Nan Robinson*; Laney Samms*; Phoebe Siegel*; Cecily Sinclair*; Sydney Sloane*; Teal Stewart*; Sgt Stone*; Catherine Swinbrooke*; Alex Tanner*; Iris Thorne*; Betty Trenka*; Robin Vaughn*; Madame Victoire Vernet; Lucy Wilton (Archer)*; April Woo*; Eve Wylie in US*

1994:   Kathryn "Kate" Ardleigh*; Cat Austen*; Kate Austen*; Johnnie Baker; Thea Barlow*; Nora Bonesteel*; Dr. Liz Broward; Brooke Cassidy (Devlin)*; Molly Cates*; Olivia Chapman; Emily Charters; Lydia Chin*; Gail Connor*; Candi and Simone Covington*; Fey Croaker*; Daisy Dahlrymple*; Peaches Dann*; Tess Darcy*; Queenie Davilov; Angie DaVito; Patricia Delaney*; Louise Eldridge*; Lynn Evans; Phoebe Fairfax in Canada*; Merry Folger*; Margo Fortier; Jill Francis*; Vicki Garcia; Angela Gennaro*; Sophie Greenway*; Mackenzie Griffin*; Anneke Haagen*; Em Hansen*; Matilda Haycastle*; Tamara Hayle*; Benni Harper*; Karen Hightower a.k.a. Bast*; Samantha Holt*; Harriet Hubbley in Canada*; Robin Hudson*; Jo Hughes in the U.S.*; Sal Kilkenny* in U.K.; Michelle "Mickey" Knight*; Sgt. Kathy Kolla* in U.K.; Thea Kozak*; Robin Light*; Margaret Loftus; Dottie Loudermilk; Joanna MacKenzie*; Gianna Maglione; Sgt Kathleen Mallory*; Saz Martin*; Angela Matelli*; Dr. Gail McCarthy*; Nuala McGrail*; Elizabeth Mendoza; Tori Miracle*; Kate Murray; Jordan Myles*; Deirdre Quinn Nightingale*; Veronica Pace*; Lorraine Page*; Daisy Perika*; Stephanie Plum*; Laura Principal*; Sarah Quillam*; Carmen Ramirez; Tammi Randall*; Mary Russell*; Desiree Shapiro*; Emily Silver; Liz Sullivan*; Jane Smith a.k.a. Stella the Stargazer*; Emily Stone*; Cassandra Swann*; Ike Tygart*; Alix Thorssen*; Penelope Warren*; Catherine Wilde*; Elizabeth Will; Jolie Wyatt*; Magdalena Yoder*; Helma Zukas*

1995: Hannah Barlow*; Ginger Barnes*; Lilly Bennett*; Sonora Blair*; Bel Carson*; Dr. Elizabeth Chase*; Ella Clah*; Eve Dallas*; Angie Da Vito; Jane Day*; Eve Elliott*; Kay Engels; Colleen Fitzgerald; Maggie Garrett; Ariel Gold*; Natalie Gold*; Gale Grayson*; Mother Lavinia Grey*; Mackenzie Griffin*; Elizabeth Halperin; Kate Harrod*; Sharon Hays*; Helen Hewitt in U.K.; Holly-Jean Ho*; Vicky Holden*; Liz James*; Elena Jarvis*; Caroline "Fremont" Jones*; Samantha "Sam" Jones*; Carol Jordan; Sara Kingsley; Fran Kirk*; Dee Laguerre; Calista Marley*; Dorothy Martin*; Lydia Miller; Michelle "Mitch" Mitchell*; Jordan Myles*; Megan O'Malley; Phyllida Moon*; Charlie Parker*; Joanna Piercy*; the Quilliam sisters*; Garner Quinn*; Savannah Reid*; Nina Reilly*; Schuyler Ridgeway*; Sophie Rivers*; Claudia Seferius*; Jo Beth Sidden*; Margo Simon*; Marguerite Smith*; Dr. Sylvia Strange*; Judith Thornton*; Melanie Travis*; Jane Turner; Jane Whitefield*; Kate Wilkinson*; Kay Williams ©; Fran Wilson* in US; (1993 in U.K.)

1996: Rachel Alexander*; Margit Andersson; Cat Austen*; Jane Austen*; Hollis Ball* in U.K.; Lily Bard*; Vicky Bauer; Jane Bee*; Sister Agnes Bourdillon in U.S.*; Lindsay Chamberlain*; Alexandra Cooper*; Ruby Crane*; Ruby Dark; Venus Diamond*; Sister Fidelma*; Suze Figuera*; Fizz Fitzgerald*; Lucy Freers; Theresa Galloway*; Sen. Eleanor Gorzack; P. J. Gray*; Beth Hartley*; Dido Hoare*; Patricia Anne Hollowell and Mary Alice Crane*; Mrs. Emma Hudson*; Cassidy James*; Texana Jones*; Lady Aoi; Julia Lambros*; Renee LaRoche; Heaven Lee*; Lt. Tory Lennox, USCG; Molly Masters*; Cassidy McCabe*; Dr. Anne Menlo; Kali O'Brien*; Alison O'Neil; Dr. Andi Pauling*; Karen Perry-Mondori*; Josie Pigeon*; Sukey Reynolds*; Emma Rhodes*; Benny Rosato*; Nicki Scott*; Barbara Simons; Lupe Solano*; Starletta DuVall*; Bert and Nan Tatum*; Abby Timberlake*; Tory Travers*; Hannah Trevor*; Lucy Wayles*; Biggie Weatherford*; Molly West; Ruth Willmarth*

1997: Mali Anderson*; Lady Susanna Appleton*; Kate Banning*; Miriam Bartimaeus; Ursula Blanchard*; Kathryn Bogert*; Helen Bradley; Temperance Brennan*; Dr. Clare Burtonall; Sister Rose Callahan*; Letty Campbell*; Carrie Carlin*; Kate Cavanaugh*; Rachel Crowne; Meg Darcy; Maggie Dillitz*;

Delilah Doolittle*; Mandy Dyer*; Kay Farrow; Lucy Freers; P. J. Gray*; Nanette Hayes*; Brett Higgins*; Marti Hirsch*; Stevie Houston*; Casey Jones*; Loretta Kovacs*; Gloria Lamerino*; Rosie Lavine; Nell Mathews*; Haley McAlister; Lara McClintoch*; Charlotte McCrae*; Sutton McPhee*; Mavis Middleton*; Brenda Midnight*; Tess Monaghan*; Ruthie Kantor Morris; Lorelei Muldoon; Jane Nichols; Tru North*; Victory O'Shea*; Martha Patterson; Karen Pelletier*; Charlie Plato*; Rachel Porter*; Amelia Sachs; Rei Shimura*; Helen Sorby*; Dr. Michael Stone*; Evelyn Sutcliffe* (one book in a different form published earlier); Rose Trevelyan; Tessa Vance; Fran Varaday; Francesca Vierling*; Connor Westphal*; Chas Wheatley; MacLaren Yarbrough

1998:   Allie Babcock*; Madeline Bean*; Nikki Chase; Wyanet Chouinard*; Venus Diamond*; Dixie Flannigan*; Carole Ann Gibson*; Meg Gillis; Susan Given; Ann Hardaway*; Annabelle Hardy-Maratos; Sierra Lavotini*; Maggie Maguire*; Trish Maguire*; Hannah Malloy and Kiki Goldstein*; Jennifer Marsh*; Adele Monsarrat*; Kellie Montgomery*; Teddy Morelli*; Taylor Morgan*; May Morrison; Laura Owen*; Sydney Teague*; Jacobia Triptree*; Charlotte Willett*

1999:   Janet Barkin*; Betsy Devonshire*; Leigh Koslow*; Claire Rawlings*

Resources and Readings for Volumes I and II

Although I read extensively on the political, economic, literary, and social period from 1860-1989, special credit should be given to the following books for their treatment of the subject and for the identification of authors and sleuths previously unknown to me.

Aburdene, Patricia and John Naisbitt. *Megatrends for Women*. Villard, 1992.

Allen, Frederick Lewis. *Only Yesterday, An Informal History of the 1920's*. Harper & Row, 1931.

Anderson, Bonnie S. and Judith P. Zinsser, *A History of Their Own*. Harper & Row, 1988.

Barnes, Melvyn. *Murder in Print, A Guide to Two Centuries of Crime Fiction*. Barn Owl Books, 1986.

Berkin, Carol Ruth and Mary Beth Norton. *Women of America*. Houghton Mifflin, 1979.

Billman, Carol. *The Secret of the Stratmeyer Syndicate*. Ungar, 1986.

Boardman, Fon Wyman, Jr. *America And the Jazz Age, A History of the 1920's*. Walck, 1968.

Burchill, Julie. *Girls on Film*. Pantheon, 1986.

Caprio, Betsy. *The Mystery of Nancy Drew*. Source Books, 1992.

Cawelti, John G. Adventure, *Mystery, and Romance*. University of Chicago Press, 1976.

Chafe, William H. *The American Woman, Her Changing Social, Economic, and Political Roles*, 1920-1970. Oxford University Press, 1972.

Clark, Homer H, Jr. *The Law of Domestic Relations*. West, 1968.

Cook, Michael L. *Murder by Mail.* Bowling Green State University Popular Press, 1983.

Coser, Lewis A., Charles Kadushin, and Walter W. Powell. *BOOKS, The Culture and Commerce of Publishing.* Basic Books, 1982.

Craig, Patricia and Mary Cadogan. *The Lady Investigates, Women Detectives and Spies in Fiction.* St. Martin's Press, 1981.

Current, Richard N., T. Harry Williams, Alan Brinkley, and Frank Friedel. *American History: A Survey,* Seventh Edition, Knopf, 1987.

Dooley, Roger. *From Scarface to Scarlet, American Films in the 1930's.* Harcourt Brace, 1981.

East, Andy. *Cold War File.* Scarecrow Press, 1983.

Edwards, Julia. *Women of the World, The Great Foreign Correspondents.* Houghton Mifflin, 1988.

Eisenstadt v. Baird. 405 U.S. 438 (1972).

Evans, Sara M. *Born for Liberty.* The Free Press (Macmillan), 1989.

Freeman, Lucy. Editor. *The Murder Mystique.* Ungar, 1982.

Freidan, Betty. *The Feminine Mystique.* W. W. Norton, 1963.

Glendon, Mary Ann. *Matrimonial Property: A Comparative Study of Law and Social Change.* 49 Tulane Law Review 21 (1974).

Gold, Annalee. *75 Years of Fashion.* Fairchild, 1975.

Gorham, Deborah. *The Victorian Girl and the Feminine Ideal.* Indiana University Press, 1982.

Grannis, Chandler B. *What Happens in Book Publishing.* Columbia University Press, 1957.

Greene, Suzanne Ellery. *Books for Pleasure, Popular Fiction, 1914-45.* Bowling Green State University Popular Press, 1974.

Greer, Germaine. *The Female Eunuch.* McGraw Hill, 1970.

Griswold v. Connecticut. 381 U.S. 479 (1965).

Grun, Bernard. *Timetables of History. Second Edition,* Touchstone, 1982; Third Edition, 1991.

Hackett, Alice Payne and James Henry Burke. *80 Years of Best Sellers*: 1895-1975. R.R. Bowker, 1977.

Haskell, Molly. *From Reverence to Rape, The Treatment of Women in the Movies*. Holt, Rinehart and Winston, 1974.

Haycraft, Howard. *The Art of the Mystery Story*. Carroll & Graf, 1983 (first published in 1946).

Haycraft, Howard. *Murder for Pleasure*. Carroll & Graf, 1984 (first published in 1941).

Heising, Willetta. *Detecting Men*. Purple Moon Press, 1998.

Heising, Willetta. *Detecting Women*, Edition 3. Purple Moon Press, 1999

Henderson, Lesley. Editor. *Twentieth Century Crime & Mystery Writers*, Third Edition. St. James Press, 1991.

Holcombe, Lee. *Victorian Ladies at Work*. Archon Books, 1973.

Hoppenstand, Gary. Editor. *The Dime Novel Detective*. Bowling Green State University Press, 1982.

Horn, Maurice. Editor. *The World Encyclopedia of Comics*. Avon, 1976.

Howell, Reet. Editor. Her Story in Sport; A Historical Anthology of Women in Sports. Leisure Press, 1982.

Hubin, Allen J. *Crime Fiction, 1749-1980: A Comprehensive Bibliography*. Garland, 1984; and its *1981-1985 Supplement*, Garland, 1988.

Hubin, Allen J. *Crime Fiction, II, A Comprehensive Bibliography, 1749-1990*. Garland, 1994.

Hubin, Allen J. *Crime Fiction III, A Comprehensive Bibliography, 1749-1995*. Locus Press on CD-Rom, 1999.

Inge, Thomas. Editor. *American Popular Culture*. Greenwood Press, 1978.

Kael, Pauline. *5001 Nights at the Movies*. Holt, Rinehart, and Winston, 1982.

Kerker, Linda and Jane De Hart Matthews. *Women's America*, Oxford University Press. 1982.

Kraditor, Aileen S. *The Ideas of the Woman Suffrage Movement: 1890-1920*. Columbia University Press, 1965.

Landrum, Larry, Pat Browne, and Ray B. Browne. *Dimensions of Detective Fiction*. Popular Press, 1976.

Maida, Patricia D. *Mother of Detective Fiction*. Bowling Green Popular Press, 1989.

Maio, Kathleen. *Feminist in the Dark: Reviewing the Movies.* The Crossing Press, 1988.

Mason, Bobbie Ann. *The Girl Sleuth: A Feminist Guide to the Bobbsey Twins, Nancy Drew and Their Sisters.* Feminist Press, 1975.

Matthews, Glenna. *Just a Housewife.* Oxford University Press, 1987.

McDowell, Barbara and Hana Unlauf. Editors. *The Good Housekeeping Woman's Almanac.* Newspaper Enterprise Association, 1977.

McLaughlin, Steve D., Barbara D. Melber, John O. G. Billy, Denise M. Zimmerle, Linda D. Winges, and Terry R. Johnson, *The Changing Lives of American Women.* University of North Carolina Press, 1988.

Morello, Karen Berger. *The Invisible Bar, The Woman Lawyer in America.* Random House, 1986.

Mott, Fran Luther. *Golden Multitudes.* Macmillan, 1947.

Osborne, Eric. *Victorian Detective Fiction.* Bodley Head, 1966, a catalogue of the collection made by Dorothy Glover and Graham Greene.

Ousby, Ian. *Bloodhounds of Heaven, The Detective in English Fiction from Godwin to Doyle.* Harvard University Press, 1976.

Peterson, Audrey. *Victorian Masters of Mystery.* Ungar, 1984.

Pruett, Lorine. *Women Workers Through the Depression.* Macmillan, 1934.

Queen, Ellery. *In the Queen's Parlor, and Other Leaves from the Editor's Notebook.* Simon & Schuster, 1957.

Queen, Ellery. Editor. *101 Years Entertainment, The Great Detective Stories, 1841-1941.* Little, Brown, 1941.

Reilly, John M. Editor. *Twentieth Century Crime & Mystery Writers, First Edition.* St. Martin's Press, 1980.

Reilly, John M. Editor. *Twentieth Century Crime & Mystery Writers,* Second Editon. St. Martin's Press, 1985.

Roberts, Gary G., Gary Hoppenstand and Ray B. Browne. *Old Sleuth's Freaky Female Detectives* (From the Dime Novels. Bowling Green State University Popular Press, 1990.

Rodell, Marie F. *Mystery Fiction, Theory and Technique.* Revised Edition, Hermitage House, 1952.

Roe v. Wade. 410 U.S. 113 (1973).

Rogers, Katharine M. *The Troublesome Helpmate*. University of Washington Press, 1966.

Routley, Eric. *Puritan Pleasures of the Detective Story*. Gollancz, 1972.

Sayers, Dorothy. *The Omnibus of Crime*. Harcourt Brace, 1929.

Slung, Michelle. *Crime on Her Mind*. Pantheon, 1975.

Solomon, Barbara Miller. *In the Company of Educated Women*. Yale University Press, 1985.

Smuts, Robert. *Women and Work in America*. Schocken, 1971.

Steedman, Carolyn. *Policing the Victorian Community*. Routledge & Kegan Paul, 1984.

Swanson, Jean and Dean James. *By a Woman's Hand*. Berkley, 1994.

Symons, Julian. *Mortal Consequence*s. Harper & Row, 1972.

Taylor, Joan Kennedy. *Reclaiming the Mainstream*. Prometheus, 1988.

Terrace, Vincent. *The Complete Encyclopedia of Television Programs 1947-79*. A. S. Barnes & Company, 1979

Tobias, Sheila and Lisa Anderson. *What Really Happened to Rosie the Riveter? Demobilization and the Female Labor Force, 1944-47*. MSS Modular Publications. Date unavailable.

Vicinius, Martha. *Independent Women*. University of Chicago Press, 1985.

Van Dover, J. Kenneth. *Murder in the Millions*. Ungar, 1984.

Ware, Susan. *Holding Their Own, American Women in the 1930's*. Twayne, 1982.

Weiss, Daniel Evans. *The Great Divide: How Females and Males Really Differ*. Poseidon, 1991.

Winks, Robin W. *Modus Operandi*. Godine, 1982.

Wrong, E. M. *Crime and Detection*. Oxford University Press, 1926.

About the Author

Colleen A. Barnett was born in Green Bay, Wisconsin, the daughter of a trial attorney and his wife. She earned bachelor's and master's degrees in Political Science from the University of Wisconsin in Madison. She remained at home to raise a family of seven children after her marriage to attorney John Barnett, but returned to work when her youngest child was in grade school.

Colleen has since worked as a volunteer coordinator and social work supervisor for a county department of Social Services. She took early retirement from Social Services, to re-enter the University of Wisconsin Law School where she received her degree cum laude.

Later she was employed as an attorney and mediator, and as a lecturer in Political Science at the University of Wisconsin Center-Richland. She is currently retired and working on Volume 3 of *Mystery Women*.

Over the years, Colleen has built a personal library of over 4,000 volumes, concentrating her collection on mysteries featuring women sleuths. She is a member of Sisters in Crime.

To receive a free catalog of other Poisoned Pen Press titles, please contact us in one of the following ways:

Phone: 1-800-421-3976
Facsimile: 1-480-949-1707
Email: info@poisonedpenpress.com
Website: www.poisonedpenpress.com

Poisoned Pen Press
6962 E. First Ave. Ste 103
Scottsdale, AZ 85251